Get the second Saul Marshall thriller for free...

Sign up for the no-spam newsletter and get NEVER FORGET, the second Saul Marshall thriller, completely free.

Details can be found at the end of FALSE PROPHET.

FALSE PROPHET

A Saul Marshall Thriller: Book One

RICHARD DAVIS

Richard Davis

TRAPDOOR PRESS

This one's for Molly.

Prologue

Aaron Woolf sat down for breakfast, opened his newspaper, and read his obituary:

Retired realtor, Aaron Woolf, died today aged 55. His body was found in his apartment on West 86ᵗʰ Street, Manhattan, hanging from the light fixture above the dining table. Police are treating it as suicide.

Setting down his newspaper on the metallic table, Aaron could see his hand shaking. Some wacko had doctored his paper into a veiled death threat. They'd done an immaculate job, too – the text was seamlessly integrated alongside the other obituaries. Aaron felt his body flooding with adrenaline, and jumped as the ring of his landline broke the silence. He hobbled to the phone and snatched the receiver to his ear.

'Hello?'

The voice on the other end belonged to Aaron's son, Joshua. This would have been unexceptional had Joshua not been missing, presumed dead, for the past two years.

He was reciting the obituary Aaron had just read, word for word. The sound of Joshua's voice made Aaron stumble.

'Josh, where are you?' Aaron said with escalating volume. '*Where are you?*'

But Joshua kept on with his recital, slow and sure, oblivious to this inquiry. When he got to the end, the line went dead.

Panic seized Aaron, and – after trying and failing to get a dial tone – he began scouring the kitchen for his cell. But it was missing. A moment later, he found himself staggering into the hallway of the seventh floor.

But when Aaron hit the elevator call button, it failed to illuminate. The elevator was down. Yet it was only when he tried the door to the stairwell and found it locked that he knew this was a trap, the stairwell door was *never* locked. With pain coursing through his chest, he clambered to the door of 232 – one of the two other apartments on his floor – and banged it hard. Nobody came. He tried the same with the door of 233. Again, there was no response.

Aaron edged back to his apartment. But before he made it, he heard the sound of hinges working. He turned around. Six men – each dressed in grey, and wearing purple hoods – were filing into the hallway from apartment 232. They seemed to be softly repeating the word 'Taprobana,' and were carrying rope and a small blowtorch. Immediately Aaron understood that the ones who'd taken Joshua had come for his father but by the time he thought to yell, the men were already upon him and silencing his mouth. He tried to resist, but it was little use. His feeble body, crippled by a stroke suffered four months prior, was no match for these six powerful men.

The men wasted no time. They dragged Aaron into his apartment, tied his hands behind his back, and removed his socks and shoes. Then they stood him on the table's edge, strung a noose around his neck, and tied the other end of the rope to the light fixture. Finally, Aaron's mouth was freed.

'Why are you doing this? Haven't I suffered enough?'

One of the hooded men slowly looked him over. 'We are here to show you mercy,' he replied. 'For your salvation. You have lived in sin. Divine justice will come through your self-annihilation.'

'You fucking lunatics!' Aaron shouted. 'Where's my son?'

Aaron spat at the man. But he didn't respond with words. Instead, he took up the blowtorch, activated the flame, and crouched beneath the table. He then put the flame to work on the table's underside. Aaron felt the metal warm and his feet prickle. Then, all at once, his senses were saturated by searing pain and he was screaming. So he did the only thing he could to switch it off: he closed his eyes, and took a single step off the table's edge…

Chapter One

I'm in a squalid motel room, holed up like an animal, and they're hunting me.

If they find me, I'll be lucky to be taken alive.

But I have experience evading the authorities as I was on the run for four years in the 1990s. And this time, I'm wiser: I've spent fifteen years working at the FBI, in some of their most elite departments. So if anyone's got a chance of staying a step ahead, it's me.

The shit hit the fan about a month and a half ago – that's when I received the call. But really, this whole mess began long before that. And perhaps had the warning come from anyone else but Solomon Teague – an inmate at Broadmoor Psychiatric Hospital, where they keep the UK's most dangerous psychopaths – things might've been different…

Teague's lawyer contacted me a year or so back, and told me that Teague had something to tell me that could save my life – something so sensitive, he had to tell me in person. If I was in any other line of work, I'm sure I would have dismissed Teague as a loon. But when you're with the

FBI, you treat circumstances like these with a bit more respect, and so I heard the lawyer out. Teague, he told me, was something of an odd-one-out at Broadmoor. For one thing, unlike the majority of inmates there, he wasn't a psychopath – he was a schizophrenic. For another, there was a good deal to suggest he'd been wrongly imprisoned. He was in for assaulting a police officer on a bus to Trafalgar Square in late 2009. But only a week earlier, Teague had taken on a new psychiatrist who'd misread Teague's notes, and prescribed him a third of what he'd needed, and apparently it was this error that'd directly caused his outburst. So the psychiatrist was to blame, not Teague.

But even more interesting than this was Teague's history pre-Broadmoor, which I unearthed by digging around myself. In 1998, he won the Pulitzer Prize for an article he wrote in the *Washington Post* entitled 'Timmy's Life,' detailing the world of an eight-year-old heroin addict. But the kicker was, he made the whole damn thing up and when the truth eventually came out, it caused so much outrage that Teague had felt his only option was to emigrate to London.

After learning all this, I decided I was curious enough to meet the guy. And so one afternoon in May 2012, during a business trip to London, I caught a train to Crowthorne, Berkshire, the tranquil patch of English countryside where Broadmoor is tucked away...

As I disembarked the train at Crowthorne Station, I immediately recognized the little man on the platform as Teague's lawyer, Ian Gillett: his round body, bulging eyes, and sparse salt-and-pepper hair were as distinct in the flesh as they'd been in the photograph he'd sent me beforehand. But though he was smiling, it was clear he was unsettled – his hands were shaking, his face flushed, his shirt checkered with sweat – and this was hardly surprising. This was a man used to spa days and fine dining, not trips to insane asylums with FBI agents.

'Thank you for agreeing to this, Mr Marshall,' he said as he shook my hand. 'Pleased to meet you.'

'That's okay,' I replied. 'You've bested all the travel agents. None of them could get me into Broadmoor. And please, call me Saul.'

He smiled a strained smile. 'Really, I appreciate it. I've not dealt with anything like this in all my years.'

'It's an odd situation,' I said.

Odd was right, it's not every day a schizophrenic at Broadmoor seeks you out with a life-or-death message. But actually it was the oddness of the man himself, in particular his unusual history of fraud, that had captured my attention more; because as it so happened, I, too, had once upon a time been caught up in the world of fraud and deception. But for me it wasn't a fabricated article in a newspaper: it was four years, between late 1991 and mid-1996, spent as a professional con-artist. And during this time, I'd been very busy: I forged historical documents, masqueraded as a psychiatrist, fell in with organized crime, started and finished a relationship with a congressman's daughter, got engaged to another woman altogether, had a child, tipped off the FBI about one of the most prolific serial killers in American history, and made over $2.5 million through illicit means. All before turning twenty-two.

'So how long am I getting with Teague?' I asked, as Gillett drove us the short distance to Broadmoor.

'Fifteen minutes,' he replied. 'And it'll just be you and

him – he doesn't want me present for the conversation. Though mind you, you're lucky to be getting that long: he's the only patient in the Dangerous and Severe Personality Disorder Unit with visitor privileges at all.'

The discovery that Teague was in Broadmoor's DSPD Unit confirmed to me what I already knew, that this was heavy stuff. But had it failed to do so, the protocol for entering the facility would have done the trick: when we arrived at the outer perimeter, Gillett's car was ransacked and our mobiles confiscated; guards armed with Heckler & Koch MP5 submachine guns interrogated us in the parking lot; and there was stringent, airport-style security at the entrance to The Wellness Centre, the facility's chosen euphemism for the visitors' complex. But finally, I was separated from Gillett and ushered into the visitors' hall – already populated by twenty or so others – where I found myself a table.

Five minutes later – when the wall clock hit 5 p.m. – the inmates entered.

Only then – as I was confronted by a cluster of men in identical orange jumpsuits – did it occur to me that I didn't know what Teague looked like. But no sooner had I thought this when a man broke away from the group, and came and sat down opposite me. A statuesque man – with a tall, slender frame, wispy grey hair, and deep hazel eyes – who held himself with a grace that distinguished him from the other inmates.

Yet for all his composure, Solomon Teague looked exhausted. He must've been about fifty, but he looked a good deal older.

'Saul Marshall. I have been so excited to meet you,' he said in a Canadian accent.

'Well, I was just in the Broadmoor neck of the woods, so thought I'd drop by,' I said, with a smile.

'As you do,' he riposted; then he added: 'I was unsure which version of Saul Marshall might be turning up, or if I'd even recognize you at all. I'd have to say my favorite of all your personas was William Martin. Just because of the sheer cheek of it, you know?'

William Martin was my first ever persona. I was sixteen, living in Brooklyn, and playing at falsifying historical documents. The next thing I knew, I was selling them for big bucks under the name William Martin, an antiques salesman from New York. Why that name? During WW2, the British created a fictitious man, Major William Martin, to feed false intelligence to the Germans. The MI5 took the body of an already dead man, planted on him papers identifying him as Major William Martin along with erroneous battle plans, before leaving him for Jerry to find. The tactic was a complete success, and so I decided to use the name for my own deception in homage to this masterful plot.

It was curious that Teague knew this detail from my past. But much more curious was his nonchalance. So far, he didn't seem remotely like a man with something urgent to say, and not much time to say it.

'I might have fooled a few experts,' I replied, opting to keep up the patter. 'But William Martin was all imitation. With you, it was fabrication. And to think how you sent those policemen and politicians running after a boy that didn't exist…'

Teague gave a wistful smile.

'Those were some days,' he said, with a note of longing, but also remorse – pride and regret slugging it out. I knew the feeling. But then, all of a sudden, Teague's body language shifted: he leaned forward, widened his eyes, hunched his shoulders. Then he said abruptly:

'Listen, Saul: I have something to tell you that could save your life.'

'Hold on,' I replied, with equal abruptness. 'If you had something so important to say, then why waste the last minute with small-talk?'

'Come on,' he said. 'You've just been taken to Broadmoor to meet with a schizophrenic. I understand how that must look. I needed to establish my sanity before I bothered to tell you a damned thing.'

I grunted. Understood his logic.

'Now, look,' he continued urgently. 'What I need to tell you starts in September 1981. I was eighteen, living in Toronto. Next thing I knew, I'd landed myself in an insane asylum. The hows and whys are unimportant. But I'd ended up at the Oak Ridge Hospital for the Criminally Insane in Ontario, an experimental facility for treating psychopaths and schizophrenics. They stripped us naked, pumped us full of LSD, then watched to see what happened. All this in what we knew as the Total Encounter Capsule.'

I couldn't see a motive for making this up.

'Describe it,' I said.

'Padded walls, with straws built into them through which they provided food.'

He said this with conviction, like it was something he'd truly seen. Then again, Teague was a schizophrenic: things he sincerely believed he'd seen could still easily be products of his own mind. Back to square one.

He continued: 'While at Oak Ridge, I was thrown in with a lot of disturbing characters: killers and sadists – much like here. But there was one I found particularly disturbing. A seventeen-year-old called Ivan Drexler. He'd been admitted a few months before me for convincing a kid to attack his own family with a crowbar. The kid's sister wound up dead. Most psychopaths don't mind getting their hands dirty. Drexler preferred to inspire others to do the dirty work.

'In short, he was lethal, intelligent, and most of all disarming. I remember him telling me about that very incident which had landed him in Oak Ridge. He told me how it had made him feel like God to have that power over another person, and how he wanted to inspire that behavior time and again. He told me that what he'd loved most was the self-abuse on the victim's part – the kid having murdered his own sister. But somehow, despite these comments, he still had a magnetism. It's difficult to explain.'

I nodded my understanding. Between late 1993 and early 1995 I had masqueraded as a psychiatrist in Salt Lake City and in the process, I'd learned a lot about psychopaths. The key is the amygdalae – the part of the brain which processes emotions. In a psychopath, the amygdalae and the central nervous system don't communicate. As a result, their brains aren't able to process another's suffering.

They're inhuman, yet they ooze charisma.

'I'm not proud of this,' said Teague. 'But I'll show you.'

He rolled up his right shirt sleeve. There was a red butterfly tattooed on his forearm.

'Drexler has one of these, too,' he said, shaking his head. 'Identical.'

'And then what?' I prompted.

'Then we both left Oak Ridge,' he said, unrolling his sleeve. 'Both discharged in June 1983. I was declared well, so long as I stuck to my medication. But Drexler was pronounced wholly cured. Supposedly the Oak Ridge experience had taught him what a psychopath can't be taught: empathy. But even then, it seemed too good to be true. There was something too polished about him – too perfect.

'And then we went our completely separate ways. I reasonably expected not to cross his path again. Why should I? I moved to DC, to pursue my dream of becoming a journalist. And as I'm sure you know, I eventually got a job at the *Post* after fudging my resume. I was ambitious, driven. Drexler didn't cross my mind for years.

'It wasn't till 1997 – fourteen years on – that I began rummaging among the skeletons in my closet. I decided to do an article on Oak Ridge: a dramatic exposé on experimental medication; a brave admission of my own personal history. I did my research and met with others who'd been through Oak Ridge, and my findings were disturbing. Here's the gist: while around sixty percent of psychopaths who go through conventional treatment reoffend, among those who'd been through Oak Ridge, the figure was eighty percent. I had questions. I looked Drexler up. I couldn't help myself.'

He paused, thinking how to proceed. I couldn't yet see what this had to do with me.

'It turned out he was serving a thirteen year prison sentence in upstate New York – the Coxsackie Correctional Institute. I paid him a visit.

'I remember the day clearly. Drexler was so pleased to see me. Ecstatic. It was unsettling how precisely he remembered me. No longer in awe of his charisma, I began to see it as part of his inhumanity. I asked him what he thought of Oak Ridge, and he gushed. "I learned how to manipulate more effectively," he said, "and to keep my more shocking instincts out of sight." Oak Ridge had taught psychopaths how to *seem* humane. It had made Drexler more dangerous, more difficult to spot what he was.'

The clock was showing ten past five. Five minutes left.

Teague needed to cut to the chase. He registered my glance at the clock and took the hint.

'But Drexler had two new obsessions,' he said, words tumbling out of him now. 'The first was the attack on the World Trade Center on February 26, 1993. He was in awe of what people would do if they thought they were serving God, and jealous of the leaders of the Jihadist militant movement. But he perceived in them a weakness – they actually believed they were implementing God's will. So Drexler, in response to this, began imagining a religion which inspired the same manic commitment, but headed by a leader who knew it was a scam, a leader who'd created the religion only to exert power over his followers.'

'And the second obsession?' I prompted.

'Was Saul Marshall,' he replied. 'The young con-artist who, the previous summer, had finally been arrested after eluding the authorities for four years. He studied you meticulously. And he saw in you the ideal traits for leading the religion he envisaged: an intelligent, detached brain, capable of getting followers to believe they're serving God, when truly they're serving their leader; capable of *conning* the believers.

'In fact, he had become obsessed with the art of the con: getting somebody to do something directly against their own interests. And really, this wasn't so far removed from his old obsession with having victims harm themselves.

'Yet while on one level Drexler admired you, on another, he truly hated you—'

'But why should he?' I cut in impatiently. 'I know I was hitting headlines at the time, so I can conceive of someone developing an obsession. But why should he hate me?'

Teague gave a quick, rueful smile. 'Does the name Eric Costana ring a bell?'

I nodded. 'When I was working for the New York mafia back in 1996 he was our only serious competitor in the drug-dealing game. But because of me, he wound up behind bars. Through a contact I'd made, I received a tip that one of our major cocaine sales was going to be raided by the authorities, so convinced my superiors to pull out. Costana, seeing an opportunity to make a quick buck, stepped in to take our place, and took the rap.'

'Right,' said Teague. 'But four of Costana's men were also busted during that raid and one of them was the thirty-one-year-old Ivan Drexler, who'd only joined Costana's outfit about six months prior. But while the other heavies received relatively small sentences, it came out that Drexler had put himself forward to do some pretty grim stuff for Costana – severing toes, driving pins under finger-nails, once even piercing an eyeball – and that won him a hefty thirteen years.

'And yet, Saul, because of what you did, he held *you* responsible for his captivity – for his losing more than a decade of his life to prison and the horrors he faced there. And, put simply, he wanted revenge.' Teague paused. 'You should have seen his thumbs, they were horrific. He told me the guards had strung him up by them his first week there…'

Teague broke off with a shudder.

'So what did you do next?' I said. 'After you visited him.'

'I did nothing. Didn't write the article and didn't tell a soul. His release was a long way off, and so I allowed myself to forget all about it. I was in London in June 2009, when that day finally came. But by the time I'd looked up where he'd gotten to a month down the line, he'd seemed to have vanished altogether, swallowed up by the earth. A little later still, I heard a rumor that he'd died in an accident. But I didn't buy it. Then all of a sudden, I was in Broadmoor. Out of contact.'

'So why are you telling me all this?' I said. 'Because next February is the twentieth anniversary of the World Trade Center attack? What exactly do you expect to happen?'

'So you see it!' he said excitedly. 'It hit me a few months ago. Drexler was intrigued by anniversaries. This'll be the twentieth. To his mind, it must seem neglected: a day unjustly overshadowed by 9/11 and its memory, when really it commemorates the original. And though he respected your skills, Saul, he also considered you both his competition and mortal enemy. I just know he will be spoiling for a fight; desperate to take you down in a way that both settles the score, and proves his superiority. And that'll be the date…'

'What exactly do you expect to happen?' I repeated.

'I've no clue,' he said, his eyes suddenly distant. Exhaustion was setting in. 'Perhaps nothing. Perhaps it's already too late. But I've warned you. It's the best I could do… given my situation.'

At that, Teague fell uncannily still, and shot me a look that spelled relief, pity, and powerlessness in equal measure; a look that seemed to stretch out interminably. And then, all at once, the stillness was shattered: the guards shouted the word "time" across the room, and all the patients, including Teague, clattered to their feet and herded towards the exit.

I was unsure what to think as Gillett and I exited the complex. My first instinct was skepticism. It seemed most likely – given that I was dealing with a schizophrenic who'd been medicated to within an inch of his life – he'd made the whole damn thing up. And even when I looked up the Costana bust that evening, and found that Ivan Drexler had indeed been among the men arrested and sentenced, I remained unfazed. After all, I'd crossed a lot of people in my time, and had never worried about it much before. And ultimately, Teague's warnings were based on wild speculations. There was no guarantee something would happen – no guarantee it would involve me.

I decided to write Teague off as a waste of an afternoon.

Chapter Two

I was in New Orleans, on a week-long vacation, when I received the call from Lucinda Parkes – Director of the Office of Intelligence at the FBI.

Immediately my stomach lurched. I didn't get a call from Lucinda Parkes unless it was Christmas day, or the shit had hit the fan. And it sure as hell wasn't Christmas.

'There's been an incident,' she said. 'More than one. Will you come back to Washington?'

'You're not asking me, are you?' I replied, knowing the answer already.

'We've booked you onto an American Airlines flight. It's due to take off at 2:30 a.m. CST from Louis Armstrong Airport. Will you come back to Washington?'

'You're not asking me, you're telling me.'

Silence. After a moment, I added:

'I'm on holiday. What's happened?'

'This is important,' she said. 'A car will pick you up from your hotel at midnight, CST. After landing, you'll be partially debriefed in the car from Dulles. You'll then attend the meeting in the Situation Room at Headquarters at 6:30 a.m., EST. Thank you.'

The line went dead. It wasn't open to debate. But her omissions and decisive action were telling. People had died, and there was a good chance more were in danger. So I returned to my room at the Jazz Quarters Hotel, and packed my carry-on bag. Then, at midnight sharp, I caught my cab.

So much for the vacation.

IT WAS A HALF HOUR'S DRIVE TO THE AIRPORT. THE CAB worked its way through the city.

Between summer 2005 and summer 2009, a call from Lucinda Parkes would've been commonplace. At the time, I'd been working in The Office of Intelligence as her right-hand man. But I had a messy past, intent on making trouble for me.

It was the early 1990s that were to blame – those years in Salt Lake City, masquerading as a psychiatrist despite a complete lack of medical training. Because I'd done more than that. I'd fallen in love – a mistake. And then I'd got the girl pregnant – a bigger mistake. Samuel was born August 7, 1994, and life, for a time, was perfect. But then disaster struck: I discovered that my co-worker was killing patients. As the body-count mounted, I *knew* I had to tell the authorities. Yet I also knew that once the authorities entered the equation, I'd be investigated as a matter of course which, given that I was on the run for stealing millions of dollars, was a major problem. So when I eventually bit the bullet on January 24, 1995 – my twentieth birthday – and tipped off the FBI, I did the only thing I could: I vanished. And in the process, I abandoned a six-month-old child, and my fiancée…

It wasn't till 2005, ten years on, that the woman I'd abandoned – now living in Washington – let me meet my son. And Parkes had understood in summer 2009 when I'd requested time off to spend with Samuel. But, unfortunately, years of absence does damage to a father-son relationship that can't be fixed with a bit of time off work; damage that leaves a son unable to recognize his father as anything more than an acquaintance, and a father ignorant of his most basic responsibilities. Damage that runs deep. And, of course, my incompetent attempts to heal it weren't helped by the fact that I was still receiving calls from Parkes. At the FBI, time off doesn't make you immune to emergencies.

But on September 2, 2010, the calls from Parkes stopped altogether. A sixteen-year-old Samuel had vanished on his way home from school. He'd been spotted leaving, but had never come home. Now you see him, now you don't. So I did what anyone in my position would've done: I dropped everything. I quit my job, and spent the rest of 2010 with a few close friends, searching high and low. Made myself sick with searching. But there were no leads, no clues. Samuel had disappeared. And I was devastated.

Quickly I realized that if I wanted any chance of keeping sane, I needed the routine of work – and this meant it was my turn to call Parkes. And when I did – on New Year's day, 2011 – asking for a job at the DC Field Office, Parkes agreed to my request. Since then, Parkes had called me only three times: twice to wish me merry Christmas; and once, in late 2011, to ask my advice about Najibullah Zazi – the Afghani national who'd been plotting to bomb the New York subway to mark the tenth anniversary of 9/11.

The cab arrived at Louis Armstrong's Concourse C. After I indulged in a quick smoke outside, I checked in and passed through security and before long, I was in a window seat in Business Class, cruising at 37,000 feet.

I only had a short two-and-a-half hour flight ahead of me, but was feeling antsy; so, to take the edge off, I ordered a small bottle of Glenfiddich. Then, making use of the aircraft's Wi-Fi, I proceeded to access the internet on my iPhone – I wanted to see if any of the major US news outlets were reporting on trouble brewing. But though it was soon clear that the FBI had kept a lid on whatever it was that was happening, there was a story on the CNN website which, while surely unrelated, immediately caught my attention: *The Silent Ripper Incites Prison Riot in Utah*. I clicked through to an article describing how the inmate, and renowned serial killer, Ernest Philipert, had instigated a riot at Utah State Prison; and how – though the situation was still unfolding – it appeared as if as many as three members of staff had been taken hostage. Then came the obligatory potted history of Ernest Philipert. He'd been a psychiatrist in Salt Lake City, and had secretly been murdering elderly patients for years. He was finally caught when the FBI received a tip off from former con-artist, Saul Marshall. And following his arrest, it came out that he'd in fact changed his name to Ernest Philipert years beforehand, and had done so because it was an anagram of 'The Silent Ripper', the insane nickname he'd privately invented for himself to celebrate his sick pursuits.

For a moment, Philipert's cold, sneering face flashed before my eyes. It didn't surprise me a bit that he was still causing misery.

Pushing him from my mind, I knocked back another

couple of whiskies, while half-watching Gene Hackman and Willem Dafoe crack skulls in *Mississippi Burning* on the in-flight entertainment. Eventually I reclined my chair, and slept the remainder of the journey.

The plane landed in Washington at 4:30 a.m., EST, and I alighted feeling groggy. A chauffeur was waiting for me in arrivals, a guy called Quinn who'd been with the FBI for years. He handed me an envelope as we got in his car, and I extracted the document within.

The page contained, in black ink, a brief outline of three incidents. The first involved a man called Aaron Woolf who'd been found dead, hanging from the ceiling of his Manhattan apartment. It was thought he'd been made to stand on a metallic table, at which point a noose was strung around his neck and the table heated, forcing him to jump. The second involved bestselling novelist, A. J. Aimes, who'd been found dead in the freezer room at the Mayflower Hotel in DC. The evidence suggested she'd been forced inside a makeshift igloo in which the temperature had been so cold that her breath had solidified on the structure's inner-surface, causing the walls to slowly close in and crush her to death. The third involved the Walsh family – a mother and father, and two infants – who'd been found dead in their suburban Philadelphia home. All signs indicated they'd been forced into a bathroom which had then been hermetically sealed. The four suffocated on their own carbon dioxide emissions.

Beneath these outlines was a short note offering two factors connecting these incidents – aside from the obvious theme of self-infliction, and the fact they'd all occurred yesterday morning. Firstly, each victim was found their right-hand index finger amputated, and tied around their neck. Secondly, each had a family member on the missing persons register. For Woolf this was a teenage son;

whereas for Aimes and the Walshes this was a teenage daughter.

I exhaled hard as that all but forgotten meeting with Teague – along with everything he'd said about Drexler and his delight in self-inflicted harm – suddenly came flooding back. And then there were the missing children. It almost felt personal.

Chapter Three

Special Agent Ali Haddad removed his headset, leaned back in his seat, and sighed.

'Another marathon conversation to end with a debate on wanking,' he said.

'Just because you're a terrorist in the making, doesn't mean you don't have urges like the rest of us,' replied Special Agent Francis Bindle, shutting the lid of his laptop.

The two men were sitting before ten monitors, each of which offered a live stream of a different room within a Chicago apartment. Occupying this apartment were six men – five Albanian immigrants and a Palestinian cab-driver – each of whom harbored Jihadist sentiments. It was the job of anti-terrorist specialists Ali Haddad and Francis Bindle – operating out of a dilapidated warehouse, just under a quarter mile from the apartment on their monitors – to catalog the activities of these six men: Haddad translating their Albanian and Arabic, and Francis recording their every word on the laptop. For the past six hours, their eyes had been glued to a monitor displaying a sitting room, where the six men had been lounging. But they had now dispersed to their respective bedrooms, and were appearing on six separate monitors.

Aside from Ali and Francis, and the three other agents involved in the investigation, nobody but the Director of the FBI knew about this operation. Not the agents' wives, parents, or children. Not even the President.

Ali sighed again, his eyes heavy.

'Are Fred and Dennis still...?' he said, motioning towards the door.

'Yes, they're in bed,' replied Francis vaguely.

'And Liam?' said Ali.

Francis checked his watch. 'Not expecting him for a while yet – at least eighteen hours.'

'You worry about him?' Ali asked.

Liam was Francis's younger brother. He'd been sent to break into the cab-driver's apartment and bug it with cameras and microphones because the Jihadists had recently started frequenting this apartment as well as the flat already under observation. It was a risky job, made all the more difficult by the cabbie's wife and two children living there full-time.

'Nah,' Francis replied with a smile.

Ali knew he was lying – Francis always worried about his brother. But Ali also knew that Liam was a capable agent, and could handle himself fine. He smiled back reassuringly.

'I know this sounds ridiculous,' said Ali, 'but when I was first asked to join this assignment, I'd thought *top secret* work meant *exciting* work. The reality couldn't be more different, just, thankless...'

Francis chuckled. It wasn't that Ali was naïve. He was simply used to a different kind of work. As one of the

Bureau's few Arabic speakers, he'd been right in the thick of things post 9/11 – he'd been given a crack at some of the key conspirators, the likes of Ramzi bin al-Shibh and Mohammed al-Qahtani, immediately after their capture. So this sit and wait business wasn't what he was used to. Whereas Francis was an old-timer – he'd done this all before.

'Given that for all intents and purposes we don't exist, we can hardly expect to be thanked,' Francis replied. 'But being away from the wife and kids – not being able to tell them you're okay, or make sure they're okay – that never gets easier…'

Ali nodded. 'Let's hope the sacrifice is worth it.'

Pure chance had brought these agents to Chicago. In October 2012, an Albanian man had entered a Wal-Mart in the Englewood district of the city, looking to transfer a VCR to DVD. But that had been stupidity, not chance. What happened next, however, was good fortune. The clerk, instead of simply making the transfer, had watched the footage and seen five men shouting "God is Great" in Arabic, as well as confessionals in which each man, in full Islamic garb, stated his hostility to America.

And then there was a second stroke of luck: instead of dismissing the video, the clerk tipped off the Chicago FBI Field Office.

A number of people could've taken the tip that day. But it happened that Fred Vitelli took the call: an agent who'd only the month before been transferred to Chicago. Not yet at home in The Windy City, Vitelli bypassed his superiors at the Field Office, and contacted Carol Taft instead – the FBI's intermediary with the NSA, and an old acquaintance of Vitelli's. But after Taft had watched the tape, she did more than simply grant authorization to monitor the men; she sent it through to Robin Muldoon, Director of the FBI. Because Taft had a nose for trouble – and as far as she was concerned, the video stunk.

Having watched the video himself, Muldoon sensed an opportunity, and hastily gathered a crack team to monitor this budding Jihadist cell. It consisted of Francis Bindle, veteran of the first World Trade Center attack; Ali Haddad, the elite linguist; Liam Bindle, Francis's younger brother; Fred Vitelli, who'd not be missed from the Chicago Field Office, having just arrived; and Dennis Ericson, the son and grandson of FBI agents, whose father led the investigation into the 1988 Lockerbie Bombing.

Of course none of this would've been any good without legal authorization from the Foreign Intelligence Surveillance Court – the only body capable of giving the go-ahead to the surveillance measures this mission required. But the chief judge trusted Muldoon, and gave the warrant without even calling a formal hearing – without asking for a single detail.

All that had remained, then, was a base for these agents to work from, and Muldoon soon found a place that fit the bill – a warehouse to the south of the gritty Englewood district, and a stone's throw from the suspects' location. The structure consisted of a large storage area in back, and an office complex to the front – all on one floor. The agents left the storage space alone, but converted the office space. The main office by the front entrance became their control center; whereas the corridor beyond – which comprised five smaller offices, a kitchen, and a bathroom – became the living space. There was a second corridor annexed to the first, consisting of five further offices. But this area, like the storage space, was left alone.

And so for the past five months, this Bureau team had

been monitoring the aspirational terrorists – bugging their homes and vehicles, watching their every move – in the hope that in the process of becoming operational, these men might provide further leads, or even reveal links to Jihadists abroad.

Since the investigation began, there had been slow progress. Initially, the Jihadists consisted of five Albanian men. But in early February, the Palestinian cabbie joined their ranks, and quickly emerged as leader. Not only did he energize the men with boasts about contacts he had in the Middle East, he also inspired them with talk of hand-grenades in malls, attacks on Fort Dix, and flying planes into the Sears Tower. Yet, despite this newcomer's leader-ship, the men had still not moved beyond talk.

But it was dangerous talk all the same, and the Director of the FBI wanted to hear it. And so every other day, at 7 a.m. CST, he called Francis for an update.

'It's kind of perverse, isn't it?' said Ali. 'Sitting about, hoping these men seek external help to carry out their attacks… willing them to do their worst…'

'I see it differently,' said Francis. 'These guys aren't likely to abandon their beliefs any time soon. And we know there are others out there with similar sentiments. So the best case scenario is for these men to radicalize further and make contact with the others. That way, we clear up.'

Ali nodded his understanding. 'Just seems perverse,' he grunted.

Suddenly, there was an urgent knock at the front door.

'Who the hell's that?' said Ali.

Francis reached forward and pressed a button on one of the monitors. The picture transitioned to a feed of the street outside the front entrance. A young, red-headed woman was standing on the doorstep. Her mouth was bloodied, her face badly bruised. The Englewood district was notorious for its crime, and clearly this woman was its latest victim. She'd seen the lights on in the warehouse, and had come seeking assistance.

'Please help me,' she wailed through the door, before knocking urgently again.

'What do we do about this?' said Ali.

'Well, one of us needs to drive her to the police,' groaned Francis. 'But we can't have her seeing the equipment, so let's walk her round back, and bring her inside through the storage area. She can sit in one of the vacant rooms and recover.'

More knocking. 'Please help. Please!'

Ali got to his feet.

'I'll do the honors,' he said.

The control room was a large square space, with white-washed walls, and grey carpeting. Along the length of one wall was a huge oak table, on which there was a mass of equipment. The wall opposite was empty, but the other two walls were not: one had a door leading to the living quarters; the other an arch leading to a five yard passage, which in turn led to the front door.

Ali exited the room and approached the front door.

'Ma'am, please remain calm,' he said. 'I'm going to open up, and walk you around back. We've got a room where you can collect yourself.'

'Thank you,' the woman sobbed.

'I'm opening up now,' said Ali. He unfastened the locks and opened the door.

The next thing he knew, it hit him in the face. Hard.

The woman came barging through with surprising power, forcing past Ali, and into the room. A moment later, two men came careering in after her. They'd been lurking in the camera's blind spot. Lean boys, all in grey, both armed with a Beretta 92F, fitted with a nine-millimeter silencer. No nonsense stuff. They seized Ali, dragged him into the room, and forced him to his knees. They leveled their muzzles at his head.

'Down on your knees,' the woman shouted at Francis, having drawn her own silenced Beretta, and aimed it at Francis's head. She was perhaps eight yards off, no longer looking quite so frail.

'We're under attack. Three assailants. Armed. Semi-automatic pistols,' Francis boomed towards the living quarters.

'On your knees, now,' reiterated the woman, her face purpling.

Francis complied.

It was then that Ali pounced, lurching back into the knees of one of the men standing over him, and hugging them with the arms he'd flung over his head. The man, unprepared for resistance, toppled into the second, throwing them both off balance. And as they swayed, arms flailing, Ali capitalized – he scrambled to his feet, and through the arch.

A third man was standing in the front entrance, Beretta in hand. He was tall and handsome and dressed in grey. He had a mess of silvery-blond hair, high cheekbones, and a strong jaw. But it was his luminous green eyes that stood out most. They seemed to laugh as the man pulled his trigger and sent Ali crashing to the ground with a 9 millimeter shell embedded in his kneecap.

The two men Ali had shaken off were on him once more, and dragged him roughly back into the room. The shooter followed them with a saunter. Francis was still at gunpoint.

Special Agent Fred Vitelli was the next to enter the room – he stumbled gingerly through the door to the living quarters, as white as a ghost. The muzzle of an FBI standard issue Glock 22 was aimed at his head, held by Special Agent Dennis Ericson – the son and grandson of FBI agents.

'On your knees, face to the wall,' Dennis said to Fred, nodding to the empty wall opposite the monitors. 'Hands behind your head.'

Fred moved to the wall and obeyed.

'You, the same,' the woman said to Francis, motioning with her head.

Francis crawled to the wall and crouched next to Fred. Then the two men supervising Ali dragged him behind Francis and Fred and patted him down, after which, they patted down the two agents by the wall, before shaking their heads to indicate none were armed.

At that, calm descended on the invading party as they realized their moment of danger had passed. Then, suddenly, all eyes turned to the man who'd shot Ali; the man who, given the way the others looked at him, was clearly their leader. In response, this man smiled softly back. He then turned to the three he'd entered with – the two men and the woman – who were now standing with their backs to the desk, their weapons trained on the agents.

'My sons, Lamed and Beth; my daughter, Shin,' he said to them, with the slightest hint of a Canadian accent. 'In a moment I will ask you to take each of these men to a separate room in the second corridor. Each must be bound to a chair, and their rooms stripped. Remove anything that might be used as a weapon or escape tool. Our whole endeavor depends on keeping these False Prophets in check. Understood?'

'Yes, my Zahir,' chimed the three.

The man known as Zahir then turned to the kneeling agents, and the supine Ali. He addressed them sharply:

'You, False Prophets, are now captives of The Order of Babylon. You shall cooperate with our revolution, or feel our wrath. The punishment for attempted escape shall be castration. Your messiah has spoken.'

'You sick freak,' said Fred venomously. 'You delusional fuck.'

Zahir laughed. 'I didn't expect you to respect my authority quite yet. But with time, you shall learn.' Zahir turned again to his invading army of three. 'Take this one away first. Do it now. Dalet and I shall keep watch.'

Fred was forcibly escorted from the room, while Dennis joined Zahir in monitoring the two remaining agents. Ten minutes later, Lamed, Beth and Shin returned for Francis and ten minutes later again, they returned for Ali. Eventually, their job done, they returned to the control room, and joined Dennis in forming a circle around Zahir. The mood among the group was now relaxed and celebratory. Zahir went over to Dennis and kissed his forehead.

'Dalet, my son, my first thanks go to you,' he said, holding Dennis's face in his hands. 'You've lived among these False Prophets for months, enduring their degraded minds. Without you, we'd never have secured this vital vessel. I am proud.'

Tears welled in Dennis's eyes. 'Thank you, my Zahir.'

Zahir then turned to the two men who'd dealt with Ali. 'Lamed and Beth. Your inability to properly subdue your False Prophet was a regrettable mislocation. But your courage and devotion have been unwavering. Thank you, my children.'

'Thank you, my Zahir,' they intoned.

Zahir then turned to Shin, the one who'd instigated the ruse and held Francis at gunpoint.

'And Shin, your heavenly deception was outstanding. It'll not soon be forgotten.'

'Thank you, my Zahir.'

He then addressed the party as a whole:

'My children, we have secured the ark. From here – this humble warehouse – we shall weather the Deluge of Euphrates and transform the world. And you, my children, are at the heart of the revolution. Your names will be passed from generation to generation. But for now, we must keep focused.

'The rooms in the first corridor shall be our living area. One bedroom shall be shared by Lamed and Beth, and another by Dalet and Shin – whereas I shall have a room to my own, and so too shall The Call to Taprobana. Go now, and prepare the rooms. And Shin: wash your cuts and change into your modesty.'

Lamed, Beth, and Shin walked purposefully out of the room. But Dennis hung back – Zahir had placed a hand on his shoulder.

'Tell me, my son,' said Zahir. 'How often has Francis Bindle been in contact with the Chief False Prophet?'

'Muldoon rings here every other day at exactly 7 a.m.,' said Dennis, 'for an update on the Chicago outliers. The next call isn't due till tomorrow morning.'

Zahir smiled broadly. 'My son, your counsel has proved invaluable. I understand how you've struggled these past months. But your sacrifice won't be in vain. The American empire has been governed by False Prophets for too long, and now must taste its self-induced destruction. Only then can we arise as the true arbiters of society's fate.'

'Our cause is true,' replied the man once known as Dennis Ericson.

'Now – prepare the room for The Call to Taprobana,' said Zahir. 'Tonight, it shall be yours to lead.'

Dalet bowed out of the door, leaving Zahir alone in the control room. This was the nerve center of the FBI's most classified operation – a location so secret, they hadn't even bothered to protect it.

The man once known as Ivan Drexler smiled to himself. It had been too easy.

Chapter Four

As soon as I got through security at the J. Edgar Hoover Building, I took the elevator down two stories to the subterranean wing: the part of the building commonly understood to be the business end of FBI Headquarters. Then, after a quick walk through its expensive white and chrome corridors, which were, even at this hour, bustling with activity, I arrived at my destination: Lucinda Parkes's office.

I entered without knocking.

The office was large, with white walls. And Parkes – who was wearing her customary slim-fitting suit and hard look of concentration – was sat at the desk on the far side of the room, writing with a heavy Waterman. The desk on whose surface sat those same old photos of her parents and brother; photos which would never be joined by ones of a spouse or child because, in Parkes's words, she was married to her work. But though Parkes knew full well that I'd entered, still she continued to write – to punish me for not having

34

knocked. So I planted myself on the sofa opposite and waited.

Eventually she looked up, and said in her clipped Bostonian accent: 'Most people knock before entering.'

'Well, I'm not most people,' I said. 'And you can start by thanking me for coming at such short notice.'

She looked at me a moment.

'I'm supposed to be on holiday,' I added, as though it were important.

'You know I wouldn't bother you unless I had good reason,' she said, leaning back and steepling her fingers. 'Don't you think I wouldn't rather be on holiday myself?' she added with a smile.

I wasn't so sure. Parkes had learned to love the abuse that came with working at the Bureau. Of course, she'd had to; because as an ambitious black woman, she'd received more than her fair share. But not only was she able to roll with the punches, she was good at it, too – which was why she'd been made Director of the Office of Intelligence. Given all I knew about Parkes, I reckoned she'd rather be in the trenches than on holiday.

'Aren't you wondering how my flight was?' I said.

'I wish I had the time to worry about such things.'

My turn to smile. 'It's been a while since I've sat here.'

'August 2010,' she said.

'We achieved some incredible things together,' I said. 'Though there's no denying we pushed the envelope with some of our methods.'

'People might not have liked our methods, but they sure seemed to like our results.'

'I heard just recently that they used to call us the Criminal Duo at the Bureau,' I said.

Parkes laughed – an unpracticed sharp exhale.

In many ways, Parkes and I were made for one

another. What we had couldn't be called a friendship. But there was a camaraderie between us, based on a good deal of common ground. It was an honor among thieves thing, because Parkes was also a controversial figure. In the wake of 9/11, the Director of the Bureau had been under pressure to expand the FBI into an intelligence agency, the consensus being that as an enforcement organization alone, it couldn't cope. So in 2003, Muldoon invented The Office of Intelligence, headhunting Parkes to oversee it. But it was her career beforehand that was divisive. She'd been Chief of Signals Intelligence at the NSA, and had run President Bush's Stellar Wind operation: the legally dubious initiative which saw the NSA spy on American citizens without a warrant – no less than a middle finger to the Constitution.

Consequently, she embraced my criminal past as a unique strength. In fact, she saw in me the makings of the ideal modern agent, because, like me, she saw the Bureau as an institutionalized con-machine, using superior intelligence to undermine the enemy. As a result, Parkes had wanted me to join The Office of Intelligence from its inception in 2003. But there was a problem: I had joined the FBI's Hostage Rescue Team immediately after 9/11, which meant I was serving in Iraq at the time. So it wasn't till 2005 – when I'd returned from my fourth tour of duty – that I quit the HRT and joined Parkes's department. Together we'd cracked some big cases. And now, suddenly, it seemed like we were back at it.

I sighed. 'Right then. Why'd you call me in? Six deaths need to be pretty special to go to the Bureau's Situation Room.'

She nodded solemnly. 'All sorts of evidence point towards not only terrorism, but also further escalation. For starters, these killings involved a good number of perpetrators. We're dealing with an organized team. Secondly, there's the date. When something happens on the twentieth anniversary of the first Trade Center Attacks, we take notice, especially when the culprits rub our face in it. And that brings me to point three. There were handwritten notes at the scenes of the crimes that made explicit reference to that attack, as well as the man who planned it – Ramzi Yousef.'

Parkes paused a beat, then added:

'Given how fascinated you've always been by the Jihadist threat, I thought this might pique your interest.'

'You can't possibly think Islamic fundamentalists were behind this,' I said.

'No. But my money's definitely on some kind of religious fundamentalism. All the hallmarks are there – it reeks of ritualism. I thought it might interest you in the same way The Liberty City Seven did.'

I understood her meaning. In 2006, the Bureau arrested seven men who'd been plotting to take down the Sears Tower in Chicago from a Miami slum. But the strangest thing about them was their ideology: it was a mad, incoherent amalgam of Judaism, Christianity, and Islam. And though they'd cooperated up to a point with Bureau operatives masquerading as al-Qaeda, they couldn't easily be lumped in with radical Islam.

'But those guys couldn't have organized an orgy at a brothel,' I said. 'Whereas, by the sounds of things, these attacks were highly planned.'

'Precisely,' replied Parkes. 'I think we're dealing with a group with a similarly odd ideology; but this time, run by folk who know what they're doing. And I'm still not writing off the possibility of collusion with Islamic radicals.'

'It's interesting,' I conceded. 'But aside from that, why bring me in?'

I knew the answer already, but I'd felt compelled to ask.

'Because, Saul, judging by the complexity and scale of these incidents, I'm certain there's more.' Parkes paused. 'And I'm sure it hasn't passed you by that these incidents have something to do with missing children. You know about that better than anyone. I thought this case would strike a chord.'

My conversation with Teague ran through my head. So much of what he'd said fit in: the theme of self-inflicted harm; a religion inspiring homicidal devotion; the twentieth anniversary of the first Trade Center attack. The missing link was how this all might involve me. And it seemed the motif of missing children was fast becoming that link.

I sighed again.

'It's a good thing you called me back,' I said. 'Do me a favor: tell Muldoon I'd like to speak at the meeting. I had a conversation in London – back in May last year – which is looking increasingly relevant to this investigation.'

Parkes leaned forward and narrowed her eyes. Then she nodded resolutely.

'Right, will do. We're meeting in the usual place in the SIOC. See you at six-thirty.'

And with that, I got to my feet and left the room, making sure to knock as I went.

Chapter Five

There was a question nagging at the back of my mind, and a person I wanted to see. So, after downing a lukewarm coffee at the nearest kitchen unit, I took the elevator up to the Criminal Investigative Division on the third floor, the epicenter of all FBI activity in the fight against white collar crime. But while this was a hugely important department, ever since 9/11 it had been forced to take a backseat to the fight against terrorism, which meant a drastic tightening of the purse strings. So it was only after walking down some considerably less glamorous corridors that I reached the Division's main office – the lecture-hall-shaped venue, teeming with technology, where its major operations were coordinated. And sitting at a computer in the front-row was a man who, though I'd never met him, I knew to be Scott Brendan: the young talent who'd walked out of Princeton and straight into headquarters; the handpicked protégé of the Director of the CID.

Brendan turned towards me and squinted through his

spectacles. Then a flash of recognition crossed his face and he stood to shake my hand.

The boy looked overworked: his hair was disheveled, his suit creased to hell.

'Pleased to meet you, Mr Marshall. I'm Scott Brendan. Though if you're looking for Morton Giles, I'm afraid you're out of luck. He left at two-thirty. He'll be back about half ten.'

'That lazy bastard,' I replied with a grin. Brendan smiled awkwardly. Joking was clearly at odds with his straight-laced sensibilities.

'Well, if there's anything I can do to help, just let me know,' he said quickly. 'Am I right in saying you're here for the situation unfolding in Counterterrorism? The whole building's gotten wind that something's happened – something big.'

I nodded. 'One minute you're on the guided tour, the next they've roped you into helping out. You know how it is.'

This time, a smile cracked his face. 'I can see why you and Morton get along.'

'Likewise,' I said. 'Good to meet you, Scott. I'll be back eleven-ish.'

'See you then.'

At that, I started towards the door. But before I got two steps I had a change of heart – it'd be fine to ask Brendan after all.

'On second thought, Scott, I wonder if you could do me a favor.'

'Sure.'

'Would you be able to run a search on the name Ivan Drexler?' I asked, keeping my tone casual.

Brendan's fingers scuttled across the keyboard.

'Here we are.' He clicked on the result. On the left-hand side of the screen appeared a mug shot, taken in '96, of a youngish man with vivid green eyes, blond hair, and a handsome face. There was a potted history to its right. Brendan started reeling off the essentials.

'Ivan Drexler – born June 21, 1964 in Toronto, Canada. His father: Canadian, though originally of Eastern European extraction. His mother: American. He immigrated to New York City in summer 1983, and was arrested in 1996 for organized drug-dealing – which earned him thirteen years at The Coxsackie Correctional Institute, New York. He was released on June 1, 2009, and went to live with extended family in Hillsborough County, Florida.'

Brendan paused, his brow crumpling.

'This is odd. He died on June 20, 2009, when the floor to his bedroom gave way due to a sinkhole caving in beneath the property, causing him to fall to his death. His body was deemed irretrievable. A freak accident. Just a day before his forty-fifth birthday.'

Brendan looked at me. I nodded casually, then thanked him and strolled out of the room.

Teague wasn't kidding when he'd said Drexler had been swallowed up by the earth. And just like Teague, I didn't buy it.

Chapter Six

After a quick cigarette outside, I made my way up to the conference room within Strategic Information and Operation Center on the fifth floor, the ultra-secure thirty-five room hub used as the Bureau's Situation Room in times of emergency, and perhaps the only part of Hoover as cutting edge as the subterranean wing. And though I was the first to arrive at the venue – a large room, with walls adorned with portraits of Bureau agents whose heroism could never be made public – the seven identical dossiers dispersed around the oversized oak table told me how many others were due to attend this meeting.

Over the next ten minutes, these six key players arrived. Stewart Eastland, the round-bodied National Security Chief. James Danahy, the Counterterrorism Director, looking fresh-faced and alert. Joseph Fairclough, the White House Counterterrorism Chief, acting as the President's eyes and ears. Alex Schneider, the Chief of the Radical Fundamentalist Unit – a handsome, well-groomed woman, looking dogged and determined. Lucinda Parkes, wearing a smile that could've been mistaken for a grimace.

And finally Robin Muldoon, the Director of the FBI, whose soft face and aristocratic mannerisms belied a shrewd and courageous man, and who was the only one to greet me with anything more than a nod: he came over and shook my hand. He'd held me in high regard ever since I'd won the Bronze Star for Valor in Iraq. He'd won the same accolade himself in Vietnam.

Before long, everyone had settled in, and at 6:30 a.m., after having thanked everyone for coming, Muldoon instigated proceedings. He began by outlining why these three incidents had been taken to the situation room, referencing the date they took place, the notes left behind, the fact they'd clearly been carried out by a fairly large group of conspirators, and their sensational nature. Next, he clarified that, while the possibility of collusion with Jihadist elements wasn't being written off, the entity behind these attacks was being treated not as Jihadist, but as an independent rogue religious group in its own right. Finally, he outlined how the meeting would unfold:

'As we go through the incidents in turn,' he said, 'Stuart Eastland will summarize the basics, then James Danahy will follow up with salient circumstantial details. Alex Schneider will then explain why this matter should come under the remit of The Radical Fundamentalist Unit, after which there will be a contribution from Saul Marshall.'

At that, Muldoon nodded at Eastland, who opened the dossier, and began:

'Bestselling author Amanda Jasmine Aimes was discovered dead in the freezer room of the restaurant at The Mayflower Hotel, Washington DC. The kitchen staff found her body at 5:32 a.m., within an igloo-type structure. It is thought she was forced within the structure on Sunday morning, then was slowly crushed to death as her breath froze upon the inner walls. Her body had been wrapped in insulative material to ensure it was the pressure that killed her, not the temperature. Her right-hand index finger had been amputated before her entrapment, and tied around her neck. The post-mortem suggests she died early Tuesday morning. A handwritten note was affixed to the igloo reading: *More to come.*'

Danahy cleared his throat and started reading:

'The restaurant's kitchen had long been in need of renovation, and its manager, Ms Nikita Prabhakar, had been putting out feelers for a quote. It appears she was approached in early January by a start-up called Larder Vixen, run by a young lady who'd identified herself as Ms Sofi Halltun. Halltun quoted an extremely competitive price for the kitchen, and suggested her team do the work from February 23 to February 25: the weekend plus Monday. Prabhakar agreed to take them on.

'Now, here's where Aimes comes in. Every year since 2009, she'd stayed at the Mayflower throughout February, using it as a writing retreat. When she moved in on February 1, 2013, she insisted on privacy – just as she'd done in previous years – rarely leaving her room, and living off room service. Apparently staff would routinely not see her for days – Aimes ordered her meals through handwritten notes, and hid when staff came by. Only a few members of staff, and a few of her friends and family, knew she was there at all.

'On February 23, the kitchen-fitters arrived. The group was described by witnesses as five Caucasian youths between the ages of eighteen and twenty-five – four men, and Sofi Halltun herself. This team quickly cordoned off the restaurant, and started work. At 7:03 a.m., February 24, the power to the hotel's security suite went down – a room occupied by a security guard monitoring multiple

CCTV feeds. The fitters claimed they'd accidentally cut the power. It is thought that during the following hour – while security were restoring power – Aimes was coerced from her bedroom to the kitchen. It was then, we believe, she was forced into the igloo, and the entrance sealed.

'The staff claim that the food delivered to Aimes's room kept on disappearing, and that they continued to receive handwritten orders. We speculate a sixth perpetrator was smuggled into the room. This would explain a second power-cut at 8:04 p.m. Monday – just as the team was finishing up – which would've given this individual opportunity to escape.

'We're going all out with forensics and eye-witness reports, but we're yet to find a substantial lead. They cleared up after themselves meticulously.'

'Thank you,' said Muldoon. 'Stewart, the Woolf incident?'

Again, Eastland spoke:

'Aaron Woolf was found dead in his apartment on West 86th Street, Manhattan – hanging from a length of rope tied to a light fixture above a metallic table – by an NYPD officer at 10:03 a.m. Though the post-mortem indicates strangulation as cause of death, it's thought that Woolf's assailants made him stand upon the table, then heated it from below, forcing him to jump. We estimate Woolf died between 7 and 8 a.m., after which his right-hand index finger was amputated and tied around his neck. A hand-written message left on the table read: *In loving memory of 02.26.1993.*'

Eastland nodded at Danahy, who took over:

'There were two parts to this operation. The first was the removal of the residents from the other two apartments on Woolf's floor. On February 26, at approximately 4:30 a.m., two men in NYPD uniforms coerced retired couple,

Mr and Mrs Roy and Belinda Benson, from their apartment at gunpoint, put them in an unmarked white van, then blindfolded them. Just under five hours later, at about 9:20 a.m., they released the couple near Cunningham Park, Queens, unharmed. Almost the identical thing happened to the occupant of the other apartment, Ms Sarah Sullivan. She was coerced from her apartment by two uniformed men at about 5 a.m., and was also released at about 9:20 a.m. on the opposite side of Cunningham Park. The Bensons alerted the police immediately after their release.

'The second part of the operation is more uncertain. Woolf's apartment is on the second-top floor. The top floor consists of a penthouse owned by a Russian who leaves it unoccupied throughout winter. We speculate that a number of perpetrators entered the building at different times during the preceding week, and squatted in the penthouse.

'On the morning of the attack, we know the building's elevator was disabled at 7 a.m. from a control box on the top floor, for a duration of ten minutes; that the phone line to Woolf's apartment was cut at 7:05 a.m.; and that the door to the seventh floor stairwell – forensics tell us – was locked for a period of time. We also found Woolf's mobile in the Benson apartment. Of course, these measures all point towards preventing Woolf from escaping; but the latter also suggests his flat might've been surreptitiously broken into in the hours prior to his attack. We speculate that the assailants staggered their departure over the hours following Woolf's death.'

'Thank you,' said Muldoon.

Eastland took this as a cue to start on the third incident:

'A family of four were found dead at approximately 9

a.m. at their isolated suburban home in Medford Lakes, Philadelphia. The bodies of Joe and Gillian Walsh (fifty-two and forty-eight years of age), and their children, Cosmo and Zenobia (eight and six years of age), were discovered by their cleaner tied up in a windowless upstairs bathroom. The cleaner forced her way into this locked room after discovering blood in the hallway. It is thought – based on forensics and post-mortem reports – that the assailants coerced the family into this room, then rendered it hermetically sealed, causing the victims to suffocate on their own carbon dioxide emissions. But this was only after each victim had had their right-hand index finger amputated, and tied around their neck, hence the blood in the hallway. All four victims died between 6 and 8 a.m. Pinned to the bathroom door was a message reading: *To do what Yousef couldn't.*'

'They suffocated on their own carbon dioxide emissions?' Fairclough broke in. 'How the hell does that work?'

Eastland looked at him intently.

'It's quite simple. You've got a bathroom of about 170 cubic feet with four people inside, each producing about half a cubic foot of carbon dioxide an hour – carbon dioxide that can't escape because of airtight sealant applied to the cracks in the doors, the ventilator fan, the light fixtures, and anything else you can think of. Even if the children were producing a bit less than that, it wouldn't take more than about seven hours before you had at least twelve cubic feet of carbon dioxide present. With that much in the atmosphere, the respiratory system can't function: death by carbon dioxide poisoning is inevitable.'

There was a moment of silence as we all absorbed this; then Danahy took the reins:

'Due to the isolated nature of the venue, it's harder for us to establish what happened. Most likely, the assailants entered this detached property sometime during the evening of February 25. However, there's no sign of forced entry meaning either the assailants had a key, a door had been left unlocked, or somebody admitted them entry. From there, the perpetrators overpowered the family. Given how few signs there are of struggle, it appears to have been a professional job. We don't know when the assailants departed.'

Danahy leaned back. All eyes turned to Muldoon.

'And then we have the element connecting these killings, aside from the amputations and the theme of self-infliction,' said Muldoon. 'Namely, missing children. Woolf was a single father who'd lost a sixteen-year-old son in 2011, and Aimes was a single mother who'd lost a fifteen-year-old daughter in 2010. Joe and Gillian Walsh had had a third child, a daughter, who went missing in late 2009 – at seventeen years of age. These three individuals are all on the Bureau's missing persons list.

'As we continue to piece things together, I've taken the reference to Yousef as a direct and serious threat. Of course, he famously failed to take down the World Trade Center. But there was also his failed Manila Plan, involving time-bombs on 747s headed for America. So I've put all aviation involving American airspace on highest alert.

'Now, I'd like to hand over to our Chief at The Radical Fundamentalist Unit, Alex Schneider, who'll provide some insights into the mentality of the people we're dealing with.'

Schneider nodded at Muldoon, then stood. She was the sort who'd see this situation not as a tragedy, but as a challenge. Something to pit her intellect against.

'Thank you, Robin,' she said. 'There are two clear indicators we're dealing with a religion. The first is the strangeness of the violence. The second is the group ritualism.

Let's start with the strangeness. In most religions, you have a clearly set out moral code which – in the religion's purest form – is to be strictly adhered to. However, sometimes you get a religion with a twisted moral code – a religion in which bizarre or violent behavior is condoned. In such a circumstance, because of the group-based nature of religion, this twisted moral code becomes legitimized to the individual by the group, as the individual sees those around them treating this dubious moral code as commonplace and good. As a result, what might seem strange or evil to an outsider, will come to appear normal and moral to an insider.

'Now, with these three incidents, there are many aspects that seem strange: the self-inflicted nature of the murders, the amputated fingers, the targeting of family members of missing persons. I feel confident that each of these peculiarities was motivated by, and can be understood through, the religion's moral code and internal logic. Obviously, we don't know what this religion, nor its logic, is, but it's easy to conjecture how a religion might justify these acts. For example, the self-infliction could've been meant as a karmic punishment; and perhaps what these people have been punished for is for negligently allowing a family member to go missing. As I say, these are just speculations, but they demonstrate the feasibility of this theory. Where there's strange violence, there's often deviant religion.

'The second tell-tale sign we're dealing with a religion is the group ritualism. Group rituals are used by all religions to create a sense of community among followers, and are usually orientated around praying, singing, and eating. In these instances, however, the group ritual was murder. This kind of violent group ritual has historically been used by radical religions who want to go a step further, and create *fanatical* bonds between the individual and group by having its followers collectively participate in something emotionally extreme. So violent group ritualism is not only a symptom of a radical religion, but a cause of it, too.

'So we're dealing with a violent religious group – what does that tell us? First off, it tells us that it's likely a *world rejecting* movement. A movement which defines itself in moral opposition to the hegemonic order – in this case, mainstream American society – which it sees as sinful and transgressive. However, a world rejecting movement only turns violent when it's also *pre-apocalyptic*. That is, when the group sees American society on the brink of collapse, and so, perceiving itself to be locked in a struggle between good and evil, violently engages the dominant order to precipitate its collapse. If this all sounds familiar, it's because al-Qaeda and other Jihadists we deal with are also world rejecting and pre-apocalyptic.'

Schneider paused, and looked slowly around the table.

'It seems self-evident that this investigation should fall under my jurisdiction,' she continued, 'because these people have more in common than not with your typical Islamic Fundamentalist. Yes, there are significant differences in the specific content of their beliefs. But insofar as extreme commitment to dogma and radical action are concerned, we're dealing with something similar.'

Schneider sat down. It was no secret that she and I didn't get along: she'd always treated me like a two-bit criminal, and I'd given as good as I got. But there was no denying this was a sharp analysis. It fell in with what Parkes and I concluded beforehand: that this was a lunatic cult.

It was now my turn to speak. But I had to wait, because Fairclough had decided to interrogate Schneider.

'I take it when you say religious group, you mean cult, right?'

Schneider nodded.

'Well, why don't we just round up all these world-rejecting cultists and put them to the sword?' said Fairclough quickly.

'Well aside from the first amendment, which might be something of an issue,' she said sharply, 'there's also the little problem of there being about 5,000 cultic groups on the American mainland. And that's just the ones we know about. At this point, we have our work cut out simply deciding where to start.'

Fairclough was about to go back for more but Muldoon raised a silencing hand, before nodding at me to begin.

'Ladies and gentlemen,' I said. 'I think I may know who's behind these attacks.'

I then proceeded to recount everything Teague had said about Drexler, plus how Drexler had come up as dead on the Bureau's computer. I concluded:

'At first I was dismissive of Teague. But so much of what he said fits in: the obsession with 2/26 attacks; the theme of self-infliction; the vehicle of religion. All that remains to be seen is what this has to do with me. And missing children has to be the key. However, I'm not convinced I'm next on the hit list. Rather, I think Drexler wants to engage me in a game – a competition.'

I took a deep breath.

'My theory? Perhaps we're not looking at missing children, but hostages. And maybe – just maybe – Drexler has my son. That's my theory.'

Silence. I had no proof Drexler had my son, but it was a compelling theory: one that had occurred to me the moment I'd read the brief in Quinn's car, and one that was plausible enough to induce a moment's disquiet within the room. But no more than a moment – because whether my theory was right or wrong, the rest of what I'd said had been potentially game-changing. And so before I knew it – amid an atmosphere of newfound excitement – Muldoon was dictating instructions to look into any cultic activity which had its roots in the last four years, to interrogate staff at the Coxsackie Correctional Institute, and to excavate the sink hole Drexler supposedly fell into. Then, after briefly recounting his plans to go public with the previous day's events, he brought the meeting to a close: he could sense the team was itching to get back to work, so he let them.

But instead of joining them, I slipped out front for a smoke. And as I took deep, calming puffs on a Dunhill in the morning gloom, I didn't know what to feel – didn't know whether to feel empty, or hopeful, or petrified. Because I couldn't quite decide what all this meant – or if it meant anything at all…

I ground the filter-tip beneath my boot, and went back in.

Chapter Seven

F rancis Bindle was bound to his chair and blindfolded. It seemed about four hours since the warehouse had been usurped but who his assailants were he could only speculate. From what little he'd heard, they appeared to be cultists of some kind. But what shocked him most was the fact Dennis Ericson was one of them. Based on everything Francis knew about Dennis, this scarcely seemed possible.

The sound of someone at the door. Francis had known they'd want to question him – press their advantage.

'Hello, Francis.' This was the one called *Zahir*; their leader.

Francis maintained his silence. Hostage takers hate being ignored. Their whole game is a bid for attention.

The man laughed softly. 'Pity – I was going to ask if you had any last requests. But since the cat's got your tongue, we might as well get down to business, eh?'

Francis heard a Beretta being loaded. Then he felt an ice-cold muzzle touch against his temple.

'I'll count you down from three,' said Zahir. 'Three.'

Had his captors already issued their demands and

decided to make an example of him? Was this being filmed – his death to be beamed around the world?

'Two.'

Francis's wife and children flashed before his eyes. His eighteen-year-old daughter he'd never see married; his sixteen-year-old son he'd never play catch with again.

'One.'

Next came the image of his brother Liam, who'd be ambushed on his return, and face the same sorry fate...

Snick – the sound of a finger working the trigger. Francis exhaled hard. The gun had been empty. Laughter filled the room.

'Look at you, shaking like a leaf,' said Zahir sneeringly. 'It's *pathetic*. You're no better than the others. Would you believe your friend Fred Vitelli *soiled* himself during our little scrap earlier? How's that for pathetic?'

Francis remained silent. But this silence was not born from passive aggression. He was too shaken to speak.

'Well, if you won't speak, then let's have a bit of eye contact,' said Zahir. He moved behind Francis, and roughly removed the blindfold.

As Francis had suspected, he was in the room next to last along the second corridor. It was completely emptied, aside from a chair three yards off. Zahir sauntered over, and sat down. He very deliberately loaded his Beretta for real.

'When I was a boy, the doctors used to run tests on me,' said Zahir casually. 'Tests like the one I just did on you. For example, they had one with electric shocks: they'd count down from ten, then hit you with a serious shock. People like you, they'd tremble during the countdown. But not me. I was cool and calm.'

He paused, looking at Francis for a response. He got only silence.

'There was another test,' Zahir continued, 'in which they showed me photographs of faces from crime scenes. One had an eyeball ripped out; another had a nose sliced in two. Fascinating stuff. Then, suddenly, they blasted the sound of gunfire into the room. Most subjects jumped out their skins. But I was unrattled.'

Again, Zahir paused. Again, he got silence. Zahir stood and started pacing.

'The others jumped because of a part of the brain called the amygdalae. This creates emotional responses, and sends them to the central nervous system. So these subjects who jumped, their emotional response was distress and when this was sent to their nervous system, it deteriorated them physically. Thus when the noise hit, they couldn't stomach it.

'I, on the other hand, am unique. By an accident of birth, that poisonous element in my brain was disconnected from my nervous system. But, of course, when people are born with an advantage, there's jealousy. So they kept me in hospital to "cure" me…'

Zahir strolled back to the chair and sat down.

'Why? Because I had a gift – a special ability.'

For the third time, Zahir paused. This time, Francis responded.

'Your certificate's in the post,' he hissed.

Zahir smiled humorlessly. 'Very amusing. But you *will* learn to respect me.'

'I've seen it all before, buddy. A whack-job thinks he's spoken to God. And guess what? God says kill 'em all. Forgive me for not clamoring for your wisdom, O Messiah.'

Zahir smiled – genuinely, this time. 'I mustn't forget that you're the man who headed the investigation into the first Trade Center attack those twenty years ago. That attack's something of a fascination for me.'

'Everybody's gotta have a hobby, right?' replied Francis flippantly.

'You have me wrong, Mr Bindle. I'm not like the Jihadists you've spent your life chasing. I'm not so deluded as to believe in any God. Religion to me is a means to an end: because nothing inspires commitment and dedication like religion, nothing affords the leadership so much power. Just look at al-Qaeda and the control its leaders have over their followers. The power to make them sacrifice their lives. But the leaders of the Jihad movements believe what they preach. Whereas I'm more powerful yet, because I believe in nothing. I preach whatever best fulfils my aims.'

'And what exactly are your aims?' probed Francis.

Zahir looked delighted to be asked.

'My aim is to be the most inspired manipulator of men. I'm looking to exert true power through deception – to persuade my victims to act against their own best interests. After all, isn't that the essence of con-artistry? But you know all about that – you're with the Bureau. You trade in exerting power through intelligence and deception. That's why it's essential not only to involve you, but to defeat you.'

Francis raised his eyebrows incredulously.

'Is this a game to you?' he whispered.

Zahir threw up his arms excitedly.

'Yes, a game! Precisely! A game I must win at all costs. I've always believed sport should model itself on war. Thank you for understanding.'

'I understand you're a psychopath,' Francis spat.

'You're not the first to call me that,' said Zahir, waving a dismissive hand. 'Now listen. As you might've guessed, I've employed superior intelligence and deception to take over your little operation. Our friend Dennis Ericson – the man who enabled me to pull it off – tells me you're in contact with the Director every other day, updating him on a local Jihadist cell. Now, what I'd like you to do is to feed the Director information that'll make him do something against his own best interests.' Zahir leaned in. 'I want you to tell him there's been a breakthrough – they've made contact with al-Qaeda.'

'And if I refuse?'

'Your colleagues and brother will die.'

Francis clenched his teeth.

'You don't have my brother,' he growled.

Zahir merely chuckled, before rising, and sauntering out of the door.

Chapter Eight

I didn't yet know if this had anything to do with Samuel. But for the time being, I had to work on the basis that it did and, as a result, the stakes felt higher for me. In fact, I felt on the verge of becoming like the family members of captives I'd seen during my hostage rescue days; of becoming incapacitated by the situation. So to stave off this feeling, I spent the next three hours energetically assisting Schneider's Radical Fundamentalist Unit at the SIOC as they began collating and scrutinizing evidence from Joint Terrorism Task Forces at the DC, New York, and Philadelphia Field Offices, with no small help from Parkes's analytical team at The Office of Intelligence. And though the situation was grave, there was still something exciting about seeing the SIOC in full swing. It was something I'd missed.

After I'd recited my meet with Teague once again – this time to an agent who'd transcribed it for future reference – I realized I was hungry. It was nearing 11 a.m., and I hadn't eaten since the flight. So I took the elevator to the third floor, and headed once more for the CID main office. This time, I was in luck.

Sitting in the audience area were ten agents, including Brendan. But it was the man before them – briefing them on counterfeit dollars from Venezuela – that I was after. This was Morton Giles, the Director of the CID: a bear of a man, whose oversized dimensions were offset by his gentle manner, soft brown eyes, and receding head of curly grey hair.

Noticing I'd slipped into the room, Giles excused himself and came over to greet me.

'Saul, my boy,' he growled in his Chicago accent, giving me his trademark car-crusher handshake. 'Good of you to drop by. How the hell are you?'

I smiled. 'I'm beat, and hungry as hell. Fancy a burger?'

'You bet. Mind if I bring Scott? The boy's grown on me.'

Giles undoubtedly knew I'd want to fill him in on the past twenty-four hours, so his readiness to have Brendan along was a clear sign he thought his protégé could be trusted. I nodded my assent.

'And here I was thinking I was the apple of your eye,' I said.

Giles slapped my shoulder affectionately, before beckoning Brendan over. A few minutes later, I was roaming up Pennsylvania Avenue. To my left, Scott Brendan. To my right, Morton Giles, the man who'd arrested me seventeen years ago following a four year game of cat-and-mouse.

AS WE ATE AT A SECLUDED BOOTH AT CENTRAL MICHEL

Richard, a low-key restaurant a block away from Headquarters, I proceeded to fill Giles and Brendan in. But once I'd finished the account, and they'd taken a little while to digest it all, we got talking about other things. And before long, we were all joking and cracking wise – Brendan demonstrating an acerbic wit I hadn't expected – in a welcome escape from the doom and gloom. Then, over coffee, the conversation turned to my time on the run all those years ago.

'Your relationship must've been very odd back then,' said Brendan intently. 'Saul, you must've seen Morton lurking in every shadow.'

I gave a half-smile. 'In a way, Mort became my only friend. Being constantly on the run like that, it isolates you. Mort was the only constant. I actually think I would've been more distressed had he not been on my trail.'

Giles nodded. 'The affection was mutual. After enough time tracking you down, I found myself caring for you. Wanted to bring you in for your own damned good. Though that's not to say you didn't piss me off.'

I smiled. Though I'd been a young man while on the run, Giles had hardly been old. In fact, he'd only been thirty when the Criminal Investigative Division at Headquarters asked him to track me down. And it was his success in sniffing me out that saw him promoted to Headquarters full time. From there, it'd only been a few short years before he was heading the Division himself.

Brendan wrinkled his brow.

'Sounds like an interesting relationship. The arrest must've been bizarre.'

'Which one?' I replied slyly.

'How do you mean?' said Brendan.

'Oh, not this again,' interjected Giles.

'So Morton hasn't told you?'

'Told me *what*?' said Brendan.

'Well, I thought I'd let you tell him, Saul, seeing that you love this story so much,' said Giles sarcastically but with the smile of a man able to laugh at his own expense.

'Kind of you, Mort,' I replied, before turning back to Brendan. 'You see, there were two arrests in all. Because before Morton had me arrested, I got him first.'

Brendan was hooked: his head was cocked towards me with interest.

I continued: 'It was June 1996, and I was hiding within New York's mafia scene. And I thought I was being real clever, too. Because on one hand, I reckoned it was somewhere Mort would never think to look for me, since what criminal hides among the most monitored group in America? Yet, at the same time, I reckoned the New York FBI Field Office would be unlikely to recognize who I truly was and alert Mort, since the chances were a local team wouldn't know the first thing about an unrelated Headquarters operation. And sure enough, this hideout did the trick.

'But then I made a mistake. I started sleeping with a woman I knew nothing about. A few weeks later, we were getting photographed by paparazzi outside a motel room, which was precisely the treatment a congressman's daughter caught having an affair would expect to receive. I knew it was only a matter of time before Mort saw these images, so I ran. Got on a Greyhound bus, and rode it all the way to Dallas. But though I'd picked Dallas out of panic, during the course of the journey I calmed and formulated a plan.

'As soon as I arrived in Dallas, I did two things: first, I forged a Texas arrest warrant for Morton Giles – the FBI impersonator who'd been causing a world of trouble in Houston; and second, I purchased a plain blue uniform, like the ones worn in Texan courthouses. Then I waited for the inevitable – for Mort to follow my trail to Dallas – and once he did, and I managed to get wind of where he was staying, I made my final move. I drove a rental car to Houston, used the uniform to gain access to the city's courthouse, faxed the warrant to all Dallas police stations, then called Dallas Police Headquarters, and left an anonymous tip as to Mort's whereabouts. Next thing Mort knew, he was being set upon by ten armed officers.'

Brendan laughed hard, but he was soon cut off by Giles. The next part of the story was the bit he liked.

'As clever as Saul's ploy had been, it didn't take long for Dallas Police to realize the truth. They soon discovered they were the only city who'd received this "statewide" warrant. And then they called Hoover, who confirmed who I was.

'Unsurprisingly, Dallas Police didn't find Saul's prank quite so funny, and were only too happy to help with my counter-offensive. First, we convinced the *Houston Chronicle* and the *Dallas Morning News* to report on the arrest of FBI impersonator, Morton Giles – we wanted Saul to think his ruse had worked. Then we traced Saul's "anonymous" tip to a motel just outside Houston. And though he was no longer there by the time we arrived, he'd read the articles and gotten complacent – just as I'd hoped – and as a result, he hadn't gotten far. We found him a few hours later, in a second motel just down the road.'

I smiled to hear this story, but I hadn't been smiling at the time. When Mort knocked on my motel room door on June 29, 1996, I'd cried in his arms like a baby. And it wasn't until after I'd grown up a hell of a lot that he negotiated me out of prison and gave me a second lease of life.

I was jogged from these thoughts by my phone ringing. The screen said: Olivia Ellis. The woman I was once due to marry. The mother of my son.

'Hello, Olivia,' I answered.

A hysterical sentence.

'I'm in DC,' I said. 'I'm heading over now.'

I hung up, trapped a twenty under my plate, then stood.

'At all costs, keep this to yourselves. Olivia's just received a message from Samuel.'

A second later, I was out the door.

Chapter Nine

I hailed a cab. 'Chichester Lane, off New Hampshire Avenue. I'll pay double if you get me there in under twenty.'

'You're on,' said the cabbie.

The car started north.

Olivia lived in a Maryland suburb, just beyond the northernmost limit of Washington, with her husband, Lester Ellis, an attorney who worked not far from Hoover. Olivia had moved to DC in the mid-1990s, looking for a way to provide for Samuel after I'd abandoned them. Within three months she'd met Lester, who'd fallen madly in love with Olivia, and married her within the year, raising Samuel as his own.

Samuel had taken Lester's surname. But he was still my son.

The cab arrived outside 29 Chichester Lane twenty-one minutes later, at 12:45. I paid the cabbie double – plus extra to get him to wait for my return – then strode up the well-tended lawn and knocked on the front door.

The Olivia that answered the door was calmer. And

though her eyes were red from crying, she still looked beautiful: her face was clustered about by delicate brown curls; and her high-cheekbones afforded her an inimitable elegance. But by the way she wordlessly turned and marched through the house, I could tell she was still distressed. I followed her to the kitchen. Immediately my eye was drawn to a red notebook on the table. A well-worn Moleskine which I recognized as Samuel's.

Olivia stood, arms crossed, staring at the offending item.

'It was on the doormat when I returned from grocery shopping. I left about eleven, and got back maybe five minutes before calling you.'

'Did it come in an envelope?'

'No, just by itself,' she said. 'At first I thought it was a prank. But it's definitely his. There's stuff in it I remember him reading to me. His name and address are within the front cover, in his handwriting.'

I pulled back the cover. In neat handwriting was the name Samuel Ellis and his address. The blue ink had turned almost brown, indicating it was written some time ago.

'The message is on the last page,' Olivia added.

I flicked through the notebook. The first two thirds were used up, crammed with exam notes, book ideas, jokes, whereas the final third appeared to be unmarked. Once I was satisfied there was nothing hidden away within this final third, I turned to the last page. There I found six lines of text in blue ink. I could tell by the color of the ink, and the impression the pen had made, it'd been written recently with a fountain tip. There was no doubt in my mind it was Samuel's handwriting. The text read:

02/25/13

I am alive, but in a desperate situation. I am a hostage. I know little of who my captors are, and do not know where I am as I write this. But I do know that Mortimer's death in Durham, NC, this Wednesday will not be an accident, and definitely not suicide. If this message makes it to you, I pray it will be enough. It is all I know. If I never see you again, I love you, Dad, whether you have a car or not.

Samuel Marshall

I read it once, fast, then a second time, more slowly. I may have looked calm, but it hit me hard. My son was probably alive – a hostage, but alive – and with that came hope. And what's more, he'd called himself Samuel Marshall – something he'd never done before.

And there was more here than just the handwriting to indicate it was actually Samuel – namely, the comment about me not having a car. On August 7, 2005, Samuel's eleventh birthday, Olivia and Lester decided I could meet Samuel for the first time since I'd abandoned Olivia, so long as I didn't tell him who I truly was. Olivia had introduced me to Samuel as an old friend with whom she'd lost contact. Samuel had asked why we'd drifted apart. '*I suppose because Saul was too pedestrian,*' she'd said, thinking on her feet, to which Samuel had replied: '*I can't believe mom stopped being friends with you because you didn't have a car!*' These words were still fresh in my mind eight years on.

I looked up. Olivia was staring at me intently.

'It's got to be him, right?' she asked imploringly.

I nodded. 'So you've no idea who delivered this?'

'As much idea as you have,' she replied.

'Have you asked the neighbors?'

'I called up the three houses opposite, and two on either side. Nobody saw a thing.'

I nodded.

'I haven't shown this to anyone else, not even Lester,' she added. 'It was clearly meant for you.'

I looked at the page again.

Somebody had my son, and that somebody was going to die. Drexler was prime suspect. And before I knew it, I was imagining tearing him limb from limb. But I quickly dismissed this from my mind: I wasn't going to get Samuel back that way. I had to assess the situation. Most central was the issue of how the notebook had gotten to Olivia's. Had some completely unrelated good Samaritan just found it and delivered it to the address within? Not impossible, but very unlikely. More likely Samuel had managed to get it to a friend of some kind – a friend who, for whatever reason, couldn't make himself known.

Alternatively, it might've been an enemy who'd delivered this message. And if this was the case, it raised doubts as to whether I could trust it. The reference to our first meeting told me it was unlikely Samuel had been coerced into writing this with a gun to his head – a man in such a position would hardly think to write something so intimate. But it was entirely possible that Samuel's captors had intentionally fed him erroneous information, then ensured this message got to me. Then again, even had an enemy not been behind the delivery, it still didn't mean I could trust it. Perhaps Samuel had misheard the information; perhaps it had once been correct information, but the plans had changed. So much was in doubt.

'Saul,' said Olivia. 'Do you know what he's talking about?'

'Which bit?' I replied.

'Mortimer's death will be neither an accident nor suicide? Durham?'

'Nothing springs to mind,' I said. This was partially true. I didn't know who Mortimer was, nor the significance of Durham. But it did remind me of something: of the six deaths I'd just been briefed about. They too had been neither suicides nor accidents.

'I think I might have some idea,' said Olivia.

I looked at her inquisitively.

'I googled *Mortimer*, *Durham* and *suicide*,' she continued. 'It came up with a theater review on the website for Duke University's student newspaper – for a play that's been on all week. Tonight's its final showing.'

She fetched her laptop, opened it on the table, and I read the webpage.

The play under review was entitled *Suicide in Stages*, by a guy named Antony Lerman, and produced by students at the university. From what I could glean, it was about a man called Mortimer who kills himself in the first scene – the rest of the play comprising a series of flashbacks revealing what had taken him to such extremes. The final performance was due to start at 9 p.m. that evening, at a venue called The Carolina Theater. To the right of the monitor was a photo of the cast and stage designers, with their names below. In it, the brown-haired boy playing Mortimer was smiling broadly. Around his shoulder was the arm of a red-headed gawky-looking friend.

This information was useful only up to a point. Because if the message wasn't a trap or diversion, and something was really set to happen at the theater, there were still a thousand possibilities as to what it might be: a bomb; a fire; a lone gunman; a mass hostage situation – to name a few. And the allusion to Mortimer didn't narrow it down much. A bomb would kill the actor playing Mortimer, plus a whole lot more. So too would a shooter with a sub-machine gun. And neither of these situations could be considered suicide. However, I had a feeling that if Drexler *had* decided to make this theater the scene of his next terrorist event, the results would be spectacular. Sensational terror and the theater have always gone hand-in-hand – from Lincoln's assassination to the shooting in Aurora, Colorado just last year.

And if something was due to happen, how would it involve Samuel? A victim? An unwilling accomplice? Or maybe it wouldn't. Maybe he'd be nowhere near North Carolina.

If the message had gotten to me without Samuel's captors knowing, and the information was legitimate, then I had an advantage. But even in this scenario, my advantage was slight. There was still so much I didn't know.

'So what's our next move?' said Olivia. 'Do you take the notebook in for analysis? Does the Bureau send a team to the theater? What?'

Olivia was urgent – caught midway between hope and desperation.

But there was a problem. I couldn't show Parkes the notebook. Because now Samuel was a hostage, the case was personal. As a result, there wasn't a chance in hell Parkes would let me be part of the investigation, let alone lead it. It's protocol: never send a parent in after their own child, because with so much at stake, you can't guarantee they'll follow orders.

The thought of being unable to control the situation made me sick to my stomach.

I wasn't sure Olivia would understand.

'What's our next move?' she repeated.

'Okay, here's what,' I said calmly, placing my hands on her upper arms. 'I'm going to take the notebook, and head to the theater myself. I don't trust anyone else to do the job.'

Olivia looked at me hard. She understood I was asking her to trust me. But though I had won back some semblance of her trust over the years, my betrayal was never far from her mind – and so I was unsurprised to see the doubts forming behind her eyes.

I needed her to see that things were different now – that this time, I wouldn't let her or Samuel down.

'Listen, Olivia,' I said. 'When Samuel was born, I wasn't there for him. Then, all those years later, when I re-entered his life, it was too late: so far as he was concerned, I'd missed my chance. As a result, he saw me at best as a vague friend – at worst, as an object of resentment. And I didn't have the first idea of how to fix it; of how to be his father.

'And then there was the day he went missing. I know we've been over this a thousand times and that I wasn't to blame. But the fact of the matter remains: I wasn't there for him. I was supposed to pick him up that day, but I forgot, and then he vanished.

'But now, by some miracle, he's resurfaced, and his message is asking me to be there for him. So you have to let me be the one to go after him. Not as a favour to me – to make me feel better about myself. But because I will go to any lengths to repay my debt to him and get him back; will do things that Parkes would never dream of.'

Olivia was silent a moment. Then, making her decision, she gave a tight nod.

'In the meantime, you mustn't tell a soul about this,' I said. 'Not even Lester. Understand?'

Lester was a good guy, and I knew he loved Samuel. But I also knew that if he found out, the first thing he'd do would be to alert the authorities. And clearly Olivia understood this too, since again she gave me a nod, before crying quietly into my shoulder. I placed a gentle hand on her head. This was the woman I loved. The woman I'd always love.

'I'll get him back,' I said. 'Mark my words.'

After a moment, I released Olivia. Time was of the essence, and she appreciated that as well as I did. And so she handed me the notebook, walked me to the front door, and watched as I headed for the cab.

'Keep me updated,' she called after me. 'Please.'

'I will,' I promised over my shoulder.

I told the cabbie I wanted the corner of 4th Street NW and I Street NW. In no time, we were blitzing down New Hampshire Avenue.

Chapter Ten

Vigilantism: when an individual takes the law into his own hands. By not telling Parkes about the note and going it alone, I was playing the vigilante and I was breaking the rules in a big way. I knew I had an obligation to tell Parkes. Hundreds of lives could be at risk – a theater full. And Parkes could send a fully equipped team, capable of dealing with any eventuality. But it wasn't so simple. Because telling meant standing down, and that I couldn't stomach.

I arrived at my apartment – located just round the corner from the DC Field Office – at quarter to two. My plan, as it stood, was to get my shit together, collect my car from the Field Office, then drive like hell – so immediately I made a start on phase one. First, I spent five minutes showering, shaving, and throwing on a fresh suit. Next, I pocketed from the safe by my bed a clip of cash – $4,000 – and two untraceable credit cards issued to nonexistent men. And then I moved onto the serious stuff: I removed a wooden box from the chest of drawers and pulled back the lid.

Within was a Ruger Mark III: a wonderfully subtle little pistol, with ten rounds to the magazine, taking .22 Long Rifle bullets – soft-nosed shells which slip easily into the target, but come out the other side in style, tearing an opening the size of your fist. And crucially, unlike the Bureau's standard issue Glock, the Ruger's bullets don't break the sound-barrier and move noiselessly through the air – meaning the weapon, when used with a suppressor, functions in perfect silence.

I took a key from the box, unlocked the gun's internal safety lock, and loaded it with ten shells, after which, I affixed a suppressor to the muzzle, before slotting the weapon into my pocket, along with ten spare shells. Then, throwing on my trench coat and grabbing a fresh pack of Dunhills, I made for the front door.

But then, just as I was about to step out, I looked down for a second. It was only a glance, but it was enough for it to catch my eye.

On my doormat was a small pile of mail which had accumulated while I was away. But the top item – a white envelope with my name and address spelt out in black ink, and a New York postmark – was written in what appeared to be *my* handwriting. And this was no mean feat, since I'd invented my handwriting anew a few years ago to make it near impossible to imitate.

I snatched up the envelope, and extracted the single page within. It was filled with this imitation handwriting, in the same ink as on the envelope:

Saul Marshall. Born 01.24.1975. The day the FALN bombed the Fraunces Tavern, Manhattan. Four dead, fifty injured.

Ivan Drexler. Born 06.21.1964. The day the KKK lynched three men, inspiring the Mississippi Burning Investigation.

The specter of the past casts a long shadow. It defines us.

Those born on 02.26.2013 will hear how their birthday was the day Ivan Drexler – the leader of The Order of Babylon – began his ingenious week-long assault on America. They will hear how Drexler's followers knew him as The Zahir, and how they believed they were serving God. But Drexler did not believe. He had created The Order as a means of control, in his effort to become the greatest manipulator of men.

They will hear how Drexler magnanimously included Marshall in this competition by taking his son, and giving him a week to live – until midnight of March 4. That is, unless Marshall told the authorities about The Order. In which case, Marshall's son would die immediately, as punishment for Marshall's cowardice.

They will hear how Marshall was bested, and how hundreds died. And they will understand that these deaths were a testament to Drexler's genius, since these victims were never simply killed. Rather, their demise was self-inflicted. The result of Drexler's awe-inspiring designs.

Because, unlike Hugh Marshall, some need just a little persuasion.

Hugh Marshall was my father. He'd shot himself three months before I was born, after a severe bout of depression. For a moment the red mist came down, and I furiously paced the apartment. But I understood this was what Drexler had wanted. So I sat down at the kitchen table and cleared my head, before reading the message again, more slowly.

There was no doubt Drexler was a psychopath. The way he talked about himself in the third person, and canonized himself in the history of terror, couldn't have been more archetypal. And his overarching motives tallied with those of a psychopath. He wasn't motivated, like most, by love, or money, or duty to nation or ideology: he

was motivated simply by a cold, calculated desire to win –
to be the greatest manipulator – and unfortunately he was
quantifying his success by how many people he killed, and
how spectacular he could make their deaths. Any yet there
was clearly also a second, more focused motive driving him
– a desire to see me suffer.

But this insight into Drexler's mentality aside, the
important thing here was that Drexler and his cult – The
Order of Babylon – had my son, were giving him just a
week to live, and had issued a threat that'd given me a far
greater reason to keep Parkes in the dark.

And then, all of a sudden, the full implication of this
hit home, and I knew I couldn't just sit there any longer.
So, with my watch reading 2:13, and the adrenaline rising
in my neck, I bolted out the door.

Chapter Eleven

The FBI is an enormous machine. Huge. We're talking fifty-six field offices, and more than sixty international offices; almost fourteen thousand agents, and an annual budget of over $8 billion. A mind-boggling operation. And it goes without saying that with great size comes great strength. But with size also comes chinks in the armor. Because in an operation that large, information gets lost.

And the Bureau knew all about this problem. In August 2001, an FBI agent in Minneapolis was tipped off about Zacarias Moussaoui, an Algerian national who'd been learning to fly 747s, with little interest in taking off or landing. The agent entreated Headquarters to secure a warrant. But the Radical Fundamentalist Unit was overloaded, and didn't have time to process the request. It was only after 9/11 the Bureau realized Moussaoui had been a key conspirator.

At the FBI, information got lost along the chain of command. My plan was to head to the Field Office and exploit this vulnerability – to find out what I could about

The Order. Because wars are won and lost on intelligence.

Meanwhile, as I paced south down 4th Street, I decided there were two people at the Bureau I could trust with the whole truth. One of them I'd last seen in a burger joint. I dialled him on my mobile.

'Mort,' I said. 'Are you somewhere you can talk? This can't go beyond you.'

'One moment.' The sound of a door opening and closing. 'Shoot.'

I gave him a rundown of the notes from Samuel and Drexler, plus my analysis.

'Of course I understand why you want to keep this from Parkes and go it alone,' Giles said, after a moment's reflection. 'If you tell her, she'll declare war on this cult in a heartbeat, and Samuel's head will roll. And yes, before you ask, you can trust me to keep my lips sealed. But if innocents die in consequence – and it sounds like many could be in the line of fire – the fallout will be huge. Parkes'll eat you alive.'

'Well, frankly, I have no choice but to leave innocents in the line of fire – because there's no way in hell I'm just going to let my son die,' I replied. Then I added: 'But besides, there'll be no casualties. Samuel *will* be there tonight, and I *will* have him back by midnight.'

This was pure bravado, as much to reassure myself as Giles. He made a noise like he wasn't convinced.

'So you're heading to Durham now?' he asked.

'Very shortly.'

'And what if Parkes wants you about, or asks where you're going?'

I grunted. 'Let's hope she doesn't.'

'Keep me in the loop, Saul.'

'Will do.'

To most Field Offices, Headquarters was far enough away that its sovereignty was merely an abstraction. Consequently, these Offices operated as laws unto themselves. But the DC Field Office was unique in that it shared a town with Headquarters. So, unlike the other Field Offices, it felt the authority of Headquarters. And no more so than during major operations, when Hoover would send over staff to manage affairs and intervene in decision making.

It was with this in mind that I entered the Field Office, and mounted the stairs towards the Counterterrorism Division, hoping to find somebody from Schneider's team whose brain I could pick.

I came into the Joint Terrorist Task Force main suite to find the large, lecture-hall-shaped venue abuzz with activity – there were maybe fifty staffers hard at work on the Aimes case, clustered in teams about the room. I looked around, and found what I was looking for.

Sitting in the corner was a pasty little man, hunched over a laptop. This was Todd Lamphere, an analyst from Headquarters who'd worked under Schneider for years. He was indicative of what was known at the Bureau as a "Brain" – a socially awkward, effacing, uneasy character, kept around for the stuff between his ears. Lamphere in particular was nothing less than a walking encyclopedia. And not only that, he liked me. The perfect prey.

I walked over, and sat down beside him.

'Hello, Todd.'

He turned towards me. 'Saul Marshall. Long time no see.'

'So Schneider's sent you over to lead the troops?'

He smiled effacingly. 'Something like that.'

I was in a rush, but this had to be done delicately.

'Todd, I reckon I could use your help. Parkes has hauled my ass back to Headquarters for this investigation. I'm sure you've been told we're now looking for cultic activity with roots in the past four years. But obviously we have little to implicate any one group at this moment. And I think I'm right in saying that despite narrowing down the time frame, there are still many candidates to investigate?'

I paused. I wanted to ensure Todd was following my line of thinking.

'Right,' he said. 'Domestically speaking, about 180,000 people join some kind of cultic group each year. That's 720,000 over four years.'

'Right. So instead of being overwhelmed by it all, Parkes wants someone to nose about a few of these groups, without worrying about warrants, in the hope of getting lucky and sniffing out some leads…'

He nodded.

'Obviously this is top secret work,' I said. 'By all means discuss it with Parkes if she brings it up – I'll tell her you know. But nobody else needs to know.'

Another nod.

'So I thought I might start with The Order of Babylon,' I said.

I'd been worried about eliciting an extreme reaction: that perhaps he'd say he'd never heard of them, or that he'd think it was a ludicrous place to start. But he looked unfazed, chewing contemplatively at his inner-cheek.

'What do you think?' I said offhandedly.

'Well, The Order has already crossed my mind. But while it *is* world-rejecting, I don't think it's likely to be a threat. As far as I know, it's a post-apocalyptic cult. We're looking for the pre-apocalyptic variety.'

I remembered what Schneider had said: groups that

locate themselves *before* the apocalypse are the ones prone to violence.

'Interesting,' I said. 'So you don't think they're behind it?'

He shook his head.

'But that's not to say someone among them might not have a lead…?' I probed.

'Cultic groups are unstable,' he said. 'They're constantly sprouting off-shoots and inspiring copy-cats. Someone at The Order *might* know something. It's a long-shot – but not impossible. There are plenty of people who *might* know something.'

'Okay,' I said, with a new resolve. As though he'd just inspired me to continue down that line of inquiry. 'Mind giving me a brief run-down on The Order?'

He smiled awkwardly. A guy like Lamphere enjoyed sharing knowledge. He began:

'They first came to the Bureau's attention in early 2010, when the NYPD alerted The NYC Field Office of what appeared to be a small religion operating out of a property in Greenwich Village. The Field Office followed up with the usual checks, and found about forty youngsters, mainly white students, living as a collective. The cult's liter-ature identified them as The Order of Babylon, and was full of the standard stuff you'd expect of a world-rejecting, post-apocalyptic cult. It claimed, for example, that the recession had been the apocalypse (or The Deluge of Euphrates, to use their language). And that the nation's fate was now to be governed along more moral lines by their leader, The Zahir.'

'Why Babylon?'

'It's based on an age-old myth of an organization in ancient Babylon which supposedly controlled the fate of the entire state – regulating everyone's lives, but operating completely out of sight. This organization was variously known as The Company, The Lottery, or The Order, depending on which version of the myth you go by. The Order of Babylon is billing itself as a modern manifestation of this organization. And before you ask, Zahir is Arabic for "notorious" or "visible," and has its own mythology as an object so unforgettable that it becomes all-encompassing to the viewer, inducing manic obsession.'

'How does this Zahir character claim to shape the fate of the nation?' I asked.

Lamphere smiled. 'Through a daily ceremony called The Call to Taprobana. The followers sit together and chant a mantra, while one throws sand out of the window. It's supposed to work in a manner akin to the butterfly effect.'

He said this with a chuckle. Found it funny.

He continued: 'Their literature urged folk to join their collective; to come and live apart from the broken society of the past. And, sure enough, its membership steadily grew. So much so that by April 2010 it had to relocate to a larger property in midtown Manhattan, West 50th Street. And in July 2010, it opened up a branch in DC – just north of Dupont Circle. According to our latest figures, the New York branch now has about one-hundred residents, and Washington about eighty. They also secretively purchased a large complex in upstate New York in late 2010, which now has about one-hundred and fifty members on site. None of this is exceptional. The Unification Church and Krishna Consciousness both outnumber them by far.

'Perhaps the most curious thing about The Order is the identity of its leader. It's common practice for cultic groups to shroud their leader in mystery: what one doesn't understand always seems more impressive. But The Order goes a step further. Nobody is allowed to see The Zahir, aside from two groups: first, his original fifteen followers, known as the Inner Sanctum; and second, a select few who've since been granted the dubious honor of seeing him. When The Zahir is with anyone else he wears a purple hood. But the situation is more complex still. Because anyone who's been allowed to see The Zahir also has the option of wearing a purple hood. The upshot? Twenty or so people in purple hoods, and any one of them could be The Zahir.'

'So not knowing the identity of their leader hasn't dampened the devotion of these followers?'

Lamphere shook his head. 'People are intrigued by things hidden from view. If there is a Zahir, he's using God's very own tactics.'

'*If* there's a Zahir?' I asked.

'I have a theory that there is no Zahir; that the leadership has created this figure of The Zahir as a symbol of their collective identity. Of course, I've no proof. But it's feasible. Wouldn't be the first cult run by a group.'

I nodded.

He continued: 'Aside from that, much of what they do is familiar territory. It makes money by pooling its members' resources, and by getting newer members to do something akin to slave labor – such as twenty hour shifts selling flowers on the street. And it employs a number of tactics to bind individuals to the group: giving each follower a new name; enforcing a dress code of all grey; dictating sexual relationships; running group confessionals which foster camaraderie through vulnerability; and, of course, teaching them a new, constricted vocabulary – some of which you've just heard – which functions not only as a private language, but also to stifle independent thought.

'In short, like many cults, it functions like a little totali-tarian state. Arguably it abuses its followers. But it does nothing that isn't safeguarded by the first amendment. And as a post-apocalyptic group, it's unlikely to exhibit external violence any time soon.'

Lamphere was winding down. I had what I needed. Time to bail.

'Right,' I said, leaning back. 'So I'm looking for folk in purple hoods?'

'Right,' he said.

I lumbered to my feet.

'Time to take a shot in the dark,' I said. 'Thanks for your help. Let's hope we find these bastards quick.'

'Fingers crossed.'

'Remember, mum's the word,' I said.

He nodded solemnly. I turned, and walked briskly away.

I STARTED MY CAR – A BLACK, UNMARKED FORD CROWN VICTORIA, owned by the Bureau, but mine to do with as I wished – and hustled her out the Field Office parking lot and onto the road.

Drexler had played a shrewd hand. By having The Order appear post-apocalyptic, he'd been able to openly grow and strengthen his cult without arousing the Bureau's suspicions – a simple ruse, but an effective one. And the purple hood tactic was nothing short of ingenious: not only did it create a mystery that enticed followers, but it also guaranteed that as and when war was declared on The Order, their leader would be difficult to find. And when combined with Drexler's faked death, it meant nobody was ever likely to realize that The Zahir was the same guy who'd spent two years in an asylum, and thirteen in prison.

Of course, I'd taken a risk by quizzing Lamphere about all this: he needed only to mention my fictional mission to Parkes, and it'd be clear that something was amiss. But given what I knew about Lamphere, it seemed unlikely he'd initiate such a conversation any time soon – and so, for now, I was safe. In the meantime, I wasn't going to lose sleep over exploiting the Bureau's weaknesses. If it were up to them, Samuel would already be dead.

It was 3:15 p.m. by the time I joined the southbound lane of I-395. My destination was Durham, North Carolina. But first I needed to make a pit-stop at Quantico, Virginia. Because it was there I would find the FBI's Hostage Rescue Team, and the second person I could trust with the whole truth.

Chapter Twelve

The final task Dalet had left to carry out before leading The Call to Taprobana was to feed The False Prophets…

The morning and early afternoon had been busy for Dalet, Shin, Lamed, and Beth. After briefly settling into their bedrooms, they'd returned to preparing the rooms containing the False Prophets. Maneuvering around the tied and blindfolded agents, they furnished each room with an army cot and a bucket for a toilet; then they fastened steel sheets over the windows and fitted peepholes into the doors. A fourth room was prepared in identical fashion in preparation for the False Prophet yet to be captured.

With the doors locked, the rooms were utterly secure.

After this, it was Shin who'd had her work cut out. As the only one with medical experience, The Zahir had given her the responsibility of tending to Ali's knee. Yet after operating for just ninety minutes with primitive materials (Ketamine, alcohol, tweezers, pliers), she'd managed to remove all the bits of shattered tibia and bullet from the wound and get it disinfected, covered in gauze, and splinted and bandaged. It was a makeshift job. But when paired with a round of antibiotics, it was likely to keep infection at bay.

These basic medical provisions were among a stockpile of items the invading team had brought along in their innocuous white van which was now parked outside the back entrance to the warehouse. Also among these provisions (as well as the army cots, steel sheets and peephole glass) was a supply of milk, bread, cheese, and tinned foods; spare Berettas and ammunition; civilian clothes; and power tools. When added to the items already brought on site by the agents, these supplies ensured that the vessel was more than well equipped to weather The Deluge.

But on top of all this, the cultists had also brought five explosive vests. And once Shin had finished operating on Ali, she'd gone into each of the agents' rooms in turn, accompanied by Lamed and Beth, and put each of them in a vest, after which, she'd untied them, put them in hand-cuffs and foot-cuffs, and removed their blindfolds. In this state, the agents were allowed to move around their cells as they wished.

But Dalet had not appeared before the agents since their blindfolds were removed. And now, with the clock in the main control room showing 2:30 p.m., the final task left for him before leading The Call to Taprobana was to feed the captives.

SHIN HAD LAID DOWN THE GROUND RULES WHILE FITTING their vests: their doors would be knocked on twice when food was to be delivered, and they were to sit on their beds as the provisions were dropped off. Failure to comply would equal forfeiture.

When Dalet entered Ali's room – with Shin covering him with her Beretta – and deposited bread, cheese, water, and a dose of antibiotics at the end of the cot, Ali was too dazed from the anesthetic to acknowledge the pair, let alone engage them. Fred Vitelli, however, was not so passive: though he stayed on his cot, he let loose a stream of vitriol, calling Dalet a 'fucking traitor,' a 'treasonous cretin.' Francis, too, didn't hold his peace. But he was calmer, greeting Dalet with 'Hello, Dennis', before telling him that his grandfather and father would be disappointed. That it wasn't too late to do the right thing.

It sickened Dalet to hear their hypocrisy. It was these agents with their degraded mentalities who'd made The Deluge of Euphrates necessary – who'd created and maintained this sinful society. *They* were the traitors. *They* were the ones who'd sold their country out. And it was Dalet who'd long since been disappointed in his father and grandfather.

It was because of these two men that Dalet had felt from an early age that his life had been determined for him – he was to be an FBI agent. He'd kept to script for years, studying hard at school and winning a place at The University of Pennsylvania. Indeed, he did everything he could to put himself on track to becoming the third generation of Ericsons with the FBI. But all the while, he felt empty and unfulfilled. As though his learnt-by-rote opinions were insufficient to explain the chaos, meaninglessness, and suffering of the wider world.

It was while he was in this muddled state that an old friend of his, studying at Georgetown University, had told him about The Order of Babylon, and the preachings of The Zahir – who spoke of the servants of big business and government dictating the lives of Americans for their own selfish ends. Dalet had seen truth in this. And in September 2010 – having just started his fourth and final year of study – he felt curious enough to attend an Order lecture in Washington.

He arrived with his friend to find about thirty people – most dressed in grey, a couple also wearing simple purple hoods – and he was greeted in a friendly manner. Then one of the individuals had removed their hood to reveal a striking young woman, who'd then addressed the room. She talked of the corrupt powers who'd once dictated the fate of society, dubbing them False Prophets; of the economic recession as an apocalypse; of the Order, who must now, post-apocalypse, reclaim their ancient role of dictating the fate of civilization along moral lines; and finally of The Zahir – their leading light and all-knowing arbiter.

Later that day, Dalet discovered that the purple hood was a symbol of status – worn only by those who'd been permitted to see The Zahir, and The Zahir himself.

Dalet had returned to The Order's Washington base three times in as many weeks. Then, on his fourth visit, he was told out of the blue that he'd been granted the momentous privilege of meeting The Zahir, without his hood on. Once Dalet had gotten over the tremendous aura of the man, it transpired that The Zahir knew all about him – about his father and grandfather, and his life. The Zahir told him he was deeply impressed that he'd been brave enough to come to The Order, given the powerful presence of False Prophets in his family. And then The Zahir told him the truth about the apocalypse: that it was yet to come – and that The Order was working to bring it about by waging war against the False Prophets. With this revelation, Dalet realized that fighting for The Order offered him a chance to effect meaningful change. Not only in his own life, but in society at large.

It was that evening that his name was changed from Dennis Ericson to a letter in the Hebrew alphabet – Dalet – a privilege reserved for The Zahir's closest.

As Dalet became increasingly involved with The Order, it soon became apparent that The Zahir had a special purpose in mind for him. He wanted Dalet to infiltrate the FBI: the False Prophet organization which – by secretly manipulating events – represented a mocking bastardisation of The Order. So instead of living at The Order's collective, Dalet kept his links with The Order concealed, and pursued his career at the FBI, joining the Baltimore Field Office in June 2011, and quickly moving up through the ranks.

Then, in October 2012, the excitement started. Director Muldoon contacted Dalet, and asked him to be a part of a top secret mission in Chicago and immediately Dalet and The Zahir realized that this was an opportunity for something exceptional. And now, because of this opportunity, the revolution – The Deluge of Euphrates – was in motion.

Dalet returned to the kitchen, ate a quick dinner, before heading to the main control room. The Zahir was sitting watching the news on the largest monitor. The anchor was talking about the murder of novelist A. J. Aimes.

'Are the False Prophets fed?' asked The Zahir.

'I've distributed water, bread, and cheese. Cephalexin tablets for Haddad.'

The Zahir smiled warmly. 'Very good. Did they give you grief?'

Dalet nodded.

'You must pity them, Dalet,' said The Zahir softly.

'Their minds have been perverted for so long that there is little hope of them ever seeing our righteousness. Pity them.'

Dalet absorbed this, and felt himself calm.

'For you to have seen the light, despite your upbringing...' continued The Zahir '... well, it took special courage and vision. You truly are unique among my disciples.'

Dalet nodded modestly. Inside, he felt a wave of pleasure.

'So you're certain we shouldn't expect Liam back before nine?' asked The Zahir.

'We should be on guard from five to play it safe – and move the van from the car park even before that. But I'd be surprised if he appeared before nine.'

The Zahir nodded, still smiling warmly.

'And if he were to be caught – by the police, or the outliers – there's nothing on him that would give this location away?'

'Nothing,' said Dalet. 'The official Bureau line is that this operation doesn't exist. And if Liam were caught, he'd hold his tongue.'

The Zahir's eyes shone with satisfaction, and again Dalet felt a wave of pleasure. He lived to please The Zahir – the man who'd spent twenty years in solitude, talking to God; who'd been sent by God to deliver justice to earth...

The Zahir looked at the clock. 2:57. The Zahir said:

'My son – it's time for you to lead our first Call to Taprobana.'

Without another word, the pair headed for the room reserved for The Call to Taprobana. Inside, Shin, Beth, and Lamed were already sitting cross-legged on the floor, eyes closed, chanting the word "Taprobana." The Zahir joined them. And then Dalet, numb with adrenaline, stood at the front of the room, and joined the chant. After five minutes, he plucked a single grain from the ceremonial bowl of sand. He then took it to the window – which looked out onto a grey, abandoned train-track – and cast it to the wind.

Chapter Thirteen

It was just gone 4 p.m. when I arrived at The FBI Academy: the 385 acre campus-like complex domiciled within MCB Quantico – known colloquially as Club Fed – where all new FBI employees go to learn the basics. And though I would usually spend time catching up with old faces when visiting, this time I didn't hang about: I made my way directly over to the Hostage Rescue Team. But when I arrived at the familiar building, and passed through its familiar doors – the ones adorned with the words *Servare Vitas* (Latin for "To Save Lives") – I was confronted by an unfamiliar new receptionist. And I could tell instantly, by his grizzled face, no-nonsense buzz-cut, and hard-set gaze, that he was hard as nails.

I needed him to comply quickly. But, at the same time, I had to play it cool. Word couldn't get back to Parkes that I was down here.

'I need to speak to Vannevar Yeung,' I said, approaching his desk.

'For what purpose?' he replied. Not rudely. But not hospitably, either.

'I've just come from headquarters,' I said. 'Need his advice, fast. I'm an old friend. We served in the HRT together. I enrolled on the selection course in May 2002. My final mission was with the Blue Operational Team in September 2005. Saul Marshall.'

He tapped at his keyboard. Then, when he clicked the mouse, I knew he was on the page with my mug-shot and potted history; the page containing details about my military history in Iraq and my Bronze Star for Valor. And though he clearly wasn't the sort of guy to be bowled over by such things, I could tell by the look in his eye that I now had his attention.

He looked up at me.

'Vannevar's at the firearms training house, taking a lesson with the new NOTS contingent. He'll be done by six.'

The NOTS stood for New Operator Training School: the grueling four-month course that any would-be HRT operative must pass after they've made it through the initial two week selection process. Whereas the firearms training house was the steel and rubber structure where live ammunition training was conducted. I hadn't tried to get Vannevar on his mobile because I'd known he'd almost certainly be overseeing HRT training – and cells are, unsurprisingly, left in the locker-room while training's in session.

I shook my head.

'Not soon enough. I need you to call through and tell whoever'll be doing the interrupting to say Saul Marshall is waiting. That should do the trick.'

The receptionist looked me over for a long moment, then picked up the landline and pressed a button.

'Drew,' he said. 'I need you to cut the kill house exercise short. Tell Vann that Saul Marshall is waiting. Apparently it's urgent.'

There was a crackle down the phone, followed by a faint melody, indicating he'd been put on hold. A couple of minutes later, he said a quick 'thank you,' then hung up.

'Vann says to wait in his office. No more than ten minutes.'

I nodded my thanks, and made off down the corridor.

VANNEVAR'S OFFICE – CLUTTERED AS IT WAS WITH knickknacks, memorabilia, and photographs – resembled more closely that of a high school coach than an HRT instructor. As I waited, I found myself gazing at a photo of the Blue Operational Team from when Vannevar and I first joined in late 2002. We were crouching side by side, looking seriously into the camera.

It was no surprise the pair of us had looked so serious. After all, the HRT – as the FBI's most elite paramilitary unit – *is* serious business. Indeed, within the American arsenal as a whole, only Navy SEAL Team 6 and US Army Delta measure up to the HRT in terms of expertise. And, really, the HRT *needs* to be among the best, given that its job is to deal with the most extreme situations that arise in domestic law enforcement – hostage situations, terrorists, bombs threats. However, to achieve and maintain the level of expertise required of an HRT operative isn't easy: operatives are required, day in and day out, to engage in complex paramilitary training. And of course this punishing lifestyle is reserved only for the rare few who make it through extensive vetting, of which there have been no more than 300 since the HRT's inception in 1983.

And even the SEALs and Deltas fall short of what

HRT operatives bring to the table, since all operatives must be able to do everything a regular Bureau agent can do – such as interrogate captives and analyze information. In fact, anyone looking to join the HRT must spend two years as a regular agent beforehand and that includes former SEALs and Deltas.

I met Vannevar at the initial two week selection process, held at the FBI Academy. This is where HRT hopefuls – who are stripped to nothing but a blue tee-shirt and shorts, and referred to only by a letter and number – are put through grueling challenges as they compete for a place on the NOTS. On the first day, I was assigned Vannevar as my partner for an open-ended trek through the Quantico wilderness – known as "The Dog Run." Ever since, Vannevar and I had grown increasingly close as we saw each other through the trials and tribulations of NOTS, then went on to save each other's lives countless times in the field.

Vannevar was closer than a brother to me. I could think of nobody better to have at my side at a time like this. And, crucially, he was now available to stand at my side – because he'd quit as an HRT operative in May 2011, and was now merely an instructor. So, unlike full-time operatives, who must be ready to be deployed anywhere in the US at zero notice, Vannevar could get away with leaving on private business.

'What kind of fresh hell have you got in store now?' came the voice of Vannevar Yeung. I turned to see him entering the room. 'One minute, I'm on the FBI Academy tour group, the next I'm being roped into meeting the mad, bad Saul Marshall.'

He said this with an anarchic grin. Vannevar had a subversive sense of humor, and loved nothing more than taking my favorite jokes, and repeating them back to me in mocking parody. He was known for cracking wise under pressure, and I could recall certain occasions when his wit had been invaluable for morale. Anyone that knew Vann knew that just because he was joking, didn't mean he wasn't taking things seriously.

He stalked across the room, and threw himself gracefully onto the chair behind the desk. The way he moved reminded me of a panther, and I knew from experience that this 6'4" giant was no less deadly than one. He ran a hand through his straight, black hair.

'You interrupted a pretty intense simulation,' he continued. 'This better be a real disaster – something to rival the worst of them.'

'Samuel's alive,' I said.

Vannevar sat bolt upright, and looked at me hard.

'Which bastard has your son?' he said, quickly inferring the nature of the situation.

'A radical cult, whose idea of morality is having sinners take their own lives,' I said. 'Run by a psychopath who wants nothing more than to see me squirm.'

Vannevar wanted me to go on, but I was worried about the time – the clock above Vann's head was already nearing 4:40. Fortunately, Vannevar caught me glancing at the time, and understood.

'Where and when?' he said as he got to his feet.

'9 p.m.' I replied. 'Durham, North Carolina.'

'Let's head to the equipment store now. Fill me in as we get what we need.'

The pair of us exited the office, and climbed the stairs to where the special equipment room was located. Vannevar unlocked the door by first entering a fifteen digit code into a keypad, and then touching his fingertip to a reader beneath. The room beyond – with its white walls, humming lights, and glass cabinets – looked like a large museum, the difference being that in these cabinets were not artifacts, but some of the world's most sophisticated weaponry. I'd been filling Vann in since we'd left his office, and by now he was starting to come to terms with the situation. Fortunately, he seemed unfazed by my plan to keep Parkes in the dark and play vigilante, his loyalty to me winning out over his loyalty to the Bureau.

'If we're heading to a theater, we're going to need snipers and night vision,' said Vannevar, as we paced down an aisle dedicated to rifles. He stopped before twelve identical black rifles, each fifty inches long, and secured within its own glass cabinet.

'Let's take a PSG1,' he added.

Vannevar and I had learned all about sniper rifles during NOTS. And by the time we'd graduated, we could both hit thumbtack heads from 300 yards with the M40 bolt action rifle – the weapon we'd trained on, and favored by the Marine Corps because of its huge effective range of up to 1,000 yards.

The Heckler & Koch PSG1, on the other hand, was only effective to 800 yards. However, to say *only* was to do it an injustice, since it more than made up for it with its ferocious accuracy. It was powerful, too: it spat 7.62mm NATO rounds at 949 yards-per-second. For these reasons, Vannevar was a particular fan of the PSG1 – and I could see it would be perfect for the task at hand. And no sooner had I said this than Vannevar extracted one, before dismantling it into its constituent elements, and stowing them in one of the metallic briefcases stacked nearby – along with a night scope.

Briefcase in hand, Vannevar then led the way to a cabinet containing maybe one hundred units of the Invisio M4 in-ear tactical headset. This was a little polymer piece that plugged directly into the inner ear and once connected to a walkie-talkie via the cable, allowed for hands-free communication. However, the exceptional thing about the Invisio M4 was that its microphone was not external – it was built into the internal earpiece, and deciphered what you said through the vibrations of your jawbone. This meant ambient noise was removed, and even a whisper could be clearly heard on the other end.

Vannevar took two of these, each in a little silver box, along with two walkie-talkies.

'We'll need these if we have to split up,' he said. He then led the way to other side of the room, found a large green sea-bag, and stuffed it with the gear we'd picked out so far.

'And we have no idea how many people we'll be up against…' He said this with a shake of the head, and a more somber tone. The magnitude of the task was sinking in. 'From what you're telling me, it could be a small army. And what if there's a get-away, an escape? Two guys don't have a hope in hell of giving chase. Meanwhile, they could be heading to a hideout – to Samuel's location.'

Before I could respond, Vann was back among the technology. He picked out five GPS tracking units plus a digital reader, which would allow us to see where these tracking units were once they'd been activated.

'These could make all the difference,' said Vann, slotting them into the bag.

'We should also think primitive,' I contributed. 'Worse ideas than a pair of blades. In case we find ourselves in close-quarters combat – or need to be stealthy.'

Vann nodded, before finding two six-inch blades, and adding them to the gear. I knew we didn't have to worry about pistols: I had my Ruger, and Vann never went anywhere without his standard issue Glock 22.

I looked at my watch. Already 5:05. On a bad day, it

could take as many as four hours to drive to Durham, meaning if we wanted to be there by nine, we had to leave *now*.

'Time to haul-ass,' I said to Vann.

At that, Vann flung the bag onto his back, and we bolted downstairs to the lobby.

'Tell anyone who asks,' Vann said to the receptionist, 'that I had a private matter to attend to and that you don't know what it was, exactly. And if headquarters calls, there's no need to tell them Saul Marshall was here. Even if they ask about him directly, there's no reason why your memory shouldn't be hazy. Okay?'

The receptionist gave a deferential nod. The next second, we were gone.

Chapter Fourteen

N ow I was back on the road – hurtling south on the I-95, on my way to retrieve my son – I was feeling better. In fact, with Vann in my passenger seat, I was feeling positively confident. A serial-killing cult? Forget about it. There was nothing the two of us couldn't handle.

The first time Samuel had gone missing, I hadn't had the luxury of Vannevar's help – he'd been with the HRT at the time, and hadn't been able to leave his post. But this time, it was different: Vann was free. And not only had he offered his assistance without hesitation, but he'd also made it abundantly clear where his loyalties lay.

As I bore down on the accelerator, I proceeded to give Vann a more comprehensive run-through. His eyes glazed as he processed the information.

'So where's Samuel been all this time?' he probed, after I'd finished.

I shook my head. 'Beats me. It's not impossible that he's been held by The Order since day one. Then again, he might've run off for some other reason entirely, and

found himself taken hostage only recently. We could speculate endlessly.'

'Perhaps it was the Russians…' said Vannevar.

I cracked a smile.

'It's almost as tricky as guessing what's in store for us at
the theater,' I said.

Vann nodded slowly. But he wasn't quite ready to talk
battle plans.

'It's always been a worry for the Bureau,' he said
thoughtfully, 'that the bad guys should gain leverage over
their agents. Not because of any concern about their
agents' wellbeing, of course. But because of the breach of
national security that could result.'

'Well, I suppose I'm a case in point,' I said.

'Parkes is lucky you're only trying to rescue your son,'
he replied. 'Imagine the rule-breaking that'd be going on if
it was your old buddy Vann they'd taken?'

I grinned. 'Or if they'd taken Schneider. Then there'd
be real trouble.'

Vann knew all about my frosty relationship with Alex
Schneider. He shot me a grin.

'I imagine after an hour or so with her, it'd be Drexler
and his lot taking their own lives,' he said.

I grinned again. I hadn't seen Vannevar for months,
but it hadn't taken long to fall back into our usual patter.

Then, with a characteristic change of tone, Vann said:

'Getting to someone through the people they love – it's
something else, isn't it? I know I've become desensitized to
this stuff, but when you stop and think about it…'

He trailed off, shaking his head.

Like Vann, I'd similarly been desensitized to hostage
situations. After just a few days on the HRT, you have to
make the choice between blocking out the emotion, or
simply becoming unable to function. But now it was

happening to me – now I was being targeted through someone I loved – there was no suppressing the emotion.

Suddenly, a memory – one that hadn't crossed my mind for nearly two decades – came rushing back. I began to speak:

'I was fifteen. It was a January afternoon, and somebody knocked at the front door of my Brooklyn home. I answered to find my mother: her eye swollen, pantyhose torn, arm broken. Without a word, I bundled her into the car, and had her direct me to where she'd been attacked. Soon enough, I spotted the culprit, swaggering along with her purse. The next thing I knew, I'd swerved the car off the road, crushing this guy against a wall, and breaking his legs. I can still remember the noise of the fender crumpling in – of his bones turning to pulp. Then I got out and laid into him. Reduced his face to a liquid mess. Eventually, a cop intervened. But he knew what the guy had done, and so he turned a blind eye…'

I trailed off. I'd never told Vann this story before. I looked at him for a response.

'Sounds like you still needed to fine-tune your insurance fraud technique,' he said. 'Crashing the car was fine; but I'm not sure you had to beat up the eye-witness, too.'

Vann's response was glib, but I could see in his face that he got the point – that if you pick on someone I love, the response will be merciless. That's not to say I was proud of this incident. But I was feeling painfully similar to how I'd felt that day.

Presently, Vann said: 'I'm not sure our friend Ivan will be quite so easy to deal with as some guy on the street. The way Drexler operates his cult – with the homogenous uniforms, the name-changing, the demand to leave individualism at the door – it's familiar, right? They're the techniques the Bureau uses when training its elite – the techniques they used on *us* when we auditioned for the HRT. And they're used precisely because they foster unquestioning adherence and loyalty. We're dealing with some committed, single-minded motherfuckers. Drexler knows what he's doing.'

'So not just your casual cult enthusiast, roped in off the guided tour?' I said.

He smiled.

Vannevar's point was an interesting one – though, really, it was no less than you'd expect from a man with anthropology degrees from Princeton and Cambridge. His education was just a short chapter in his privileged upbringing. He was born on May 7, 1977, into exceptional wealth: his mother a Scandinavian-American from old money; his father a Chinese-American who'd made a killing on Wall Street. As a result, after a more than comfortable childhood in a brownstone on Manhattan's Upper West Side, he was treated to the best schooling money could buy. And when it turned out he had a good head on his shoulders, his enrolment at Princeton, and then Cambridge, had been the next logical steps. What might've seemed less logical to an outsider, however, was his decision after graduation to join the rough-and-tumble world of the FBI…

What led him to this decision was, in fact, pure chance. It was because his father's brother happened to work in IT solutions, and in August 1998 his company happened to send him to Nairobi, where they'd been commissioned by the US embassy to update their technology. And it was during his time in Nairobi that two Jihadists happened to detonate a ton of explosives in the embassy's parking lot.

Twelve Americans died that day. Vannevar's uncle was one of them.

After that, any plans Vannevar had had went out the

window. All he was interested in was preventing such a thing from happening again. So once he'd returned to New York after his Masters in England, he'd joined the city's FBI Field Office. It didn't take the Field Office long to realize that Vann was someone special and, soon enough, they'd placed him with the Joint Terrorism Task Force – the front-line at Field Office level. Vann was happy there. He was making a difference. But then came 9/11, and with it Vann's decision that he had to do more. The HRT was the answer.

'It's the all-or-nothing mentality – that's the kicker,' Vannevar continued. 'In mainstream religions, there's a mentality of moderation: here are the rules, follow them as best you can, don't sweat it if you fall short. But in a cult like Drexler's, it's all-or-nothing: every rule must be followed to the letter, you must seek absolute purity, or you cannot be said to exist in the eyes of the religion. This is known in academic circles as "dispensing of existence" and it's a sure-fire way of radicalizing followers.'

I thought back to what Lamphere had said about The Order's membership at last count. The image of over three-hundred wide-eyed fanatics flashed before my eyes.

'We can't possibly be looking at three-hundred entirely obedient fanatics…' I said tentatively.

Vannevar shook his head.

'Unlikely. It doesn't work that way. There are different levels of susceptibility to this sort of thing. Whereas some completely submit themselves to an ideology, others simply don't have the discipline. And still others will turn against an ideology if pushed too hard to obey. Drexler will have handpicked the ones most susceptible to full-blown radical-ization in order to create his core, while still radicalizing others to varying degrees, depending on how far he can push them. The result will be, no doubt, different levels of radicalization within the one religion… Though you'd think his core must be pretty large, given the amount of bravado with which he's declared his war.'

I nodded.

'And if The Order is as much like the Jihadists as you're making them sound,' I said, 'then there will surely be unequal knowledge within the movement about what's going on. A great deal of the rank-and-file will be blissfully unaware because it's foolhardy to spread vital information among those only tentatively involved. Whereas more radical followers will've been told more, and sent out to get their hands dirty.'

'But nobody told too much,' said Vannevar, 'in case someone winds up captured.'

A few minutes later, at 6:07, we hit the stretch of the I-95 which cuts through the heart of Richmond. And as we did so, my mind turned to Olivia. It'd been almost five hours since I'd left her home and I felt I owed her an update. However, I decided I was better off keeping her in the dark about Drexler's note.

'Going to check in with Olivia,' I said to Vann as I dialled her number.

She answered after a single ring.

'One moment,' she said hastily. Then the sound of footsteps, and a door slamming.

'Sorry,' she said. 'Lester's been home ten minutes. I didn't think I could conceal my distress under ordinary circumstances, so I told him I'm sick. I'm doing my best to keep him from calling a doctor.'

'So he's still in the dark?'

She paused. 'I hate lying to him.'

'So he's still in the dark?' I repeated.

'Yes.'

'You mustn't tell him, Olivia.'

'I know.'

'I appreciate this is difficult and I know the urge to do something is strong. But you need to keep quiet. Vannevar and I are passing through Richmond as we speak. We'll be in Durham before you know it.'

Silence. I could sense she was working up to saying something.

'And you're sure we shouldn't tell Lucinda Parkes?' she said.

Olivia didn't know about Drexler's note nor The Order, so were she to reveal what she knew to Parkes, she wouldn't be putting Samuel's life immediately at risk. But it'd certainly make things messy.

'Listen,' I said, stepping up the bravado. 'Vann and I are experts. There's nobody better at this. We've got all the equipment, and we're prepared to do things that Parkes would never allow. I'm going to get our boy back, okay?'

'Thank you, Saul,' she said, her voice cracking with relief.

Then, in the background, I heard footsteps, followed by Lester's muffled voice.

'Good luck,' Olivia garbled, before abruptly hanging up.

I could see Vann was about to say something, but before he could, my cell started ringing. It was Lucinda Parkes. And immediately I felt tense. Because when it came to Parkes, I could afford to give nothing away.

'Hello,' I answered.

'You've not been seen at Hoover since eleven,' she said curtly. 'Where are you?'

'Have there been any breakthroughs?' I said, in a tone implying she was wasting my time if there was nothing new to go on.

'Not yet. But I want you here as soon as we get one.'

'Okay.'

'Where are you driving to?' she snapped, picking up on the sound of the engine.

'Back to DC from Olivia's. Can't a guy visit the mother of his son without the third degree?'

'I hope you haven't told her anything. No matter what theories you have about your son, classified is classified.'

'I'm not an amateur, Lucinda.'

Parkes paused a beat.

'I heard you visited the Field Office,' she said. 'Any particular reason?'

For a moment, this question put me on edge, because I couldn't help but wonder if she'd heard anything specific. But her tone wasn't accusatory, so I reckoned I was safe. I opted for a tactic of sarcasm and nonchalance.

'I know, it's strange that an FBI employee should turn up at his place of work, isn't it?' I said coolly. 'Unless, of course, you're asking why I was there instead of New Orleans?'

'Funny,' she said with equal sarcasm. 'Look, I want you nearby. Understood?'

'I wouldn't have said what I did about Samuel if I didn't think there was something to it. So I can assure you, I intend to stick around.'

'Make sure you do,' she said brusquely before hanging up.

Parkes clearly didn't have time to talk in circles with a stubborn agent. Undoubtedly, she had Muldoon breathing down her neck; who, in turn, no doubt had The President breathing down his. But meanwhile, Drexler's neck was getting off scot-free. And it was high-time I did something about it.

Twenty minutes later, we got to work on our battle plans.

We immediately decided to work on the premise that we were dealing with neither a trap nor a diversion. But even then, it was obvious – considering the sheer number of possibilities we faced – that it was impossible for two men to make sure all bases were covered. However, we didn't bemoan our situation. We began methodically sizing things up.

It didn't take long for Vann to get photos of the exterior and interior of The Carolina Theater – plus a floor plan, and map of the surrounding area – on his phone. It was located on West Morgan Street: a stretch of road in downtown Durham, running from east to west. The building was side-on to the road and was accessible by foot via a diagonal walkway which ran from the sidewalk to the front door. On the opposite side of the building from the road was a car-park, which was accessible via a service road which ran behind the theater.

The building was comprised of three stories. Immediately beyond the front door was the main lobby – on the far side of which there were doors to the main theater and the orchestra seats – while on the left-hand side of the lobby there were doors leading to offices and backstage facilities. On the second floor, however, there was not only a second lobby, with doors to the Lower Balcony, but also two small cinemas. The third floor, by comparison, was considerably smaller, and consisted only of a modest third lobby, with doors to the Upper Balcony. The theater itself – when you combined the orchestra seats, two balconies, and the boxes – sat a total of 1,016. Yet according to the theater's website, only about 700 tickets had been sold for that night's show, meaning the Upper Balcony was due to be closed.

We kept our plan simple and adaptable. On our arrival, I would exit the car with the discreet suitcase containing the sniper-rifle, and enter the theater, while Vannevar parked in a second parking-lot a little further up the road. I would then buy a ticket, before stealing into the offices on the first floor, and the cinemas on the second – to survey these areas for threats. Meanwhile, Vann would take up a position outside the front of the building where he could monitor people arriving at the premises – both by foot and car – and keep me updated via the Invisio M4s. And while Vann held his ground, I would then head to the Upper Balcony, and use this vantage point to keep an eye on things, with the PSG1 at the ready.

And then we'd wait and see.

Chapter Fifteen

WEDNESDAY, FEBRUARY 27, 2013, 7:17 P.M. CST -
ENGLEWOOD, CHICAGO.

Liam Bindle was feeling good as he swung his sedan off West 76th Street and onto South Laflin. Planting those microphones and cameras in an apartment occupied almost twenty-three hours a day hadn't been easy. The task had required not only subtlety and precision, but also a steady nerve, since the operation was entirely off the books – meaning that had he been caught by police, he would've been treated like a common crook. In short, there'd been no safety net.

But the job was done now, and Liam felt eager to soak up the kudos from his colleagues and, more importantly, his older brother. Because although Liam was now well into his thirties, he still sought the approval of his older brother, the person he admired most in the world. In fact, he'd only become interested in joining the Bureau after his brother had taken up a post at the New York Field Office all those years ago…

Liam parked in the large parking lot which catered to the back-end of both their warehouse, and the warehouse next door. And as he walked the passageway between the two warehouses and towards the front entrance, all that passed through his mind was how fortunate it was that their neighbors, a metal-cutting company called Lakeside Steel, seemed to be having a quiet evening. All too often the agents had been kept up at night by the sound of metal cutting metal and, after sleeping two nights in the back of the car, Liam felt he'd earned a night without disturbances.

Liam unlocked the warehouse's front door and entered. But as he lumbered through the arch into the main control room, and announced his arrival with 'Honey, I'm home,' he wasn't met with familiar faces. He was met with the sweet smell of chloroform, and overpowering darkness.

Chapter Sixteen

The moment we arrived at West Morgan Street at 8:28, I jumped out the car with the sniper suitcase. Then, as Vann drove on ahead to park, I made my way along the sidewalk, and across the diagonal walkway leading to the theater's entrance, keeping my head down.

The main lobby was the perfect amount of busy – filled with enough bodies for me not to be conspicuous, but not so many as to disorientate me. I strode to the box-office, bought a ticket, then headed out of the lobby towards the toilets. Then, once I was sure nobody was looking, I stole away into the private area, placing the Invisio M4 in my ear.

'Vann, I'm in. Commencing surveillance. Do you copy?'

'I copy,' he said, his voice loud and clear. 'Just parked. Heading over now.'

I spent the next eight minutes searching every room I could access on the first floor, with the exception of the backstage areas, to avoid arousing suspicions among the actors. Once satisfied the coast was clear, I leapt up a staff stairwell, and proceeded to investigate the cinemas on the second floor. Beyond a pair of teens fooling around, I found nothing.

'Nothing as far as I can see,' I whispered. 'Heading to the Upper Balcony.'

'People are arriving,' Vannevar replied. 'Plenty by both foot and car. But, likewise, nothing doing.'

'Fire escapes?' I asked.

'Three in all. One at the back, two on either side. They're all shut, and can only be opened from the inside, so anyone wishing to enter by one needs internal help.'

I headed to the third floor, where I found the lobby deserted, and the door to the balcony unlocked. I crept through the door at a crouch, and remained hunched as I moved down the steps, towards the front of the balcony, and the murmur of audience chatter.

When I came to the bottom, I crouched behind the parapet at the centermost point of the balcony. Then I began putting together the rifle and within a minute, it was ready. But while I was reluctant to start poking its muzzle over the parapet until the lights went down for the start of the show, I decided I was happy to take a glance – so I did.

On the face of it, the place looked like any theater in the minutes before a production: people filing in; people already sitting and talking. From my vantage point, the entire stage and the orchestra seating area (which was divided into three sections – left, right, and center) was in clear view. However, I could see nothing of the Lower Balcony, which was tucked beneath me – and there was nothing I could do but accept this considerable blind-spot.

I ducked back behind the parapet. 8:55. Five minutes till lights down.

'How we doing out there?' I said. 'I'm all set up and ready.'

'They're herding in,' Vann replied, with an edge to his voice – the sound of someone doing a five man job alone. 'It's hard to get a good look at everyone. But, so far, I've seen nothing suspicious.'

I started counting down the seconds. Four minutes to nine... three minutes...

Then Vann's voice came again. His tone told me instantly it was something major.

'Saul, we've got something developing. I've got a visual on Samuel. He's just arrived in a blue Ford Escort, driven by a red-headed man... Red is killing the engine and getting out... he's 5'7", skinny, pale – in jeans, a red-checked shirt, and windbreaker... his left hand in his jeans pocket, grasping something... now he's at Samuel's door, and Samuel's getting out... he's wearing black jeans – a plain blue shirt under a red windbreaker... now they're both heading for the entrance... they've entered the crowd... I'm going to get closer.'

A pause.

'Shit,' he whispered – evidently closer now, and needing to regulate his volume. 'I reckon Red has a pistol in his windbreaker's right pocket. I can see the outline. And he's aiming it at Samuel's back. And there's more. I think I can see... yes, I can see a wiring at Samuel's neckline and a bulge under his shirt. Can't be sure, but think it's a bomb vest. If it is, I bet that's a detonator in Red's left.'

I could feel my heart working. My son in a bomb vest... a gun to his back...

I had to keep calm. Think clearly.

'No chance of a clean head shot?' I whispered.

'Too many people. All on the move. Collateral damage assured.'

'And others can't see what's going on?'

'You wouldn't see unless looking for it. They're entering now. I'll follow.'

No sooner had he said this than the lights went down.

I leveled the rifle's muzzle over the parapet, and put my eye to the night-scope.

It seemed like Drexler's plan was to blow the place to kingdom come, and my son was to be the bomb. Both unwilling accomplice and victim.

Should I tell Vann to shoot Red before he sends Samuel in? Wasn't the collateral damage preferable to the alternative? Would Vann be able to get the sort of head shot required to stop Red's finger involuntarily activating the detonator on the bullet's impact?

A handful of people were still entering. Silence was falling. And I was just about to tell Vann to risk it and take the shot, when he said:

'They're both entering the main theater. Orchestra seats. Left-hand side.'

So Red was entering too. Did this mean a suicide mission? On one hand, this spelt trouble – because when a man's willing to die for a cause, you know you've got a problem. On the other hand, it was promising – because it meant Red could be about to stray into my far more precise line of fire.

I waited. Seconds ticked by.

Samuel appeared first in my lens, moving quickly down the aisle between the left and central seating areas. This was the first time I'd seen him in over two years. And though I recognized him instantly, I'd never seen him move this way before – he was walking with stiff, jilted movements, as though his bones were rusted with fear. I'd no doubt the bulge just visible beneath his shirt was the cause.

Did the bomb only have a very small blast radius, so Red could watch from afar then escape unscathed? I doubted it. Because Drexler was behind this, and he'd want fireworks.

Samuel stopped two rows from the front and turned right into the central seating area. People stood to let him pass. There was an empty seat, roughly in the middle, towards which he was moving. It was the position of maximum impact. The optimum place to target both cast and audience.

Before Samuel had gotten to his seat, Red entered my field of vision, just as the orchestra music was starting. A second later, I had him in my scope's illuminated optics and watched as he moved along the left-hand aisle in close proximity to three other stragglers, his left hand planted in his jeans pocket. I recognized him instantly as the boy who'd had his arm around Mortimer in the photo on Olivia's laptop.

Almost in the same moment, Mortimer walked on stage, and started speaking.

What I needed to do was lodge a bullet in Red's brain-stem. Only by hitting this small area on the back of his skull, an inch wide, could I ensure that no post-death muscular spasms would cause Red's finger to activate the detonator when the bullet struck. But making this shot was easier said than done, since Red remained on the move *and* in close proximity to innocents. So I did the only thing I could: I waited as he continued down the aisle, then at last ducked left, and began shifting along the sixth row of the left-hand seating area…

Eventually Red sat down in the fourth seat from the left.

Finally, I had the back of his head in my crosshairs. But there was a big problem. The two rows in front of Red were full – and since the rifle had a muzzle velocity of over 929 yards-a-second, this meant that from whatever point along the Upper Balcony a shot were to be taken, the bullet would go through Red's head, and into the neck of someone in the row in front. And then probably into the chest of someone in the row in front of that...

'I've got the brainstem shot,' I whispered to Vann. 'But impossible to make it without collateral.'

'I'm at a fire alarm. Give me the word, and I'll set her off,' he replied.

Samuel's vest could blow at any moment. So surely it was worth sacrificing two lives to prevent the whole place going up in flames? But even as I thought this, I caught a glimpse of the two empty boxes to the right of the stage, and realized the higher one would afford me a clear shot at Red's brainstem through the side of his head, with zero collateral damage – since all three seats to his left were empty. But it'd take at least sixty seconds to get over there and be ready: ten to pack the gun, forty to sprint over, ten to unpack.

Was it worth risking all our lives in the hope of saving two?

But maybe I had the time. After all, there must've been a reason why Red hadn't done the deed already. Perhaps he was waiting for a specific time: for the entire cast to be on stage, or a particular part of the play. Or maybe he was psyching himself out. The way he was restlessly bobbing in his seat said this was a real possibility...

I made my decision.

'Stand by,' I hissed. 'Getting a cleaner shot from the box.'

With only the sound of Mortimer speaking onstage to mask the noise, I speedily dissembled the gun. Then I bolted out the balcony door and began charging down the stairs towards the box on the second floor. Despite running flat-out, I felt like I was moving in slow motion – like I was destined not to make it before the all-engulfing fire-ball hit. But then, the next thing I knew, I was in the box and reassembling the rifle. And as I did so, I could hear how the character Mortimer was planning to kill himself, and registered in the back of my mind that this was how the play started: with Mortimer's suicide. And I wondered if, because of my own decision to delay, I'd end up losing my life – a kind of self-induced destruction…

Then, before I knew it, the gun was ready, and the muzzle over the parapet, trained on Red's head. I'd made it in time.

I steadied my breath and prepared to squeeze the trigger.

But then, suddenly, there was a rapturous noise: a mixture of screams and standing ovation. The woman next to Red jumped to her feet and shrieked, pointing at the stage.

I panned over. The actor playing Mortimer had slit his throat for real. There was blood everywhere, sputtering from the gash like a garden sprinkler.

This must've been the moment Red had been waiting for to detonate the bomb. But I hadn't fired; hadn't neutralized the target.

'Hit the alarm,' I shouted to Vannevar.

The fire alarm joined the screams. The hall descended into anarchy.

Chapter Seventeen

The lights went up, and the staff came hurrying in. But there was no explosion. No fire-ball.

Both Samuel and Red, however, were already on their feet, and pushing towards the fire-exit on the far side. They were both ahead of the rush, having begun their evacuation the moment Mortimer slit his throat.

'They're heading for the car-park,' I said.

'I'm there already,' Vann replied. 'Their car's bugged.'

I tore the rifle apart with savage pace and barged out the theater, exiting via the fire-door on the opposite side. I then bolted to the back of the building, just in time to see the blue Ford careering down the small service road, before turning left onto West Morgan Street. And though it'd passed quickly, I'd clearly seen Samuel behind the wheel, no doubt following the instructions of the red-headed man sitting to his right. I sprinted back to the building's front to find Vann among the panicked bodies. Without a word, the two of us powered across the walkway and towards the car-park where Vann had left the car. But we weren't quick enough: by the time we were in the car, and trying to turn onto West Morgan, the road was at a standstill with emergency vehicles.

'Shit!' I said.

'Easy now,' said Vannevar.

I looked over. He already had the GPRS receiver on his lap.

'I've got them,' he said. 'Looks like they're heading towards the I-85.'

It calmed me to see that Vannevar had things in hand. With the GPRS on side, I knew we had every chance of catching them up.

I nosed onto West Morgan, and began worming my way through emergency vehicles. As I did so, Vann turned towards me and said:

'What on earth happened in there?'

'You remember the kid playing Mortimer – the character that was supposed to kill himself in the first scene? Well, the prop knife was switched for a real one. So the kid ended up accidentally slicing his own carotid artery. He's dead. No doubt about it.'

'Shit.'

'It was right before our eyes. Neither an accident nor suicide. Well, if the knife swap was premeditated – which undoubtedly it was – then it follows that we're looking at murder, not suicide. This is Drexler flaunting a new method of getting his victim to take their own life. This time, instead of trapping his victim in a situation, Drexler's fooled him into self-murder. And the results were sensational.'

Vann's eyes were glazed in thought.

'The target was only ever Mortimer,' I continued. 'The bomb was merely there to force Samuel to watch – to facilitate some bizarre psychological torture.'

'How did they get out the building so quickly?'

'They were both on their feet the moment the actor slit his throat.'

'Does that mean Samuel knew what was coming?' Vann probed.

I paused a moment: 'He *may* have known. But if he did, I don't think that necessarily means he knew at the time of writing his note. It's just as likely that some days ago he'd picked up on a vague hint which he put in his note, and then was told exactly what was going to happen just before entering the theater. Then again, maybe he never knew more than a vague hint, and was simply told to evacuate when he received a certain cue, such as a pager vibrating in his pocket.'

'Or,' said Vann thoughtfully, 'he knew precisely what was in store when writing the message but for some reason, felt unable to spell it out…'

During the silence which followed this comment I finally finished weaving my way past the last fire truck and turned right onto North Duke Street.

'Do me a favor,' I said. 'Look up the online review for that play in the Duke University student paper, published a day or so ago.'

Vann brought up the page on his phone.

'You see the photo?' I said.

'You bet. Red's real name's Dean Lofkin. And the way he's got his arm around Mortimer is about as sick-making as it gets.' He paused. 'It says Lofkin was a set designer.'

'So now we know how the knife wound up behind the scenes.'

I hustled the Crown Vic onto the I-85, joining the eastbound lane, just as the GPRS told us Lofkin had done. Then, as I crushed the accelerator, my mind turned again to Olivia. I knew that not only would news of the actor's death already be all over the internet – in various incomplete and embellished forms – but also that Olivia would be at her laptop reading these accounts. Even if I couldn't tell Olivia everything, I felt obliged to tell her Samuel was alive.

But more than that, I was also aware that while everyone else would consider this incident a freak accident, Olivia knew better. If she suddenly lost her cool, and told Parkes the truth, the consequences could be fatal.

I dialed her on my mobile. She picked up immediately

'Tell me it wasn't Samuel,' she said tensely. 'Tell me he wasn't the one with the knife across his throat.'

The news had traveled fast. But as I'd suspected, it was incomplete.

'It wasn't Samuel,' I replied quickly. She exhaled hard.

'So where's Samuel?' she said.

'He's alive and in one piece. He was at the theater. But we don't have him. He's now being transported by a solitary hostage-taker. Vannevar and I, unbeknown to this hostage-taker, are tailing the vehicle. You have to trust us.'

'It wasn't an accident, was it? The boy cutting his own throat? That's what people are saying on the internet.'

'No, Olivia, it was the people who've taken Samuel.'

There was a heavy silence, and I knew what she was thinking: if these people are capable of this, what might they have in store for Samuel? I could sense her panic stirring.

'We've got to tell Parkes,' she said suddenly. 'We've *got* to.'

I had to make Olivia understand.

'Look, Olivia. If you tell Parkes about what's just happened in Durham, the Bureau will descend on the theater, and Samuel's captors will see that the FBI know this was no accident. And then they'll get to thinking that maybe the FBI had known something was going to happen in Durham beforehand, and maybe they'd had people in the area at the time. Which would mean that maybe their man is being tailed. It'd take no more than that for Samuel's escort to receive a warning, and for Vann and I to lose the element of surprise... And that could be fatal.'

Olivia ground her teeth as she took this in. 'Why didn't you get Samuel if he was at the theater?' she said accusingly. 'What went wrong?'

I could tell by the way she'd dropped the subject of telling Parkes that she'd accepted my point. But she was still feeling angry and frustrated. There was only so much I could say to reassure her.

'There was a mix-up,' I said gently, leaving out the bomb vest in what I considered a merciful omission. 'It's a tricky place, a theater: lots of innocent folk, lots of scope for collateral damage. But we'll get him, Olivia. I promise.'

There was a heavy sigh, followed by a considerable silence. Eventually Olivia's voice came again, only this time it was tired, weary.

'Lester's so worried about me. I told him I was too sick to see anybody this evening, and quarantined myself in the bedroom. He thinks I'm out of my mind. Maybe I am...'

'You're being incredibly brave.'

'Please get him back. Please.'

'I will.'

Chapter Eighteen

After traveling along the I-85 for 125 miles, Lofkin went north on the I-95, clockwise around the westernmost limit of Richmond, then joined the westbound lane of the I-64. And as Vann and I tailed him, we discussed the situation. We agreed that attempting to take Lofkin out in transit was too risky, and that ideally we'd neutralize him with the sniper once he'd stopped. We also agreed, after an internet search of Lofkin's name came back with nothing, that he must've joined The Order in secret while continuing to lead a seemingly ordinary life.

But when we got about twenty miles along the I-64 – putting us some two-hundred miles, and three hours away from The Carolina Theater – our conversation turned to how we would set about ambushing Lofkin were he to stop for food or gas, since such an eventuality was looking increasingly likely. And, sure enough, scarcely had we started discussing this when Lofkin made a decisive move: taking Exit 158 off the I-64 and joining a single carriage road leading into the heart of Louisa County, Virginia. We followed suit, but held a little further back, since we were more conspicuous on this country round.

After Lofkin traveled fifteen miles along this road, the GPRS told us he'd entered a town called Mineral, a small settlement comprising a main drag running from south to north; a grid of residential roads to its west; and a small park to its southeast. Lofkin entered the town at the south of the main stretch. Then, instead of passing straight through, he slowed near the top and took a left, following the road down to the end, before finally coming to a halt. The map on the receiver told us he'd stopped outside a large isolated property.

Vann and I were still some four minutes behind, and Vann used this time to throw Mineral into a search engine. From this we learned that the place took up less than a single square mile; that it had a population of about 400; and that it was named after the gold-mining which had once gone on there. In short, it was the sort of generic backwater town where nothing ever happens.

Yet when we finally arrived at the bottom of the main stretch, it was clear that something *was* happening here. Though there was nobody about – as you'd expect at midnight – the town was crammed with parked cars. The parking lot of a small supermarket a third of the way up the road was playing host to maybe two-hundred vehicles.

'I bet whichever bastard owns all these cars isn't too popular with his neighbors,' said Vann. 'Not sure he got the memo about the whole carbon footprint business.'

'How the other half lives,' I replied.

Our joking took the edge off; but it was clear there was something not right here.

I turned left off the main stretch, and eventually found somewhere to park on the road seven blocks south of where Lofkin had stopped, which was equally full of cars.

Then, with Vann taking the sea-bag, we returned to the main drag, and headed northwards, walking through the gathering darkness of an overcast night. The barely visible words on the shop-fronts – The Mineral Community Bank, The Municipal Building, Robin's Nest Nursery – confirmed the impression of a generic backwater town. Eventually we came to the turning down which Lofkin had gone. But instead of heading that way, we continued straight on, coming to the town-square on our left, and a gas station on our right. The town square was little more than a glorified parking lot (also full of cars), bordered on one side by the road, two by shops, and the last by a motel whose sign read: *No Vacancy*. The whole thing looked fast asleep. The petrol station, however, had lights on and a guy manning the till.

I looked at my watch. 12:33.

'These cars,' I said to Vann, 'they've got something to do with The Order.'

'Either that, or the Hell's Angels' little-known automobile division happens to be passing through.'

I smiled. 'I'm going to talk to the guy in the petrol station. See what he knows.'

Vann nodded, and I made for the entrance. An electronic ding-dong sounded as I crossed the threshold. The guy at the counter was young – perhaps still in high-school – with a wide, obvious face, and long, greasy hair. He had the look of someone bright, stubborn, a bit of an outsider.

'Got any Marlboros?' I said.

'Should've known,' he said. 'Why else come in at this hour?'

He retrieved the smokes and placed them on the counter.

'You tell me,' I said, handing over a ten. 'Why stay

126

open through the night if nobody comes in for anything else?'

The kid fished out my change. 'Ask my boss. Just because the town has a few visitors, he thinks he'll make a killing by staying open all night. Doesn't seem to realize that visitors sleep much the same hours as anyone else. After all, not much to stay awake for in Mineral.'

'You tell your boss this?' I said.

He shook his head.

'I'm happy to look after the place and take his money. Not hard work.'

'Some boss,' I said.

'It's no wonder he's hit the big time,' he said facetiously.

I grinned. 'So what's with all these out-of-towners, anyway?'

'So you're not here for the event?' he asked.

'Not last time I checked.'

'I should've known,' he said with a grin. 'Not too many amateur Civil War re-enactors walk around in suits.'

It was clear he disliked the event, and liked that I wasn't associated with it.

'Are Civil War re-enactments a common fixture in Mineral?' I asked.

Again, he shook his head. 'Obviously there are plenty in this part of the world, but it's a first for Mineral. An events company contacted the Mayor five months ago, and suggested they put on Mineral's very own re-enactment. The Mayor's always wanted to bring us into the circuit, so jumped at the opportunity.'

I nodded. 'And this is set for tomorrow?'

'Can't slip one by you,' he said, with wink. 'About 500 participants – due to commence at 6:30 a.m. over at Elizabeth Trice Walton Park. Since the motel's full, the Mayor's even allowed folk to camp in the park.'

'Cold night for camping,' I said.

He shrugged.

'So what's this company organizing the event?' I asked.

He crumpled his brow. 'They're called True Shape. Hadn't heard of them before. Think they're a start-up.'

'Get a chance to meet any of them?' I said in a tone of idle curiosity.

'Sure. They've been in town the past four days or so. Maybe ten of them, young and enthusiastic, though plenty more interested in making money than the history. They're renting the Peterson house at the bottom of West 2nd.'

'Nice place?'

'Forget about it,' he said. 'Nicest place in town. Four stories. Tennis court and swimming pool in back. The works.'

'You seem keener on the house than the event. Re-enactments not your thing?'

'Well, I don't care too much for this particular re-enactment, not least because I had to walk a mile to get into town due to there being nowhere to park my car. But I do like re-enactments when they're done properly. Tomorrow's event, you see, is a Public Demonstration, meaning it's open to any member of the public willing to buy a ticket. One for the FARBs, basically. Not faithful to history.'

'FARBs?' I asked.

'Fast and Researchless Buying. The sort of half-assed re-enactor who leaves almost everything – the muskets, uniforms, equipment – to the organizers. These FARBs do ridiculous things, like bringing cameras onto battle-fields. Whereas I'm what they call a Progressive. I take it seriously. If I'm doing a public re-enactment, I'll only do Scripted

Battles where everyone's prepped on what to do. But my favorites are Total Immersion Events. It's like group method acting. The real deal.'

Just as I'd thought, this kid was a bit of an outsider. But I liked him, and understood the appeal of playing parts.

'You Progressives, always a handful,' I said.

He grinned. I pocketed the smokes and made for the exit.

I FOUND VANN WHERE I'D LEFT HIM, STARING AT THE sky. Thick clouds were continuing to gather, submerging the town even deeper in shadow, and conjuring a bitter chill.

'Here's the deal,' I said. 'An events company called True Shape are putting on a Civil War re-enactment at 6:30 a.m. in the town park. There's due to be about 500 participants – hence the cars. Meanwhile, approximately ten True Shape employees are renting the four story mansion where Lofkin has parked.'

I paused, then added:

'My bet is that True Shape is another front for The Order. And given what we've just seen in Durham, I think it's obvious what's on the cards: The Order intends to switch the blank ammunition in the rifles they distribute with the real thing. Their plan is to have the participants wreak carnage on themselves on a spectacular scale…

'Now, I reckon Lofkin is here taking a rest stop. After all, a safe house is the perfect location for Lofkin to let down his guard and get some sleep, since alternative arrangements can be made to look after the hostage. But I don't think Lofkin will be directly involved in pulling off the atrocity. It seems to me more likely that True Shape –

like the team behind the Aimes murder – are a self-contained unit. So I reckon at some point, Lofkin will leave with Samuel. But when that will be, I don't know. Perhaps Lofkin plans to stick around for the action, and again force Samuel to watch. But more likely, Lofkin will want to depart sooner because he'll know this attack won't be mistaken for an accident, and he'll want to avoid the huge response that'll inevitably follow…'

I trailed off. Vann gave a low whistle.

'So you're sure these cultists are providing the participants with weaponry?' he asked.

'That's what I've been told. I wouldn't be surprised if they're preparing the weapons within the house as we speak.'

There was a silence as what I'd said sank in.

'So what are you suggesting we do?' probed Vann. 'Storm the whole damn house – two men versus eleven?'

I nodded solemnly. 'Most likely, Samuel will be locked in a room, perhaps with someone watching him, perhaps not. But either way, it's a preferable situation to when Lofkin had his finger on the detonator at all times. And remember, we have the element of surprise. We'll sneak in, and eliminate the lot of them. I can think of no other way to both retrieve Samuel, *and* eliminate the terrorist plot.'

Vann gave another low whistle, then looked me in the eye.

'Is there no way you'd consider calling Quantico and getting in the HRT?' he said. 'I understand you wanting to have things in your own hands. But a team of twenty with all the technology… they'll stand a far better chance.'

I shook my head. It wasn't just about being in control.

'It'll take the HRT four hours to get here – three at the least. Yet we've no guarantees how long the cultist are planning on keeping Samuel here. He could be whisked away well before the boys arrive. And then Drexler kills Samuel anyway, because I've told the Bureau.'

Vann sighed. 'Is there no way this atrocity can be prevented if we wind up captured? Can't we get Giles to call the local police at 6 a.m. and tip them off if he doesn't hear back from us after we've entered the house?'

Again, I shook my head. 'We wind up captured in Mineral, Drexler will know we were wise to his plans, and will know we were the ones who organized the tip-off. That's reason enough for Samuel's head to roll.'

Vannevar fell silent with a pained expression. The cause of his distress was plain: if we failed to eliminate these cultists, countless innocents would die and this bothered me, too. But this was the situation Drexler had put me in. He was making me choose between my son, and the security of hundreds of others. And I'd made my decision: I was going to get my son back at any cost.

And besides, if anyone was going to be able to pull this off, it was me and Vann.

I sighed. 'It's in our hands, Vann. If we wipe out these bastards, it's crisis averted. Then we can let the Bureau go after Drexler, all guns blazing.'

He nodded slowly. He was coming to terms with the fact that having my back meant sharing in my decision…

Suddenly, there was new resolve in his face. 'Eleven versus two? Piece of cake. They'll be dead before they know what hit them.'

'Thataboy,' I said.

A smiled flickered at the corners of his mouth.

'We should enter only with the gear we absolutely need,' he said. 'That way, if things go pear-shaped, but we manage to get out, we'll still have vital items such as Bureau IDs, phones, cash. Though we shouldn't leave them in the car, they'll find that. Somewhere else.'

This was good thinking. I looked around, and spotted the white steeple of the town church two minutes to our north.

'How's that for a sanctuary,' I said, nodding towards the steeple.

'As good as any,' he replied.

I led the way to the church, and found a place to stash the bag between a hedge and the building. We then extracted from the bag everything we reckoned we'd need on top of the pistols we were already carrying – which amounted to the pair of blades and the Invisio earpieces – while leaving behind the sniper-rifle, the remaining GPRS bugs and receiver, our mobiles, FBI IDs, and cash and credit cards.

On the way back to town, a slash of lightning cleaved the sky, momentarily turning night into day. Then came an almighty bellow of thunder. I looked over my shoulder. Through the dark, I could just make out the words on the marquee outside the church:

'What if you had only a week to live?'

Chapter Nineteen

The rain began as we started down West 2nd Street, and quickly escalated to a torrential downpour. Vann and I trudged along what was little better than a dirt track, guided by the dim lights from a small number of properties, until we finally came to the large house at the end. It appeared in the shadows like an undifferentiated mass of grey, punctuated by the occasional light at the window. But despite the gloom, we could clearly see that there were five vehicles in the drive – including Lofkin's Ford – and that there was nobody on guard. Crucially, it looked like we still had the advantage of surprise. And to make it count, we knew the answer was back-to-basics guerrilla warfare.

Suddenly, a second shock of lightning set the scene brilliantly alight. For a moment, the place looked like a house from hell.

I turned to Vann, and said over the sound of rain pummeling the ground:

'Samuel will most likely be in a locked room on the fourth floor at the top of the house. Perhaps with someone standing guard, perhaps not.'

Vann nodded. We'd both seen enough hostage situations to know captives are usually held higher up the building. It complicates their route of escape.

'Our only option is to slaughter every last one of them,' I continued. 'Silently working through the house until Samuel is secured. The gas station guy said there were maybe ten of them. So eleven in all, including Lofkin. But we mustn't take that for granted. There may be more. And blowing our cover with just one remaining could prove fatal.'

I condemned the cultists to death with a clear conscience. Once upon a time I might've considered them as misguided youths, deserving of mercy – as victims of brainwashing. But dealing with Jihadists had changed my way of thinking. Because they'd taught me that once someone is infected with the mind-virus of religious extremism, they are not only happy to carry out unspeakable acts of violence, but they're also impossible to dissuade from their line of thinking. When an opponent is obsessively trying to do you mortal harm, there can be no room for mercy.

Vann nodded. He was on the same page. He then said:

'But they're going to be reluctant to detonate Samuel's vest. Because even if they're willing to be in the same house as a bomb going off, they still have a job to do this morning and the blast would blow their cover. So if they want to stop us by directly threatening Samuel's life, they'll probably have to put a gun to his head. And if Samuel *is* in fact unattended, then we might have a chance of getting to him before they can do so…'

I rocked my head side to side. This was all speculation. Yet, at this point, we had no choice but to speculate. I looked again at the house, and wished for a glimpse of how things stood within, an idea of what to anticipate. But as things were, there was so much we didn't know. And in the field, the less you know, the worse your chances.

'Point of entry?' asked Vann.

The front door was out of the question. But there was an opening in the fence to the left of the house, leading down the side of the property, presumably to the garden.

'With a house like this, there's bound to be an entrance round back,' I said. 'More than one.'

'No time like the present,' replied Vann decisively.

We went for the opening, and followed the pathway. Soon we came to a door on the side of the house. I could see from the crack between the door and jamb that it was unlocked.

'I'll enter here,' I whispered to Vann. 'You head round back and find a second entrance. We'll enter simultaneously. Work our way to the front of the house.'

He gave me thumbs-up, inserted his Invisio M4, then skirted round the building. I thumbed my own Invisio into my ear, extracted my Ruger from my pocket, and waited. Presently, Vann said to me through the earpiece:

'There's a conservatory round back – lights out, doors unlocked. From what I can see, it leads to a kitchen. Ready when you are.'

I pressed my ear to the door, but could hear nothing over the rain.

'On the count of three,' I whispered. 'One, two, three.'

With my pistol upraised, I burst silently through the door. The room was still, with a TV in the corner, and the door to the next room ajar. Only after a moment did I realize there was a man sleeping on the sofa, under a comforter. And when I pulled it back to find him dressed in the grey uniform of The Order, I promptly put a bullet in his head. A quick pat down told me he was unarmed. Playing it safe, I recovered my shell case, and shifted the body behind the sofa and out of sight, before pausing to listen for noise beyond the room. But all I could hear was the roar of rainfall. I'd made my first mistake: I'd forgotten to close the door on entering and the noise coming in was inviting attention. And sure enough, no sooner had I closed the door than I heard footsteps approaching. A male voice said:

'Gimmel, are you going for a cigarette, too?'

I dived for the sofa, and drew the comforter over me. I didn't expect this to fool anyone too long – it was clear there'd been an intrusion from the water I'd trailed inside. But all I wanted was to induce a moment's confusion. And then, when I heard this guy enter and stop mid-sentence, and I knew that moment had come, I threw off the comforter and aimed a bullet into his forehead. He crumpled to the carpet with a low thud.

Again, I pocketed the shell case and quickly searched the body. This time, I found a Beretta 92F tucked into his waistband. It was a serious weapon and if this guy was carrying, I had to assume the rest would be, too. It was the noise that worried me most: if someone fired a unsilenced Beretta, the whole house would know about it.

I slipped the Beretta into my pocket, then cautiously poked my head around the door. The next room was a large living space, with a door on the far side opening onto a corridor. I made for it at once, whispering as I went:

'Two down. Heading towards a central corridor.'

'Ditto,' replied Vannevar.

I hit the corridor. To the right, it led round a corner to a central foyer, just out of sight. To the left, it led to the kitchen. Approaching from that direction was Vannevar. He was holding his blade which was red with blood. When we were engaged in combat at the same time, it was difficult to determine what he was up to, since the sound of his heavy-breathing through the earpiece was drowned out by my own. But he certainly looked like he'd been busy. He arrived at my side and I motioned to him that I was going to investigate the foyer. Then I glanced round the corner. There were two men: one sitting on a sofa, perhaps fourteen yards away; and another standing in front of him, with his back to me. I couldn't make out what they were saying over the drone of the rain.

But this setup presented a problem, because both men were right near the foot of the stairs. So while I could deck one with the Ruger, by the time I was ready to take my second shot, the second man would already be mounting the stairs and raising the alarm. And not only did the angle make it difficult for Vann to take a shot at the same time, but it would be foolish to attempt it in the first place – since his Glock's muzzle velocity surpassed the speed of sound. His bullet would create a sonic boom, regardless of his silencer. The solution was simple: I'd have to eliminate one with my Ruger, while Vann neutralized the second by hand.

I turned to Vann and whispered:

'There's two of them – one on a sofa, one standing, but both near the stairs. Would be a mistake to try shooting both from here. Too slow with the Ruger to guarantee one doesn't make the stairs. Too much racket with the Glock.'

He nodded.

'So I'll shoot standing guy from here; then you run in and take down sofa guy.'

He nodded again.

I edged round the corner and drew a bead on standing guy's head.

'Ready?' I whispered.

'Ready,' said Vann.

'On three,' I said. 'One, two, three.'

I worked the trigger and hit the bull's-eye and by the time my guy had hit the floor, Vann was already bolting across the foyer. Sofa guy managed to get no further than hobbling to his feet before Vann arrived at his side, and snapped his neck with awful ferocity. The whole thing made a little noise, but nothing that wasn't masked by the rain.

Quickly, I checked the two rooms on the far side of the foyer. Both were empty. I then returned to find that Vann had extracted a pair of Berettas from the bodies – which he pointedly displayed to me before pocketing – and a purple hood. I remembered what Lamphere said about the purple hood: it was a sign of status, worn by the Inner Sanctum – those who'd been allowed to see The Zahir's face. So we'd taken out a high-ranker, making it six dead in all. But while this was progress, there was still a mountain to climb. We were still outnumbered – with at least five more to deal with – and my son was in a bomb vest.

With a sense that it may come in handy, I pocketed the hood, before stealthily leading the way up the stairs. The stairs opened onto a wide corridor. At the end was a second flight of stairs to the third floor. On the left-hand side were two doors, both shut, and both concealing rooms with their lights out. Whereas on the right-hand side, about halfway down, was an open set of double doors and I could hear from within what sounded like three people shifting equipment and quietly talking. The echo told me it was a spacious room.

'Cover me,' I whispered to Vann. 'I've got a plan.'

Vann laid himself across the top seven steps – with his head peeking over the top step – and leveled his Glock at the empty hallway. Neither of us wanted to see it fired; but it was there as a last resort. I then put on the purple mask and made for the double doors. Again, I didn't intend to fool anyone long term. I just wanted to induce a moment's hesitation…

I stepped into the room. Just as I'd expected, it was a large space. On the right was an enormous pile of replica Springfield Model 1861s – the preferred musket of the American Civil War – and several large canvas bags of gunpowder and Minié ball rifle bullets. On the left, there were piles of blue and yellow uniforms, with the words "True Shape" on their breast. And standing amid all this were three cultists – two men, one woman – in the process of preparing the muskets.

The first man had his back to me, and went down before he realized I was there – a bullet to the head. The woman froze – paralyzed by the suddenness of the attack and the purple hood – and similarly went down without a fuss. But though the third guy didn't draw a Beretta, he made it clear he wasn't going down so easy, taking a run at me, and body-checking me hard. My Ruger flew from my grasp, and landed among the rifles. The clangor wasn't enough to blow our cover. But I was worried about this guy raising the alarm himself. More so than I was of the threat he presented to me personally.

I acted fast, delivering a savage blow to his solar plexus and knocking the wind from his lungs. He keeled over. I then grabbed his head, and forced it against my knee before seizing a fistful of his hair, tugging his head back, and exposing his throat. I then snatched the blade from my pocket, thrust it behind his windpipe, and ripped forward. He died before he'd hit the ground. And then, after removing the hood, I allowed myself a second to catch my breath. Because I could see in my peripheral vision that the towering frame of Vannevar had just entered the room, which meant I could relax.

But then I turned around and suddenly I wasn't so relaxed.

The man standing in the door wasn't Vannevar. It was a Goliath of a man – two inches taller than Vann, and at least a stone heavier – dressed in grey. He was soaked through; his eye swollen to the size of a baseball; his nose pouring blood; and he was aiming Vann's Glock at my head. Immediately I understood. This guy had been having a cigarette outside when we'd entered the house which was why he was wet, and why the second man I killed had asked the first if he was *also* going out for a smoke. Then, when Goliath had re-entered the house, he'd discovered Vann on the stairs and staged an ambush. The black eye and broken nose told me that a struggle had then ensued – a struggle Goliath had won.

My first thought was: is Vannevar dead, or merely incapacitated? But I didn't have the luxury of worrying about this too long. Judging by the way Goliath was carefully lining up his aim with my forehead, he was moments away from pulling the trigger.

But then he threw me a lifeline. He bellowed: 'False prophet. Now is The Deluge of Euphrates, the end of your reign.' And as he did so, I took a gamble that he'd chosen his aim before he'd started speaking, and was intending to stick with it. So when he finished, I dived out the way of where I predicted the bullet was headed. Sure enough, he failed to alter his aim, and the bullet screeched past me as I landed among the muskets.

But the danger hadn't passed. Goliath was lining up a second shot. And not only could I not spot my Ruger, but I was also lying on the pocket containing the Beretta. There was no other choice: it'd have to be a musket. I hoisted one into my arms and began raising it, hoping to get a head-shot. But as I was still in the process of raising it, I saw

Goliath was about to shoot again. I had to take my shot *now*. So I did, unleashing hell right into his stomach. He bellowed, shuffled back, threw up his arms, and took an involuntary shot at the ceiling. He then dropped the gun.

I scrambled to my feet and pulled out the Beretta as Goliath retreated from the room. I went after him. And this time, I wasn't to be denied my headshot: I blew a gaping hole right in the middle of the bastard's face. And yet with this came not even a second of respite, for almost in the same moment, a man burst out of the room at the end of the corridor, took a split-second glance, then belted up the stairs – all before I could line up another shot.

None of this was a shock. I knew that Goliath had blown my cover, and that the time it'd taken to eliminate him had thrown me off the pace. So it was no surprise that cultist number eleven had reacted first, and was now a crucial step ahead in the race to secure Samuel. My only option was to give chase, in a last desperate bid to salvage the situation.

Five seconds later, I was up the stairs and on the landing of the third floor. But there was a bend in the corridor which the guy had already gotten beyond, meaning I couldn't take a shot. So immediately I began chasing him with every fiber of my being – and yet, in what felt like slow motion – following the sound of him repeatedly calling the name "Resh" at the top of his voice. As I did so, I desperately attempted to comprehend what was happening. It seemed almost certain this guy knew who I was, or at the very least why I was there. But who Resh was, I wasn't sure. The gas station man had estimated there to be ten members of True Shape but I was chasing number eleven. So while Resh might've been Lofkin's cult handle, it was possible that the estimate had been even further off, and that Resh was another cultist altogether.

But at the same time, it seemed unlikely the estimate would be *wildly* out. At the upper limit, I reckoned I was dealing with maybe three or four cultists, including Lofkin.

And then as I turned the corner, and glimpsed the guy disappearing up the stairs to the fourth floor, my mind turned to what was waiting for me there. Perhaps they'd still be fumbling to unlock a door to get to Samuel, giving me chance to stop them in their tracks. Or perhaps they already had a gun to Samuel's head in the hope of stopping me in *my* tracks. Or perhaps they had a gun to his head, and were planning to slaughter him as soon as he entered my field of vision, forcing me to watch. Or perhaps they'd set off the bomb, and send us all up in flames… And as still more eventualities occurred to me, I continued to worry about Vann. Was he alive? If so, in what state?

The next thing I knew, I was mounting the stairs. I cleared my head, tightened my grip on the Beretta, and prepared to deal with whatever they threw my way. But when I arrived on the landing – before I could take in even an inch of my surroundings – something happened. There was an ungodly bang, and a flash of light that made the lightning look like a fire-cracker, and all at once I was blind and deaf. This wasn't a bomb blast, it was a stun grenade. And barely had I thought this when I was set on by what felt like at least six powerful bodies. Too scared to shoot lest my bullet accidentally found Samuel, I thrashed wildly against these invisible assailants, hitting someone's jaw, and glancing off a collar bone. But that's where my dance ended. Because then I took a dizzying blow to my carotid sinus, followed by another to the back of my head, and my world turned to black.

Chapter Twenty

When I came round, the only thing I knew was the thumping inside my head. I sat for a long while, breathing deeply, then finally I opened my eyes. I was confronted by a powerful wave of nausea, and had no choice but to close them again. A minute or so later, I tried to move, but I couldn't. I was tightly bound.

I continued breathing deeply, unable to hear anything but the thumping. Eventually I tried opening my eyes again. This time I did better and through the haze I could just about make out where I was: the foyer on the first floor. The next thing I registered was the limp body of Vannevar, bound to a chair two feet to my right. My first thought was relief: you don't restrain a dead man.

I tried taking in the rest of the room. I could see somebody standing a few feet away. And though I couldn't quite bring him into focus, the blur of blue and yellow told me he was wearing one of the uniforms I'd seen on the second floor. A moment later, he left the room; and when he returned five minutes down the line, I could see his face clearly – as well as the faces of the five others he'd brought with him. I didn't recognize the newcomers, but the original guy was the runner who'd led me into the trap. They were all wearing the blue-yellow uniforms emblazoned with the words *True Shape*.

Though the thumping continued, my brain was kicking into gear. A number of signs told me it'd been a few hours since the stun grenade: the fact that these men were now in uniforms; that the mess Vann and I had made in the foyer had been cleaned; that both Vann and I had been moved and bound. However, the windows by the front door told me the sun was yet to come up. My guess was that I'd been out for about two to three hours, which put the time at 4 or 5 a.m. – and meant the re-enactment was yet to begin.

But for all this on-the-spot deduction, there was one thing that'd been painfully clear even before I'd gone down for the count. Namely, that my gas station guy had been way off with his estimate of ten *True Shape* members. We'd killed ten, and at least six still remained. More than enough to pull off the atrocity.

But where was Lofkin? And where, more importantly, was Samuel?

Runner came over, and brought his face up to mine. He had black hair, bushy eyebrows, and crooked teeth. He was maybe twenty-five-years-old, and pig-ugly.

'False Prophet, we are at war. But you shall not win. The Deluge of Euphrates is upon you. The old system must make way for the just and righteous order; the will of The Zahir.'

I looked him in the eye: 'Where's my son?'

'Today, people will die by their own hands,' he continued, ignoring my question. 'It's symbolic of how society's own transgressions have caused its downfall. Only through self-punishment can society truly be redeemed; can society reach salvation. And we, The Order of Babylon, must be stage-managers, silently shaping events, to prepare the people for the time when we shall shape *all* events, in our just, moral society.'

The guy was nuts – brainwashed to oblivion.

'Where's my son?' I repeated. Again, I was ignored.

'But you are a steward of the old, sinful order,' he said accusingly. 'You are responsible for maintaining this morally bankrupt society through your silent manipulation of events. So now it's time for you to taste your own medicine – for you to be placed in a position of powerlessness.'

Runner paused, then added:

'Now, False Prophet, you will have the great honor of talking to The Zahir himself.'

I was confused. Was Drexler here? About to walk into the room? But these speculations were quickly dispelled by the sound of a cell-phone ringing. Runner answered.

'Yes, My Zahir... we have him here... ten minutes ago... thank you, My Zahir.'

Then Runner held the phone to my ear.

There were many things I wanted to say to Drexler. But to say them as I sat completely at his mercy would be to undermine their seriousness. Instead, I opted for an uncooperative silence. Eventually he spoke:

'Hello, Saul. It sounds like you've been having fun. I certainly have.'

His voice was smooth, nuanced, precise. I could tell by the air of ceremony this was a big moment for him: the first one-on-one with the man he'd obsessed over. He continued: 'I understand you've killed ten of my men. I hope you enjoyed it. Killing another human is a rare pleasure – one that most never get to enjoy.'

I was listening carefully, hoping he might let something slip that could, at some point, give me an advantage. Drexler remained silent, patiently waiting for my response.

'Where's my son, Drexler?' I said.

He chuckled. 'Really, Saul, I'm impressed. I don't know how you managed to track him to Mineral. And I won't ask you how you managed it, either. After all, I can't have you revealing all your secrets – that'd ruin the fun of our little game.'

'Game?' I replied incredulously.

'Oh, don't play coy. You've surely read the note I left at your apartment. And I admit you did well to find your way to Mineral, better than I thought you'd do. But once you'd gotten there, you had a fighting chance of retrieving Samuel, and you fell short. That's nobody's fault but your own.'

I remained silent. I wasn't going to disclose anything I didn't have to. After some time, Drexler said:

'But of course you had *more* than a fighting chance, because you had Mr Yeung along for the ride – an ex-HRT boy, no less. But last I checked, Mr Yeung was with the FBI. We both know you read the note, Saul, and you've broken the rules. I'd be well within my rights to kill Samuel right now.' Drexler paused. 'But seeing as Mr Yeung *seems* to've kept his knowledge of The Order to himself, I'm going to let you off. The game will continue. But Vannevar, I'm afraid, is mine. Think of it like losing a piece in a game of chess.'

I could tell by the playfulness and drama in Drexler's tone that he perceived what he was doing as glamorous. That he had envisaged between us a rivalry worthy of Hollywood: the pair of us wise-cracking and joking, and in the process discovering that we're just alike, as happens so often in the movies. And this was all precisely because he was a psychopath and psychopaths suffer from delusions of grandeur.

But the truth was far removed from Drexler's world-view. What he was doing wasn't glamorous – he was a sick freak hurting innocent people. And what's more, we were nothing alike. Even when I'd lived outside the law, I'd never murdered, maimed, and tortured. And so I was unwilling to engage him; unwilling to become the other half of his fantasy double-act.

'Where are you taking him?' I replied in deliberate monotone.

He chuckled again but with a note of impatience.

'It's not so fun when something you value is taken from you, is it, Saul?' he replied with sudden malice. 'I should know: I lost my freedom, and was left to rot in a god-forsaken hole where I was tormented by jailers, and forced to fraternize with the scum of the earth. And I owe that privilege all to you. Yet, strangely, you don't seem to be enjoying things quite so much now that *you're* the one up against it.'

This, I knew, was the crux of his seething animosity towards me. But it was bullshit. My actions may have led to his arrest; but I sure as hell wasn't responsible for the dark, sadistic crimes. And I wasn't going to bite – which was still what he wanted.

'It was nobody's fault but your own,' I said flatly, using his own phrase against him. He hissed with exasperation.

'Come now,' he said slowly. 'You sound so *melancholy*. If you're going to be such a spoil-sport, maybe there's no point *bothering*? That'd be a shame, wouldn't it? To blow little Samuel's brains all over the fucking wall because of daddy's poor sportsmanship. Huh?'

Again, I was silent. I wasn't keeping to the script and my refusal to engage was riling him. But then, abruptly, there came a new noise from his end. A loud, grinding screech – the sound of heavy machinery. Then Drexler said:

'Like I said, because I'm a good sport, the game will continue, and that means I'm going to set you free. But the stakes are higher now. Not only because you cheated, but because this is chance number two. So it's double or nothing.'

But suddenly Drexler was talking with urgency. This noise hadn't been something I was supposed to hear, and it'd thrown his rhythm off. He continued without his usual pause:

'Should you fail, both Vannevar and Samuel shall die at midnight March 4, EST. If you compete nobly, their deaths shall be noble. But should you fail to treat the game with respect, they'll suffer. Death by castration. And tell anyone else at the FBI about The Order, then it's game over. Understood?'

There was another screech. It sounded like metal cutting metal. Then, when the noise let up, Drexler immediately continued speaking, even more hurriedly than before:

'Now, as I'm sure you've already deduced, I have big things planned for Mineral this morning. But while I can't have you running about as they unfold, I can't have you missing them, either. So let's have you *conscious enough*, and give you an indirect view of things. Oh, and I'll ask the boys if they'll let you have a quick glance at Samuel before he leaves; though I'm not sure how keen they'll be to do you any favors. After all, you did kill ten of their brethren. But really, I must get on.'

This time, Drexler did pause – though he was clearly weighing up whether to end the call prematurely, or hear my response. He made his decision.

'Any last words?' he said.

I decided to land a punch.

'It's a shame, Drex. Despite all your efforts, you can't

even execute a simple phone call without a slip-up. That's what happens when you locate your base next-door to a metal works. I'll be seeing you soon.'

It was clearly a bluff, but that was beside the point. I was drawing attention to the one thing that hadn't gone to plan. He didn't like it.

'Good luck,' he spat. 'You'll need it.'

The line went dead.

Runner – with no way of knowing the conversation was over – continued to hold the phone to my ear. But then the phone rang again, and he picked up. No doubt it was Drexler with further instructions. But already my mind was ticking over. What had he meant by conscious enough? By an indirect view?

In the next instant, Runner hung up, and started issuing instructions to the others in hushed tones. One of the men then ducked out of the room, returning a moment later with a vial of clear liquid and a hypodermic syringe. He approached the unconscious Vann, and administered about 250 milligrams to his upper arm. Then all the men – aside from Runner – untied Vann, and carried him out the front door. I heard car-doors slamming and an engine starting, followed by wheels crunching stones. When only four of the five cultists returned I understood that one had been given the responsibility of transporting Vann.

On one hand, I felt anxious: now Drexler had my best friend as well as my son. On the other, I felt relieved: not long ago, I'd thought Vannevar was dead.

But my thoughts about Vann were soon cut short as the man who'd injected him again took up the vial and syringe, and came my way. He was a big guy with a bruised jaw – the one I'd hit after the stun-grenade. I looked carefully at the liquid as he administered about a third of what he'd given Vann to my upper arm. My gut told me it was Ketamine, a powerful anesthetic and hallucinogen, commonly used to tranquilize horses. If this was the case, then not only was this dose not enough to knock me out, but it was also not even enough to put me in a K-hole – that state of waking death Ketamine can induce in which the subject is unable to talk or move. Rather, they'd given me enough to put me in a state just shy of that. Enough to severely impair my motor skills and speech, but not disable them altogether. In short, for approximately ninety minutes – the time it'd take for the drug to work through my system – I'd be conscious, but would appear as though I was blind drunk.

What Drexler had meant by *conscious enough*.

I had about ten minutes before the stuff kicked in. Clearly, they were planning to execute their atrocity while I was under the influence. But what was less clear was what they planned to do with me during the action, since it seemed to me that all five would be needed to execute the plot. And I couldn't see them leaving me alone in the house, as that hardly constituted an "indirect view" of events.

Unable to decide between a number of feasible possibilities, I turned my mind instead to Samuel. If Drexler's word was anything to go by, then Samuel was still in the house and so too, presumably, was Lofkin. But then again, Drexler might've lied, and the two of them might've left hours ago…

I was jogged from these thoughts by Runner shouting upstairs. Then, a few seconds later, I got my answer about Samuel and Lofkin – the two of them came downstairs and entered the foyer. Samuel first, followed by Lofkin, holding a Beretta to Samuel's back. They both paused before me, and I was able to take a good look. Lofkin – with his other hand buried in his left pocket, clutching the detonator – had heavy bags under his eyes and a deathly pallor. At the very least, it was clear I'd managed to disrupt his rest-stop and had kept him in a state of advanced fatigue.

And then there was Samuel. The bomb-vest remained, and was now complimented by handcuffs and a gag. He looked no less exhausted than Lofkin. But whereas Lofkin avoided my eye, Samuel looked me dead-on. At first I saw pure surprise in his face – clearly, he'd had no idea I'd come after him. But then – as it sunk in that I, too, had been captured – his eyes became dead and empty. The drugs were now, very suddenly, taking their toll and I knew a garbled attempt at speech would only demoralize him further. So, instead, I mustered all my self-control, and shot him a look that said: *hang in there; I'm coming for you; I love you…*

The next thing I knew, both Lofkin and Samuel were out the front door. Sixty seconds later, I heard the growl of an engine and the crunch of wheels. Immediately I wondered: were they still using the Blue Ford? Had they found the GPS tracking device? Were they headed in the same direction as Vann? But whatever the answers, I felt relieved. Samuel was alive and therefore there was hope…

I took deep breaths as the drugs continued to take their toll. The world was slowing down, time distorting, and it took all my concentration to flex my muscles against my restraints. My mind was becoming increasingly detached from my body – a signature effect of Ketamine. Then, an indeterminate time later, Runner picked up the mobile and dialed.

'Hello, is this the Sheriff's Office? This is Owen Lodge, managing director of True Shape – yes, the ones organizing the re-enactment this morning… well, I'm afraid we've had an incident. We've had a man break in and assault one of our team... He's still here, inebriated – would you be able to send a squad car? ... Thank you – and please be quick, our event's due to start in fifty minutes. Don't want to let folk down... It's O-W-E-N L-O-D-G-E... Yes, bottom of West 2nd.'

With that, he hung up. It was now clear what they were planning: they were going to hand me over to the local police. And not a moment after I thought this, one of the men produced a bottle of whiskey and doused it over me, completing the effect of a lunatic drunk.

I'd certainly get an "indirect" view of things from local police headquarters: it would undoubtedly be the first place to hear about the disaster when it struck. And it became perfectly clear, when I was then unbound and led to the sofa by two of the men, that resistance was impossible – it was the most I could do to move my legs enough to stop them having to carry me. And so I sat slumped on the sofa – as my son was being whisked away, as the men around me prepared to murder innocent people – waiting to be arrested.

Utterly powerless.

Chapter Twenty-One

The cultists worked like men possessed, shifting five-hundred muskets from the second floor, out the front door, and into what sounded like two separate vehicles. By the time the squad car arrived about ten minutes later they were done. I could hear the policeman get out the car and talk to the men in the driveway. It was the Sheriff himself – a guy called Galbraith. And I could tell instantly from his lazy, loud-mouthed drawl and dense laughter that this was not an intelligent man. I could already see the son-of-a-bitch in my mind's eye: overweight and bloated; sweat dribbling from his brow; a few lank strands of hair atop his head.

First, Runner, who was operating under the pseudonym Owen Lodge, told Galbraith how I'd entered the house thirty minutes ago through an unlocked front door, struck one of his men, before collapsing into a stupor. Next, Galbraith marveled at the bruising on the big guy's jaw. Then, finally, he said:

'Well, let's take a look at old rummy, then.'

Galbraith, followed by the five cultists, entered the

foyer, looking exactly as I'd pictured him. He boomed with laugher at the sight of me and said:

'Not one I recognize. Well, if it weren't for you boys, these out-of-towners wouldn't be here in the first place. Brought this on yourself, didn't you? Well, no problem, I'll take him in. No problem at all.'

He waddled over, cuffed my wrists, and said to me:

'You've had a busy night, haven't you, son? Smells like you've had an evening with Jack Daniels! Well, suppose I'd better give you your Mirandas.'

He did. In response, I tried to speak. But all that came out was an incoherent slur.

'Thought so,' he said through fits of laughter.

Clearly, I'd no hope of alerting this guy. He wasn't an evil man, but he was incompetent and, as he continued with his lowbrow conversation, I could see even the cultists were getting impatient. Eventually, Runner hurried things along by offering to escort me to the squad car, and before long I'd been bundled into its back-seat. Then, after telling Runner and Swollen Jaw they needed to visit the police station in the neighboring town of Louisa to give statements, and that one of his four officers at the re-enactment would give them a ride a little later, Galbraith got behind the wheel, and we set off. It was then I realized my watch had been removed. The dashboard clock showed 5:59.

Galbraith hummed a nonsensical tune as we went. I did my best to resist the effects of the drugs, but it was little use, and my mind continued to become increasingly detached from my body – a sensation which filled me with devastating impotence. At one point, as we powered down a country road, I attempted to talk, and managed to choke out: 'terrorists.'

'You're not quite a terrorist, son,' Galbraith replied through dumb laughter, 'but definitely a pain.'

It was 6:09 when we arrived at the large redbrick police station in Louisa, some six miles away from Mineral. Galbraith whistled over a colleague to help escort me to the building, and during this short walk I managed to slur:

'True Shape terrorists. I'm FBI.'

'And I'm the President,' boomed Galbraith, to the delight of his colleague.

Once inside, Galbraith gave me over to an efficient, disinterested policewoman, who took my mug-shot and fingerprints all in the space of ten minutes. I sat through the process in a slack-jawed daze – detached and incoherent – and soon found myself in a cell within the squad room, sitting with my back to the wall. I counted nine police-officers around the room: eight men (including Galbraith), and the woman who'd dealt with me. There was a clock above the front entrance, and I stared at it dumbly. When it hit 6:25, I took a deep breath, mustered all my energy and said at the top of my voice:

'Organizers using live ammunition.'

A few of the officers looked over, but the desk sergeant coughed loudly, and gave them a look that said I was a crackpot, and not to waste their time. Galbraith was sitting on the far side of the room, ignoring me altogether. It'd been almost an hour since I'd been injected, and I could feel myself slowly coming down. But too slowly and I was still unable to do anything more than what I just did.

Then, since I could do nothing else, I started muddling through my thoughts. I thought about the irony of my situation, given the measures I'd taken to remain in control; about Olivia, and how this was the way she'd been feeling the whole time; about Vann and Samuel, who were in situations of equal powerlessness; and then about the innocent people whose lives were about to be pointlessly destroyed…

When I next looked at the clock, it read 6:29. With a

sudden surge of energy, I struggled to my feet, raked my cuffs across the bars, and said as loudly as I could:

'I'm with the FBI. Organizers using live ammunition. Running out of time.'

It took me thirty seconds to say all this. This time, the woman was the only one to look up. However, she wasn't curious, but annoyed. I knew how I must've looked: like a drunk, slurring his paranoid thoughts. I slumped back to the floor in defeat. The seconds ticked by with awful inevitability.

It wasn't till 6:32 that the news finally came. A phone rang, Galbraith picked up, and his face dropped like a ton of bricks.

'Live ammunition?' he exclaimed.

Every officer turned to look at him.

'Jesus Christ – but that's impossible. I'll send everyone over immediately.'

Galbraith put down the receiver. He was shaking.

'What's happened?' demanded the female officer.

'A terrorist attack at Elizabeth Walton Park,' he stuttered. 'The organizers put live ammunition in the muskets. It's a bloodbath.'

All at once, crisis was in the air. Galbraith couldn't stomach it, and collapsed into his chair. The next instant, the power vacuum was filled as the female officer, with fearsome authority, started barking orders across the room to every officer at hand. She told them that a suspected terrorist attack, involving the sabotage of muskets at the re-enactment in Mineral, had taken place; that they should assume the perpetrators to be armed and dangerous; that there'd been casualties already; and that every officer was to head over there immediately, aside from the desk sergeant who was to stay and call every hospital that could conceivably help, plus the Richmond FBI Field Office. As soon as she finished speaking, all the subordinate officers rushed for the door, save for the desk sergeant, who hurried to my cell.

'Who are you?' he bellowed.

The woman joined him. The badge on her breast told me her name was Matthews.

'Who are you?' she demanded.

'Saul Marshall – FBI.' I paused for breath. 'You need to take me with you.'

'What's happening?' she pressed.

'Take me with you,' I repeated.

There was no more hesitation. The door to my cell swung open and before I knew it, I was being escorted to a squad car by Matthews and a somewhat recovered Galbraith. My state was steadying by the second, and I was able to pump my legs faster and with improved coordination. I was put into the back of the car, the officers got in front and in no time we were bombing down the road, sirens blaring. I knew, at our current velocity, it'd take about four minutes to cover the distance between the two towns. And I knew also that the other officers, because they'd left a few minutes before us, would be arriving in Mineral imminently. I was jogged from these thoughts by Matthews, who asked me once again:

'What's happening?'

'Give me a minute,' I said. 'They drugged me. Ketamine. I'm coming down—'

I was interrupted by a panicked voice on the police radio. It quickly became apparent this was one of the four officers who'd been at the event, and he spoke hysterically about bodies everywhere; about *so much blood*. It sounded like the stuff of nightmares and suddenly I felt crushed by the awful weight of responsibility: this was the price for not telling Parkes what I knew, for not sacrificing my son.

We sat in tense silence for the next thirty seconds. I could see – as we belted down the country road connecting the two towns, and Mineral came into view – that we were approaching it from the north. And the fact I'd picked up on this detail told me I might be sufficiently recovered to speak coherently, so I gave it a go:

'The people who organized this event are terrorists, and they've been planning this for months. But they're not interested in sticking around and doing more harm, they're only interested in the kinds of sensational scenes which arise from innocent people gunning each other down. They will vanish, if they haven't done so already; and a local police operation doesn't have a hope in hell of catching them.'

Before either officer could respond, another voice came through on the radio. Chillingly somber.

'Peterson's place on West 2nd – it's up in flames. Heading over there.'

Now that it'd been brought to our attention, there was no missing the cloud of grey billowing out of north Mineral. Twenty seconds later, the same voice came again:

'It's a huge fire. The vehicles the organizers were using are outside, also in flames.'

This news came like a punch in the gut. I wasn't sure if the officers understood but I was certain what this meant: the cultists were in the house, completing the last phase of a suicide mission. I'd been wondering how they were intending to escape; how they were planning to cover their tracks. But now I saw that their plan had been annihilation: of anyone who could be made to talk and of any space where evidence might've been left.

Then, almost involuntarily, I started imagining what'd happened in the park. I could see the calm before the storm, the people preparing to enjoy their day-out; then I could see the moment when the shots went off, and the fear, panic, and suffering that had followed – and were still no doubt ongoing. Then I imagined footage of this – taken on someone's phone or camcorder – showing on every news channel, spreading like wildfire across the internet.

However, whether this footage existed or not, one thing was certain: over the next half hour, the entire world would be turning its attention to the town of Mineral and every law enforcement body and news outlet in the land would be descending here *en masse*. This meant I needed to get out of town *fast*. Because there was no doubt the Bureau would discover that I'd been in Mineral before the atrocity, and had prior knowledge of the attack. And given the extent of my rule-breaking, they'd almost certainly want to detain me, and that was something I couldn't allow...

We were now less than sixty seconds from Mineral.

'Listen carefully,' I said, speaking fast. 'There's little you can do about catching the perpetrators – these people will be dealt with by the FBI. Your best course of action is to help coordinate the rescue effort and instill some calm. But right now, I need you to do two things for me. First, I need you to promise to keep my presence in Mineral out of the public sphere. It'll be critical for morale if people discover that the terrorists had bested a Bureau agent sent in to take them down. You got that?'

They both nodded.

'And the second thing I need from you is to stop the car *right now.*'

Matthews slammed the brakes. The car screeched to a halt directly outside the church.

'Why here?' she asked.

'Because the second thing I need is a gun. The terrorists took mine, and I'm gonna need one. But I understand
that while I'm claiming to be FBI, the only things you
know for sure about me is that you found me among
terrorists, and that I had prior knowledge of the attack.
Given all this, I can hardly expect you to arm me. But I've
got my FBI ID stashed in a bag outside this church. So
how's this: I show you my ID, *then* you give me a piece?'

Matthews looked to Galbraith, saw his bottom lip quiv-
ering with uncertainty, then made the decision herself.

'Deal,' she said.

I got out the car, and – feeling greatly recovered –
sprinted to the bag, back to the car, and handed Matthews
the ID through her window. She studied it for a good few
seconds, then finally gave a nod and handed it back. She
then produced her weapon and handed it over. It was a
Swiss made Sig Sauer P229 pistol; and when I checked the
magazine, I found thirteen rounds of .357 bullets. I slipped
it into my pocket with a nod of thanks. Then Matthews
said:

'Now what?'

'You get down to business,' I said. 'I can manage from
here. Good luck.'

She gave me another nod and then, a second later, the
squad-car was powering south into town. I took a moment
to transfer a few choice items from my bag to my pockets:
my cash and credit cards; my phone, which said I had
missed calls from both Parkes and Olivia; and, finally, the
GPS receiver, which still seemed to be picking up the bug
Vann had attached to Lofkin's Ford (it was, apparently,
heading north up the I-95). Then, with no time for further
consideration, I bolted southwards. The sun was rising as I
hit the main drag, and the deserted road – in spite of the
wails of out-of-sight sirens, and the column of smoke to

the west – seemed incongruously tranquil in the morning rays. But this tranquility was quickly shattered as I came through the door of my destination – the town petrol station – and was greeted by the sound of a pump-action shotgun chambering a round.

'Where the fuck do you think you're going?'

There was an old guy behind the counter – not the young man I'd spoken to earlier – and he was pointing an Ithaca Mag-10 at me. This was not a clever weapon. If he worked the trigger, a quantity of lead would undoubtedly perforate a wall and find a gas-pump, sending the whole place up in flames.

'FBI,' I said quickly. 'I can show you my ID.'

He nodded and I reached slowly for my pocket, produced my ID, and displayed it clearly. He nodded again and lowered his weapon.

'I ain't gonna shoot you, but I sure as hell ain't pleased to see you. What do you want with me? Seems like you boys have your work cut out as it is.'

'I *don't* want you. I want the kid who was working here last night. Who is he? What's his address?'

'Clint Macfarlane. Lives on West 10. Number 11. Should've known that good-for-nothing kid was trouble.'

The next second, I was back outside. Before I could draw breath, five ambulances screamed past in the direction of the park. Clearly, the emergency response was gathering momentum, and my instinctive reaction was to ensure I was spotted by as few first-responders as possible. So I crossed the road, turned down one of the streets to the west of the main drag, and worked my way south through this residential grid. I wanted to find my gas station guy because he'd complained about there being nowhere to park his car. And a car was exactly what I needed right now, since I felt sure the cultists, during my stint of unconsciousness, would've found and removed mine. After all, although it was unmarked, it was still easy enough to spot for those in the know, by virtue of it being a Ford Crown Victoria, a model unavailable for private purchase, and almost exclusively used by police and government agencies. And sure enough, no sooner had I digested this thought than I arrived at the parking space to find the car gone. So I just kept on sprinting towards West 10.

Before long, I arrived at Clint's house. There was a run-down red Toyota Yaris in the driveway. I rapped the door, and jabbed the doorbell repeatedly, and when Clint opened the door a moment later, I already had my FBI ID on display.

'Clint, I need you to listen carefully.'

'You're with the FBI?' he exclaimed. 'I knew there was something—'

I cut him short. 'Clint, listen. There's been a terrorist attack in the town park. The organizers put live ammunition in the muskets, and the participants unwittingly gunned each other down. We're talking front-page news the world over. But the terrorists stole my car and that leaves me high and dry. So I need to borrow yours.'

For an instant, he just looked at me blank-faced. But then he took himself in hand, and said: 'Of course.'

He darted into the house, and quickly returned with the keys.

'Thank you, Clint. I'll look you up when all this blows over, and see to it you're fully reimbursed.' I paused. I wanted to tell him to lie to anyone from the FBI who asked after me – in order to delay them working out my movements. But I knew that getting Clint to mislead the Bureau could land him in serious hot-water. So I decided on a middle line.

'And when the law enforcement agencies arrive here throughout the day, tell them what you know. But don't go looking for them. Wait for them to come to you. That way you'll know you're talking to the right people. Understand?'

'Got it.'

I gave a final nod of thanks. Then, with no time to lose, I ran to the Yaris, threw my bag on the back seat, and started the engine. A few seconds later, I was belting down West 10th, with Clint fading away in the rear-view mirror. I was surprised, however, when I turned left onto the main drag, to find it still empty and tranquil − this façade of calm maintained by the wall of trees blocking the park from view. But as I headed north, I shot a glance down the road leading to the park, and caught sight of a scene that turned my stomach. A man was sitting on the ground, and in his arms he held a small child drenched in blood. Immediately I understood that the man must've carried the child the 600 yards or so from the park to the main road, perhaps in search of aid, perhaps merely to escape the trauma. And though the pair passed from my sight a moment later, I'd seen enough.

Soon I was on a country road, heading north, with the dashboard clock reading 6:55 a.m., and the I-95 in mind as my immediate destination. I was recovered enough from the Ketamine to think clearly and function with coordination; but it had still left a nasty hangover, which was combining with the ache to the back of my head to induce an unrelenting assault of nausea. And the thick stream of emergency vehicles passing by in the opposite direction with sirens whirring were only exacerbating my condition. But I was glad to simply be out of town – away from the gathering storm.

I'd chosen to head for the I-95 because the GPS receiver had told me the bug Vann had placed on Lofkin's car was traveling north along that route; and, even now, the receiver said it was continuing to do so and was just outside DC. And though there was obviously a possibility that somebody else was now driving the Ford, or that the cultists had discovered the bug, it was my only lead…

Of course, another possibility had also occurred to me: that perhaps Lofkin knew about the bug, but had neither removed it nor taken another vehicle – that perhaps he wanted me to follow him. But even if this was the case, the I-95 remained my only option.

It wasn't until I'd gotten onto the Interstate and put a good few miles between myself and Mineral that I decided I was ready to talk. But it wasn't Olivia or Parkes I called – it was Morton Giles. And when he answered, I could hear the news playing in the background.

'Do I really want to know what you're about to tell me?'

Chapter Twenty-Two

THURSDAY, FEBRUARY 28, 2013, 6 A.M. CST - 7505
SOUTH LAFLIN STREET, ENGLEWOOD, CHICAGO.

'F rancis, the reason you're sitting here,' said Drexler slowly, 'is because I'm not convinced we have your full cooperation. But you see, Francis, your full cooperation is *vital*. So, to secure it, I've decided to demonstrate to you how serious we are. And the reason you're bound and gagged is to show you that once I make a decision, there's nothing you can say or do to change my mind.'

Drexler paused. Francis looked at him, expressionless. Drexler then stood, and moved to the monitors.

'The first thing I have to show you is this.'

Drexler pressed a button below one of the monitors. The screen jumped to life. It was a recording from the news, taken from perhaps ten minutes prior. First, it gave a rundown on events in Mineral – a rundown which included graphic amateur footage of townsfolk gunning each other down. Next, it summarized the event that had happened a few hours previously in Durham, which the experts now realized was not an accident, but a terrorist attack; a precursor to the events in Mineral. Finally, it briefly recapped the six deaths of two days beforehand.

Francis watched this stoic-faced. After eight minutes of footage, Drexler shut it off and returned to his seat.

'As you might've guessed, Francis, *we* were behind what you've just seen. But of course I was planning to show you this anyway, since it seemed likely to crop up in conversation with Muldoon. Now, however, I'd like to show you something to help you understand what the consequences will be if you don't achieve the results we want.'

Again, Drexler paused. This time there *was* emotion in Francis's eyes – fear. Drexler licked his lips.

'We're about to welcome Fred Vitelli. When he enters, he's going to be gagged, nailed to the wall, then castrated. Then we'll let the blood loss run its course. And the reason for all this, Francis, is so that you may see *precisely* what'll happen to you, Ali Haddad, and your brother, Liam, if you don't play ball. So I do hope you pay attention.'

Drexler nodded to Shin. She opened the door to the corridor and called out. By the time Lamed and Beth arrived with Fred Vitelli, tears were streaming down Francis's cheeks.

THIRTY MINUTES LATER, FRED'S BODY HAD BEEN removed from the main office, and only three people were now present: Francis, no longer bound or gagged, but still in cuffs, sitting by the telephone; Drexler, sitting opposite; and Dalet, standing at Drexler's side, training a Beretta at Francis's head. Francis had been horrified by what he'd seen – disgusted. But he had now taken himself in hand, and was ready to put in the performance of his life. It was, after all, his only option. Because there was no way he could let what'd happened to Fred Vitelli happen to his brother. No way in hell.

At seven, the phone rang. Francis, as he'd been instructed, let it ring once before activating the speakerphone.

'Hello, Robin.'

'Francis,' said Muldoon. 'How are you keeping?'

'Just fine. Yourself?'

'Well, other than having to deal with the worst terrorist attacks on American soil since 9/11, I can't grumble.'

Francis made a sympathetic noise. Muldoon continued:

'It's a madhouse over here, Francis. We're completely out of our depth. We still don't even know who's behind this all. And unsurprisingly, The White House isn't impressed.'

'If anyone can handle it,' replied Francis, 'it's the man who had 9/11 fall into his lap a week after becoming Director.'

Muldoon grunted.

'Robin, I know you have some big fish to fry right now, but there's been a development with our Chicago lot; in fact, precisely the development we were hoping for. And I don't think it can be seen as an unlucky coincidence that it's happened now. Rather, I think the drama of the past few days was exactly what put wind in their sails.'

'Tell me the details,' said Muldoon.

Francis proceeded to tell Muldoon everything he'd been told to relay.

'Obviously, it could scarcely be a worse time for this,' Muldoon sighed, after a moment's contemplation. 'It must be said, however, that this was exactly the result we wanted. And we're America, for God's sake. Given the number of enemies we have, we simply have to be prepared to deal with multiple threats at once. And like you said, a successful string of terrorist attacks is precisely the sort of thing that galvanizes another enemy into action.'

Francis hummed his agreement. 'All they want is some cash and the ego trip of dealing with the FBI Director. In return, we're getting two serious catches served up on a plate. The CIA have been trying to find AQAP's Norwegian convert for five years now.'

There was a pause. Even the level-headed Director wasn't above the one-upmanship which had long existed between the FBI and the CIA. Then Muldoon said:

'Francis, if we're going to go ahead with this, then I need you to take the reins. I'm talking making sure everyone's in the right place at the right time, sorting out the cash, and organizing with the guys in Yemen precisely what's going to happen. All I want to worry about is showing my face. I simply don't have time for anything more. Okay?'

'I've already been thinking along those lines,' said Francis assuredly. 'I intend to use Glenview here in Chicago, away from prying eyes in Washington, as our starting point on March 5, and, of course, to book you onto a flight to Chicago earlier that day. And I'm confident that getting the money together and liaising with the boys at the embassy in Yemen shouldn't present a problem. All would be in hand.'

Muldoon took a moment to absorb. 'Okay, let's do it. I want you to get everything sorted over the next twenty-four hours. I'll call tomorrow, same time, for the details. Meanwhile, I'll organize for you to have the powers of The Office of the Director at your disposal for the next seven days so you can get things authorized.'

'You can count on me,' said Francis.

'I know I can, Francis. You're one of the rare few I can trust.'

WITHOUT CEREMONY, SHIN AND DALET ESCORTED Francis back to his cell. Alone once more, Drexler felt more than pleased – he felt ecstatic. Never had he imagined everything, every little detail, to go *this* smoothly. And as he turned on the news, his mood only improved. Because the provisional figures from Mineral were in.

Six dead, eighteen injured.

Not bad at all.

Chapter Twenty-Three

I t was just gone quarter past twelve when I entered The Holland Tunnel, the subterranean highway connecting New Jersey with Manhattan Island. About an hour earlier, the bug had come to a rest on Manhattan's West 59th Street, just to the south of Central Park. And this worried me. Because Drexler undoubtedly knew that in November 1991 – after selling my forgery of Stephen Daye's 'The Oath of a Freeman' (the first printed document to be produced in the colonies) to The Library of Congress for $1 million – I had moved into a suite at The Essex House Hotel on West 59th Street, and stayed for four months. And the only reason I could think of why Drexler would want to include a place from my past in his designs was to use it to torment and outdo me.

In other words, I had a feeling Drexler had plans to take my old haunt and somehow make it his own. And my gut told me his methods would be extreme…

Before long, I was working my way up 6th Avenue with urgency, all too aware that if Drexler *did* have something planned, the shit could hit the fan at any moment. Then, when I got as far as West 58th Street, and found myself caught in traffic, impatience got the better of me and I abandoned my car and continued on foot at a dead run. But this short sprint – because of my sleep deprivation and hangover – exhausted me far more than it should have. And so, when I arrived outside The Essex House, my head was swimming.

The next thing I knew, a man with a headset and clip-board was approaching me. He said curtly:

'Are you a wacko or an extra? Because if you're a wacko, then, I'm sorry, but you need to leave. We're shooting a film.'

I wasn't surprised my appearance elicited this reaction: my clothes were creased to hell, my face unshaven, and I was trembling with fatigue. But I *was* surprised by his comment about shooting a film. And in the next second, I realized the stretch of road outside the hotel had been cordoned off, and no vehicles were passing through.

'Saul Marshall, FBI,' I thundered, displaying my ID. 'I've reason to believe a terrorist attack may occur immi-nently within this location. Tell me *exactly* what's happening.'

The guy saw I wasn't kidding.

'I'm with Paramount,' he said quickly. 'We're producing an action film. We've rented a metro train, and the portion of track directly beneath us. We're shooting a scene involving the release of nerve gas into a number of carriages.' He glanced at his watch. 'The shooting should begin any second now, if it hasn't already.'

'Where's the director?' I growled.

He pointed westward, where one-hundred yards up the road a small marquee had been erected on the sidewalk.

About fifteen people were standing in its vicinity, crowded around a number of monitors outside the tent. Immediately I started running towards them.

'Stop production,' I yelled. 'The nerve gas you're using is real.'

Chapter Twenty-Four

I was fifty yards off, still bellowing, when I heard a shrill, blood-curdling scream. Its source was one of the women standing before the monitors. Then others joined in.

Five seconds later, I was among the crowd, watching the tragedy unfold on three screens. Minus sound, they showed nerve-gas filling every inch of two separate carriages, each one crammed with actors. And there was no ambiguity: these people, with their bodies twisting and seizing, and their faces contorting into expressions of fear and panic no actor could simulate were dying before our eyes. I was watching a mass execution.

I'd remained calm when I'd discovered Samuel strapped into a bomb, and when I'd spoken to Drexler over the phone. I'd remained calm when he'd taken Vannevar, and when people had died in Mineral. But in that moment, as I watched these people clawing at their throats, suffocating slowly, I was tipped over the edge and a thirst for revenge, mad and animalistic, took over. I understood that Drexler, for now, was out of reach. But I reckoned I knew where Lofkin was. And so I decided Lofkin was going to pay.

In the next instant, I was tearing back towards The Essex House. By the time I burst into the lobby and approached the reception desk, I could already hear the first few sirens starting up outside. The man behind the counter, clearly oblivious to what was happening, sneered at my appearance. He opened his mouth to speak, but I got in first.

'FBI,' I barked, presenting my ID. 'I'm looking for two Caucasian men, one with distinctive red hair. What've you seen?'

Ignoring my ID, he gave me a look that spoke caution and contempt. He thought I was a nutcase from off the street.

'Well, *sir*, if you wish for us to disclose such information, you'll need a warrant. Otherwise—'

I reached over the counter, grabbed the guy by his throat, and lifted him off his feet. His pupils dilated with fear.

'Listen very carefully,' I hissed. 'There's been a terrorist attack outside your hotel. People are dying. So I haven't got time to fuck around. Now, I'll ask you only once – what room are they in?'

No sooner had he choked out a number than I was hurtling up the hotel stairs. 502, he'd said, and I wasn't surprised. 502 was the suite I'd stayed in all those years ago. And as I climbed, two steps at a time, I pictured the interior of this room in my mind's eye. But I didn't use this knowledge to devise a subtle approach to the situation. I was out of patience. All I was interested in was getting inside and blowing Lofkin's brains from his head. And so, when I arrived on the fifth floor and outside 502, I didn't hesitate: I extracted the SIG, chambered a round, and with one vicious kick cast the door aside.

By all rights, it should've been the last thing I ever did.

Chapter Twenty-Five

I t was just sitting there, a few yards before me: a simple bomb, made of Semtex. It looked so harmless, so innocent. Yet it was crystal clear that this device, connected as it was to the door, had been meant to go off as I'd come in; that it'd been meant to kill me. And, courtesy of my HRT bomb disposal training, I could see exactly what'd spared my life: a small fault in the fuse's circuitry. Otherwise, the bomb was sophisticated – a very capable effort.

By killing me at The Essex House, Drexler had intended to achieve a symbolic victory. But I'd been spared by the tiniest of errors.

I was, however, too busy berating myself to feel any kind of relief. I'd allowed my temper to get the better of me, and the result had very nearly been fatal. If one thing was clear, it was that I couldn't afford to make the same mistake twice, because next time, I might not be so lucky.

As suddenly as my rage had come, I summoned my composure, and took myself firmly in hand. Then I took a closer look at the device. Fortunately, as I'd first supposed, the bomb presented no threat: it needed modifiction before anything would set it off. However, I didn't let down my guard, because it occurred to me I may not be alone. It was possible, given what'd happened in Mineral, that there were cultists somewhere in the suite who'd been intending to bring a suicide mission to its conclusion. But while I was willing to consider this eventuality for the sake of caution, it seemed more likely that if anyone was in this suite, it'd be Samuel. After all, Drexler had only taken Samuel to goad me. So it was possible that he'd want to get rid of us both at the same time. Though, if this was the case, then I had to hope Samuel had been gagged and restrained. It was just as possible the cultists had taken the easier option, and simply put a bullet in his brain.

Looking around the suite I could see that, although there'd been some superficial refurbishment since the 1990s, the layout had remained unchanged. There was a living room (in which I was standing), a bedroom, and a bathroom. So, closing the door to the suite, I quickly rounded the living room, checking any spaces where a body, living or dead, might be concealed. Then I did the same for the bedroom. In both the coast was clear. But then I entered the bathroom and what I found there turned my world completely upside down.

I found a body alright, but it wasn't Samuel's. It was Lofkin's. It was floating, naked, in a body of water that − with the help of sealant applied to the drain and doors − had been trapped in the shower unit. Both his hands and legs had been tightly bound. And immediately I understood. He'd been placed, while in a state of sleep deprivation, in this body of water which, due to its height, had required Lofkin to stand on tiptoes to breathe. The bindings, of course, had stopped him getting free. Then, when he'd finally reached a point of exhaustion in which the urge to sleep had been overpowering, he'd been forced to let himself drown.

Lofkin had been targeted by The Order and, just like The Order's initial victims two days earlier, he'd been placed in a situation in which he'd been forced to self-inflict harm. Of this, I was sure. But what was wildly unclear was *why* they'd chosen to target one of their own. Of course, there were a number of possibilities – perhaps he'd wronged the cult, perhaps he'd known too much, perhaps Drexler simply ordered it on a whim – but it was impossible to be sure. And the questions didn't stop there. Who, precisely, had done this? And, more importantly, where the hell did this leave Samuel?

But I didn't have time to ponder all this. I needed to get moving. And already, I'd formulated a plan. If I could modify the bomb to go off after I'd escaped, I could convince Drexler that his plan had, in fact, succeeded and in doing so, I could put myself in a perfect position to plot a sneak offensive. But first I knew I ought to search the place, since whoever had been here had assumed the suite was going up in flames, so the chances they'd negligently left something behind were higher than they might otherwise have been.

Starting in the bathroom, I began rifling through everything that could conceivably contain a clue – the cabinets, the toilet, Lofkin's discarded clothes – before moving onto the living room. However, it wasn't until I got to the bedroom that I found something: a small rucksack, tucked beneath the comforter. Immediately, I emptied its contents on the bed. And although at first my heart sank at the sight of empty potato-chip packets, flattened juice boxes, and apple cores, in among this rubbish I also spotted a crumpled piece of writing-paper. But when I read what was on this page, written undoubtedly in Samuel's hand, two things happened. First, my world was turned the right side up again. And second, it was smashed into a thousand pieces.

02/28/2013 – Third Day of Euphrates

 5:30 a.m. Depart for NY.

 11 a.m. Check in Essex House, Room 502. Lofkin's salvation.

 11:15 a.m. Depart for NJ, after preparing father's salvation.

 1 p.m. Collect kerosene, restraints. 407, Bloomfield Avenue, Montclair.

 1:15 p.m. Spender's salvation. 141 Highland Avenue, Montclair.

 1:25 p.m. Depart for home.

 Resh, for The Zahir.

All at once, I understood.

Samuel was no hostage. Samuel was Resh – a member of Drexler's cult. And suddenly everything made sense. The note Olivia had received had indeed been written by Samuel, but it had been a trap. Drexler had planned all along for me to go to Durham, to follow Samuel and Lofkin to Mineral, then finally to die in New York. And while Samuel had worn the bomb-vest to make it appear to me that he was the hostage, in actual fact Dean Lofkin had been the real hostage the whole time, and had only pretended to be Samuel's captor *because* of Samuel's bomb-vest. Because Samuel was threatening to detonate it and kill them both if Lofkin didn't play ball. And as I absorbed this, I realized that both Samuel and Drexler had known there was a good chance I'd storm the house in Mineral, but hadn't warned the other cultists. That is to say, they'd allowed their own loyalists to be blindsided to facilitate their plot. But then my son had done worse than that. He'd then killed his hostage in the most chilling of fashions and attempted to kill his father.

I understood this intellectually. Yet emotionally, my brain short-circuited. I couldn't process it. Everything was broken.

But then, for the simple reason that it had to, my training kicked in. Samuel's itinerary suggested he was plotting another attack in Montclair, New Jersey, at 1:15, and the bedside clock was already showing 12:37. I needed to haul-ass. So I headed back to the living room and got to work modifying the bomb. First, I removed a quantity of Semtex – enough to ensure the bomb would take out nothing beyond the suite, but not so much that Drexler would realize there'd been tampering. Next, I fixed the fault in the fuse's circuitry. Finally, I added a rudimentary countdown, a mechanism which created a lag of approximately sixty seconds between when the device was activated, and when it actually went off.

Then, with the device sufficiently modified, I pocketed the excess Semtex and started the countdown. The next instant, I was in the corridor, which I was relieved to find deserted, and sprinting towards the staff staircase. However, despite taking the stairs at a tremendous pace, I was still within the building – approaching the fire-exit leading to the service road behind the hotel – when the bomb went off, the blast shaking the place like an earthquake. But the shock didn't slow me and a moment later I was bursting through the fire-door with an overwhelming sense of relief.

But then I spotted the man with the gun.

'Police,' he shouted. He was standing seven feet off, wearing the blue uniform of an NYPD officer, and aiming at my head. 'On your knees. Hands behind your head. Don't think I won't shoot.'

I had a split second to decide on a course of action. I could see by his steady hand and serious gaze that this guy meant business. And though I recalled that during the Aaron Woolf incident impostors dressed in NYPD uniforms had coerced Woolf's neighbors from their apartments, I knew this couldn't be a set-up. As far as The Order was concerned, I was dead.

I decided to cooperate.

I got to my knees, and put my hands behind my head, saying as I did so, 'I'm with the FBI. My identification is in my inside, left jacket pocket.'

He nodded curtly. 'If you are who you say you are, then you'll understand my need for caution. A bomb goes off at The Essex House, then I find you running out of the building ten seconds later. And you don't exactly *look* like a Fed.'

'I understand,' I said calmly.

If I was in this guy's shoes, I would've had the same reservations. So I cut him some slack, and kept still as he came close, extracted the ID from my pocket, then finally moved back beyond my range. After a few long seconds of examination, he was satisfied.

'I believe you,' he said, throwing me my ID and holstering his gun. Then, once I was back on my feet, he added:

'So what the hell's happening here?'

There was no way I had time to get into that now. I needed to get to Montclair, pronto. But then it occurred to me that this chance encounter could in fact be a blessing. Because in my current situation – stranded in a city undoubtedly on lockdown – a ride from an NYPD officer was exactly what I needed.

'You got a car?' I asked.

He nodded. 'On 58th.'

If I wanted his cooperation, I had to let him in a little.

'What I'm about to tell you is classified,' I said. 'And I'm only telling you because the situation is desperate. Lives are on the line.'

He nodded again. I continued:

'Everything that's happened in Manhattan this past half hour is linked to the attacks of the past three days. That bomb you just saw, however, was intended specifically to kill me. As far as the people who made it know, it has. They're now plotting an assassination in Montclair, New Jersey, within the next forty minutes. The situation's complex but the crux of it is, I have to be the one to stop it. But as things stand, I've no means of getting there—'

'Let's roll,' he interjected, before leading the way to 58th Street at a sprint.

FOR YEARS I'D HUNTED JIHADISTS, SUICIDE BOMBERS, and terrorists in general without a second thought. To my mind they'd been nothing more than murderers; the scum of the earth. But now my son had joined these ranks, suddenly all my certainties were out the window. Suddenly all the terrorists I'd ever hunted, including the cultists I'd dispatched only that morning, weren't just terrorists. They were somebody's children. And I didn't want my child hunted down in the same way. I wanted him regained and rehabilitated – saved from himself.

Yet not only had this revelation forced me to see terrorists as human – it'd also forced me to see my son as capable of the very worst monstrosities…

But though this was a big shock to my system – a tremendous and disorientating blow – I'd suddenly gained two significant advantages in my fight against Drexler.

Firstly, he now thought I was dead. And secondly, I'd gained *genuine* information regarding The Order's plans, namely, the information contained within Samuel's itinerary. And it was because of this information that I knew Samuel was on his way to assassinate somebody called Spender, since it was clear "salvation" was a euphemism for murder.

But on the face of it, there was a problem, because there was no way I was going to get to Montclair by 1:15 when Spender's salvation was set to begin. This seemed to suggest that if I wanted to save Spender, I'd have to call ahead and warn Spender or The New Jersey Police Department and thus reveal to Drexler I'd survived the assassination attempt, found the itinerary, and passed on the information. However, in actual fact, it seemed to me the situation was more complex. I reckoned, based on the itinerary's reference to kerosene and restraints, that this attack, like almost every other Order attack so far, would be a drawn out affair; that what I was probably dealing with was a house set on fire, and the target left for dead within. And if this was the case – and I felt certain it was – then there was a distinct chance that when I arrived in Montclair, there'd still be time to save Spender.

However, there was also the issue of Samuel himself. The itinerary said he was planning to leave Montclair by 1:25. So if I arrived before then, there was a chance we'd come face-to-face. And if this happened, I'd have no choice but to try and safely neutralize him – not least because if he got away, he'd tell Drexler I was still alive. But although one part of me wanted to encounter Samuel, a much larger part told me that it was something I wanted to avoid. That attempting to neutralize my hostile son while an assassination attempt involving extremely flammable materials was underway was asking for disaster. Better, I thought, he should be gone by the time I arrived so I could concentrate on rescuing Spender. Because really, if I could save Spender while keeping Drexler none the wiser that either of us were still alive, then I was in as good a position as I could reasonably hope to be.

And then it occurred to me that Spender may in fact be an extremely useful person to get hold of. As far as I knew, the only other people who'd faced incineration these past few days were the cultists in Mineral. So perhaps incineration was a means of death reserved for cultists. But Spender's death wasn't going to be willing, so perhaps he was a cult defector – somebody who knew too much.

Spender could be an invaluable lead.

I looked to the policeman sitting to my left, expertly guiding the car through traffic, and then to the dashboard clock which was already reading 12:55. I knew I had to emphasize the need for haste: Montclair, under normal circumstances, was at least thirty minutes from Manhattan and there were only twenty till Samuel's attack began. But just as I was about to broach this subject, the box of donuts on the dashboard caught my eye and suddenly, all I could think about was the hunger in the pit of my stomach.

'Mind if I help myself to those?' I said, nodding at the donuts.

'Go crazy.'

Within twenty seconds, I'd gotten through the three remaining donuts. The policeman gave a low whistle.

'Boy, you've really been through the trenches.'

I nodded. 'That's one way of putting it.'

'Look,' he said abruptly. 'I know this might be confidential, but why does it have to be you? Why can't we call the NJSP and have them deal with this?'

I'd expected this question. And, really, I was happy

about where he was steering the conversation. It was ground we needed to cover.

'If we call ahead, the people who put the bomb in The Essex House will infer I'm not dead. And from a tactical standpoint, it's very important these bastards think I'm dead.'

'So you plan to save this person without giving away the fact you're alive?'

'That's correct.'

He crumpled his brow. 'I take it you've some idea about how this assassin intends to carry out his attack?'

'I reckon the assassin will get to work at quarter past one, and will leave the scene no more than ten minutes later. I've reason to believe, however, that his method of execution won't be instantaneous, and thus I should have a window of opportunity to save the target –though I'm not sure how long this window will last, or whether it'll extend past the assassin's departure. And it's entirely possible there will be no window at all…'

The guy glanced at the clock and tensed his jaw. This was the effect I'd sought: to have him sweating about the time as much as I was. He then said:

'So you're gambling with this person's life to maintain a tactical advantage?'

I nodded. 'I'm gambling with this person's life because it may mean saving more lives down the line.'

'And this is all happening in Montclair?'

'141 Highland Avenue,' I said.

He grunted as if to say he knew where that was.

'And when we get near,' I added, 'you need to kill the sirens and drop me a block or so away. Then you need to make yourself scarce. There can't be any record of an emergency response arriving too soon.'

'I get it,' he said. 'If the authorities are spotted turning up early enough to suggest prior knowledge, these people will know you've had a hand in it.'

'Precisely.'

There was a prolonged silence. The officer continued to navigate the roads. At last he said: 'It was a chemical attack, wasn't it?'

'Nerve gas,' I said. 'And just like the atrocity in Virginia, the damage was unwittingly inflicted by innocent people, in a situation engineered by a terrorist organization.'

His knuckles turned white on the steering wheel, and he ground his teeth. When folk find their city under attack, their response is often more personal than you'd expect. Suddenly the vast population becomes a tight-knit community, standing as one against a common enemy. It happened to New York after 9/11 – and no doubt it'd happen again after.

'Look,' he said, his voice tight with emotion. 'I may not be as qualified as you Bureau boys, but you learn a thing or two after fifteen years on the beat. So if there's anything I can do once we get to Montclair, then I'd be only too happy to lend a hand.'

I understood what he was saying – that he was willing to put himself on the line to help me out. And I could tell he wasn't messing around.

'I appreciate the offer,' I replied seriously. 'But trust me, what needs to be done in Montclair needs to be done by me alone.' I paused, then added: 'Really, the best thing you can do is return to Manhattan and help deal with the aftermath.'

He stared ahead for a long moment. Finally, he gave a slow nod.

'The name's Rex, by the way,' he said, extending his hand. I shook it.

'Saul,' I replied, despite knowing full well that he knew my name already from my ID. But while I appreciated his gesture of companionship, I didn't dwell on it long, because we were now fast approaching The Lincoln Tunnel, the other subterranean passage between Manhattan and New Jersey, and I needed to focus on the task at hand.

1:31 P.M.

Rex pulled over a block from 141 Highland Avenue. I jumped out the car and by the time I'd accelerated to a run, Rex was spinning away in the opposite direction. As I'd expected, the road was lined with large detached houses – each one set back behind concealing trees – and the over-whelming impression was one of quiet suburban harmony. But I knew better. And as I went, I speculated as to how things stood within the house. I decided, given that it was now sixteen minutes since Samuel had started Spender's "salvation," that Samuel had probably left. Yet whether or not Spender was still alive, I had no idea.

The next thing I knew, I'd reached 141, and was ducking through a gap in the trees to bring the house into view. It was a large, grey affair, looking perfectly innocuous in the afternoon gloom: no flames dancing in the windows; no signs of life at all. There was, however, a pathway to the left of the house, and I made for it immediately, deter-mined to get a look at the house's rear. A moment later, I was in a large back garden, complete with swimming pool, skirting along the back of the house. But it wasn't until I reached the plate-glass patio door that I found the action.

On the other side of the glass there was a grand-looking living room. But more than that, there was also a woman bound in thick rope, gagged, and strewn across a sofa, and a fierce blue fire that had all but engulfed the far-side wall. And though I experienced a flash of relief at the fact that this woman, who I assumed to be Spender, was still very much alive, it was short lived. Because the situation was critical: not only was the fire growing at an incredible rate – latching onto the adjacent walls, colonizing the ceiling – but the sofa was positioned only about four yards away from this tremendous blaze. And even as I was absorbing this, the situation deteriorated further, the sofa suddenly catching light, and burning even faster than the kerosene-soaked walls.

I needed to act fast.

Scarcely had I thought this than I removed my jacket – containing my valuables plus the Semtex – and lobbed it on the grass behind me. Then, after trying the door and finding it locked, I seized a clay flowerpot, and hurled it at the glass. There was an enormous crash as both the glass and clay burst into a thousand pieces, followed by a scream of air as the fire heaved in oxygen from the outside. Fed by this newfound fuel supply, the flames surged, showering the room with flecks of scorched paint – flecks which ignited puddles of kerosene dotted about the floor, spreading embers all over.

Spender, now very much aware of my presence, stared at me panic-eyed.

I dived through the door bowing below the smoke gathering overhead and started sprinting across the room. Five seconds later, after upturning a coffee table to stifle some intervening flames, I was at Spender's side, scooping her off what now looked more like a continuous body of fire than a sofa, and swinging her over my shoulder. Then, feeling my skin prickle as the flames passed from her clothes to mine, I turned around, and charged back across the room and back into the garden. And then I did the only thing I could think of to divest us of the flames: I made for the pool, and plunged us into the water.

Holding Spender's head above the water's surface, I tore off her gag, and said:

'Is there anyone else inside?'

'Nobody.'

'Do you have a car?'

'In the garage.'

'And the keys?'

'On the windowsill. By the front door.'

At that, I heaved the two of us out the water, and untied Spender's restrains. Then, grabbing my jacket, I led Spender back to the front of the house, where I unceremoniously kicked down the front-door and grabbed the car-keys from the windowsill. And once I threw back the garage door to reveal a blue Nissan Murano SUV, I didn't hang about: I got us both inside the car, and drove away at speed.

Chapter Twenty-Six

I t was an itch – an itch that *needed* scratching. And besides, he'd be back on the road again within half an hour. He had the time to spare.

Resh pulled his rental car – the one he'd had waiting for him in Manhattan – into the car-park of a small motel in Riverdale, NJ. Then, after paying in cash at reception, he got inside his room and locked the door at which point, he slowly and carefully began readying himself. He changed into the simple grey clothes he had in his bag. He produced the small ceremonial bowl, and filled it with sand. Then he assumed the position: he sat on the floor, legs crossed, and eyes closed.

Then, finally, he started softly chanting the word "Taprobana." The effect it had was immediate: the physical world dissolved and Resh felt himself fall into a deep calm. As he continued, this calm became more and more profound, until eventually, all at once, it spilled over into the ecstatic, the divine. And it was then – in a state of rapture – that he stood, took a grain of sand from the bowl, opened a window, and cast it to the wind.

Chapter Twenty-Seven

'How you feeling? Any calmer?'

It'd been ten minutes since we'd left Montclair, and we were on the Garden State Parkway, traveling north. And though we were both still dripping wet, I'd judged that the worst of the shock had passed. It was time to break the silence.

Spender nodded diffidently.

'I'm feeling… I'm feeling better. And thank you. For all your help.'

I nodded and smiled. She was trembling all over – the result, no doubt, of both the cold water and the adrenaline come-down. But despite her bedraggled clothes (which by the looks of things had borne the brunt of the flames), sodden blonde hair, and shell-shocked demeanor, she was clearly a beautiful woman. Her eyes were dazzling blue; her skin was soft and creamy; and she held herself with poise and grace.

'Well, you had a close shave back there,' I said warmly. 'So if you're already feeling better, you're doing well.' I paused, then said, 'Not many people are targeted by The Order of Babylon and live to tell the tale.'

She looked at me questioningly. 'So you know about The Order?'

'I do.'

'Who are you?'

'I'm with the FBI.'

She shook her head. 'You can't be. If the FBI knew about The Order, it'd be all over the news.'

I regarded her carefully. I had decided I was going to tell her a lot of the truth because I reckoned this was the best way to get her to open up about herself. And already this approach was paying off. With this last comment, she'd revealed she knew The Order was responsible for a lot more than setting her house on fire. This knowledge alone, I understood, was enough for Drexler to want her dead.

'I really am with the FBI,' I said slowly. 'And I *do* know about The Order and everything they've done these past few days. But here's the thing: I haven't told my superiors because I'm being blackmailed. The Order have people I love. They'll die if I talk.'

'It's a relief,' she said after a moment's reflection, 'to hear I wasn't the only one who knew. The guilt's been terrible, knowing I'd been in possession of information that might've saved so many lives. But I was too scared to tell anyone.'

I nodded sympathetically. I understood the guilt. And she didn't need to explain why she'd been too scared to tell – I felt sure Drexler had threatened her to keep her silent. Though clearly he'd now decided she was too much of a liability to be allowed to live.

'So how did you know about the fire?' Spender said. 'That my life was in danger?'

I'd been expecting these questions. But though I'd

already decided to tell her plenty of the truth, there was one detail I wasn't yet ready to reveal – that it was my son who'd attempted to kill her; who'd attempted to kill us…

'It's simple,' I said. 'The guy who set your house on fire also tried to kill me just over an hour ago in New York. But he didn't realize his attempt failed. So I did what seemed the logical thing: I followed him.'

She absorbed this calmly. I continued:

'But that means as far as The Order is concerned, we're both dead. So we don't need to worry about anyone coming after us.'

She gave a strained smile. 'That's a relief.'

I smiled back reassuringly. On the whole, I was encouraged by how things were going: she seemed to trust me. However, she was very clearly still in shock and I knew that if I wanted to get her talking freely, I needed to get her to relax.

I had a plan.

Fishing into my jacket pocket, I withdrew my cigarettes, lit one up, then handed the packet to Spender who gratefully lit up herself. After five minutes of puffing away in silence, just as I'd hoped, Spender had loosened up considerably – her arms were no longer crossed, her face was brighter, and she'd stopped trembling. We flicked our cigarette butts out the window, both lit up a second, then I restarted the conversation:

'My name's Saul Marshall. It's good to meet you.'

She smiled a more relaxed smile. 'Lilly Spender. Good to meet you, too.'

'So, Lilly, I've just had The Order of Babylon try to kill me. Makes sense, really – I'm a nuisance. But it turns out you are, too. You know too much.'

She nodded meaningfully.

I was still unsure what her relationship with The Order

was. But I had a feeling she knew more than just that The Order were responsible for these recent attacks. I had a feeling she had other information Drexler didn't want getting out.

I cut to the chase:

'Tell me, how did a girl like you wind up in a situation like this?'

'That's a question I've asked myself many times.' She shook her head. 'What do you know about The Order already? So I know where to start.'

'I know they're a terrorist organization, headed by a psychopath, and responsible for the string of attacks these past three days. And I know a little bit about their history – a handful of facts, figures, dates – starting with the house in Greenwich Village in early 2010. I've also heard a brief outline of their screwy theology.'

She rocked gently back and forth. At last she said:

'They want me dead because, as you say, I know too much. I'm the only member of the Inner Sanctum to defect from The Order.'

She was, just as I'd guessed, a lapsed cultist.

'The Inner Sanctum,' I said. 'The first fifteen members plus anyone who's been allowed to see The Zahir's face. The ones with purple hoods.'

'That's right.'

'And which were you?'

'I was there from the start,' she said ruefully.

She finished her smoke and flicked the butt out the window. Then she gave a big sigh. The floodgates were about to open.

'It was Summer 2008, I was eighteen, and I was in New York,' she said. 'I was there to audition for a popular ice show because before all this I wanted to be a figure-skater and my parents had organized for me to stay at a hotel in Midtown. But unbeknownst to them I'd made alternative plans to stay with a friend at Columbia University. A friend my parents didn't know about.'

She paused a moment. Sighed again.

'I remember the day clearly,' she continued. 'It was the height of summer and I was in my friend's apartment on West 111. Then her boyfriend arrived. He was tall, handsome, and much older. But above all, he was incredibly charismatic. He had a way of talking that made the rest of the world fall away. Well, that was my first meeting with The Zahir – only then he went by the name William Martin.'

My skin crawled. Drexler had used the same handle I'd used when starting out as a con-artist. I felt violated.

Spender shot me a piercing look. 'It's difficult to admit how I felt about him then, given what I know now.'

'You weren't to know,' I replied gently.

Spender nodded and went on:

'I fell under his spell so quickly, I can hardly believe it looking back. But after just three days of knowing him, he demanded I cut off all ties with my past, insisted I broke all contact with everyone I knew, and give them no indication where I'd gone – and I did. I berate myself to this day that I could've been so gullible, but I take solace that I wasn't the only one. In fact, by November there were fifteen of us – both men and women – living in that small apartment. Sleeping with each other, on top of each other, sharing everything. And The Zahir was our leader. He'd preach to us about the corruption of society; about how one day we'd go to war with the old order and triumph. About how we'd oversee a moral utopia. It sounds ridiculous, but we believed. We thought he was a god; that together we were The Order of Babylon – the ancient arbiters of fate, reborn.

'We dressed the same, spoke a private language, and each had special names. Before long, I felt like I couldn't function without them.

'It was about this time, November 2008, that The Zahir started preparing us for expansion. He insisted that before we could expand, we needed to create titles and ranks. So it was established that he'd go only by the name "The Zahir," and that the fifteen of us would collectively be known as "The Inner Sanctum." He then introduced two tactics that were necessary, he explained, to safeguard us from the old order as we expanded. The first was that nobody from then on would be allowed to know his identity or see his face who wasn't in The Inner Sanctum. That way, when The Deluge of Euphrates came, our enemies would struggle to find our leader. To police this, aside from forbidding anyone from photographing him, he came up with the idea of the purple hoods. Not only would he wear a purple hood when among anyone not in The Inner Sanctum, but, at the same time, anyone in The Inner Sanctum was entitled to wear one whenever they wished, thereby protecting against attempts to unhood The Zahir.'

'The Deluge of Euphrates,' I echoed. 'The final showdown with civilization.'

She nodded solemnly. 'Right. And that leads me onto the second tactic he introduced – namely, that we were to conceal publicly that Euphrates was yet to come. Instead, we were to pretend it had already happened. That way, the old order wouldn't suspect we were a threat. Only when he saw fit, The Zahir told us, would any new member be told the truth.'

I nodded. She went on:

'And so we moved to Greenwich Village and expanded. Obviously, we knew we'd come up on the authorities' radar in some capacity; but so long as we kept to these tactics, we knew their scrutiny would be cursory. Yet I suspect they still had a fairly good idea of what we got up to, day to day—'

I broke in: 'They knew about you raising money through slave labor and obligating members to surrender property and wealth; about the strict regulations on sexual relations, and the exploitative use of confessionals.'

Spender nodded at each item.

'The confessionals were a particularly potent tool,' she said. 'Of course they're routine in cultic groups, but The Zahir put his own twist on it. A typical session involved perhaps ten members standing in a circle. Then the person who called the session – either an Inner Sanctum member or The Zahir himself – would pick on individuals to confess. But they wouldn't confess things they'd done recently: they'd confess sins from their previous life, before The Order. The upshot was that people would re-live their shame time and again… Somehow, this humiliation only redoubled people's hunger for acceptance.'

There was a pause for thought. Then I asked:

'What was the turning point?'

'It happened in New York – summer last year. There was a couple, both Order members, with a young child, maybe three years old. The kid threw a tantrum, and kicked The Zahir. He didn't do any damage, of course, but The Zahir demanded the child apologize. He wouldn't. So The Zahir ordered the father to spank the child with a wooden board. The father followed orders. Thirty minutes later, the child was unconscious. He was lucky not to die.

'I was very close to The Zahir: he told me things he told nobody else. For this reason I decided I should be the one to talk to him about this incident – I felt that some-body had to. So in private, I challenged him for the first time. I asked whether a child could be held responsible for its actions; whether the crime warranted the punishment.

The Zahir's reaction, however, was as extreme as it was unexpected. He took me by the throat, slammed me against a wall, and told me he ought to crush me; that I was no better than an insect. But no sooner had he done so than he let me go, and suddenly he was livid with himself. It was like he'd accidentally shown me a side to him that he'd desperately wanted to keep hidden. He dismissed me. Then the next time I saw him, he acted like it'd never happened.

'It may've taken me three days to fall under his spell, but it took a lot longer to break free. Simply entertaining a negative thought about The Zahir was difficult: when everyone around you thinks one way, you get to believing you're insane if you think differently. But slowly I began to see the truth. I began to see that The Zahir wasn't a religious man – he was someone who got his kicks from controlling others. And I began to see that so much of what he did was geared towards breeding dependence. The way he forced followers to break contact with their past and renounce their wealth. The way he sent individuals to live in closed-off safe-houses. The confessionals.

'Finally, I began to see that the religion itself was a lie. It was a way of justifying violence – making it appear not just necessary, but urgently moral. The Zahir was creating an army of fanatics who'd go to any lengths…'

She paused a moment, thinking, then continued:

'His powers of manipulation were never more on show than when he got wind that a child of an influential person – say a celebrity, or high-powered businessman – had displayed interest in The Order. He'd drop everything to groom these individuals. His aim was for them to join The Order secretly – to go missing without trace, like I did – and he was *always* successful. The boy who attempted to kill us, he was one of them. I can't remember who his father was exactly, some government official, but I do remember the lengths The Zahir went to seduce him. This boy was even given a place in The Inner Sanctum – the ultimate honor.'

She was, of course, talking about Samuel. But though I'd been too embarrassed to tell her he was my son the first time I'd had the chance, I knew that if I wanted to get the right information out of her, I'd have to tell her the truth eventually. So I bit the bullet:

'That was my son. The boy who tried to kill you is my son, Samuel.'

I looked at her, half-expecting to see shock. But she simply narrowed her eyes, and said, 'He looks like you. Is he the hostage you were referring to?'

The question revealed she knew what I did – that Drexler was capable of killing his own men without batting an eyelid.

'He's one of them,' I muttered.

All at once, my body was hot with emotion. But I couldn't let my feelings cloud my head – not when so much needed doing. So, taking myself in hand, I moved the conversation on: 'So you broke free of The Zahir's spell. Then what?'

'Well, at first I tried to hide my reservations from The Zahir. But of course it was little use – I was too close to him – and gradually, over the course of many weeks, he began to see a change in me. A tension grew between us. Then, one day, he took me aside and told me that if I ever told anyone what I knew, he'd kill me. He understood that he'd made a mistake with me, he'd allowed me to learn too much. Now I was a liability.'

Again, Spender sighed.

'But even then, I didn't leave,' she continued. 'Yes, I was scared; but I was even more scared of leaving The

Order, so dependent had I become. But eventually, after many weeks working up the courage, I finally did it. In December last year. I've been living at my parents' house in Montclair ever since. They don't know I've returned. They're in Europe…'

'And now their house has been razed to the ground,' I said, 'because Drexler decided it was safer you were dead.'

'Drexler?' she replied quizzically.

I'd suspected she wouldn't know his real name. After all, given that he'd gone so far as to fake his death before starting The Order, it would've made little sense if he'd then revealed his true identity. So, since it was now my turn to talk, I proceeded to tell Spender everything I knew about Drexler's past – right up to him faking his death. Then, after a brief pause, I added with an air of positivity:

'But we're in a unique position to fight this man. Because we're in a similar position to which Drexler himself was in after he'd faked his death: we're alive, but our enemies think we're dead. We're perfectly placed to launch a sneak-attack…'

But the moment I said this, terror flashed across her face and her body tensed up again, arms crossing over her chest, nails worrying at her forearms. I understood. Now Drexler thought she was dead, Spender was finally free, after months of fear. Having only just tasted this freedom, she wasn't ready to start thinking about going after Drexler. So, for now, I decided to let it drop. But I felt encouraged by what she'd told me so far, and confident that she knew things that could help me. One thing had particularly caught my attention: The Order safe-houses. Perhaps Samuel was living in one. Perhaps so was Drexler.

Ten minutes later, a calmer Spender broke the silence, asking me where exactly we were going.

'My friend has a holiday home in Stonington,

Connecticut,' I said. 'The neighborhood will be deserted this time of year so it'll be a good place to lie low.'

The property belonged, in fact, to Vannevar's parents. But Spender was content with the details she'd been given. And, after yawning twice and leaning back on the headrest, she did what anyone would've expected considering what she'd been through: she fell asleep.

For the first time in a while, I was left alone with my thoughts. But my mind didn't turn to Samuel. It turned to the two women in my life: Olivia and Parkes. There was no question Parkes now knew I'd had foreknowledge of the attacks in Mineral and New York: she would've spoken to the Louisa County Police and eye-witnesses in Manhattan. And I knew she'd be livid with me; that she'd be holding me in no small way responsible for what happened, and would want to bring me in for interrogation. And I also knew it was immaterial whether or not Olivia had shown Samuel's note. Parkes wouldn't care a damn if I'd been trying to save my son – she wouldn't consider this, nor *anything* else, an excuse. As far as Parkes was concerned, employees of the FBI must be loyal, above all, to the Bureau, regardless of the situation.

On one hand, I could understand Parkes's point of view. Dozens of people had died, at least in part because I'd withheld information. But, on the other hand, I felt angry with her mentality – the extremity of it.

But when it came to Olivia, all I wanted was to reassure her. Not because I had any interest in stopping her showing Samuel's note to Parkes – that was immaterial now – but because I felt terrible about the position I'd left her in. I'd told her I'd keep her updated when I left Durham, but then I'd not been in contact since, even though there'd been two large-scale terrorist attacks. Doubtless she was terrified. But, at the same time, I wondered if the truth was really any better than the silence.

Yet one thing was clear: if I wanted to call her or anyone else, I'd need a new phone and SIM card. Because the iPhone was out the question. With it on, Parkes could triangulate my location. This was why it'd been off since my conversation with Giles outside Mineral. It wasn't enough to stay ahead of Drexler anymore. I had to stay ahead of the Bureau, too.

Chapter Twenty-Eight

A n Oval Office Address, all because of him?
Drexler was flattered: it's not every day the President addresses an enemy before the entire country. Not that he didn't deserve it, of course – the events which had elicited this response had taken *years* of planning. Not only that, they'd each come off without a hitch. The latest two were no exception: the gassing of the Manhattan Metro had been a resounding success – the preliminary death count was already well over thirty – and so too had the bombing of The Essex House Hotel. And Drexler had been able to see them both because not only had an amateur cameraman caught the explosion at The Essex House, but Paramount Pictures had made public their footage of the actors suffocating on the train.

Sadly, however, Drexler would have to miss the live showing of the Address. It wasn't due to start until 8 p.m. EST, and Drexler had already made plans.

With this thought, he looked at the wall-clock in the main control room. The time was fast approaching four, and Dalet was due back any minute. He'd gone out to collect Vannevar Yeung from the nearby city of La Porte, Indiana. Drexler hadn't wanted anyone outside his most trusted four to know the location of his hideout, so had organized for Dalet to take custody of Vannevar for the last leg of the journey. And Drexler felt relaxed about this change of hands. He knew he could trust Dalet, who'd proven his worth and reliability time and again. His FBI training in particular seemed to be the gift that kept on giving. Earlier today, for example, his expertise had been invaluable when it'd come to organizing things at Glenview Naval Air Station, the naval military base to the north of Chicago. Dalet had known precisely what language to use, precisely what Francis should say. As a result, everything had been sorted exactly to specification.

On balance, Drexler reflected, he would be unhappy if anything happened to Dalet. It'd be like losing a loyal, well-trained dog. A shame. Though, of course, that's all it would be to him, and this was crucial, because it was symptomatic of Drexler's unique ability not to have an emotional stake in anyone outside of himself. Both Francis Bindle and that worm, Saul Marshall, lacked this ability, and it was incredible to see how vulnerable it made them; incredible to see the lengths they'd go to for the life of just one person.

Drexler was jogged from these thoughts by Shin knocking at the door.

'Dalet has returned,' she reported.

Drexler rose, and followed Shin to the storage area out back. Then he watched as Lamed, Beth, Shin, and Dalet retrieved Vannevar's unconscious body from the van parked outside the warehouse's rear-door and carried it through to the room in the second corridor that'd been stripped in preparation for Vannevar's arrival. He then supervised as Vannevar was put into a bomb vest and bound to a chair. Vannevar wouldn't be allowed to roam about his room like the other agents – he was in a different league.

Once this was done, Drexler ushered Dalet into his bedroom.

'Do you have the items for me?' said Drexler.

Dalet nodded, then produced a Ruger Mark III and a blade from his person.

'Thank you, Dalet,' said Drexler. 'Once again, you've done me proud.'

Dalet blushed.

'So you've resolved to carry out the next task yourself, My Zahir?' asked Dalet.

'I have, my son. And in my brief absence, you must take charge. It'll be your responsibility to ensure Francis relays all the necessary information to Director Muldoon tomorrow morning. As you know, it's *crucial* that job is done correctly... I will return no later than Saturday morning.'

'I won't let you down,' said Dalet.

Drexler placed his hands on Dalet's cheeks, held his face a moment, then kissed him.

'I know you won't, my son,' said Drexler. 'Now, you must leave me to prepare for my heavenly voyage.'

Once Dalet had left the room, Drexler packed a valise with the Ruger and blade, a roll of cash, and a mobile, before changing into civilian clothes. He then exited the warehouse, started Liam Bindle's car, and nosed it onto South Laflin Street. Drexler knew he had disciples who'd beg for the honor of doing this task for him. But though he took great pleasure in having others do his bidding, some-times, just sometimes, it was more satisfying to do things himself. And this particular task was so enthralling, he couldn't resist getting involved. Even if it meant a long car journey. Even if it meant exposing himself to the vulnerabilities that came with leaving his safe haven.

Time to get in on the fun.

Chapter Twenty-Nine

I t was just gone 5 p.m. when we arrived at 84 Wilcox
Road, a large, isolated house by a lake. Spender and I
went inside – making use of the keys hidden under a
flower-pot – and both showered and put on a change of
clothes, Lilly opting for a simple blue dress while I went
with one of Vannevar's father's suits. Then, looking a lot
less conspicuous, we headed to a nearby supermarket
where we picked up food and an outdated Nokia cell with
a SIM. When we returned to the house, we started working
on the roast we were planning for dinner. And as we
worked, we made some light conversation, joked around a
little. Of course, it was impossible to properly unwind with
so much on our minds but I felt glad for Lilly's company,
and got the impression she felt the same. However, when it
hit 7 p.m., I knew I had to return to business, and went
upstairs to call Morton Giles.

'Hello?' he answered gruffly.

'It's Saul. I'm on a new phone. New SIM.'

'Give me a moment.' I could hear footsteps. Then:
'Right, you're on a new SIM, meaning you know you

should be lying low. But you need to know just how much trouble you're in. The extent of it.'

'Okay.'

'The good news, at least as far as you're concerned, is that Parkes still doesn't know about The Order. The bad news is she's spoken to Louisa County Police. She knows you were in Mineral before the incident and had prior knowledge.'

I said nothing.

'She's also spoken to witnesses in Manhattan, who've said they saw you there just before that incident, too – again, seemingly with knowledge of what was about to happen. And then there's the receptionist at The Essex House who told Parkes that after accosting him, you'd headed for Room 502 which was the room destroyed by a considerable quantity of Semtex ten minutes later. But though the receptionist was the last eye-witness to see you, Parkes knows you weren't killed: there's CCTV showing you leaving the building seconds after the blast. She doesn't know where you went from there but she *does* know you didn't return to the car you came in. She's figured out that the abandoned Toyota on 6th Avenue – containing thousands of dollars' worth of HRT property, including a PSG1 rifle – was how you got from Mineral to Manhattan, not that it took much figuring.'

Giles paused a beat. 'And there's more.'

'More?'

'Olivia has shown Parkes Samuel's message, and told her about you and Vannevar going to Durham. By all accounts, Olivia was hysterical.'

'And let me guess, Parkes didn't care a damn that our son's been taken?' I said darkly. 'Didn't think trying to get him back was an excuse for doing what I did?'

'What she cares about, Saul, is that you had prior

knowledge about all three incidents, but didn't tell her. She's livid. She wants you arrested and prosecuted under the Espionage Act. Remember, she doesn't know about The Order and their threats to kill Samuel if you told the Bureau. She thinks you withheld information *only* because you wanted to be in control of Samuel's rescue and then stubbornly continued in that vein even when you saw things were going to escalate and many more people were going to die.'

I scoffed. 'Even if we explained the entire situation to her – that Samuel would've died if I'd passed on the information – she would *still* say I should've told her. She'd have sacrificed my son in a heartbeat, Mort.'

'I know,' he said.

He really did. It was why he'd kept The Order's involvement secret all this time.

I sighed. 'So now they know Vannevar was involved?'

'That's right. Parkes got the receptionist at the HRT to corroborate Olivia's story that you'd picked up Vann, though apparently he was plenty tight-lipped about it. But he wasn't the only one to give Parkes confirmation. She traced the Toyota to the guy in Mineral you borrowed it from. He told her that the first time he saw you, you were with a man fitting Vannevar's description. What Parkes wants to know is where Vannevar is now, seeing that the next time you surfaced – when the terrorists handed you over to the Sherriff – he was gone… She's assuming he's either been taken hostage or killed.'

'So losing a highly-trained Bureau asset has been added to my list of sins?'

'Precisely.'

'How do you know all this? The Director of the CID isn't usually kept updated on the minutiae of Counterterrorist investigations.'

Mort sighed a big sigh.

'That's the problem. I know because I've been interrogated. Parkes and Schneider are suspicious that I've been in contact with you; that I also had prior knowledge of the attacks, but held my tongue at your request. I've denied it, naturally, and I'm too senior for them to do anything more than question me. But the tension between our departments is now beyond acrimonious. And needless to say, if the truth comes out, I'll also face charges.'

For a moment, I didn't know what to say. At last:

'I'm sorry to have put you in this position.'

Mort sighed again.

'I can cope with the personal fallings out at Hoover, and with the threat of prosecution. But what I'm coping less well with is the guilt. I had information that could've saved many, many lives, but I didn't pass it on. In a way, I feel responsible for all those deaths. I've not slept a wink since that boy died in Durham.'

His voice was tormented – like I'd never heard it before. It was uncanny: Spender had said almost the exact same thing.

'Mort, I really do know what you mean,' I said. 'I went after Samuel like I did because I felt I had no choice, and I stand by that decision. But now all this damage has been done – it's not easy for me to stomach, either. And the faces of those people suffocating on the train – those faces will haunt me forever.' I paused. 'This guilt was a torture Drexler designed for me but I've brought you in on it, too. I'm sorry.'

He ground his teeth. 'Well, that's the crux of it. We're not responsible, Drexler is.'

I'd told myself the same thing over and over. It didn't dispel the guilt.

'I'm sorry,' I repeated.

He grunted. A grunt that said he could cope; that we didn't have time for hand-wringing.

'If we're not telling Parkes about The Order, then you need a plan of action,' he said decisively. 'But before you tell me your next move, tell me, what happened in New York?'

'It's bad, Mort. Real bad.'

'Do I want to know what you're about to tell me?'

'It's bad.'

'Go on…'

'It's my son. He's part of The Order.'

There was a heavy silence.

'Tell me from the beginning.'

I told him about my arrival in Manhattan; my discoveries in Room 502; my detonating the Semtex to throw Drexler off the scent; and, finally, my rescue of Spender.

'So you're with a cult defector, Drexler thinks you're both dead, and you're laying low in Stonington?' he said, after a brief pause. 'And you're hoping this ex-cultist will point you in the right direction?'

He sounded doubtful.

'She mentioned the existence of Order safe-houses,' I replied. 'I haven't had a chance to ask further questions – it's a sensitive situation. But I reckon she may know the location of key cult strongholds. Perhaps Samuel's whereabouts. Perhaps Drexler's.'

'And we still can't tell Parkes about The Order because Vann will die?'

'Right. If we tell, Drexler will realize I'm still alive, or will assume I told somebody in the Bureau who'd kept it secret up till this point. Either way, I've no doubt it would be enough for him to carry out his threat. And I reckon he won't hesitate to kill Samuel, too. We know he's not fazed about slaughtering his own loyalists.'

'What exactly do you hope to do about Samuel? The boy… well, he's a terrorist.'

'I can't just leave him to die. He's still my child.'

'All terrorists are somebody's child.'

'Don't pretend it doesn't make a difference.'

He groaned. 'So what do you hope to do?'

'Get him back, Mort. Get him back.'

'Even if this woman leads you directly to Samuel, it's not going to be easy,' he said. 'He won't come peacefully… and we know from the bomb he's been wearing that he's probably willing to give his life for this cause…'

'But I have to try. Right?'

He grunted. 'If the Bureau figure out he's a terrorist, you won't just have to worry about Drexler killing him. The Bureau'll hunt him down.'

'I know. So I have to try to get him back myself. What choice do I have?'

'Your choice is simple,' he said calmly. 'Either you hang up your gloves and tell Parkes about The Order – which means throwing Vann and Samuel to the wolves – or you squeeze the right information out of your ex-cultist and act on it immediately.' He paused. 'Though if she doesn't have the right information, then the decision's made for you. If the trail's gone cold, then you might as well tell Parkes about The Order and give her a fighting chance of averting any further atrocities.'

I contemplated this a moment, then said forcefully, 'I *will* get the right information from Spender. And then, after calling Parkes first thing tomorrow and telling her I have no intention of turning myself in, I *will* act.'

Mort was quiet a moment. 'Keep me updated, Saul.'

'I will.'

I FINISHED THE PHONE-CALL FEELING SHELL-SHOCKED. But after I came downstairs and tucked into the meal already on the dining table, I soon started feeling better. And once again, I was glad of Lilly's company. But I knew this relative good-feeling couldn't last – I had urgent questions. And when we finished eating, at about nine o'clock, I finally bit the bullet, and steered the conversation sharply in that direction.

'Lilly, listen, I need your help. My son's been converted to The Order. My best friend's been taken hostage… will you help me?'

Immediately there was a change in her body language. She tensed-up and started trembling slightly. Her face flushed.

'I'll try,' she said softly.

'Please, put yourself in my shoes,' I persisted, 'and think what it must be like to have loved ones threatened like this.'

She nodded almost imperceptibly. 'I'll try,' she said, with a little more force this time.

All the same signs of fear she'd displayed in the car were reappearing. But I had anticipated as much, and had already decided to power through.

'What I need, Lilly, is information. In the car you mentioned Order safe-houses. Now, I'm assuming these are properties owned by the Order, but whose existence are unknown to the authorities. If this is the case, and you know the location of any of them, I need to know, okay? Because I need to find Samuel or Drexler – or both. I understand you're scared of what might happen if you tell. But I promise you you'll be fine. I'll protect you.'

She breathed heavily, then said, 'Okay. I know of one house, only one, in Boston. I visited it once, with Drexler, almost a year ago. It was home to ten Order members, one of whom was a member of the Inner Sanctum…'

She trailed off.

'It's okay. You can tell me.'

She looked at me, then glanced down at the table.

'It's okay,' I repeated.

'Ten Order members live there,' she said slowly. 'And the Inner Sanctum member is your son.'

This was a major breakthrough. But though her discomfort was building, and she was clearly struggling to keep herself under control, I couldn't stop there. I needed more.

'The address,' I said gently. 'I need the address, Lilly.'

She looked at me like she was about to speak. But then, suddenly, she got to her feet and shook her head.

'I can't do this,' she exclaimed, 'I can't.'

Then, before I could respond, she dashed out the room, and I could hear her rapidly mounting the stairs and slamming a bedroom door behind her.

I leaned back in my chair and reflected. What Spender had just said was promising – it seemed as if she knew where Samuel lived. And not only was I not worried about getting the address out of her, I was also not particularly taken aback by the fear she was exhibiting: after everything I'd seen of Drexler, I'd have been surprised if she wasn't scared of antagonizing him. But what I *was* worried about was the prospect of entering a safe-house containing nine cultists in an attempt to remove my hostile son.

But worse than this prospect was the possibility that Spender's information was stale; the possibility that, almost a year on, Samuel was no longer living there. Because if this was the case, and Spender knew no further information, then the trail had gone cold…

With that thought, I made my way upstairs to an empty bedroom.

Twenty minutes later, there was a knock on my door. The next thing I knew, Lilly was in my bed. She was looking for comfort; for some escape, if only temporary, from everything. I craved the same things. But then it turned hot and frantic, as though the end of the world was upon us. Maybe it was.

Chapter Thirty

I woke at 5:30 a.m., dressed without waking Lilly, and crept out the room. Then I booted up the desktop computer in the living room, and started downloading and installing the software required to place untraceable calls. Once the software was ready, I plugged in a headset, and dialed Parkes's number. She answered immediately, sounding wide awake and alert.

'Yes.'

'It's Saul.'

There was a tense pause.

'You're not using a telephone,' she said.

'That's right.'

'Where are you?'

'If I wanted you to know that, I'd have used a telephone.'

Another pause.

'You need to come in, Saul.'

'That's not going to happen.'

'I'm not asking you. You're coming in.'

'I don't think so.'

Parkes took a labored breath. 'I'm sure it'll come as no surprise to you that I've spoken to eye-witnesses, and know you had prior knowledge of all three incidents: Durham, Mineral, and Manhattan. And yes, I've spoken to Olivia, too, and have seen the note from your son – so don't bother telling me why you did it. It doesn't fly.'

I said nothing. She continued:

'You need to come in, Saul. You need to tell us everything you know and everything that's happened to you. Then you need to explain yourself. Why you thought it was okay to solicit Vannevar Yeung's help, and why you stole HRT property. Why Yeung seems to've vanished, and why you left a rifle lying about Manhattan. Why a bomb went off in The Essex House, and why the remains of a body were found among the rubble… Why you withheld information which could've averted three major terrorist incidents.'

She said this with awful calm.

'My son was taken hostage,' I replied squarely. 'What did you expect me to do?'

'You arrogantly withheld information because you knew you'd be sidelined if you told the Bureau. For that reason alone, you put hundreds of lives in jeopardy. It was beyond reckless. You *will* be held to account.'

'You know only half the story.'

'Is that so?' she said darkly. 'Well then, I'd love to hear the other half.'

'On the day I returned to DC I received a message from Ivan Drexler. It told me a number of things. Firstly, it disclosed some extremely pivotal information. Secondly, it told me that he had Samuel, and would kill him immediately if I told the FBI this information. Thirdly, it told me that if, by midnight March 4, I'd failed to rescue Samuel, he would be executed.'

Parkes breathed deeply, processing the information. I knew what was coming.

'It still doesn't fly,' she said calmly. 'You didn't have the authority to make that kind of decision. It wasn't your place to prioritize Samuel over the lives of so many others. You were out of line.'

Intellectually, I understood her point. But on an emotional level, I snapped.

'So you just wanted me to sacrifice my son, is that it?' I growled.

'I can't have a terrorist's leverage over one agent jeopardize the entire nation's security,' she said coolly.

'It's just a numbers game to you, isn't it? You're happy to sacrifice one man for "the greater good." But it's a human being you're sacrificing – it's not that simple.'

'My job is to protect the country. It involves making difficult decisions.'

'Well, believe it or not, sacrificing my son wasn't a decision I was prepared to make.'

Another tense pause.

'So this note you received,' she said slowly, 'you say it disclosed *pivotal* information. I'm guessing this information, *if* it included details of the attacks over the past few days, wasn't limited to that, otherwise you'd be able to admit it now.'

I said nothing.

'Well?' she said.

'My situation hasn't changed. If I tell you, Samuel dies.'

Parkes hissed through her teeth. 'Look, my patience is wearing thin. I know the note disclosed information about The Order of Babylon. And to save you the effort of feigning ignorance, yes, I've spoken to Todd Lamphere.'

Suddenly, my heart was in my throat. How did Parkes

know about The Order? If it was anything less than Drexler disclosing this information, and Parkes took action, then Drexler would assume I'd spilled the beans. That spelt major trouble.

'Okay, it's true, I spoke to Todd Lamphere about The Order of Babylon,' I said evenly, giving nothing of my panic away. 'When did you speak to him?'

'Last night, when I approached him for a run-down on this cult. But lo and behold, Saul Marshall had already paid a visit the previous day, asking the same questions on my behalf which was, of course, news to me.'

'So if Lamphere didn't tell you, how did you find out about The Order of Babylon?'

'How do you think?' she snapped. 'There's been another murder. This time, a woman called Sylvia Loft-house in Hastings-on-Hudson, New York. They stripped her, tied her up, trailed electrical fencing between her legs, then force-fed her water. You can guess what happened next. But Lofthouse wasn't just anyone: she was the chair of a small group called Concerned Family and Friends which has been opposing The Order of Babylon for years. The note left at the scene read: *The Grand Reveal.*' Parkes paused. 'So it transpires that all these kids we thought had gone missing had in fact joined this cult. The members of this anti-cult group were the rare few who'd figured out where their children had gotten to. And now one of them's dead – yet another tragedy that might've been avoided had you come forward.'

This was a lot to take in. Drexler had finally revealed The Order to the authorities. And this was unsettling. It meant he now believed disclosing this information was no threat to whatever plans he still hoped to achieve. But at the same time, I felt relieved. Because although this murder was yet another burden on my conscience, it seemed both

Vann and Samuel would live another day. Drexler still had no reason to kill them before midnight of the 4th.

'The note specifically mentioned The Order of Babylon,' I conceded.

'Good of you to let me know,' Parkes said sarcastically.

'I did what any father would've done.'

'Do you even have a clue where Samuel is now?'

'I haven't seen him since Mineral. They paraded him before me when I was bound and drugged then drove him away.'

I was happy to tell Parkes this much, but had no intention of telling her about Samuel's conversion to The Order. I had enough to worry about without the FBI hunting Samuel on a shoot-to-kill basis.

'And that's when you lost Agent Yeung?' she probed.

I sighed. 'Yes. They drove him off, too.'

'Where did they take them?'

'They didn't seem too keen to tell me, funnily enough,' I said facetiously.

'You've got to come in and tell us this in full. I'm not scared to take you in by force.'

'We both know you don't have the spare manpower,' I replied.

There was yet another pause. But when Parkes finally broke the silence, her tone surprised me.

'You need to give yourself in,' she said gently, almost maternally. 'Yes, there are going to be repercussions – big ones – you know that already. But if you *don't* give yourself in, there may be far bigger repercussions.' She sighed. 'You betrayed me these past two days, Saul, but I'll tell you this out of respect for the professional relationship we once shared. People are talking about you here. They're suggesting that perhaps... well, that perhaps you're *involved* in The Order of Babylon. That perhaps you're *running* it.'

'Ludicrous,' I whispered.

'I agree. But for those willing to entertain the idea, there's a convincing case to be made. The cult seemed to come into existence roundabout when you took time-off from the Bureau, and it would explain how you knew about all of these attacks beforehand. And an event like the cult handing you over to the police in Mineral could've been a ruse to make it appear as though you'd been outmaneuvered by the cult, when in fact you're orchestrating events. When in fact you're orchestrating everything—'

I broke in. 'Ludicrous! You're buying into this?'

'I'm not buying into anything,' she said calmly. 'But there's talk.'

At first, I'd been numbed by this news. But suddenly it started hitting home: there were people at the FBI who thought I had it in me to slaughter innocents by the dozens. And I was more than angry, I was bitterly hurt.

'Enough,' I shouted. 'Enough. Let me make one thing absolutely clear: there's not a chance in hell I'm coming in to cooperate with people who think this of me. Tell them they can shove their conspiracy theories where the sun don't shine because I don't have time for this bullshit. Goodbye, Lucinda.'

And with that, I hung up, took myself upstairs, and shook Lilly awake.

'Lilly, I *need* that address.'

Chapter Thirty-One

L illy sat up, immediately wide awake, nodded once, then said:

'Nine Columbus Square.'

Already Lilly had readopted her closed-up body-language; but this time there was a new look in her face – like she'd now resolved to tell me what she knew.

'Thank you, Lilly,' I said meaningfully.

She nodded again, seriously, then continued:

'It's a terraced house, four stories plus a basement. When I visited with Drexler, we entered via the backdoor, which leads into the basement. They use this door instead of the front because it's hidden from view: the small back garden is fenced off *and* there are concealing trees in the space between the garden and the service road. So, with our hoods on, we knocked on the backdoor and one of the junior residents let us in – there's always a junior member posted by the door of any cult building to deal with visitors. Then, once he saw we were senior members, he led us to the fourth floor – to the front bedroom – to meet with your son. This was Samuel's bedroom.'

I nodded. She continued:

'I can't remember exactly, but I'd say that the house consisted of maybe twelve rooms. The nine cultists living there aside from your son, though not Inner Sanctum members, were still very much radical and all undoubtedly belonged to a class of cultist whose families thought they'd gone missing without trace.'

'And you're sure these same people will still be living there? That Samuel will still be living there?'

'I can't be certain; but there's a strong chance.'

Silence fell for a moment, then Lilly said:

'I'll give you some time to digest this while I shower. I'll answer any questions when I'm out.'

I glanced at the bedside clock, which read 6:32 a.m., then nodded.

'I'll be in the living-room.'

The first thing I did when I got downstairs was call The Eliot Hotel on Commonwealth Avenue, Boston, and book a room for the night under the fictional name on one of my emergency credit cards, organizing for it to be ready for our arrival in under three hours' time. My instinct, drilled into me from my HRT days, was to establish a command-post in close proximity to where an operation was due to take place. The Eliot seemed as good a place as any, given that at just under a mile away from Columbus Square – which I knew to be in the South End of the city – it was neither too near nor too far from the action.

Then, back on the computer, I brought up maps and satellite images of Columbus Square. It was a line of twelve terraced houses, set back from the main road behind a slither of greenery. Just as Spender had said, between the service road which ran behind the houses and the gardens there was a space populated by a number of tall trees which concealed these gardens from view. The image I found of the front of Number Nine also matched Spender's account, showing a four story town-house. But what Spender *hadn't* mentioned was the fact that the front entrances to Nine and Ten were side-by-side. I knew this could imply something potentially pivotal: that at one point, Nine and Ten might've been one property.

Spurred by this theory, I scoured the internet, and managed to find the floor plan of Number Nine. Sure enough, it showed that in the back bedroom on the fourth floor there was a door leading to Number Ten. Immediately, I started thinking about how this could be exploited. And though my gut said I couldn't use it to enter Number Nine – there was no way the neighbors would believe that a lone FBI agent wanted to launch a surprise attack on the next-door property – I reckoned I *could* use it to exit Number Nine. If I could get Samuel unconscious, I could put him over my shoulder, knock down the partitioning door, and make my escape through Number Ten before the neighbors could even think to call the police...

But if I wanted to use this escape plan, I needed to figure out a way of getting to Samuel on the fourth floor. Because I knew fighting my way up wasn't an option: not only would one of us probably end up dying, but the racket would undoubtedly attract police well before I'd made it to the top. So I had to think of another way... Then I recalled how, back in Mineral, I'd momentarily confused a group of cultists by wearing a purple hood.

I was jogged from these thoughts by Lilly entering the room. She was wearing a soft rust-colored dress, but her body was still hard and tense. She looked at the computer monitor, which was still showing the floor-plan, then said:

'Scoping out the place?'

I nodded. 'According to the floor plan, in the bedroom down the hall from Samuel's there's a door that used to connect the property to the neighboring house. Did you see it?'

She narrowed her eyes in thought. 'I think I did… during a brief tour of the house. I seem to recall a big door on the right-hand side as you enter that room. It was thoroughly bolted, as far as I can remember.'

'Right. Well, I'm thinking that if can neutralize Samuel, I could use this as a getaway route, and escape through the neighboring house. But the question is: how do I get to Samuel's room in the first place? I can't fight my way up, it's too dangerous.'

Again, Lilly's eyes went thoughtful.

'You could just do what I did,' she said at last. 'I mean, if you put on a purple hood, you could pretend to be an Inner Sanctum member. That *ought* to be enough to get you a private reception with Samuel in his room.'

This was precisely the idea that'd occurred to me when Lilly had walked in but I hadn't been sure it was feasible.

'Obviously they wouldn't see my face,' I said. 'But won't they realize I'm not who I say I am on the basis of my body shape, height, skin color…?'

Lilly shook her head.

'There are members of The Inner Sanctum who the other nine cultists living in that house will have never met. And even Samuel, who *has* probably met everyone in The Sanctum at some point, will not remember certain members well enough to recognize them without seeing their faces.' She paused. 'What *might* give you away, though, is your voice – your son might recognize that.'

'That won't be a problem, I can alter it,' I said assuredly. 'So which member of The Inner Sanctum should I impersonate?'

She closed her eyes a moment. 'I reckon your best bet is Ayin. Aside from the fact he's a good match physically –

he's white, about your height, similar build – he's also a particularly reclusive character. He's one of the original fifteen and, crucially, doesn't like to mix with anyone below his station, including newer members of the Sanctum. This means he's likely to have had minimal contact with everyone in the house, including your son.

'Also, his accent isn't *too* different from yours – you both sound like New Yorkers – though his voice is a little deeper, with a slight Harlem twang.'

'A bit like this?' I said, altering my voice.

She looked impressed. 'Yes, that's good.'

'Okay. So I need to get into the garden, put on a hood, then knock on the door…'

'Right,' she said. 'And when the person within asks who it is, say: *It is Ayin of The Sanctum – Taprobana.* Then, once inside, greet the person – calling them 'my son' if they're male or 'my daughter' if they're female – and ask to meet with Samuel; though you must call him by his cult name, *Resh.*'

'Got it. But give me a bit more of this cult vocabulary just in case I find myself in a position in which I need to say more.'

She nodded. 'They call members of the establishment *false prophets*, the uninitiated *systemites*, and blood relatives *flesh-manacles*. A *mislocation* is a mistake, and any kind of behavior that goes against the cult's code of conduct is described as *degraded*. If you find yourself needing more than that, you're saying too much – Ayin's not a talkative personality.'

'Understood,' I said. 'So I get inside, say I want to meet with Resh, and they'll lead me upstairs to Samuel's room? And then they'll just leave us alone to speak in private?

'I can't guarantee it but that's what I'd expect. Though bear in mind that once you're alone with Samuel, you'll be expected to remove your hood immediately. So whatever you have planned at that point, well, do it quick.'

I took a deep breath, let out a low whistle, then said:

'Right, the plan as it stands. We drive to Boston as soon as possible, park around the corner from Columbus Square, then take a cab to The Eliot Hotel on Commonwealth Avenue where I've booked a room. Then, once we're ready, I'll take a cab back to the service road behind Columbus Square, and put what we've just discussed into action. After I have Samuel, and have made my escape through Number Ten, I'll throw him into the Murano and drive…'

I trailed off. There was no denying this plan was beyond mad. And there was so much that could go wrong. What if this door was harder to break down than I anticipated? What if the neighbors had obstructed the other side with heavy furniture? What if the cultists *didn't* take me up for a private meeting with Samuel? What if they realized I wasn't Ayin?

But at the same time, of all the courses of action open to me to try and get Samuel, it was the one most likely to work. And it was of utmost importance that I *did* try something, because I knew I might not get another chance. And there were so many things that could happen that would make rescuing Samuel a lot harder, or even impossible. I could end up arrested; Drexler could realize I was still alive, and take measures to put Samuel out of reach; or the FBI could realize Samuel was a terrorist, and start hunting him themselves.

My plan was mad but I had to try it.

I looked back to Lilly and was struck by her appearance: she was shaking a lot. And suddenly I remembered the risks *she* was facing. By infiltrating this safe-house I was telling Drexler that Lilly was still alive *and* had leaked secretive information about the cult and this meant she was going to be incurring his wrath. And judging by her appearance, this was something she knew only too well. In exchange for this information, I had a responsibility to ensure her safety.

'Lilly,' I said gently. 'Once I've retrieved Samuel, I think it's best we part ways – I don't think it's safe for you to be around him. But obviously as a result of me doing this, you'll be back on Drexler's radar and you'll need protection. I think the best option is for you to seek refuge at the Boston FBI Field Office. I received notice from a source within the FBI that last night they finally discovered that The Order was behind this past week's attacks, so they'll be *very* interested in keeping you safe when they hear who you are. Their address is: *One Center Plaza, Suite 600, Somerset Street.*'

I wrote this on a nearby piece of paper and handed it to Lilly.

'Get a cab there twenty-five minutes after I've left for Columbus Square,' I added. 'That way, you can tell them the truth about why you're in Boston without jeopardizing my plans. If you tell them any sooner, there's a chance their response will cause me trouble. But it's important that you *do* tell them the truth about why you're in Boston – and everything else: the more truth you tell them, the safer you'll be.'

'Okay.'

'And thank you,' I said sincerely. 'I know by telling me this, you've put yourself at risk. I really appreciate your bravery.'

'Okay,' she repeated. This time, her voice wavered and she avoided my eyes.

With that, an uncomfortable silence stretched out between us. But then I noticed the clock on the computer was already showing five past seven, and quickly put an end to it. We needed to get moving.

'Do you think you could fashion me a purple hood on the way there?' I asked.

She nodded. 'I saw a sheet in the airing cupboard I could use.'

'Perfect. I'm just going to make a quick phone-call, then let's get out of here.'

Once again I retreated upstairs and dialed Giles.

'Saul. What've you got for me?' he said.

'Have you heard about Hastings-on-Hudson?'

'Not a thing.'

'Another murder,' I said. 'But crucially it was the chair of a small anti-cult group that's been opposing The Order for years. In short, Drexler has used this to reveal to the authorities that The Order was responsible for everything that's happened this week. I heard this from Parkes not ten minutes ago.'

'So we're moving into open warfare – FBI versus The Order?' he said.

'Right'

'Did she give you shit?'

'I gave as good as I got. But there's more.'

'More?'

'Spender has information. She told me about a house in Boston where she thinks Samuel could be living along with nine other cultists. I'm going to try and retrieve him.'

'What's the address?' he said.

'Nine Columbus Square.'

'And you're sure Samuel's there?'

'No. But there's a good chance.'

'So what's your plan?'

'To masquerade as a member of the cult, get Samuel

alone, then knock him out. From there, I have an escape route lined up…'

Giles was quiet a moment. I could tell he was weighing up whether to ask for more details. But in the end, he decided against it.

'Foolproof,' he said at last.

'The next time I speak to you,' I said forcefully, 'I *will* have Samuel.'

'Good luck,' he replied. 'You're gonna need it.'

When I came downstairs, I found Lilly looking on edge, but ready to go. So I didn't hang about. I led the way to the car and fired up the engine. But despite what I'd said to Giles, I wasn't feeling assured, I was feeling anxious. And not just because of the magnitude of the task ahead. But also because I was beginning to think that maybe Lilly's unease didn't indicate fear. That maybe it indicated she was deceiving me.

Chapter Thirty-Two

O nce again, Francis Bindle was sitting by the
telephone in the control room, waiting for a phone-
call from Director Muldoon. About thirty minutes ago he'd
been shown a second segment of news, which had
informed him about a gas attack and bombing in Manhattan. The person who'd shown him this footage – and was
instigating proceedings in general – was not, this time, the
man Francis knew as Zahir, but Dennis Ericson, flanked by
the woman he knew as Shin. Yet Francis wasn't thinking
about where Zahir might be, nor about the victims in
Manhattan. He was thinking about the information he had
to convey to keep his brother alive.

At seven, the phone rang. Francis activated the speakerphone.

'Hello, Robin.'

'Francis.'

'We're still on?'

'We are,' said Muldoon firmly. 'Headquarters is
chaotic, because aside from Manhattan, we also had a
revelation last night: we discovered who's behind this all –

a small, esoteric cult called The Order of Babylon. They were nowhere near our radar; a bolt from the blue. But on a personal level, there's very little I can do at this point. I've got all my heads of departments calling the shots in their respective areas, doing all they can. So I'm happy to go ahead with this. After all, if I *do* need to make decisions, I can make them remotely.'

Francis responded with a reflective silence.

'So I'll have the details when you're ready,' Muldoon prompted.

'Here's what I've got,' said Francis. 'The provisional plan is to get the operation at Glenview underway at 12:30 CST on March 4, though that time is flexible, since we have complete autonomy over the area beyond the East Gate from midnight tomorrow. The money has been made available, and has already been delivered to Glenview.

'As far as your transportation to Glenview is concerned, I've organized for you to be picked up at Hoover at 9:20 a.m. EST by Quinn, who'll take you to Dulles. Your flight from there is chartered at 11:00 EST, and your estimated time of arrival at O'Hare is 11:20 CST. In the VIP Reception Room you'll be met by Dom McElroy, from the Chicago Field Office, who'll drive you to Glenview, where you should arrive no later than 12:05. To get beyond security at the perimeter you'll need to display Bureau Identification and quote the code-word *Saturn*. I'll be there to meet you within the perimeter.

'In terms of who knows what, I've told people only what they need to know. McElroy knows that he'll be transporting you to Glenview, and nothing more; whereas the Station Commander at Glenview knows only that this has something to do with Yemen.'

Francis paused a moment: 'You got all that?'

Muldoon quickly repeated the details.

'Precisely,' said Francis.

Robin grunted his satisfaction. 'Then I think that's everything. I'll call you the same time Sunday morning for final confirmation. Thank you for organizing this, Francis.'

'You can count on me.'

Chapter Thirty-Three

As soon as the cab dropped us off outside The Eliot Hotel, I *knew* Lilly had betrayed me to The Order. I knew because there were two Order men staking out the hotel – one standing on the opposite pavement, on the phone, and another half a block away, to my west, smoking a roll-up – both looking perfectly innocuous and relaxed. Of course, it was precisely this heightened nonchalance that gave them away. There's an almost imperceptible gap between at ease, and a capable imitation of at ease, but I could spot the difference.

I responded to these men the only way it was wise: I acted like I hadn't seen anything, and calmly led Lilly into the hotel and over to reception. But despite my cool exterior, I was furious with myself because I'd made a cataclysmic error. I'd realized there was a possibility that Lilly was concealing something, but I'd treated the situation lightly. I'd decided that if she *was* concealing something, it had to be something relatively minor and, of all things, that it couldn't possibly be that she'd told The Order I was still alive. After all, there were only two conceivable reasons why she'd have done such a thing – either in the hope they might spare her life in return, or out of some perverse residual loyalty to the cult – and both had just seemed too far-fetched to seriously entertain. So I'd decided to dismiss the issue for the time being, and question her at The Eliot.

However, it was now abundantly clear that she *had* betrayed me to The Order and must've done so after I'd told her about The Eliot. And because I hadn't taken my suspicions about Lilly seriously enough, this situation was now a whole lot worse than The Order merely knowing I was alive. They now knew *exactly* where I was…

But when we got in the elevator and started making our ascent, I knew I couldn't afford to berate myself any longer. These watchers were a sign that my life was under threat since it stood to reason that after what'd happened in Manhattan, they were going to try and finish the job. And not a moment after I thought this I began speculating where an attack could come from and what form it might take. It seemed to me the danger could be lurking extremely nearby: in the corridor at the other end of the elevator, or in the bedroom… And the forms it could take were endless… Perhaps a gunman… Perhaps another bundle of Semtex, wired to the bedroom's door… Perhaps – well, perhaps just about anything.

My hand hovered over the pocket containing the SIG.

When the elevator doors opened, I was relieved to find that the corridor seemed all clear. And when we arrived at the room, I was relieved again to find two housekeepers – both looking relaxed – filing out into the corridor, suggesting there was nothing untoward within our room. But I wasn't about to take any chances. So the moment Lilly and I were inside, and the door was closed behind us, I took her firmly by the arm, pulled her close, put the SIG to her back, and whispered in her ear:

'When I let go of your arm, go sit on the sofa with its back to the window and wait there while I sweep the room for threats. Understood?'

'Understood.'

I let go, and immediately started combing the room. Once I was content the place was clear, I drew the curtains, sat down beside Lilly, and pointed the muzzle at her stomach. Tears were streaming down her cheeks.

'Don't fuck me around,' I said with brutal directness. 'I saw two Order men outside the hotel. Tell me everything you know, about how they came to be here, and what they're planning, or so help me God...'

'They know you're alive,' she said pleadingly.

'Of course they know I'm alive,' I spat. 'You clearly told them after I informed you about The Eliot Hotel, when I went to make a call. You used the landline, no doubt. Now tell me what I want to know.'

'You don't understand,' she said desperately. 'They've always known you were alive. The bomb in Manhattan – it was *designed* to fail.'

'WHAT ON EARTH—'

'I would've told you,' she said hysterically. 'But they have my daughter – I couldn't.'

'Lilly,' I said forcefully. 'Get a grip, and explain from the start.'

'Okay.' She took a few deep breaths; then at last she said, 'Okay, here's what happened. Before you arrived in Mont-clair, your son came over, overpowered me, and tied me up. Then he told me that I was going to be complicit in a set-up. He told me that his father was on his way to my house, an

FBI agent called Saul Marshall who believed not only that he'd just dodged an attempt on his life perpetrated by his son after a bomb had failed to go off, but also that he'd successfully faked his death to The Order by altering the bomb and detonating it. In actual fact, he told me, the bomb had been *designed* not to go off. And the "clue" you'd then discovered – which pointed you to my house – had been planted.

'From there, your son started telling me his plan. He said he was going to set my house of fire and make it look like he'd tried to kill me. Then, when you turned up and "rescued" me, I was to conceal the truth of the situation by pretending I was surprised to be saved; as though I, too, believed The Order thought we were both dead. After I'd won your trust, I was then to tell you the story about Samuel living in a safe-house on Columbus Square and to convince you to try and infiltrate the house by masquerading as an Inner Sanctum member. Obviously, I knew I was sending you into a trap – and I didn't want to deceive you – but I had no choice. The Order have my daughter, and your son said that if I wanted to get her back alive, I had to.'

I took a deep breath, bracing myself against the weight of this revelation. Once again I felt as though I'd been hurled through the looking glass. After I'd detonated the bomb in Manhattan, I'd been convinced I'd escaped the web of events Drexler had created for me. But on the contrary, I'd been as firmly ensnared as ever and all the more vulnerable precisely because I thought I'd gotten free. And my stomach turned as I contemplated how exactly Drexler had predicted my actions. He'd guessed that I would believe the bomb had been meant to kill me; that I would search the suite and find the itinerary; that I would rescue Spender; and when it came to entering the safe-house, that I'd choose the strategy that involved acting a part...

I wondered if the guy who'd given me a ride to Montclair was truly an NYPD officer or just another of Drexler's lackeys...

It suddenly felt painfully obvious that Drexler wouldn't have been content to simply kill me in a bomb blast. *Of course* someone like Drexler, a personality obsessed with controlling others, would've preferred to use the opportunity to create a situation in which his nemesis thought he was a step ahead, but really was two behind. He'd done this to prove that he was *the* master manipulator and if one thing was clear, it was that Nine Columbus Square in no way represented an opportunity to retrieve Samuel. It was a trap. And it was almost certainly where Drexler was planning to kill me. In a fashion, no doubt, befitting the complexity and ingenuity of the plot which had brought me there.

To figure out how to respond, I needed all the information available.

I looked Lilly in the eye.

'So you were complicit in a plot against me because The Order have your daughter?'

She nodded, tears still streaming her cheeks.

'I had Abigail two years ago, while in the cult. But when Drexler saw I was having reservations, he shipped her off in the night to some hidden location. What better leverage to keep me in line? Your son told me that if I succeeded in everything he'd asked of me, I'd get Abi back... But if I didn't, she'd die.'

My response to this was ambivalent. I felt angry, disgusted even, that she'd been so willing to send me to the slaughter. But at the same time, I could empathize with her situation, and felt deeply sympathetic. In fact, I could see how her situation – having her *infant* child held hostage – was even worse than mine. I couldn't say for sure I wouldn't have done the same thing. And with this thought, sympathy won out over anger.

I lowered my gun and softened my voice.

'Lilly, I understand why you betrayed me, and I forgive you. You were put in an impossible situation. But the cat's out of the bag, now. So you need to tell me *all* the details. The more I know, the better equipped I'll be to try and fix this and help you. Okay?'

'Do you really think you can help? That you can get her back?' she said wildly.

'First I need the details.' I said authoritatively. 'Okay?'

'But—'

'No, Lilly, first the details.'

There was a pause as Lilly grappled with her emotions. Eventually, she brought herself under control, and said with relative calm, 'Okay, the details.'

'So what exactly was the plan once I left for the safe-house?' I said. 'Obviously this location, The Eliot Hotel, impacts on proceedings in some key way, otherwise you wouldn't have risked calling them to tell them about it... clearly you *did* call them.'

She nodded. 'I'll explain as best I can. Samuel told me that after you'd learned about the safe-house on Columbus Square, you'd almost certainly organize a base-point in Boston – either a hotel room or rented property. He made me memorize a cell-phone number, and told me to call once I knew where this base-point was. So after you told me about The Eliot, I called and disclosed the location and time we were set to arrive. I didn't recognize the voice on the other end, but it told me how things were going to go down. It told me that five minutes after you left for Columbus Square I was to head to the hotel lobby, and tell anyone who asked I was meeting a friend and his daughter. Then, the moment you entered the house, Abigail would be escorted into the hotel by an Order chaperone, and I was to invite them both to the room. There Abigail would be dropped off, then the chaperone would leave.'

I was silent a moment, then said:

'And so the watchers outside the hotel are there as a precaution?'

'That's right. The last thing the person on the phone told me was that they were going to have people watching the hotel and surrounding area, and if there was the least suspicion we'd plotted something, Abigail would die. It was enough for me to write-off the option of telling you the truth.' She paused. 'But ironically, it was this measure they put in place to deter me from telling you the truth that gave them away.'

I nodded slowly. Up till this point, Drexler's plot had been astonishingly complex, and astonishingly successful. But now he'd slipped up. By placing his men outside the hotel, he'd given his game away…

'Tell me about Nine Columbus Square,' I said. 'Firstly, have you any clue what this trap could be? What's waiting within?'

She shook her head emphatically. 'I honestly have no idea.'

'Secondly, have you actually visited the property before? Or did Samuel just give you a run-down of where it was and what it looked like?'

'No, I actually did visit about a year ago with Drexler; and it actually was inhabited by ten cultists, one of whom was an Inner Sanctum member living in the front bedroom on the fourth floor – though it wasn't your son. Drexler and I entered the house just as I said – through the back-door – and really did have a private meeting with the most senior resident in his bedroom followed by a tour of the house. And I really did see that connecting door to the neighboring property you mentioned…

'I think they chose this house specifically because I'd seen it, so it'd be easy for me to describe it without coming across unsure. And though obviously I lied to you about Samuel living there, I really don't know the location of any other Order safe-houses.' She paused a half-second, then said feverishly: 'So what do you think? Can you get Abigail back?'

I rose a hand in a gesture of patience. 'Let me think.'

I got to my feet and began pacing. What were my choices?

On one hand, I could just run away; simply depart the city. But there were two big problems with this. Firstly, I didn't have anywhere else to go, or any other leads to follow up. Secondly, and more urgently, leaving now meant consigning a two-year-old child to death.

So the only alternative was to enter Nine Columbus Square anyway, thereby initiating the chain of events that'd see Abigail returned to Lilly. I knew just about anything *could* be waiting within the house. But by far the most likely thing I'd find there was a group of nine cultists who knew who I was, but who'd been told: a) to pretend that they believed I was an Inner Sanctum member; and, b) to lead me to a trap situated in the front room on the fourth floor – whatever this trap might be. If this was the case, and I felt sure it was, then the solution was simple. I would enter the house, then would play for time – that is, do everything I could to delay arriving on the fourth floor. Then, once Abigail had been safely returned to Lilly, she would somehow contact me, and I'd make my escape.

Yet while this plan seemed feasible, like something I could pull off, there was a part of me that said it was futile:

Drexler would probably just kill Abigail, anyway. But surely I had to try. Because at least that way there was an outside chance of saving this child which was better than no chance at all…

And then there was the feeling in my gut that said I simply had to enter the house, because I was out of leads – and maybe, just maybe, I'd discover something…

I stopped pacing and looked at Lilly. Her teeth were worrying at her lower lip.

'Here's the deal, Lilly. I'm going to enter Nine Columbus Square anyway, masquerading as Ayin of the Inner Sanctum—'

Her eyes rounded, and she made to speak. But I put up a halting hand.

'No, just listen. You need to listen. I'm going to enter the house, pretending I don't realize it's a trap. That way, The Order will believe you've kept your side of the bargain and your daughter's return will be set in motion. But I don't intend to make this a suicide mission; so I need you to listen carefully because I'm going to need your help.

'What I think I'm most likely to find is a group of nine cultists who'll know exactly who I am, but who'll pretend they believe I'm Ayin, and who'll try to lead me into some kind of trap on the fourth floor. What I'm going to do – while staying in character, and without giving away that I know it's a trap – is delay being taken to the fourth floor. Obviously that'll be tough as they're going to expect me to want to get upstairs as fast as possible to get to Samuel, but I'll find a way. Now, here's where you come in. The moment Abigail's been returned to you, I need you to get in a cab to the Boston FBI Field Office – you still have their address, right?'

'Yes,' she said.

'Okay. Then as soon as you get in the cab, I need you

to turn on this phone –' I handed Lilly my iPhone '– and call my Nokia, which'll be in my pocket, set to vibrate. That way, when I feel it ring, I know I can make my escape. But don't turn on the phone any earlier, that's very important. Understand?'

'I understand.'

'It's also very important, Lilly, that the number to my Nokia doesn't find its way into the wrong hands because it can be used to track the phone's location. So I need you to memorize it. Will you do that for me?'

She said she would, and I spent the next few minutes repeating the digits until she'd committed them to memory. Then there was a pause as we both digested what'd been said. A minute or so later, Lilly broke the silence.

'Saul,' she said.

I looked at her. Her eyes were intense.

'Saul, thank you for doing this… I can't tell you what it means to me. But I have to confess that, well, that I'm scared…'

I sat back down on the sofa, put my arm around her, and held her close. It was an embrace that said I understood her situation, that I believed in her. And when I let her go a couple of minutes later, I could see it'd had the desired effect: her expression was now hardened and resolved.

I took this as a cue to get the show on the road.

'Lilly, it's time for me to go. The sooner I go, the sooner we'll get your daughter back. And waiting doesn't help us: the longer we delay, the more we allow our anxieties to fester.'

She took this remarkably well, with a stoic nod.

'Okay, let's do it,' she said.

'And you remember everything I told you?'

'I remember.'

'Good luck, Lilly. I know you can do it.'

And with that, I got to my feet and left the room.

I EXITED THE HOTEL AND HAILED A CAB, PRETENDING not to notice the two new watchers who'd replaced the earlier pair. Four minutes later, the cab dropped me off by the service road behind Columbus Square. I lit a cigarette, took three drags, then crunched it underfoot. Then, after darting into the service road and following it until I drew level with Number Nine, I started cutting across the space between the service road and the back garden: a paved area, dotted with a number of trees, each about fifty feet tall, whose branches interlocked to form a dense canopy of greenery. Then I hit the fence at the end of Number Nine's garden.

Here I made my final preparations. I made sure the SIG was ready and loaded. I switched the Nokia to vibrate, and placed it in my pants pocket. I extracted the purple hood and put it on. And then, for a brief moment, I fell into thought. Working on the assumption that I was indeed up against nine cultists and a trap on the fourth floor, my thoughts turned to what this trap could actually be. But when I tried to picture it, I drew a blank: the possibilities were too vast. However, seeing that my plan involved avoiding the trap altogether, I decided to stop speculating and instead turned my thoughts to my tactics. It was simple, really: I needed to play for time. But in the process, I needed to make it seem like my priorities were playing the part of Ayin convincingly and getting upstairs to Samuel.

But then, all of a sudden, I was struck by a disturbing thought. What if Drexler had intended me to spot the watchmen? Had intended for me to get the truth out of Lilly, then to hatch this exact plan to get Abigail back? However, the very next moment I pushed this notion from my mind. This was the kind of paranoia that was only going to shoot me in the foot. And so, returning my mind firmly to the task at hand, I opened the gate in the fencing, crossed the small garden, and knocked on the door.

'Who's there?' came a voice from within.

'It is Ayin of The Sanctum – Taprobana.'

The door opened.

Chapter Thirty-Four

Standing beyond the door was a young man with a long, swarthy face, dressed in grey. He looked me over then broke into a broad smile.

'My father,' he said in a hushed, reverential tone. 'What a pleasure to have you visit.'

I stepped past him into the room, saying as I went, 'Thank you, my son.'

I glanced quickly around. I was in a large rec room, which took up the entirety of the basement, and contained nothing more than sofas, a television, a book-shelf. A staircase ran along the left-hand wall, leading up out of sight. I turned back to the man who said:

'To what do we owe the honor of your company? Am I to assume you wish to hold council with Resh?'

'That is correct.'

'Do you come bearing news of Euphrates?'

I wanted to engage this guy in conversation and kill as much time as possible. But I had no idea how an Inner Sanctum member would respond to this, so had no choice but to shut the conversation down.

'What I have to say is for Resh alone,' I said sternly. 'If it were intended for your ears, I'd have told you so.'

The guy played his part well: his eyes fell, and he looked genuinely shamefaced. And as I studied his expression, I felt torn. On one hand, I felt ruthless towards him: it was the HRT Operative in me responding to the knowledge he was conspiring to trap and destroy me. But at the same time, I felt an involuntary mercy. Because ever since I'd discovered Samuel was in The Order, I'd been unable to think of these cultists in the same way. They were no longer just inhuman killers. They were somebody's children.

'I apologize for my degraded mentality,' he said.

I regarded him for a few long seconds, then finally conceded a nod.

'See to it that it doesn't happen again.'

'Yes, my father,' he said obsequiously. 'Please, come this way.'

Before I could respond, he moved to the staircase, and began leading the way to the first floor. I followed suit, keeping myself alert and ready. But when we hit the first floor, and started through the corridor, it was quickly apparent that, on this floor at least, there was nothing to respond to. The rooms we passed – a kitchen, a living room, a dining room – were empty and non-descript. And before long, we were mounting the stairs to the second floor, and alarm bells were going off inside my head: I was progressing up the house too fast.

But when we got to the top of the stairs, I spotted something I could work with. Straight ahead was a second living room, and inside were six cultists, all in grey, clustered around a sofa by the far side wall: some sitting, some standing; four men, two women. For a second I thought my guide might simply continue past this room without entering and I found myself desperately thinking up excuses to go in. But a moment later, I saw this wouldn't be necessary, because my guide walked directly into the room. I followed him in, and discovered two further cultists, a man and woman, sitting at a small table I hadn't been able to see from the corridor.

Clearly, I'd been right about who I was going to find within this house: together these were the nine cultists I'd predicted, the ones who'd been drilled to pretend to believe I was Ayin. But while I was relieved that it looked like I was going to have a chance to interact with these cultists and buy some time, I knew that if I failed to capitalize on this opportunity I was in serious trouble. So far, I'd only been inside the house for about two minutes and this didn't nearly cover the time it would take for Abigail's handover to complete.

I could feel the adrenaline coursing.

My guide cleared his throat and addressed the room:

'Brothers and sisters. Please join me in welcoming Ayin of The Inner Sanctum – one of our heavenly fathers who's granted us the privilege of his company.'

Everyone in the room turned in my direction. Then, all at once, they rallied themselves – those who were sitting getting to their feet – and came over to form a loose crowd around me, smiling maniacally, and saying in clumsy unison: 'Greetings, my father.' But though they were taking the time to greet me, I knew that very soon they were going to try and get me moving again in the direction of the trap upstairs.

But barely had I thought this when a plan crystallized in my mind. If I could instigate a confessional, then I could get the cultists talking, while its closed-off form would stop the conversation straying into areas I didn't know about.

And I remembered that Lilly had said that anyone in The Inner Sanctum could initiate one.

It seemed like my best bet.

Returning my attention to the cultists, I moved my gaze over them slowly. Then, after along pause, I said with quiet authority:

'My children, what a pleasure it is to see you; what a joy to be welcomed into this precious oasis of morality. It warms my heart to know that, hidden away within this broken city, your humble devotion goes on.'

I paused, and my words were met with smiles. Then, just as I'd expected, my guide placed a hand on my back and said quickly to the room:

'But now you must excuse our father, for he wishes to hold council with Resh and—'

I cut him off by raising a silencing hand.

'Really, there's no rush, my son. I can meet with Resh in a short moment – it will do no harm. But for now, I am enjoying meeting with my children… In fact, I would rather like to engage with them more fully, which is why I propose we hold a confessional right this moment, before I head up to meet with Resh. This would please me greatly.'

I said this in the tone of an order and it was immediately apparent that the cultists had been warned I might try to expand on my role, because they didn't exhibit any surprise. Instead, they unhesitatingly obeyed, and quickly shifted around me so that a moment later we were all standing in a circle. Then they looked at me expectantly.

'Wonderful,' I exclaimed. 'Now, how about you my daughter–' I nodded at one of the three young women in the circle '–would you care to start us off?'

She gave a tight nod, paused, then said:

'When I was thirteen, I encountered a man a number

of times at my local bowling alley who took a kind interest in me. But instead of responding with modesty, I led him on – a fact I was unable to admit at the time – and so, when one day he took sex from me by force, I had myself to blame. I now understand that my body should only be used at the behest of The Zahir; and that only through The Order can I find redemption for my degraded behavior.'

She reeled this off like it'd been rehearsed, and I recalled what Lilly had told me: that Order confessionals involved members divulging transgressions from their pre-cult days, often repeating the same confession time and again. But while this confession was disturbing, what I was more worried about was that it was killing time. And though I'd been concerned about how I should respond to a confession, I discovered in the next instant I didn't need to.

'You were a whore,' exclaimed one of the young men sanctimoniously. 'You were degraded and wayward.'

'It is because you have willed yourself to change that we accept you,' said another.

Silence fell and I gave a nod of satisfaction. But just as I was about to pick someone to go next, my guide piped up.

'My father,' he said, his voice still deferential. 'I hate to interrupt, but I think Resh should very much like to see you right away…'

Clearly, it was the guide's job to keep me moving in the direction of the trap. However, I simply couldn't afford to let him cut me short quite yet.

'I'm sure it'll be fine,' I said casually, waving a dismissive arm. Then I quickly nodded towards one of the men who hadn't yet spoken and said: 'My son, will you go next?'

Just as the woman before him had done, he nodded, then started speaking:

'One day, during my early teenage years, I was fighting my younger brother – my flesh-manacle – on a jungle gym, when part of the structure broke, and my brother sustained a fall that paralyzed him. Though I was told by those around me it was an accident, and I believed them for a time, the truth was plain: I was degenerate. And I understand now that violence is a holy thing which must only be used in advancing the will of The Zahir and that what I did was blasphemy. Only through The Order can I find redemption.'

'You were irresponsibly violent,' another of the women responded immediately. 'You besmirched and squandered a holy thing.'

'It is because you have willed yourself to change that we accept you,' repeated the guy who'd said this last time.

I was just about to nod at a third cultist and get another confession going when my guide did what I'd both expected and feared: he butted in again. And this time, though his tone remained deferential, it took on a hardness that demanded a proper response.

'My father, I really must suggest we bring this to a close,' he said. 'I believe Resh would be *very* upset to discover that you delayed so long to meet him.'

I looked at him hard, then said softly:

'And what if I would be *very* upset to bring this to a close?'

My guide narrowed his eyes, and I read a hint of suspicion creeping into his expression. I was sailing close to the wind. It'd been plausible that staying a little longer to engage, and even exerting Ayin's authority in a small way, had been part of an effort to convince them I was Ayin. But such reticence to progress upstairs must've seemed odd from a man whose main objective they believed to be retrieving his son from the fourth floor.

I was running a big risk. But I had no choice. I had to buy as much time as possible.

My guide's suspicions, however, weren't yet advanced enough for him to drop his act. Instead, he gave me another chance.

'I don't ask you to bring this to a close for my sake,' he said slowly. 'I ask you out of respect for a fellow member of The Sanctum – that is all, my father.'

I studied him, thinking desperately how I could prolong this. But it was quite clear: if I persisted any longer with the confessional, I'd betray I knew this was a trap. I now had no choice but to head upstairs.

I laid a relaxed hand on my guide's shoulder and emitted a deep chuckle.

'Of course, you're quite right, I must see Resh,' I said, patting him twice on the shoulder. 'You must forgive me: it seems I allowed myself to get carried away in the society of my children. But you're quite right, my son.'

Just like that, my guide's suspicions evaporated.

'That's quite alright, my father,' he said amiably.

Then once again he put his hand on my back, and this time, after I'd given the rest of the cultists a slow nod of farewell, I let him lead me out the room. As I did so, I thought to myself: it's been over six minutes since I entered the house, Abigail's handover *must* be on the verge of completion. So, with this in mind, I proceeded to follow my guide at as leisurely a pace as I could get away with, hoping to ensure I'd receive the call in the time it'd take to reach the fourth floor. But though it took me ten seconds to walk the second floor corridor, ten to climb the stairs, and another ten to walk the third floor corridor, in all that time there was *still* no call. And then, before I knew it, I was mounting the stairs to the fourth floor...

When we hit the landing, straight ahead was the door to the room I knew contained the connecting door to Number Ten. My guide stopped in front of it – with his back to it – then pointed down the corridor to the room at the front of the house whose door was shut.

'That's Resh's room,' he said. 'Just knock and enter straight away. I'll leave the two of you to meet in private.'

Then he gave me a maniacal grin.

I nodded, stepped past him, and started down the corridor. And as I did so, I made a decision: I couldn't afford to wait any longer for the call. I was now ten strides away from danger, meaning I had to make my escape. And while I knew that doing so would tell the cultists that Lilly had tipped me off, I just had to hope that by the time word got back to their men at The Eliot, it'd be too late for them to do anything about it.

I decided that when I got halfway along the corridor – five strides – I would turn, take out my guide with the SIG, then make my escape through Number Ten...

So I carried on walking. Two steps... Three...

But just as I took my fourth step, I was taken by surprise.

Phut.

It was the unmistakable sound of a silenced automatic weapon firing. Working on instincts alone, I turned and drew my SIG. But the weapon wasn't necessary. My guide was already dead. The silenced Berretta by his body, together with the blood pooling from his head, told me he'd just put a bullet in his own brain.

I was confused – disorientated. Clearly, this was the big reveal; the moment in which they'd intended to let me know that Samuel wasn't really here, but rather this was a trap. But I didn't understand why they'd revealed this to me *before* I'd entered the room. What was compelling me to enter? What was stopping me from attempting to escape right now?

But hardly had I thought this when I discovered the answer.

'Help,' came a shrill cry from beyond the door. It belonged to a young boy, no older than ten, and there was no question the fear in his voice was genuine. 'Please help, he's going to kill me.'

I hesitated. My plan had been to get out as soon as possible. But I couldn't just leave a child to die, could I? But what if there was nothing I could do? But what if…

'*Please.*'

There was no time to analyze further. I had to make a call.

I darted to the door, threw it open, and stepped inside.

Opposite me was a man in his mid-twenties, dressed in grey, with a round face, wispy blond hair, and manic eyes. He was down on one knee, holding a Beretta to the head of a young child, while clutching him tight with his other arm. The child, whose coarse brown hair was soaked with sweat, and whose face was white with terror, was wincing as the guy ground the muzzle into his temple. But that wasn't all there was to see. On the floor, in the center of the room, were two bodies, a man and woman, who, judging by the state of them, had only very recently been killed. And to the left, in front of a window with its curtains drawn, was a monitor on a desk, displaying a live stream of the back of the house from the viewpoint of a camera mounted on the property's rear wall.

I understood immediately what the monitor was for. This cultist had used it to tell the team at The Eliot when I'd arrived. However, it took me a second longer to realize who these victims were. But all of a sudden I recognized the dead man as Franco Rinaldi, the antiques specialist who, in the summer of '93, had figured out that the documents I'd been selling were phonies after he'd picked up on minutiae that experts in their dozens had missed. He was the man who'd turned me into a fugitive. I hadn't seen him in almost twenty years, but I was certain it was him. And once I realized this, I was sure that the woman next to him was his wife; that the child in the cultist's grip was his son.

I drew a bead on the cultist's head and said:

'Release the kid.'

'Listen carefully,' he replied. His words were soft, chilling; spoken with an unnerving staccato. 'First: if you take another step, I *will* shoot. Second: remove the hood and rip it up.'

I bore my eyes into him, thinking hard. But there was no escaping it: *he* was in the position to call the shots. For starters, I couldn't get closer to him – I'd learned by now that The Order were serious about their threats. And second, given that his finger was resting on the trigger, I couldn't shoot him in the head, either. A head-shot would induce post-death muscular spasms which would cause him to pull the trigger anyway.

'Apologies, I wasn't clear,' the cultist said. 'Rip up the hood *now*, or I will shoot.'

There was a mania in his eyes that said he wasn't kidding. And there was a panic in the child's eyes, begging me to comply.

I took off the hood and tore it along the seams.

'More,' the man said.

Savagely, I ripped the material apart, then scattered the pieces behind me.

'Now,' I said. 'Release the kid.'

The man shook his head…

I didn't understand – why had they engineered this standoff? In what way did this constitute a trap? Were they hoping I'd eventually lose my patience and either try to make a head-shot or try and get closer, so that when the child died, his blood would be on my hands? Or was this situation an end in itself? A kind of bizarre psychological torture in the form of a never-ending standoff?

And why the family of Franco Rinaldi?

The seconds crawled by. The kid was trembling all over, too terrified to speak. The man stared at me from eyes set deep within his face.

Still, there was no call from Lilly.

At last I said again: 'Release the kid.'

The man shook his head.

'What do you want?' I said, nothing in my voice. 'If it's me you want, then give up the kid. Take me instead.'

Yet again, the man shook his head. But this time, his face broke into a demented grin. It made my skin crawl.

'Release the kid,' I boomed.

Not even a head-shake – just more of that unhinged grin…

And that's when I heard it, just as the echo of my voice was fading – the silence. It was a Friday afternoon in Boston, and we were right by a main road in a room situated at the front of the house. I should've been able to hear pedestrians working the sidewalks, vehicles pounding by. But there was only silence. And when a Friday afternoon sounds like a Sunday, something is seriously wrong.

But suddenly my attention was drawn back to the cultist, because he'd started talking, at a volume barely above a whisper:

'The False Prophet will die at the hands of his own kind,' he said. And then, not a second later, two things happened in quick succession. First, an almighty blast shook the house, and I recognized the sound of it instantly: it was an explosive charge blowing down a door, a sound I associated with SWAT team maneuvers. Then, second, there was a *phut* of an automatic weapon firing, and the kid's head burst all over the room.

The cultist tried to turn the gun on himself. I shot him before he could.

Chapter Thirty-Five

Suddenly, everything clicked in my mind, and I understood the situation perfectly. Drexler had tipped off the authorities – presumably telling them that there was an Order safe-house at this address – in the hope that a SWAT team would be sent into the building and would end up taking me out. Essentially, he wanted to engineer a situation in which American national security eliminated its own agent.

But there was another dimension to Drexler's trap. He'd made it look like I was personally behind The Order's latest atrocity – by killing the Rinaldi family in a setting that made it seem plausible that I'd used the cult to settle an old score. And by making me destroy the hood, he'd ensured that, if I *did* escape, I'd almost certainly be identified in the process.

In short, Drexler wanted me to die at the hands of American national security. Failing that, he wanted me framed for a crime I didn't commit.

Yet immediately after this moment of clarity struck, my survival instincts kicked in. I'd no doubt a SWAT team had just entered via the front entrance: I'd heard SWAT explosive charges a thousand times, and the sound had clearly emanated from the front of the house. But more telling was the fact that Drexler was unlikely to have made the tip-off more than about ten minutes ago, for fear of first responders arriving before I'd entered the house.

Firstly, this told me *who* I was up against – since there was only one SWAT team that could've gotten here that fast *and* were senior enough to enter with that little planning-time: the FBI SWAT at the Boston Field Office. They would've been able to get here quickly because in the weeks following a domestic terrorist attack, every Field Office is obligated to ensure it has between five to seven SWAT operatives ready for immediate deployment. And they would've been allowed to enter with so little planning because they're exceptionally qualified. Aside from the HRT boys, Field Office SWAT operatives are the most highly trained in domestic law enforcement.

But the promptness of their entry told me more than this: it told me they'd probably been informed there was an extremely high-powered target inside the house. Because although these operatives were highly trained, they still would've needed a very good reason to have entered so quickly. And finally, their speedy entry also told me something of their mentality. When operatives are sent in without a proper plan, they're encouraged not to take any chances and to shoot-to-kill at the first sign of resistance.

So a group of operatives had just entered the house, and I had a good idea what was likely to happen. First, in a single-file formation known as "the snake," they would survey the first floor for threats, before one or two would briefly splinter off to check the basement. Then, after regrouping on the first floor, they would head up to the second, and when they encountered the eight cultists presumably still there, they would immediately deploy stun grenades. Then, once they had the cultists prone on the floor, two or three operatives would splinter off and head upstairs to survey the rest of the building. This was how I reckoned things would go down. And on that basis, I had about thirty seconds before the splinter group was upon me...

I had a choice, then. Either give myself up peacefully, which meant incarceration by the FBI, and the end of any hopes of saving Vann and Samuel by March 4. Or attempt an escape through Number Ten, which was still very much a feasible option. Because not only was there a distinct possibility that the SWAT team hadn't yet realized the properties were connected, there was also a distinct possibility Number Ten had been evacuated – meaning I was unlikely to encounter anyone within.

And then, if I could escape through Number Ten's rear entrance, I reckoned I had a realistic chance of getting away since it was unlikely the authorities had done much more than cordon off a few hundred yards of road out front, and evacuate the houses immediately neighboring Number Nine.

Of course, there were also snipers to consider. One was probably positioned with the front of the house in his sights, and one with the back. But I could worry about them later. Right now, I had to act. Trouble was closing in fast.

I dived out the door, pelted down the corridor, and burst into the room to the back of the house. Sure enough, to my right, completely unobstructed, was a large wooden door. But when I took a closer look, my heart sank. It was secured in place by five heavy-duty bolts. I knew it was unlikely that the SIG and my boot alone could break down this door quickly enough but I had to give it a try.

So I aimed at the top bolt and waited for the stun grenade I felt sure the operatives would use on the cultists downstairs, since this would mask the sound of my bullets and thus deprive the operatives of further encouragement to hurry in my direction. Then when the blast came about five seconds later, I instantly unloaded two bullets, one at the top bolt, one at the bottom, and kicked the door twice with savage force.

But it didn't budge. In fact, the bullets seemed to have done very little damage. The top bolt looked only partially dislodged, the bottom almost completely unscathed.

I could hear muffled voices from downstairs. The first sounded like the authoritative voice of an operative demanding surrender; the second like a cultist complying.

I knew the arrival of the splinter group on the fourth floor was now imminent. And it was painfully clear: even if I went at the door with everything I had, I didn't have a hope of breaking it down before they got here.

What I needed was a shotgun that could blow it in one.

What I needed was a plan to deal with the operatives who'd be with me any moment…

I pivoted around, looking for inspiration. Then I spotted a wardrobe to the left of the door to the room, and a plan flashed into my head.

Without a moment's pause, I closed the door to the bedroom, before opening the wardrobe and getting in. Then, after unleashing another bullet at the connecting door, I closed the wardrobe and listened intently. Sure enough, I could already hear two sets of footsteps hurtling up the stairs, undoubtedly honing in on the sound of my gunfire and my first thought was relief that it was two men, not three. Then, as they got nearer, I found myself picturing them in my mind's eye: wearing bullet-proof body armor, reinforced goggles, Kevlar helmets; cradling

Heckler and Koch MP5s, fitted with flashlights and laser-pointers; and carrying Springfield .45 pistols in holsters on their thighs, and Remington Model 870 pump-action shot-guns on their hips…

Their steps thundered closer, then stopped abruptly. I knew they were now outside the room, conferring about their entrance strategy. And as they did so, I contemplated the difficulty of the task at hand. I knew these operatives, at the first sign of resistance, would respond with lethal force. Yet despite this, I knew that in incapacitating them, I couldn't respond with lethal force of my own. After all, these were the good guys. Their only crime was unwittingly becoming pawns in Drexler's designs.

All of a sudden, I heard the bedroom door open and in came the stun grenade I'd been expecting. And this time, unlike in Mineral, I was ready for it: my head was turned away, my eyes were tight-shut, and my fingers were stuffed in my ears. Of course, in spite of both this and the wardrobe, I still felt it – the noise shook me, and the light slammed against my eyelids – but just as I'd hoped, its disorientating effect was neutralized by my defensive measures. And so, a second later, I was watching through the crack in the wardrobe door, feeling completely alert, as the two operatives came careering in. Then, suddenly, they both came to a stop, one with his back to the wardrobe, the other on the far side of the room. And I knew *this* was the moment in which their confusion at my absence would be at its height. In which they'd be most susceptible to attack.

With this thought, I launched myself at the guy directly before me and pistol-whipped him across the back of the neck while reaching round with my other hand to direct the muzzle of his MP5 away from the operative opposite. The guy squeezed his trigger as he lost consciousness sending a stutter of bullets into the wall, then finally dropped the weapon.

But I didn't let him fall to the floor, I strapped my right arm around his chest, and held up his body as a shield. And then I ground the muzzle of the SIG into the underside of his chin in a warning that said to the second operative: shoot me, and run the risk of my post-death spasms finishing your friend.

Only then did I finally look the second operative in the face and our eyes met with a flash of recognition. This man was Milton Coleson, one of the agents I'd met at HRT's New Operator Training School. He'd passed the training with flying colors, but had pulled out at the last minute and had clearly joined the Boston SWAT instead. But though he was plainly flustered at the sight of me, I knew that an agent of Coleson's quality wasn't going to stay that way for long. So I had to act *now*.

The next moment, I began charging him down at full-pelt. Then, when I was about a yard away, I released the unconscious operative from my arm, catapulting him at Coleson who finally reacted, meeting the body side-on with his shoulder – since he no longer had time to dodge it – and sending it across the room. But by the time he'd corrected his stance, I'd gotten right up to him, too close for him to use his MP5 on me.

But before I could draw breath, Coleson took a half-step back and delivered a vicious elbow to my jaw, turning my whole head numb. And this told me Coleson was ready to fight. Only I didn't fancy my chances: he could hit me anywhere whereas my options were vastly limited by his armor. So I had to do something drastic, fast. And even as I thought this, Coleson swung a second elbow that had enough force behind it to knock me cold. Quickly, I dodged back, just in time to avoid the brunt of the blow, his elbow glancing off my chin instead. And then, as he was following through, slightly off-balance, I decided to take a chance.

With a burst of speed, I lunged forward, slid my left arm underneath his MP5, and pressed it up against his body. Then, after crouching down, threading my right arm between his legs from behind, and grasping his belt, I lifted him off the ground so that his legs were above his torso and drove him chest-first into the floorboard. There was a brutal crack of ribs, followed by a heave as the air was forced from his lungs.

A risky maneuver, beautifully executed.

But there was no time to savor it. Coleson was still lethal, even with a couple of broken ribs. So immediately I landed my weight on top of him, looking to press my advantage. Yet Coleson had expected that, and thrashed his head back, smashing my nose with his helmet. Blood began pouring from my face, and my head started to swim. But I forced myself to focus – knowing that this was life or death – and in the next instant, my hand was on the back of his head, forcing his face to the floor, and exposing the nape of his neck. Then, with my free hand, I struck out...

Coleson was out cold.

I took a deep breath, before staggering to my feet, ears ringing. Then, still in a daze, I removed the Remington from Coleson's waist, chambered a shell, and squeezed the trigger at the connecting door. The job was done. There was now no connecting door – only splinters.

But then I realized I couldn't simply start making my exit with the situation as it stood. If I tried, there was a distinct possibility that the operatives downstairs would come up, discover my strategy, and tell their colleagues outside – all before I managed to exit Number Ten. So I

needed a tactic that would get the operatives to stay put…
And I knew just the thing.

I moved back over to Coleson, removed the earpiece from his ear, and placed it in my own. Then in a Connecticut twang, in my best impression of Milton Coleson, I said: 'One target, barricaded behind furniture. Shotgun round deployed. Await further update.'

I knew I was talking to the assault net, the name given to the team of people who wear the earpieces in a SWAT operation; a team that would, in this instance, most likely consist of the operatives currently in the house, the agent in charge of the operation (who was probably in a temporary command post outside the house), and the snipers I felt sure had been deployed. And I delivered these words with confidence: I knew precisely how to address an assault net and I knew that my impersonation was convincing.

'Holding positions,' came the response. 'Awaiting update.'

The moment I heard this, I pounced through to Number Ten, and began hurtling down the stairs at top speed. And as I went – stepping lightly to ensure no noise filtered through to Number Nine – I was relieved to discover I'd been right: the house was empty. Fifty seconds later, I arrived at the rear door, in the basement of Number Ten, my mind hazy. But once again, I forced myself to concentrate…

If there was a sniper, he'd probably be positioned up and to my right on the roof of one of the houses on the road adjacent to Columbus Square, since this was the spot that'd afford him the best view of Number Nine's garden. But, for now, it was immaterial whether he was up to my right, or left – my objective was getting to the safety of the tall trees beyond the back fence, and a sniper in either position would be equally dangerous as I crossed the garden. So what I needed was a way of disrupting the sniper's concentration. Because while I knew that my exiting from the neighboring property would surprise him, I knew this wasn't enough to throw off a seasoned professional.

But then it occurred to me that I could simply tell the assault net that the target had been secured. Of course, this wouldn't break the sniper's concentration completely but there was a chance it'd do enough to see me across the garden.

There were no guarantees. But I had no other options.

I took a deep breath.

'The target is secured,' I said. And with that, I burst through the door, and began sprinting across the short stretch of tarmac. Before I knew it, I was a quarter way across… then half… then three-quarters – and suddenly I was wondering whether a bullet would come at all. But then, when I was a half-step away from the back fence, it came: fizzing over my head from the direction of the rooftops to my right, and pounding the tarmac behind me. Close, but not close enough. And in the next second, I was through the gate, and cutting towards the service road, under the safety of the tall trees.

'Target has just exited Number Ten's rear. I missed the shot. He has access to the assault net. Shut it down, *now*.'

I'd known the sniper would alert the rest of the assault net. But although they were now aware I'd exited the building, I knew I still had a more than fighting chance of escaping the vicinity. For starters, the members of the assault net were going to struggle to coordinate a response, seeing that they'd just had to shut down their primary means of communication. And secondly, I knew there'd be a good minute or two delay before the news of my escape had been conveyed to police officers at the scene.

Yet despite all this working to my advantage, I knew I had to be *completely* on guard as I made my way.

A moment later, I hit the service road – which was, to my relief, empty – and without hesitation turned left, for the simple reason that I had no choice: if I turned right, I'd wind up back in the sniper's line of fire. Then, after hurrying to the end of the service road, I was cautious: I stopped and poked my head round the corner. But, just as I'd hoped, the road itself was un-cordoned. And while there was a small police presence about sixty yards to my left – six officers in all – I could tell by their easy demeanor that they'd not yet gotten wind of my escape… None of them were even looking in my direction.

Aware this was the best chance I was going to get to cross this road, I started bolting across at top speed and, sure enough, five seconds later, I'd ducked into a second service road on the opposite side, certain I hadn't been spotted. Then, knowing that the hardest part was now behind me, but time was still of the essence, I continued east as quickly as I could, ducking in and out of service roads. And as I went, I took the opportunity to divest myself of my blood-soaked jacket, and to shift the blood caked on my face using saliva and my hand.

It wasn't until I'd gotten a good four blocks east that I began heading north up a main road at a fast walk rather than a run so as not to arouse suspicions. And I knew already my next destination had to be The Eliot. I'd left Lilly there, entirely at the mercy of The Order. And though there were a thousand things that could've happened that would've resulted in Lilly not making the call, my instincts told me to expect the worst.

I had to see if she was okay.

When I neared the hotel, just under ten minutes later, I slowed my pace, so I could survey the surrounding area for threats. But, as far as I could see, there were no longer any Order watchers on the scene. So, without hesitation, I strode into the hotel, and into one of the waiting elevators.

ONCE AGAIN, I EXITED THE ELEVATOR, AT THE READY TO deal with unknown dangers, and found the corridor empty. And once again, as I approached the room, I found the door not closed, but ajar. Yet this time, there were no staff filing out. Instead, from within came the sound of the room's telephone ringing. I lingered outside a moment, seeing if I could hear anything else that'd give me a clue. But I could hear nothing but ringing. So I pushed open the door…

The first thing I did when I laid eyes on the scene was gag and I had to fight hard to hold back the urge to heave. Once the initial physical impact of the scene passed, it was replaced by profound disquiet.

Inside the room was a body. Lilly's.

It was strewn, naked, on the sofa we'd sat on not thirty minutes ago, with a sticky-tape gag secured across the mouth. However, it bore little resemblance to the Lilly I'd left behind. A knife had been taken to her face and neck, and had mangled her features almost beyond the point of recognition. Her breasts had been completely severed from her body. A complex series of patterns had been painstakingly cut into her remaining flesh, down her arms and legs; across her navel. And there was a small entrance wound on her left temple, along with a far larger exit wound on her right – the work of a soft-nosed slug.

Lilly had been butchered.

On the floor, by the sofa, were two objects. The first was the Ruger I'd lost during the ambush in Mineral. The second was the blade I'd lost at the same time. There was no doubt they'd been used to perpetrate the scene before me.

There was a unique sadism behind this murder, an unbridled monstrosity, that made me think this wasn't just The Order's doing. It was the handiwork of Drexler himself.

I had a feeling this same person was on the other end of the landline that was still ringing and ringing.

And then, all of a sudden, I found myself struck by an overwhelming sense of guilt. Not because I felt responsible for this atrocity – I'd done everything I could to try and prevent disaster – but because it was a chilling reminder of just what I'd done to Samuel. From the moment I'd discovered that Samuel had been converted to The Order, I'd understood that I was to blame; because by abandoning my son, I'd created a vacuum which had driven Samuel into Drexler's arms. But this atrocity was a reminder that the man I'd driven him to wasn't just a manipulative ringleader – he was an unspeakable monster.

Taking a deep breath, I closed the door to the bedroom and moved over to the dresser where the phone was sitting. Then, without yet picking up the receiver, I picked up the entire phone unit, and carried it to the window where I had a view of the main road. Finally, after another glance at the carnage, and another shiver of disgust, I lifted the receiver.

'Oh, there you are,' came the chilling voice of Ivan Drexler. 'That's sixty-two rings before you answered. How coy of you, Saul. Treating me mean to keep me keen?'

His voice, just as it'd been during our last conversation, was jokey and playful. I could hear in the background the hum of an engine. He was in a car.

I responded with a bitterly ironic laugh.

'So funny, so clever,' I said softly, my voice dripping with sarcasm. 'I just don't know how you do it… This time you managed to kill an unarmed woman and *still* found time to write your own jokes. Perhaps tell me how she begged and pleaded? Or perhaps a joke about how she fell to pieces under pressure? Now that would be funny, wouldn't it?'

Drexler paused a moment, weighing up how to respond to my facetiousness. But in the end, he didn't get angry. Instead, he used my mocking words against me.

'You should have seen how she *begged*,' he purred. 'How she *pleaded*.'

There was something in his tone that made even these clichéd words skin-crawling.

'You had a child executed,' I said in a voice pitched barely above a whisper. 'Do you have any idea what they do to people who hurt children in prison?'

Drexler laughed long and heartfelt. Then he said:

'Well, my boy, thanks to you, I actually have a *very* good idea what they do to such people in prison. But of course, *you're* the one who should be worrying about that, not me. After all, if you look at the evidence, it seems you're the one who had that poor Rinaldi boy executed. And then you had your wicked way with Ms Spender. Shame on you, Saul.'

He laughed again. As he did so, I saw once more, in my mind's eye, the little boy's brain bursting across the room. I looked again at Lilly's mutilated body.

'You did this, didn't you?' I growled. 'You were here, and you did this to her.'

He made a clucking noise. 'Why, you sound upset, and here I was, thinking you'd be happy I did it after Lilly betrayed you like that—'

'And where's her daughter?' I broke in coldly. 'Another slaughtered child?'

'Oh, so she told you about Abigail, and you naively entered the house anyway?' he said, with what sounded like genuine surprise. 'I must admit, I didn't think she would. But then again, I imagine she still left out *some* details like, for example, the fact that I'm the girl's father. I dare say she was ashamed of that.' He chuckled. 'In the end, I decided not to kill her – if you're going to spare anyone, it might as well be the person carrying your DNA – though to be clear, I'd sacrifice her in a heartbeat if I needed to.'

The fact the child had been spared was some small relief. But I felt a deep sympathy for Lilly – she had been intimately and irrevocably bound to this monster.

'Really, Saul, I find this emotional stake you have in other people quite amazing,' Drexler continued musingly. 'It's a great weakness, you know. And it's because I don't share this weakness that I'm the better manipulator.'

'It's why you're a monster,' I responded icily.

Drexler tutted impatiently. 'Spare me, I've heard it all before. Come now, Saul, you cannot deny the genius of my designs. I've deceived you not once, but twice. *Twice* I tricked you into believing you had the tactical advantage, when the reverse was true; when in fact you were, at all times, in my thrall. And I must admit, watching as you were drawn into the chain of events I'd created, and as each of my masterful predictions about how you'd respond came true – well, it felt incredible. Infinitely more enjoyable than merely taking a life. When I've taken lives, while the sense of control has been absolute, it has always been over too soon – whereas what I've done to you has not only given me an enormous sense of control, it's also lasted a good deal longer. And, of course, the fact it was Saul Marshall, the so-called greatest manipulator, made it all the sweeter.' He paused. 'What I've done to you is nothing short of a work of art.'

After a speech like that, I knew Drexler would be hoping for a substantial response. But I didn't give him the satisfaction.

'Where's Samuel?' I said flatly.

Drexler sighed. 'Come now,' he said, like it was a stupid question.

'So what, then? Your sick little game continues? And what perverted plan do you have in store for me next?'

'No more plans,' he said simply. 'Surely you can see that the game is finished, and I've won. The trap at Number Nine was my final move, and I would've been very happy if the SWAT gunned you down. But I was aware you might escape, so I made provisions to ensure you'd be hunted down if you did. And in many ways, I'm *glad* you did. It means you got to see the show at The Eliot, and that, if you last long enough, you'll get to see my grand finale; whereas I get to see Saul Marshall as fugitive once again.

'And, of course, if you survive till midnight of March 4, it'll make killing Samuel all the sweeter.' He chuckled softly. 'I'm excited to see his face when his messiah – his *father* – turns on him. That's how he sees me, Saul, as his father. Though I've done things with him that most fathers don't with their sons. Or, rather, I've had him do things to me. It's a power thing – it excites me to see how far someone is willing to debase themselves.'

White-hot anger rose inside me, but I squashed it immediately. I knew there was every chance he was lying to get a rise. He continued:

'But in short, Saul, the reason why I haven't killed you myself, why I'm in no hurry to see you dead, is because, at this point, you represent no threat to me. Even if I hadn't framed you, and you had nothing to worry about but stopping me, you wouldn't stand a chance.'

Instead of anger, I now suddenly felt a creeping fatalism, since a large part of me couldn't help but believe him. I was, after all, completely out of leads. And if Drexler's previous form was anything to go by, then what he still had planned was likely to be meticulously safeguarded against error and interference… But a moment later, I again took myself in hand. I couldn't allow this kind of thinking.

'So in the meantime you're happy for me to take all the credit?' I asked. 'For people to think that *I'm* behind The Order of Babylon?'

Drexler snorted. 'I know, it's *preposterous* – what I've done is *way* beyond your pay-grade. But yes, I'm happy for people to believe it for the time being, while it's convenient. And if they *do* believe it, which I have no doubt many will, I shall take it as another sign of my powers of manipulation – that I have managed to get people to believe something so absurd. But don't worry. It won't be long until the name Ivan Drexler is known world over.'

It was unsurprising that Drexler was looking for universal fame – the desire for admiration was a key psychopathic trait. But what set Drexler apart from most psychopaths was that he seemed capable of delaying the gratification of claiming credit: he'd kept The Order's responsibility quiet for days on end, and he was still keeping his identity hidden. And because of this, he'd reaped huge tactical advantages.

'Now really, I must be off,' said Drexler, his voice suddenly bored and efficient. 'You've served a purpose to me, but now I'm done with you. Though you should probably know that since your employers *do* still have designs against you, I thought it'd be polite to lend them a hand, you know, just to get them off the mark. The time now is 10:31. At exactly 10:30, one minute ago, I organized for the Boston Field Office to receive a second tip concerning your location—'

I didn't wait to hear any more. I hung up the phone.

I'd expected Drexler to organize a second tip-off about my location. It was why I'd stood by the window – to keep an eye out for any law enforcement approaching. And though, as of yet, the coast was still clear, I'd no doubt the hotel would soon be crawling with FBI.

I needed to get outside, hot-wire a car, and haul-ass.

I jumped into action. First, I pocketed the Ruger and the knife. Then, after uncoiling a wire hanger from the bedroom closet and folding it into my pocket, I left the room, and made my way down a staff stairwell and through a back exit.

I came out onto the hotel's parking lot. But I understood I couldn't use any of the cars there. When the authorities arrived, I knew they'd promptly investigate the vehicles on the premises, and quickly ascertain which, if any, were missing. So I passed straight through the car-park, hit the service road behind the hotel, then began heading west, along the back of the buildings neighboring The Eliot. Sixty yards later, I found what I was looking for.

Hidden behind a brick wall, there was a small parking lot, sign-posted "Staff," which appeared to belong to a private members' club. And immediately I knew this was a better place to take a car. Not only because there'd be a considerable delay before the authorities started investigating neighboring properties. But also because at a staff car-park, people come and go less frequently, meaning my theft was more likely to go unnoticed for longer.

With this in mind, I approached an unexceptional silver Toyota Corolla, took the wire from my pocket, and negotiated one end of it under the rubber seal at the top of the window and penetrated the vehicle's interior. Then, threading the wire into the car, I hooked it around the inner handle and popped the door. I then quickly went to work on starting the car, removing the casing from beneath the steering column and searching out the two wires which had to be brought into contact and not a moment later, the engine came roaring to life.

Then, getting behind the wheel, I wasted no time: I hustled the Corolla first onto the service road, and then onto the westbound lane of the I-95, which ran directly behind The Eliot. And then I bore down on the accelerator with everything I had, wishing it was Drexler's throat.

Chapter Thirty-Six

As soon as I finished unpacking my equipment onto the bed of the master bedroom in the Manhattan Suite at The Gansevoort Hotel, I sat down and started thinking…

After I'd gotten out of Boston, I drove to New Haven. There I purchased a suit, a briefcase, two large maps (one of mainland America, one of just the eastern seaboard), two pads of paper, and a pack of biros, then checked into a motel and used their facilities to ice my bruising, and shower. Then, abandoning the car, I rode a Greyhound to Manhattan, after which I took a public bus to the Meat-packing District and checked into one of the more expensive suites at the five-star Hotel Gansevoort, using the second of my false credit cards. The logic behind my choice of hideout was simple: hide in plain sight, because it's the last place anyone will think to look. And when I got inside the safety of the suite, I was overcome by a sudden urge to sit and think.

The first thing I considered was my status in the eyes of the authorities. I knew that by now the authorities would definitely know I'd been at Nine Columbus Square – there was no doubt that Milton Coleson had recognized me, and that the sniper would've seen enough to corroborate Coleson. However, what was more difficult to ascertain was how convinced they'd be of my guilt. Lilly's body, and even more so those of the Rinaldi family, looked pretty damning. And I knew from my conversation with Parkes that there'd been speculation about my potential complicity with The Order even before Boston. Yet, at the same time, I knew there was plenty to cause them uncertainty. The forensic evidence, it seemed to me, was likely to offer them an inconclusive picture. And I reckoned there'd be significant question marks about why I'd been so careful not to kill the operatives.

And then there was the not inconsiderable factor of my history. After all, while I may have played fast and loose with the law early on in life, I'd then served my country for a decade and a half, risking my life on countless occasions. This had to count for something.

On the whole, I reckoned that opinions within American national security were likely to be divided: some would be convinced of my guilt, others of my innocence, and the rest would fall somewhere in between. And in all probability, this was what Drexler had been aiming for. He would've known it'd be impossible to completely convince the authorities of my guilt, so would've aimed instead to turn a significant enough number against me. Yet precisely who and how many had been turned, and thus what kind of approach American national security was going to take towards me, remained to be seen. It seemed to me most likely that the overall consensus would be that I needed to be brought in as a matter of top priority, and that serious steps were already being taken to achieve this. However, I was aware that if more people than I expected had bought

Drexler's ruse, the response could be more extreme. They could even be willing to make an attempt on my life.

This seemed less likely, but I had to be ready for it.

But though I was under threat, there were a couple of factors allowing me to stay a step ahead of the authorities. Firstly, there was the fact they couldn't go public with their manhunt – it would be a fiasco to end all fiascos if they announced that one of their own men was wanted in relation to these attacks – and this meant they couldn't use the public to help track me down. And secondly, there was the unique skill-set I'd accrued during my time spent as a con-artist, and then as a Bureau agent, which was allowing me to makes decisions that best kept me off their radar. And it was this which had led me to the safety of the suite.

But this suite wasn't just going to be my hideout. It was also going to be the place from which I would figure out how to get to Drexler, because this was precisely what I'd resolved to do. This resolve had set in soon after I'd left Boston. Once I'd left the city, I had promptly rid myself of defeatism and started calmly analyzing the situation. Before long, I'd begun to see that although I was out of obvious leads, I wasn't completely empty-handed. On the contrary, I had a wealth of information about Drexler – about his history and personality, as well as the attacks he'd already instigated – and I knew from experience that occasionally *crucial* things can be inferred, or second-guessed, from this kind of information. Things like what someone is planning next, or their whereabouts. Of course, I was under no illusions: I was aware that often when this kind of information is analyzed, it tells you nothing. But I'd resolved that if there *was* anything to be gleaned from these details, I was going to find it.

And once I'd decided this, immediately I'd begun to see there were factors working in my favor. For starters, I had time: there were more than three days before Drexler was set to execute Samuel and Vann, and *a lot* could be achieved in three days. And what was more, I was dealing with an enemy who'd complacently dismissed me as a threat which meant, if I *did* manage to track him down, I'd have on my side the all-important element of surprise.

So with a plan of action clear in my mind, and my spirits rallied, I'd gone to New Haven and purchased the items I needed to catalog and analyze what I knew – items which were now laid out next to me on the bed, along with a laptop which belonged to the hotel. And while I was aware that these tools were laughable compared to the FBI's sophisticated gear, this didn't dampen my hopes that I'd be able to see something they hadn't. For one thing, I had a unique perspective on things – the perspective of having been on the run myself. For another, the Bureau were wasting their resources by focusing on irrelevant pursuits such as attempting to track me down.

Yet although I fancied my chances of finding some-thing the Bureau had missed, there was somebody I desperately wanted to consult. Somebody who could not only give me a valuable insight into how I stood in the eyes of the authorities, but also had exceptional expertise when it came to tracking people down. Morton Giles. But so far I'd held off from calling him because I knew there was a good chance, given that he'd already been under suspicion for being in contact with me, that his activities were now being watched.

So I had to wait for him to contact me.

But then, just as I was thinking this, the Nokia abruptly started ringing, displaying an unknown number. And immediately I thought: it has to be Giles, calling from a new SIM…

'Hello,' I answered.

'How the hell has this happened?' growled Morton Giles. 'The last I hear from you, you're about to embark on a mission to recover your son. Then, all of a sudden, a string of bodies appear – most noticeably those of the entire Rinaldi family – and you're being discussed as a serious candidate for the mastermind behind The Order.'

'So these suspicions are big news?' I said calmly.

'The whole of bloody headquarters is talking about this, Saul, though of course it's not been allowed to get any further. Could you imagine the outcry if the public got wind of this? Hell, I've even had to use a new SIM to call you because frankly I'm not sure at this point if they would hesitate to tap my calls, goddamn it!'

Giles was seething, and understandably so. But I kept a cool head.

'Just how seriously are these suspicions being taken?' I asked.

'You answer my question first,' replied Mort. 'How the hell has this happened?'

'It was a set-up,' I said. I then filled him in with everything that'd happened, right up to my escape from Boston.

When I finished, Giles was quiet for a bit, then said:

'So things have gone from bad to worse.'

His tone was dark, but at least he was calmer.

'Please Mort,' I said gently, 'I need to know: just how seriously are these suspicions being taken?'

Again he was silent a moment. Then he said:

'It's bad. But it could be worse.'

'Go on.'

Giles sighed exhaustedly. 'Well, from what I've heard on the grapevine – because of course I've not been told anything directly – the suspicions have gone all the way to the top. Fortunately, from the sounds of it, both Muldoon and The President have come down on your side: they don't believe for a second you're behind The Order, and think Boston was an attempt to frame you. However, as I understand it, there are some high-powered people who aren't so convinced – namely, The Chairman of the Joint Chiefs of Staff and The Director of the CIA. The latter, in particular, is apparently very ready to believe that an FBI agent is behind The Order. Meanwhile, analyses from forensics and post-mortems are still coming in and I've no idea whether they will help clear your name, or indict you further.'

'And what's the feeling within Hoover?'

'Well, the official line – established by Muldoon – is that you're *not* responsible for The Order. But, nonetheless, there's still a significant minority who feel the accusations shouldn't be dismissed outright, even if they're not entirely convinced by them, and this group includes the likes of Alex Schneider. Parkes, on the other hand, is remaining poker-faced and is just reiterating that she wants you brought in for withholding information.'

I wasn't surprised by any of this. It was almost exactly what I'd expected.

'This was precisely what Drexler wanted,' I said. 'To turn enough people within American national security against me so that they'd take their eye off the ball. He wanted them infighting and wasting their energies chasing the wrong man, so he could be left in peace to get on with his own plans.'

Giles grunted. 'Well, I can tell you that American national security is already wasting a whole lot of its energies on trying to get something out of the elements of The Order they've managed to get their hands on. As you might have seen on the news, there have been major raids on the Order properties in Manhattan, DC, and upstate New York, but the subsequent effort to interrogate the hundreds of young men and women arrested has been as time consuming as it's been useless. Either these kids are incredible actors, or they've genuinely been kept in the dark about nearly everything.

'What's more – and you won't have seen this on the news – the FBI managed to sniff out the team behind the Aimes murder, right here in DC. There were six of them, holed up in a place on Chesapeake Street. And you won't be surprised to hear that not only were all six of them on the Bureau's missing person register, but one of them was none other than Aimes's missing daughter… But these six also yielded next to nothing during interrogation. Incredibly, they seem to know nothing outside the logistics of their own attack.'

'It makes sense Drexler has ensured nobody knows too much,' I replied. 'After all, you can't compromise plans you know nothing about, it's an elementary safeguard.'

Giles grunted again.

'So what now?' he said, with an air of defeat. 'Your son's still at large. Vannevar's still a hostage. And whichever way you look at it, you're on the run. So what now?'

'Well, I have a choice,' I said evenly. 'Either I lie low and do nothing. Or I try and find Drexler and put an end to this. I personally prefer the latter.'

'And how, tell me, do you intend to find him?' said Giles skeptically.

'The same way you found me. By taking everything I know about Drexler, everything that he's done so far, and seeing if I can find some kind of pattern in it. I may be out of leads, but I still know a lot about him – surely more than anyone else does.'

'It took me years to find you,' said Giles slowly.

'Well, obviously I don't have years,' I said. 'I have just over three days. But that's not going to stop me trying…'

'Look, at midnight of March 4, Vann and Samuel are set to be executed. But that's not all: Drexler told me on the phone that there's going to be a "grand finale" and that says to me that he's planning another attack, even bigger than what we've seen already. Now I for one can't just sit around waiting for all this to happen. I've got to do something. I've got to at least try and work with the information I've got and see if there's anything there. And I'm just going to come out and say it: I want your help. Because if there *is* something hidden within the information, my chances of extracting it will be a whole lot better with you on side – the man who caught Saul Marshall…

'And don't pretend like you've had no desire to get involved in this these past few days. I know you, Mort. I know you've been *itching* to get your hands on all the information – to have a proper crack at this. Well, here's your chance.'

Giles sighed. 'It's true: it's been frustrating to be so cut off from the investigation. And frustrating, too, to watch them waste their time on so many misguided pursuits.'

Giles sighed again, then fell silent. I knew he was weighing up whether it was worthwhile to help me or whether this was simply a fool's errand. At last he said:

'Fine, I'll do it, I'll come help you… Like you say, it's worth a shot.'

I smiled broadly to myself.

'Where are you, Saul?' he added.

'In Manhattan. The Hotel Gansevoort on 9th Avenue.'

Giles made a knowing noise. 'So no motel in backwater America for Saul Marshall?'

'That's where they'd expect me to be.'

'Alright,' he said. 'Well, I'm in DC, but I'll leave right away. But before I do, two quick questions. First: does anyone else know about Samuel's defection?'

'As far as I know, we're still the only ones.'

'And second: what about clearing your name?'

'It's not an immediate concern. Drexler made it clear that he has every intention of taking the credit for The Order *very* soon – that this whole business of framing me is only temporary. Besides, I haven't got time to worry about it.'

'Right,' said Giles. 'Then I'll see you soon.'

'Bring money,' I said. 'And a laptop. I've got one here, but another will help.'

'Anything else?'

'Yes. Make sure you're not followed.'

Chapter Thirty-Seven

At ten past nine, Mort called again to tell me he was in the hotel lobby. I went down and found him looking serious-faced but pleased to see me. He was clutching a brown deli bag; and over his shoulder was a laptop satchel.

'How was your journey?' I asked. 'How did you get here?'

'I was careful,' he rumbled. 'I took a cab to Dulles, then rented a car from there. I queued up with a bunch of new arrivals so that the staff at the rental company wouldn't remember me in particular. The valet's just taken the car off my hands, and I've grabbed us some sandwiches from the deli down the road.'

At that, I nodded my appreciation, then led Giles up to the suite, and through the living room directly off the large, meticulously tidy foyer. But while the living room had also been tidy, it wasn't anymore, because over the past few hours I'd converted it into my situation room, which had involved shifting all the furniture to one side, and using the floor-space as a canvas for information. The two maps

285

were now unfurled on the floor, and on both I'd marked every place I could think of that had remotely anything to do with Drexler or The Order. Nearby, there were piles of paper, on which I'd written all the potentially important information I'd accumulated: what I could recall from the SIOC, and from my talk with Lamphere; what I'd learned from Lilly, from my conversations with Parkes and Drexler; and the name and description of everyone I'd met since February 26 – be they now alive or dead.

In brief, the last four hours had been a painstaking exercise in recall; an attempt to bring together *all* the raw information.

Giles gave a low whistle as he looked the room over. Then, after we both sat down on the floor and Giles handed me a sandwich, we began, at a slow and focused pace, to discuss it all, hoping to spot a cosmos in the chaos.

Chapter Thirty-Eight

D rexler put his eye to the peep-hole. Just as he'd
expected, Vannevar was sitting in the middle of the
room, fastened to his chair, strapped into a bomb-vest. But,
more unexpectedly, he was also wide awake, despite the
lateness of the hour.

On seeing this, Drexler made his decision: he *was* going
to talk to Vannevar before resting from the drive. And
scarcely had he thought this when he unlocked the door
and stepped inside. But before he could say anything,
Vannevar beat him to it.

'Are you the guy in charge of this theater? Because for
the last time: I'm *not* David Blaine. You've got the
wrong guy.'

Vannevar said this with nothing in his voice; with his
face completely blank. In response, Drexler smiled. Then
he pulled up another chair from the side of the room,
placed it opposite Vannevar, and sat down.

'Actually, I think I've got *precisely* the right guy,' replied
Drexler at last. 'Just the man for the job.'

'Well, if the job is musical chairs, then you could be

right,' said Vannevar. 'Though, truth be told, I'm a cheat: the reason I've never lost my chair is because I'm tied to it.'

Once again, Vannevar said this without cracking his face. Drexler arched his brows.

'Are you sure you're taking this situation quite seriously enough?' asked Drexler, with a playful air.

'I may like to joke around,' replied Vannevar. 'But at the end of the day, my message is perfectly serious: I will *not* let you cut down this beautiful chair.'

Drexler leaned back and regarded Vannevar carefully. He was encouraged by what he'd seen so far: Vannevar, unlike Marshall and Francis Bindle, had exhibited a sense of humor. And though he was currently using it to make light of the situation, Drexler had expected no less. After all, Vannevar hadn't been informed about any of the events that had happened since his capture – so as far as he knew, the situation *wasn't* that serious…

And what was more, Drexler knew there was a distinct possibility Vannevar hadn't yet realized who he was talking to.

Drexler leaned forward. 'Do you by any chance know who I am, Mr Yeung?'

'My friend Jason Bourne also had the misfortune of suffering memory loss,' replied Vannevar. 'But I'm sure if you keep at it, you'll work it out eventually.'

Again Drexler smiled. 'Very good. It's always nice to see someone retaining their sense of humor in a tight spot. But since you won't answer my question, I'll have to tell you. Does the name *Ivan Drexler* ring a bell?'

For the first time, Vannevar smiled. 'You bet. Ivan Drexler, the sickest son of a bitch this side of the equator. Pleased to meet you.'

'Likewise.'

'And since we're friends and all now, you wouldn't

mind loosening these ties, would you? I've got to say: it comes across a little desperate when you tie up your guests for anything more than twenty-four hours.'

'So these are the thanks I get for trying to look after your posture?' replied Drexler with a grin. But Vannevar didn't smile. His face had reverted to a blank.

'Now, Vannevar,' Drexler went on. 'Do you have any idea where you are?'

'Do I get any lifelines for this one?'

'Afraid not.'

'Well then, I'd have to say Chicago.'

Drexler narrowed his eyes. 'How did you know?'

'I didn't,' replied Vannevar.

Drexler unleashed a big laugh.

'Very quick, Vannevar. It's refreshing; it really is. But truth be told: I don't mind you knowing where we are, seeing that you won't be getting the chance to tell anyone. On the contrary, I was planning to tell you – I've been wanting to discuss the subject with someone capable of understanding for quite a while now.'

'Oh, I bet you say that to all your hostages,' replied Vannevar.

'You'd be surprised,' said Drexler. 'But now, here's the big money question: do you have any idea where in Chicago we are?'

'The Sears Tower?'

'I think the real answer is going to impress you a whole lot more,' said Drexler. 'Because while this may look like any old dilapidated warehouse, it's not. It belongs to the FBI. It was purchased so that five Counterterrorism agents could conduct a highly classified operation here in Chicago – an operation so classified that outside those five agents, only the Director of the FBI was supposed to know about it. But, as you might've guessed, I found out about the warehouse, and usurped it – and the Director remains none the wiser. What better place to hide from the authorities than in their own most classified location?'

Drexler paused, and looked at Vannevar hard. Then, for the first time, Vannevar gave him a serious answer.

'So you had a mole on the inside?'

'Bingo,' said Drexler.

Drexler was gratified. After telling Vannevar about just one small element of his ingenious designs, he'd already impressed him enough to put an end to his glib responses. But he had no intention of stopping there.

'But that's just the tip of the iceberg,' continued Drexler. 'I've pulled things off this past week you wouldn't believe and because so many of them have come since your capture, you've missed quite a show. So I'll fill you in. First there was Mineral. Not only did the plot you deduced – the live ammo at the re-enactment – come off without a hitch, but the results were awesome: eight dead, fourteen in intensive care. Then there was the spectacle in Manhattan later that day. Paramount Pictures were filming a scene on a metro train, involving fake nerve gas. But I managed to replace their gas with the real thing, and the actors ended up suffocating themselves to death. It was *beautiful* – thirty-seven dead in one fell, *spectacular* swoop.

'And then there was the run-around I gave your friend Saul Marshall. I released him after Mineral but he was still very much ensnared in my designs. And I'm not sure what's taken more of a toll on him: the discovery that his son is in fact one of my loyal disciples; or the fact that I've ingeniously had him framed as the mastermind behind The Order – a maneuver which has forced him to go on the run from the law.

Drexler chuckled, then went on:

'And so now I've got American national security so

distracted chasing their own man that I've got nothing standing in my way from carrying out my final attack – the grand finale. It's due to take place on the Tuesday morning, March 5. Unfortunately, I can't tell you much about it: I've decided that only the team carrying it out are allowed to know the details. But what I can tell you is this: I'm hoping it'll surpass 9/11 – if not in terms of the death toll, then certainly in terms of psychological harm. But already I've said too much…'

Once again, Drexler paused to let what he'd said hit home. And it did: Vannevar's face hardened, his eyes widened, and he began slowly shaking his head. He was coming nearer, Drexler thought, to understanding the complexity and genius he was up against. But still this wasn't enough. And so it was at this point he began telling Vannevar the part of his plot he was most proud of – his escape strategy. And, sure enough, as Vannevar took it in, it had the desired effect: his face hardened still further, and his eyes glared.

'So Vannevar, what do you think?' Drexler added after he finished. 'You said yourself I was sick. So wouldn't it be great if I went viral after pulling this off?' And even as he said it, he felt certain he'd now more than secured Vannevar's respect; that Vannevar would finally engage him in a proper back-and-forth.

But Vannevar's response surprised Drexler. Because he didn't reply with words – he burst into laughter; a kind of uncontrollable, hysterical, out of all proportions howl, accompanied by a stream of tears. It seemed to go on and on.

'Enough,' commanded Drexler, after a full ten seconds of laughter. 'I really don't see what you find so amusing.'

Vannevar took a deep breath, bringing his laughter under control.

'You really don't get it, do you?' he said. 'You come in here, and I ridicule you because you're a pathetic and contemptible worm, who gets his kicks from hurting inno-cent people. But you don't realize this. You think I simply don't comprehend how impressive you are, so you brag about your atrocities, thinking it'll win my respect. But it hasn't. It's just made you all the more laughable.'

And with that, Vannevar started howling once more.

All at once, Drexler understood. He'd been wrong about Vannevar – he was, just like the others, blinded to his genius by the cancer of empathy. And with this realiza-tion, Drexler suddenly found himself overcome with anger. And so he let it out: he leaped off his seat, and punched Vannevar square in the face – then again, and again, and again. But despite the assault, Vannevar kept up his manic laughter.

'Torturing people again, eh, Drex?' said Vannevar, when Drexler finally stopped to catch his breath. 'Just like all those years ago, working for Costana. Weren't so smart back then, were you? Landed yourself in prison for almost a decade and a half.'

Again, Drexler saw red and in one fluid motion he whipped out a small switchblade, seized Vannevar's left pinky, and smashed the tip of the blade under his nail. As Vannevar gasped and recoiled, Drexler snatched the next finger along, and drove home yet again.

Then Drexler raised the blade to Vannevar's throat. For a few moments he held it there contemplatively; then, with his anger subsiding, he backed off.

'If you'd shown some respect, there was a chance I would have let you live,' Drexler hissed. 'But now you have no chance: you *will* die.'

Vannevar gulped in two deep, composing breaths.

Then, the next instant, an anarchic grin crossed his face, and he said:

'And here I was thinking I was going to live forever.'

'You won't be laughing when midnight of March 4 comes around,' Drexler spat. 'I'll be remotely detonating your vest, and the explosion'll blow your head straight off your neck.'

'Shame you won't be here,' said Vannevar. 'Or you'd have been able to follow it up with a witty quip, like: *looks like he lost his head.*'

Yet again, Vannevar broke into hysterical laughter. Drexler scowled, then stormed out of the door.

Let the clown laugh.

Chapter Thirty-Nine

I t was about five minutes after Mort had left the hotel – in search of some food following a nine hour fruitless discussion – that I realized someone was inside the suite. I was sitting in the living room, and then suddenly I could hear the faint footsteps of someone moving across the lobby; someone who was, by the sounds of it, already halfway across the room. And immediately I knew I should be worried. Because this person had navigated the front door and penetrated a good way into the suite in utter silence, and this wasn't something that could be done by accident. This person was making a deliberate effort to catch me off-guard, and probably had special training.

Most likely, this was someone sent by the authorities to bring me in, or perhaps even to take my life…

There was no doubt this person was coming for the living room. And, judging by the volume of the footsteps, I had about three seconds before he arrived. But I didn't have access to my weapons: I'd left them in the bedroom on the other side of the lobby. So I had to use what was available in the room. And I knew that whatever I used, it was critical I got the first blow in. If I could land a hit before this person realized I was wise to his presence, it'd greatly increase my chances of coming out on top.

With these thoughts rushing through my mind, I snapped to my feet, grabbed a small wooden coffee table, and hurled it with everything I had at the door four yards away. And I timed it perfectly: no sooner had I released the table than a man appeared at the threshold.

In the brief moment during which the table was in flight, I took a good look. He was in his mid-twenties, 6'2", in perfect shape; he was wearing a plain grey sweater, durable black pants, lightweight boots; and in his right hand was a Ruger Mark II, the older version of mine, with a silencer. And it was this weapon that told me he was an assassin. Because not only was the Ruger a make famously favored by assassins, but this was also an outdated, non-standard-issue model, and I knew from experience that very few in the armed forces other than assassins have the autonomy to use non-standard-issue weapons.

But there was something about this man that said he wasn't *just* an assassin. After working at the HRT for years, I'd come to recognize a certain quality which belonged exclusively to those in the most elite special forces – a kind of supreme confidence and calm – and this guy had it. And since I didn't recognize him, my guess was that he was from the Navy SEALs or the US Army Deltas – one of the two groups that measured up to the HRT.

And if this was the case, then there were only two organizations that could've sent him: the FBI or the CIA…

In the next second, the table hit the target: it clattered hard against the guy's abdomen and hands, breaking as it did so, the shattered parts flying past him into the lobby.

And, crucially, so too did the Ruger, which had slipped his grasp with the contact.

I was unsurprised to see that the guy still looked unfazed: he was too well trained to lose his cool. And I knew that he'd now be weighing up whether he should retrieve the Ruger, or reach for the blade inevitably on his person. A moment later, he made his decision: he took a half-step back in retreat. But this wasn't what I wanted. So immediately I began charging towards him, hoping to force him to engage. And sure enough, it worked: he paused abruptly, and whipped from his boot a black Ka-Bar – a seven-inch, military-standard bowie knife. But this was exactly what I'd expected, so I reacted fast. I suddenly halted my charge a couple of feet from him, and threw a vicious front kick at his knife-wielding hand. The contact sent the Ka-Bar clattering into the lobby.

I'd managed to disarm him because I'd realized what he was planning without him knowing, and had thus been able to surprise him first and so now, it was a level playing field. Only it wasn't really, because if he had in fact been sent by American national security, then he would've been extensively briefed on my strengths and weaknesses. And what's more, he was fresh whereas I was exhausted.

If I wanted to survive, I'd have to finish him fast. Stamina was on his side.

Our eyes met for a brief, electrifying moment. We both knew only one of us would be leaving alive.

And then, all of a sudden, I went for him, throwing myself forward with a flurry of punches, and forcing him to backpedal into the large lobby. But my first four blows he comfortably blocked, and my next two missed the target altogether – he was thoroughly outpacing me, and it was disorientating. Then the next thing I knew, his fist struck me hard between the eyes and my vision went hazy. A half-second later, he followed this with a tremendous blow to the upper-right of my abdomen after which, he took my feet from under me with a leg-sweep. I fell hard onto my lower back.

Yet at this point, he didn't straddle my body full-mount but leaned across my torso instead. And the fact he'd chosen this position, which was universally considered weaker, told me that he had indeed been briefed on me – he knew about my unusual capacity for disabling assailants in the full-mount position.

But the next instant, these thoughts were disrupted by screaming pain. The guy had forced my hand to the floor, slipped his other arm under my elbow, and started forcing it up and the pressure on my shoulder was excruciating. But then, more worryingly, as my shoulder popped from its socket, and the guy started working my face with his elbows, the pain was replaced by an encroaching darkness. Unconsciousness was closing in. With every ounce of my being, I fought to keep my brain online but still the elbows kept coming. And I found myself thinking dimly: this is it, I've finally met my match…

But then suddenly he lifted one of his legs, and began swinging it over my body. Clearly, he'd decided that I was now subdued enough that it'd be safe to adopt the full-mount position. And instantly I knew: this was my only chance – it was now or never. With this thought, I bucked my hips wildly, and my pelvis struck his with force, throwing off his balance. Then, before I knew it, I'd rolled him over. I was on top.

For the first time, calm left his features. I had to capital-ize. I shuffled up his body, and clamped his head between my knees, locking my ankles while grabbing one of his hands with my right hand, since it was my left shoulder that'd been dislocated. Then, with everything I could muster, I proceeded to squeeze his head with my knees and to crush his hand with mine. Soon the bones in his hand began to crack, and his face began to purple. But the pain didn't subdue him, and, with his free hand, which I was unable to defend against, he lashed out viciously at my kidneys. Yet I persisted in spite of the punishment, driven by a primal urge to survive, until finally, what felt an eternity later, he gave up struggling, and blacked out beneath me.

Drenched in sweat, I rolled off him. Then I made my decision: he was too dangerous to let live. And so I took his head, and snapped his neck.

TEN MINUTES LATER, MORT CAME THROUGH THE front door.

'Holy shit,' he said, as he set eyes on the scene before him: the assassin lying dead; me sitting nearby, battered and bruised.

'Help me put my shoulder together,' I said. 'I'll tell you what happened.'

Mort came over and slammed my shoulder into its socket. The pain was intense but a walk in the park compared to what I'd just been through.

'Our friend here crept into the suite with a silenced Ruger,' I said, after taking a moment to catch my breath. 'He was undoubtedly an assassin; and, judging by the way he handled himself, I'd say special forces – a SEAL or Delta.'

'But only the FBI or the CIA could've deployed such an assassin.'

I nodded solemnly. 'I know.' I paused. 'It had to be the CIA. It would've required Muldoon's authorization had it been the Bureau. You said yourself he's got my back.'

Mort nodded. 'It was the CIA. Their Director must've authorized this on the sly – against the President's expressed wishes.'

'Meanwhile this guy' – I gestured at the body – 'was only doing his job. Died for no reason.'

Again, Mort nodded, this time looking guilty. The reason why was obvious: he knew he'd been followed; that he'd led the assassin here.

'It could've gone either way back there,' I said, as I probed my injuries with my fingertips. My head was the least of my worries: though aching, it was stable enough. My shoulder, however, was extremely tender – I'd sustained, I reckoned, a closed fracture to the upper-humerus. But worst of all was where the guy had struck my abdomen, because he'd gotten my liver. I probed the area a second, then said:

'I took a big blow to the liver. I reckon it's lacerated: filling with blood as we speak.'

Mort gave me a serious look, then said: 'A ticking time bomb.'

I nodded. It was a ticking time bomb because such a hematoma will almost certainly infect the abdominal cavity. And once the cavity is infected, you have three or four days to treat it before it kills you.

But I didn't have time deal with it right now. Treatment would have to wait.

I sighed, then looked at Mort resolutely.

'Right, it's no longer safe here,' I said. 'I say we take your hire-car and haul-ass. It should still be safe to use, given that it's unlikely that anyone will be staking out the hotel. After all, assassins, as we both know, usually operate in isolation, so they can't be traced. And even if the assassin passed on the details of your car to the CIA, I don't see how that'll help them. They won't have brought the police in on this, so I can't see who they could possibly have out on the roads on the lookout for it.'

'The car could be bugged,' said Mort.

'You're right. So we'll have to pull over once we're out of town and comb it.' I paused. 'Then we'll have to find somewhere safe to go next, but we can decide on that in the car. Right now though, we need to get going.'

At that, Mort shot me a nod, then we fell to action. First, we carried the body into one of the bathrooms, and locked it inside by breaking the door-handle. Then Mort left the suite to get his car from the valet, leaving me to pack our equipment and papers. When I finished, I had just enough time to wolf down the coffee and sandwich Mort had left in the lobby before he called my Nokia and told me he was waiting outside. So, after affixing the *Do Not Disturb* notice to the front door, I flung everything over my right shoulder, and, with my head bowed, made my way quickly through the hotel and out onto the street.

Mort drove assertively, and before long, we'd left Manhattan via the Lincoln Tunnel, and were traveling west along the identical route Rex had taken when driving me to Montclair. As we sat in silence, I thought darkly about the success of Drexler's designs, about how American national security was squandering its energies chasing their own man, just as Drexler had hoped. But after a few minutes, these thoughts trailed off and my mind slipped into neutral – I was too exhausted to think.

About thirty minutes later, Mort came off the Interstate and pulled over on a deserted road near the small town of Rockaway, NJ, so we could comb the car for bugs. Within fifteen minutes, we were back on the westbound lane of the I-80, satisfied the car was clean.

'Where we going now?' I asked.

'Don't sweat it,' Mort replied. 'I know a place.'

I didn't have the energy to inquire further, I was happy just to let Mort take the reins. And so, divested of responsibility, I surrendered to the overwhelming urge to sleep.

Chapter Forty

I f I'd felt bad immediately following my bout with the assassin, I felt a whole lot worse when Mort woke me four hours later. My left shoulder had tightened up, and was in desperate need of ice. My head was swollen. And my liver was generating an agonizing pain. Together, these injuries culminated in a wave of nausea which took me a good few seconds to curb. Then, finally, I gazed out the window. We were in a settlement little bigger than a hamlet, looking tired and run-down beneath the bleak, overcast sky.

'Whitesville, New York,' said Morton. 'Used to have a uncle who lived here. We're more than three-hundred miles from The Big Apple.'

Mort pulled up outside a weather-beaten structure on the main drag with neon letters on its front reading *The Whitesville House Motel*, after which he led the way inside, and paid for the two rooms on the top floor. Soon enough, we were alone inside one of these rooms. And as Mort started unpacking our gear, I laid myself out on the bed, too incapacitated by pain to do much else. When Mort finished, he came over and shook his head concernedly.

'Mort, we've got to do something about my injuries,' I said in response. 'I'm no good to anyone like this.'

Mort nodded slowly. 'You don't lock horns with a Delta or SEAL and not have anything to show for it.'

I grunted. 'You can say that again. Look, my arm's broken: it needs a sling and splint. And my head needs ice. My liver's giving me hell, and may need surgery down the line. But in the meantime, I need painkillers.'

Mort glanced at his watch. 'There's a pharmacy up the road. A pizza parlor and a grocers, too. I'll go stock up on everything we need. We might as well get comfortable – no telling how long this process will take…'

Barely had Mort said this than he ducked out the room. But I was struck by the tiredness in his voice…

Fifty minutes down the line, Mort returned with provisions, and we both immediately felt better after getting through the pizzas. Mort then proceeded to splint my arm and put it in a sling, ice my bruising, and dose me full of ibuprofen and once all this was done, he lost no time getting back to work. His tiredness, I was glad to see, had been replaced with a quiet energy – this shift no doubt the result of the food, as well as the hour he'd had to clear his head. However, it wasn't until four hours later, about six o'clock, that I felt fit enough to join him and it was then that we finally, with an air of cautious optimism, continued with the discussion we were having in Manhattan.

In the hours that followed, we discussed a host of things. We discussed, for example, the Japanese cult, Aum Shinrikyo, which, on March 20, 1995, killed fifteen people after releasing sarin gas into five subway carriages in Tokyo. This obviously resonated with Drexler's attack on Manhattan. And what was more, the leader of this

Japanese cult had also exerted power by casting himself as a messianic figure: he claimed to be Christ reborn. But while Drexler's attack on Manhattan did seem to be an intentional homage, it looked to be no more than that. The Aum Shinrikyo plot didn't appear to offer any answers.

We discussed also the TRIBOMB incident. This was the first ever bomb plot conceived by Arab terrorists against America – the brainchild of Iraqi born Khalid Mohammed el-Jessem, who, on March 4, 1973, planted car-bombs in three separate locations around New York, then met with disappointment when all three failed to detonate due to an identical fault in their circuitry. I'd brought this incident up because I'd suddenly remembered the photographs of the fault in el-Jessem's bombs I'd seen years ago at bomb-disposal training, and realized the fault in the explosive at The Essex House was identical. And immediately it was clear that this had been an intentional allusion. Drexler, the man obsessed with Islamic radicalism, had of course been aware of this first Islamic plot on America. And by using a replica of one of el-Jessem's failed bombs, he hadn't simply been making a homage to this plot, he'd also been showing off. He'd been demonstrating that he could succeed using the same faulty circuitry that had caused el-Jessem's plot to fail.

But what grabbed our attention most was the fact that in two days' time, it would be TRIBOMB's fortieth anniversary, and this was also the date Samuel and Vann were due to be executed. Clearly, this was no coincidence. Drexler had undoubtedly known that if he started a week-long assault on the anniversary of the first Trade Center attack, he'd get a chance to commemorate TRIBOMB, too. But though this told us the reason why he might want to stage something on this date, it appeared to tell us little more. After all, given that he hadn't remotely imitated

Ramzi Yousef when commemorating the first Trade Center attack, it seemed unlikely he'd commemorate TRIBOMB by imitating el-Jessem…

We discussed all this and more; and time and again we discovered patterns and hidden meanings in Drexler's designs. Yet time and again, we fell tantalizingly short of cracking the code; of glimpsing something he hadn't intended us to glimpse. So, not to be deterred, we persisted through the evening and into the night, fueled by a conviction that there had to be answers somewhere. Then we persisted into the early hours of the morning, until exhaustion overcame me, and I found myself dreaming I was lost in a labyrinth without an exit.

Chapter Forty-One

Francis Bindle was ushered into the control room, and sat down in the chair next to the phone. The man known as Zahir had returned, and was sitting opposite him once more. Dennis Ericson was standing at his side.

At 7 a.m., the phone rang. Francis activated the speakerphone.

'Hello, Robin.'

'Francis.'

'Are we still on for tomorrow?'

'We are.'

'Great,' said Francis. 'The plane is now waiting on the runway, with all the money on board. Everything's ready to go.'

'Perfect.'

'Is there anything more we need to cover?'

'Not that I can think of.'

'In which case, I won't keep you any longer,' said Francis. 'I hope you're making some headway your end.'

'Don't get me started,' replied Robin.

'See you tomorrow, then.'
'See you tomorrow.'

Chapter Forty-Two

I t was mid-afternoon, and I was sitting on the bed in the attic of the Whitesville House Motel, holding a sheet of paper containing a detailed description of the events that had occurred in Mineral. But I wasn't reading it, I was simply staring at the page…

I'd woken at 6 a.m. to find Mort, who'd resisted the urge to sleep, still at work and instantly, we'd resumed our conversation. However, during the hours that followed, we used up our last dregs of calm and optimism and when we'd hit midday, desperation had set in, and our conversation had suddenly become muddled and frantic. And unsurprisingly, when this panic had at last subsided two hours later, it'd been followed by skepticism, exhaustion, and despair.

And so, it was in this downbeat mood that I sat, staring at the page. Staring at the words *True Shape*, the name of the events company The Order had used as a front, because it was precisely the true shape of Drexler's designs we were failing to grasp.

Then, just when things had seemed like they'd hit rock

bottom, Mort, who was sitting by the desk, pivoted to face me, and said solemnly:

'You're in the news.'

My heart jumped into my throat. Had American Counterterrorism come to a consensus after all, and decided I *was* their man? Had they announced to the whole country to be on the lookout for Saul Marshall, the mastermind behind The Order of Babylon? All of a sudden I saw in my mind's eye my face on every television in the country, on every computer screen, on the front page of every newspaper.

I saw an entire nation hunting me down.

I scrambled to the end of the bed. 'Does this mean I'm public enemy number one?'

Mort shook his head. 'You're a footnote in an article on CNN. Something to do with that serial killer you put away, and a prison riot?'

Mort shifted so I could see the laptop screen. On it, underneath a headline reading *The Silent Ripper Killed in Prison Riot Raid*, there was a sneering-eyed mug-shot of Ernest Philipert. Next, there was a body of text describing how the Utah prison riot – which had been instigated a week beforehand by Philipert, and had led to a hostage situation – had come to a close when state troopers raided the prison, killing Philipert. Then, finally, there was a rundown of Philipert's past: how I'd gotten him arrested back in the 1990s; and how it'd then come out that he'd in fact legally changed his name so that it was an anagram of "The Silent Ripper" – the private nickname he'd created for himself.

At first, all I felt was relief: I had not, as I'd first assumed, been publicly named as the mastermind of The Order. But then, suddenly, I was struck by a staggering realization…

I grabbed a piece of paper, and wrote in block capitals across the top the words "True" and "Shape." Then, a moment later, I wrote underneath the word "Euphrates."

'Look,' I said thickly, brandishing the page at Mort. '*True Shape*, the name of The Order's front in Mineral – it's an anagram for *Euphrates*. The Order's word for apocalypse.'

Mort's eyes widened with tentative excitement. 'So Drexler encoded a hidden message within the name he used?'

'Yes, but there's more to it than that. Don't you see? When Drexler used the name *True Shape*, it was *before* he wanted the authorities to know about The Order. In other words, he'd left a clue hinting at The Order's responsibility which he hadn't wanted anyone to find.' I stood and started pacing the room. 'All this time I've been wondering how Drexler had been so restrained about claiming responsibility. Typically, psychopaths are desperate for acclaim. Typically, they suffer from an overwhelming urge to show-off their achievements. But here was this psychopath who was very patiently waiting for the optimum time to reveal himself. Only, he hadn't waited. Just like Philipert, he'd found a conduit by which he could secretly claim responsibility. He'd left a mark, but one which he'd paradoxically hoped – calculated, even – nobody would find.'

Mort looked at me hard.

'But are there more of these codes?' he asked seriously. 'And more importantly, if there are, do any of them contain information Drexler *still* wishes to keep secret?'

I nodded, then lowered my eyes in thought. Mort was right: though the discovery of this code was promising, it would amount to nothing if there were no further codes – or, equally, if there were more codes, but they told us nothing we didn't already know.

The only thing to do was to look for more. And, if we found any, to see what information they contained.

On this thought, my mind turned back to The Order's early killings – the six initial deaths. Then, almost in the same moment, I saw it.

'*Larder Vixen*,' I said at once. 'The front he created to perpetrate the Aimes murder. It's an anagram for—'

'—for Ivan Drexler,' Mort broke in, snapping his fingers.

There was no need to double-check: it was clearly the case.

'Alright,' he said. 'So clearly these names are intentional anagrams, but we need more. On what other occasions did Drexler give something a name?' Then, before I could answer, he added: 'Didn't one of the cultists who perpetrated the Aimes murder use a pseudonym? I think it might've been Aimes's daughter herself…'

I knew exactly what Mort was referring to. The one female member of *Larder Vixen* – who later transpired to be none other than Aimes's daughter – had used a pseudonym during her dealings with the Mayflower Hotel. I'd seen the name written in the dossier I'd been given at the briefing in Hoover. And though I couldn't bring it to mind, I'd written it down the day before when my mind had been fresher.

I went over to my notes and produced the relevant page.

'Sofi Halltun,' I read aloud. 'Spelt S-O-F-I H-A-L-L-T-U-N. The one who claimed to be their managing director.'

'Precisely,' said Mort. 'You remember I told you that the kids behind that attack were arrested the other day? Well, somebody repeated that name to me just after their arrest; and I remember it struck me as slightly odd that the cult used that less common spelling – as opposed to S-O-P-H-I-E – for the sake of a pseudonym.'

I nodded thoughtfully; then I wrote the name in block capitals on a clear page, and began rearranging the letters. After a minute, I looked up.

'I've got the word South,' I said. 'And with the remaining letters I've got Fallin. F-A-L-L-I-N. Could that be a place name?'

Mort consulted the search engine, then shook his head slowly.

'It's a place, alright – there's a South Fallin Avenue in Oklahoma. But it doesn't look promising: it's a tiny residential street in the middle of nowhere…'

I looked at the map Mort had brought up on the screen. Sure enough, the road in question was underwhelming – a four-hundred yard stretch of dirt-track in the back of beyond. And then suddenly I felt increasingly pessimistic again. After all, just because the names Drexler used for his fake companies were intentional anagrams, it didn't guarantee that this pseudonym was also a code. Perhaps it wasn't and we were seeking hidden information where there was none.

And even if it was a code, there was no guarantee the information it contained was going to change the game – no guarantee it'd tell us something Drexler wanted to keep secret. On the contrary, it seemed more likely – if Sofi Halltun was in fact code for South Fallin – that South Fallin Avenue simply had a personal resonance for Drexler. In other words, the chances were this was another dead-end—

'How about Laflin?' Mort said, pulling me from my thoughts.

'What?'

'South Laflin. L-A-F-L-I-N. Same letters as Fallin.'

Mort keyed these words into the search engine then cocked his head in interest.

'South Laflin Street, Chicago,' he said. 'It's over ten miles long, and runs from north to south through the Englewood district of the city.'

Peering over his shoulder, I had to admit this place looked more promising – like the sort of place Drexler *could* have something to do with. But nevertheless, my reservations remained. I turned to Mort.

'Mort, clearly this is the more promising place of the two. But there's a big problem here: this pseudonym may not even be a code at all. And even if it is, what's to say the information it contains will help us track Drexler down or scupper his plans? Surely it's just as likely, if not more so, that one of these locations just has some personal meaning to Drexler, and that's it.'

Mort nodded slowly. 'I was thinking the identical thing.'

At that, a thoughtful silence stretched out between us. I lit one of the Marlboros Mort had bought down the road and sat on the bed. Then, after a good few minutes, Mort said:

'Look, I understand that even if there are more codes here, there's a high chance that cracking them won't help us. But all the same, I still think it's out best line of inquiry.'

I chewed my cheek in contemplation.

'You say that because of *True Shape*, don't you?' I replied.

'Yes. That choice of name, at least for a period of time, constituted a rare vulnerability. So if there *are* more codes, then there remains an outside chance one of them may leave Drexler vulnerable yet again, and that's reason enough to keep pursuing this.'

I gave a slow nod, then again lowered my eyes in thought.

Mort had a point: so far, the only vulnerability we'd identified in Drexler's designs – the only thing that could've caused him trouble had it been spotted earlier – was this anagram of Euphrates. And so, because a code had left him vulnerable once, I decided to allow myself to entertain the possibility it could happen again.

With that decision, my thoughts turned to the two locations Mort had brought up on his laptop – South Fallin Avenue and South Laflin Street – but no matter how much I thought about it, I couldn't see how either had anything to do with Drexler. So, instead, I once more cast my mind to the six initial murders, and ran through them one by one. But this also appeared to be a dead-end: not one seemed to throw up a clue.

And then, almost involuntarily, my mind wandered back to Mineral, and began, very slowly, replaying the events: my arrival with Vannevar; my conversation with Clint; the storming of the house and my capture; my conversation with Drexler and my brief glimpse of Samuel; my being handed over to the police—

Suddenly, something clicked.

I looked up at Mort.

'Mort, what was it you said about South Laflin Street?'

'Over ten miles long. Runs north to south through Chicago.'

'No, the other thing. The district it cuts through.'

'Englewood. It cuts through the Englewood district of the city.'

Calmly, I rummaged through the papers on the bed, found the page detailing the events in Mineral, and looked it over.

'Just as I thought,' I said, as I stood and approached the

desk. 'After I was captured in Mineral, their ringleader gave his name to the sheriff as *Owen Lodge* – I remember, he even spelt it out. But look –' I took a blank piece of paper, wrote the name, then rearranged the letters '– it's an anagram for *Englewood*.'

For a second time, Mort eyes rounded with tentative excitement.

'So that means—' he began.

'It means,' I cut in, 'that these pseudonyms are indeed intentional codes that are supposed to be taken together – it's simply too far-fetched to suggest that they just happened to contain the words *Englewood* and *South Laflin*, and that there also just happened to be a South Laflin Street in Englewood, Chicago.'

I took a step back, and looked at Mort. Then he said what we were both thinking:

'So now we have a ten mile stretch of road in Chicago which may be absolutely pivotal, and may be completely inconsequential. Merely a place of personal significance to Drexler.'

'Right,' I said.

'So what do we do now?' he asked.

Once more, I began pacing the room.

'Well, there's only one thing we can do,' I said. 'We need to go through this road with a fine-tooth comb and investigate every single property. See if we can find *anything* that grabs our attention.'

I trailed off and continued my pacing.

And then, without warning, I stopped. I'd remembered something – a detail that I knew could be crucial. And this time, I wasn't calm.

'Mort,' I said excitedly. 'Quickly, have a look and see if there are any metal cutting enterprises on or near South Laflin Street.'

'Why?' asked Mort, clearly taken aback by my sudden intensity and by the seeming randomness of my request.

'When I was on the phone to Drexler in Mineral,' I explained hurriedly, 'our conversation was repeatedly interrupted by a noise from his end that sounded like metal cutting metal; a noise that, judging by his reaction to it, was beyond his control to stop. So if there's a metal-cutters on South Laflin, then there's a chance that's what I heard…'

Hardly had I finished speaking than Mort typed what I'd asked into the search engine. A second later, it came up with a single result – Lakeside Steel, at 7504 South Laflin Street – and my first thought was: this is promising. But then, when Mort brought up a satellite image of the address, which gave us a view of the surrounding area, I started feeling positively excited. Because not only was there a dilapidated warehouse directly next door to the north of Lakeside, but these two warehouses were alone on what was effectively a cul-de-sac: to their north, South Laflin was interrupted by an abandoned-looking railway running east to west; and to their south, the road was traversed by West 76th Street. And this meant that this dilapidated warehouse, located as it was at the end of this cul-de-sac, was precisely the sort of place someone who knew what they were doing would locate their hideout in an urban environment. A property that nobody was ever likely to walk past or see in day-to-day life.

I had no doubt this was where Drexler had called me from when I was in Mineral. And finding it was a big deal. It was somewhere Drexler had used as his base – somewhere he *still* might be using as his base…

I turned to Mort. 'Mort, you beautiful bastard. We might've just sniffed out our rat.'

The next thing I knew, Giles had scooped me up into

an enormous bear-hug, completely forgetting my injuries. But I didn't mind. Not a goddamn bit.

'So we need to get to Chicago,' said Mort.

I was sitting poised on the edge of the bed and Mort was standing in the middle of the room, rocking foot-to-foot. All of a sudden, he'd become a different man, a man full of energy and life. And so too had I.

Our discovery had changed everything. We now had purpose, hope, direction.

'Right,' I replied. 'But we can't fly there – for one thing, we're packing heat, for another, the CIA will undoubtedly be alerted if I attempt to go through security – so we'll have to drive. How long do you reckon that'll take?'

'Maybe nine hours,' replied Mort. 'So if we leave in the next half hour, we'll be there sometime between eleven and midnight local time, given that Chicago's an hour behind.'

I nodded resolutely. 'Then, when we get there—'

'Then,' Mort broke in forcefully, 'we're going to ambush the place. Though we're not doing it as a two-man army. I know you've gotten used to those kinds of odds this past week; but this time, we're bringing reinforcements.'

'Reinforcements?'

Mort grinned. 'Saul, my boy. You forget I oversee an entire division at the largest law enforcement agency in the country. I'll make some calls to DC and rally some of the best agents from The Organized Crime Unit. No, they may not be quite as elite as Parkes's lot at The Office of Intelligence, but they can definitely handle themselves. And frankly, I bet they'll be only too glad for a chance to outdo Counterterrorism at its own game.'

'Can we trust them, though? – to keep my whereabouts secret, and with the truth about Samuel?'

Mort smiled. 'Would I suggest we use them if we couldn't trust them?'

'Fine, let's bring in reinforcements,' I said decisively, then added: 'I suggest I find the floor-plans to Drexler's warehouse and organize a command post in Chicago right now – since these jobs will be a lot faster using the laptop – while you pack up. Then let's hit the road immediately and organize reinforcements from the car.'

With that, we both got down to business. Then fifteen minutes later – with the floor-plans and satellite images of the warehouse downloaded, a house round the corner from the warehouse rented, and all our stuff packed – we departed the hotel. And before we knew it, we were back on the Interstate, with Mort behind the wheel.

Then, as I churned my way through the remaining Marlboros, Mort got to work organizing his reinforcements from Washington. First, he called each of his five most trusted agents in turn, explained to them the situation – that he was with Saul Marshall, and that we'd found what could well be the leader of The Order's base – and asked them if they'd come to Chicago to aid in an off-the-books operation. Then, after receiving five affirmatives, he expressed his desire in a series of follow-up phone-calls that the men coordinate with one another, and make the journey to Chicago in two separate parties. The first was to come in a white surveillance van, bringing with them silenced firearms and walkie-talkies; the second in a rental car, bringing with them three pairs of Illinois number plates. And the men were quick to comply: no more than ninety minutes later we received confirmation that they'd split themselves into two groups, that the equipment and vehicles were in the process of being secured, and that both parties, if all went to plan, would be in Chicago by 5 a.m. CST.

And then, with this job done, we fell into a relaxed silence. For now, there was nothing more we could do.

Chapter Forty-Three

R esh knew that he shouldn't do it; that if he was caught, it'd be critical. But the urge to take a brief look inside the house at the end of the road – small and isolated, with the white shutters – was just too much to bear.

Resh had been eating dinner at the bar and grill in the small town of LaGrange, Indiana, when he'd spotted a waitress who looked uncannily like his mother. The like-ness had fascinated him. But then, when she'd finished her shift, a friend of hers had dropped off the waitress's son – no older than ten – and Resh had overheard the friend ask the waitress whether she was starting to cope better with the strains of single motherhood.

At that, Resh was no longer fascinated: he was spell-bound. It was like a time warp; like glimpsing into a scene from his own past.

So, when the waitress left with her son, Resh slipped out the restaurant and followed them. Followed them through Main Street, and then through the unlit residential streets, where the modest houses were set back from the road and sparsely distributed. And now he was standing at the end of their drive, in the pitch blackness of an overcast night, watching the downstairs lights pop on and illuminate the windows.

Getting closer was a risk. Because if he was spotted, they'd call in False Prophets, and it was possible he'd end up arrested, or have to take extreme evasive measures. And given that The Zahir needed him tomorrow, this was tanta-mount to running the ultimate risk, that of letting down The Zahir.

But he'd be careful. He wouldn't get caught.

Resh made off towards the house, then started down its left-hand side towards the illuminated windows. And though the room beyond the glass was partially obscured from view by a tree which had grown up right by the outer-wall, as Resh drew nearer, he began to make out a kitchen. Then, all at once, when he came within about five yards, he was able to clearly see the scene beyond: the mother frying eggs at the stove; the son playing on a gameboy at the kitchen table.

But then, the next thing Resh knew, he was struck by a crippling sense of impotence – struck so suddenly that he quickly had to find his footing to stop himself falling into the branches and blowing his cover. Immediately he under-stood the cause. The scene before him so closely resembled his youth that it induced in him the helplessness that had pervaded his young life. This boy, with his drawn, unhappy face, was just like how he used to be when he was Samuel: a completely powerless entity, whose fate resided in the hands of others. That was how Resh had felt throughout his childhood – like he was someone who others could just forsake or abandon or adopt or readopt as they pleased.

Then, when Resh had gotten a bit older, he'd come to understand that the world was split into two: a minority that dictates how things are run; and a majority that's dictated to. And as far as he was concerned, the people calling the shots had grown corrupt and immoral.

Ultimately, it was this sense of helplessness that had driven Resh from home. And it was only once he'd found The Zahir – the man who'd been sent by God to bring about a new world order – that this feeling had died away, to be replaced with purpose and empowerment.

But now, as he stood watching this ghost of his mother serve up eggs on toast, and the unhappy child prod them with a fork, this feeling had returned for the first time in years. And Resh knew that it wasn't simply inspired by sympathy for this child. He was also feeling this way because peering into the house felt like peering into his own past and he knew that while he might be able to sever himself from his past through The Order, he was powerless to *change* his past. That was something he could never change.

Yet barely had Resh thought this when he broke free of the spell. After all, he reminded himself, he was no longer powerless; and this scene unfolding before him *wasn't* in the past: it was happening right now, and he *could* do something about it. He looked again at the child, and his slim white neck. He had a blade in his pocket, and he could break in and mercifully cut this child's throat, mercifully save him from the impotence he himself had had to face. And, suddenly, with this thought, Resh was filled with a powerful urge to act, mingled with an anger that this was a world in which it was more merciful to kill this child.

But of course he couldn't, because this wasn't part of the plan. In fact, acting in this way would almost certainly endanger The Zahir's plan.

And then, as suddenly as his urge to act had come on, he felt himself calm. Because he remembered that after

The Zahir's plan was complete – once Euphrates had been wrought – this would no longer be such a world. He remembered that by acting together with The Zahir he was acting on a much greater scale – to bring about a revolution – and this was infinitely more important than a small act of mercy.

Resh laid a hand on the tree-trunk, and reflected on the worthiness of his cause.

Almost in the same moment, the boy looked up and out the window; looked Resh directly in the eye.

A cold panic seized Resh. He'd acted against The Zahir's wishes. And now, as a result of his degraded behavior, he'd endangered Euphrates. He'd endangered everything. And for what?

His chest ached like a heart attack.

But then, to Resh's surprise, the child didn't scream. He simply looked back to his plate and continued eating. He hadn't seen Resh. He'd just been gazing into the distance.

Resh exhaled hard. He'd been lucky – *very* lucky. And as the relief washed over him, he turned, and retreated through the night.

Euphrates was calling louder than ever.

Chapter Forty-Four

We arrived at our destination – 6451 South Racine Avenue, Chicago – at about five past midnight. And the moment the landlord turned over the keys and left, Mort went for a power nap, while I found my way to the living room, and began unpacking our weapons and the laptop onto a low table. Then, when I was done, I sat and tried to clear my head. I didn't want to start planning our assault without Mort, but nor did I want to start fretting, either. Yet despite my best efforts, there was a thought I couldn't shake: it was now less than twenty-four hours till Samuel and Vann were due to be executed…

At about half one, Mort finally joined me in the living room and in the process he not only dispelled my fretting, but also galvanized me with the energy the sleep had given him. As a result, it was in a mood not dissimilar to the one we were in after our revelation in the motel that we then set about poring over satellite images and floor-plans, planning our assault. Soon enough, we'd devised a plan – one which, given that we didn't know who or what exactly was inside the warehouse, was simple and flexible enough that it could be adapted on the spot to a host of situations.

Not long after we finished, at just gone 4:30 a.m., the first party – consisting of Rand Dotman, an old boy who'd been retired for a couple of years now, and Chris Burnett, a short, squat, powerful field agent – arrived in the white surveillance van. Immediately, Mort and I went out to inspect the vehicle, and we weren't disappointed. For one thing, it looked perfectly innocuous, like any white panel van you'd see in a warehouse context. For another, the surveillance suite in the back was comprehensive: there was a computer linked to the FBI's database; four monitors, linked to cameras on the front, back, and either side of the van, so you could see everything going on outside; and a number of further monitors which could be linked to any one of the small wireless cameras stacked in the corner. Satisfied with what we'd seen, we helped Dotman and Burnett carry the valises containing the silenced Glocks and walkie-talkies into the house.

Scarcely had we done so when the second party – consisting of Adrian Sayle and Henry Childs, two tall, lean, eminently handy young agents, plus Fabio Rodriguez, a deadpan Hispanic agent, and an old friend of Mort's – pulled up in a suitably unmemorable grey sedan. After Mort and I once again came out and offered our greetings, Mort made a start on fitting the Illinois number plates they'd brought with them to all three of our vehicles.

Before long, Mort had finished the job, and all seven of us were assembled in the living room. As I sat there, I was struck by the atmosphere: it was, though serious, tinged with an excitement; an electricity. But really, this was unsurprising. After all, while these agents had been told only the bare-bones, they knew enough to know that what they were doing was taboo. For starters, they knew this operation was completely out of their jurisdiction. Secondly, they were working with Saul Marshall. And although it was unlikely that they knew about Counterterrorism's suspicions that I was behind The Order, they almost certainly knew I was wanted by the Bureau for withholding information.

A moment later, Mort stood, and addressed the room in his trademark growl:

'First off, I'd like to thank you all for coming. Although I dare say that many of you are relishing this chance to beat Counterterrorism at its own game, I'm under no illusions about the risks you're taking. I know you're not only risking the dangers of the field, but also your professional careers. So thank you.

'Now, as you already know, the reason we need your help and the reason we haven't gone through the usual channels is because Saul Marshall is on hostile terms with FBI Counterterrorism: he's wanted for withholding information. However, the situation is more complex than this. So let me explain...

'Over this past week America's been under attack by a cult called The Order of Babylon – this much is all over the news. But what *isn't* on the news is that the mastermind behind The Order is a man called Ivan Drexler. Earlier this week, Drexler targeted Saul: he took his son, Samuel, and his close friend, agent Vannevar Yeung, hostage, then he put Saul in a bind by disclosing to him sensitive information and threatening to execute the hostages if Saul passed on what he knew. It's for this reason that Saul withheld information.

'However, three days ago, Saul's situation went from bad to worse: Drexler attempted to frame him as the leader of The Order. And though his attempt failed to convince a majority, enough high-powered people have been swayed to cause Saul serious problems. In fact, two days ago Saul had to fend off an assassin who we believe was sent by the CIA. As you can see, Saul has his fair share of souvenirs from the encounter.

'But after this assassination attempt, we had a stroke of luck: we found one of Drexler's secret locations – a warehouse where, we believe, Drexler could be residing. And it's imperative we follow up this lead and ambush this warehouse because we know Drexler plans to do more damage. We know at midnight tonight, EST, he intends to execute Samuel and Vannevar. And we know, also, that he's planning at least one further terrorist attack.

'So we've assembled this off-the-books team to storm this warehouse. And it's true: we've rejected the usual channels because of Counterterrorism's stance towards Saul. However, there's another reason – one that's equally important…'

Mort paused. I knew what was coming.

'The other reason we've solicited your help is because, shortly after the atrocity in Manhattan, Saul discovered that Samuel has, in fact, been converted to The Order. We've good reason to believe this won't stop Drexler executing Samuel as he's already sacrificed a number of his loyalists. But what we're hoping is that this team will be less hasty to pull the trigger than a counterterrorism team would be if it encounters Samuel in the course of this mission… We'd like to take him alive.'

Again, Mort paused. I looked around the room, anxious to see their reaction. And I was relieved. There was understanding in their faces.

Mort continued: 'It must be said at this point that we don't know who or what exactly is inside this warehouse. Yes, we know it's a secret Order location, but we haven't had an opportunity to put it under observation. Now obviously, we're hoping that Drexler's inside, and we believe there's a realistic chance he is. And it's worthwhile saying that if he *is* there, then he's probably got backup; though, given the size of the property and their need for discretion, I can't imagine he'd have more than maybe ten men.

'But bear in mind: we have to be prepared for all kinds of eventualities, because all sorts of things are possible. If there are cultists there, then perhaps Samuel is among them. Perhaps there are hostages there, and if there are, then perhaps Vannevar is one of them. And maybe there are cultists there, but not Drexler himself. You get the picture. We have to be prepared for a number of possibilities.

'However, what I *can* say with some confidence is: if there are cultists there, they *will* be armed – it seems that Order members are ubiquitously equipped with Beretta 92Fs. But despite the fact any hostiles we encounter will be armed and dangerous, we *must* try to take them alive. It may be that the only way we can stop the final terrorist attack, or find Vannevar and Samuel, is through information they have. And I should add that just because you have a cultists in your sights doesn't mean they're likely to surrender. On the contrary, they seem happy to die for their cause; so you may have to incapacitate them.

'But of course, if your life's on the line, and you have no choice, shoot to kill. No matter who it is.'

At that, I nodded to the room. I meant it, too. Yes, I wanted Samuel back alive. But I couldn't ask these guys – who were already taking such huge risks on my behalf – to give up their lives for that end.

'But on the plus side,' Mort went on, 'they're probably also using sound suppressors, since it's in their interest to keep a low profile. So even if gunfire's exchanged, it's unlikely anyone'll hear it, meaning we shouldn't have to worry about local law-enforcement turning up and making a mess of things.'

Mort paused, as though contemplating if he'd covered everything; then, with a look of satisfaction, he said:

'Now I'll hand you over to Saul, who'll brief you on our assault plans.'

I got to my feet, and, dispensing of formalities, jumped straight in:

'The first phase of our plan, which we'll put into action as soon as this briefing is over, is to put the warehouse under observation, because if we can find out more about what's going on inside, it could radically improve our chances.

'Now, before I go on, I'd like to show you satellite images of the warehouse.'

I picked up the laptop, which was already pre-loaded with satellite images, and handed it to the nearest agent. Once it'd been round the room, I continued:

'As you just saw, the warehouse in question, 7505 South Laflin Street, is at the far end of a cul-de-sac. Also on this cul-de-sac is one other warehouse, directly next-door, which contains a metal-cutting business called Lakeside Metals. And when you enter the cul-de-sac, there's a right turn, just before Lakeside, leading to a large parking area which caters to the backend of both warehouses.

'I suggest for this observational phase we place our main surveillance van on the far side of this parking lot, in an intermediate point between the warehouses. That way, the men inside will be able to monitor the back of Drexler's warehouse via the van's camera system and people at both warehouses will hopefully assume the van belongs to the other.

'At the same time, I suggest we have a second party of three parked on South Laflin Street itself. But I don't think this team should be parked directly in front of the ware-house: while our images show there are no windows on the warehouse's front, I think this is pushing our luck. Rather, I suggest that someone in this party plants a wireless camera opposite the warehouse's front, so that we get a live stream of the vicinity fed to the surveillance van and that this second party parks in front of Lakeside Metals instead.

'Finally, I suggest we have a single man parked on West 76th Street – the road adjacent to South Laflin – so that if at any point someone leaves the warehouse, we have a man ready to tail them.

'So by taking up these positions in the first instance, we can put the place under observation, and in doing so we may learn something that'll change the game. However, 11 a.m. will be the cut-off. If by then we've seen nothing that either, a) forces us to act, or b) gives us cause to rethink our approach, then we will storm the warehouse... Because there's only so long we can hang around.

'Now, at this point, I'd like to show you the floor-plan of the warehouse.'

At that, I loaded the image of the floor-plan onto the laptop. After everyone had seen it, I continued:

'As you can see, the warehouse consists of one floor. Beyond the front door is a large main office. This office leads onto a long corridor, which is divided into two by a partitioning door. The first half of the corridor has seven rooms – five offices, one kitchen, one bathroom – whereas the second half has five rooms, all offices. At the end of this second corridor is a door leading to the warehouse space. And at the back of this warehouse space is the rear-door, leading onto the parking lot.

'I reckon the best method of attack is simply to have the two teams of three enter via the front and rear entrance simultaneously, then work their way through the building from either end. I'm hoping the element of surprise will make it a quick, easy operation.'

I paused, then said: 'Any questions?'

'Who'll be in the surveillance van, and who'll be on South Laflin Street?' asked Burnett pragmatically.

'Let's have Giles, Burnett and myself in the van; Sayle, Childs, and Rodriguez on South Laflin; and Dotman on West 76th. That sound okay?'

There were nods all round.

'Any more queries?' I probed.

The men shook their heads. But in their faces, there was a confidence, a belief we could actually pull this off. It gave me hope.

'Right,' I said, with all the bravado I could muster. 'Let's go earn ourselves a parade.'

Chapter Forty-Five

As soon as we finished the briefing, we began preparing to leave. Silenced Glock semi-automatics were passed around. Each team, as well as the lone Dotman, was given a walkie-talkie. And Childs went and retrieved one of the wireless cameras from the van – the one which was to be planted opposite the warehouse's front. My personal perpetrations, however, also included a large dose of ibuprofen, because my liver was aching worse than ever. But while I was able to do something about my liver, even if it was only taking over-the-counter painkillers, there was unfortunately nothing I could do about my left arm, which still hung limp and useless in its sling.

I decided to supplement my Glock with the assassin's Ka-bar to compensate.

When we were ready to leave, at about five past six, we staggered our exit. Sayle, Rodriguez and Childs were first to go, taking Mort's rental. Three minutes later, Dotman followed suit in the grey sedan. Then, after a further three minutes, Burnett, Mort and I finally got in the white van – Mort and I getting in back, Burnett getting behind the wheel. And as Burnett peeled away from the curb, I found myself thinking: this could be the beginning of the end – my chance to bring this nightmare to a close.

Mort and I sat in silence as Burnett navigated the roads. Then, no more than four minutes later, I felt him turn right and right again feeling certain this meant he'd turned onto South Laflin, then into the car-park. And sure enough, I was right: a moment later, the van stopped and the engine died. Then, after the sound of a door opening and closing, Burnett appeared at the van's rear-door and jumped in.

'Anybody spot you drive in?' I said.

'Not that I could see,' he replied. 'There's nobody out there.'

I nodded at Burnett. Then, losing no time, we began setting up our equipment and within sixty seconds we had the computer booted, and a view of our surroundings displayed on three separate monitors. Sixty seconds later, these streams were accompanied by a fourth of the ware-house's front. Immediately, Mort communicated over the walkie-talkie that we were receiving the stream from the wireless camera, and that we were in position, in response to which both the South Laflin team and Dotman confirmed they were also in position. Then Mort told Dotman about the two vehicles parked outside Drexler's warehouse – a medium-sized white van, and a black sedan – quoting their make and number plates, in case Dotman should need to tail them later.

After this, Mort inputted these number plates, both of which were from Illinois, into the FBI computer. But they were rented, which meant tracing them was pointless. Because a rented vehicle in this sort of context doesn't mean the person using it doesn't have their own vehicle, it means they've rented a vehicle with fake identification to cover their tracks.

Then, finally, we got started on the most important job – the observation of Drexler's warehouse. We were all experienced enough to know that in a stakeout, sustained concentration is paramount, since the situation can change in a second. And so it was with hawk-like attentiveness that we watched the morning slowly unfold. We watched as the staff at Lakeside arrived for work between 7:30 and 8. We watched as a truck arrived with a delivery for Lakeside at 9, as the workers unloaded the cargo, and as the truck departed at 10 and the staff returned indoors. And then we watched emptiness for minutes on end.

This wasn't a two-minute Hollywood stakeout. This was the tortuous real deal.

At half past ten, however, there came a palpable rise in tension as Mort announced on the walkie-talkie we were thirty minutes from launching our assault. It was looking increasingly like we weren't going to get a clue – like we were simply going to have to go in blind. But still I kept watching the monitors as Mort continued his countdown – as he announced we were twenty-five minutes away… then twenty… fifteen… ten…

But the countdown never got further than that. Because suddenly, about twenty seconds after Mort announced the ten minute mark, the warehouse's rear-door swung open.

'Look,' I exclaimed, pointing at the monitor.

A half-second later, two men exited the warehouse, one ahead of the other. The first man looked happy and healthy. He was wearing a black suit, and a broad, charismatic smile under a mess of blond hair. His left hand was in his pocket, clutching something, and his right was holding a car key fob. This was undoubtedly Ivan Drexler.

The second man, however, I didn't recognize. And though he was also wearing a suit, he didn't look remotely as happy or healthy. He looked wan and gaunt, like he'd been deprived of sunlight.

Drexler quickly surveyed his surroundings, his gaze flickering unsuspectingly over our van, then he pressed his fob and the sedan's lights flashed. Then he paused, turned back to the warehouse, and said something – a word or two – to someone standing just out of sight beyond the door. Then he walked to the sedan's passenger door and got in, while the second man got in the driver's seat. And then, just as the car began to move, the unseen person closed the rear-door.

All this happened fast. There'd been no more than six seconds between the warehouse door opening and shutting. And no sooner had I processed it than Mort gave me something else to think about.

'What the hell is an FBI man doing chauffeuring Drexler?' he exclaimed.

Chapter Forty-Six

'An FBI man?'

'That's Francis Bindle,' said Mort. 'One of the most senior agents in FBI Counterterrorism.'

There was no more time for talk as the sedan was already rolling across the back of Lakeside. I needed to react, or else lose control.

I snapped up the walkie-talkie and held down the button.

'Dotman. Drexler's just left the premises in the sedan, with a second man who we think is Bureau agent Francis Bindle. Bindle's driving. It's unclear whether Bindle is accomplice or hostage. Track the vehicle, but don't be seen. It's exiting the car-park *now*.'

I took my finger off the button.

'Got it,' said Dotman.

I held the button down once more.

'South Laflin party, the warehouse appears still to be occupied. So we will proceed with the ambush as soon as Dotman confirms he has the sedan under observation. I want your party to enter ten seconds before ours. Understood?'

I released the button.

'Understood,' said Childs.

I knew Dotman would've heard this broadcast. But since he was concentrating on spotting the sedan, I knew there was a chance he hadn't actually processed what'd been said. So after a tense minute, I held down the button once again.

'Dotman. Have you got the sedan in your sights?'

I released the button. Five seconds later: 'Yes. Traveling east along West 71st Street.'

I couldn't worry about whether he'd keep track of the sedan, it was out of my hands. I just had to worry about launching our assault, pronto.

I held down the button.

'South Laflin team. Head to the front entrance immediately. Contact when you're about to enter.'

I released the button.

'Right,' said Childs.

There was no further discussion among my party. Mort opened the van's door, and the three of us jumped out, paced quickly across the blacktop to the warehouse's rear-door, then withdrew our weapons.

Childs's voice came again through the walkie-talkie: 'Entering now.'

Almost in the same moment we heard a clang – undoubtedly a bullet striking the front door – followed by a second, slightly louder clang, signifying the door getting kicked in.

I aimed my Glock at the bolt between the door and the jamb. The door's lack of reinforcement told me it'd be easy to force.

Ten… Nine… Eight… Seven… Six…

We heard a short, muffled yell from inside. It wasn't loud enough to make-out what was said – but it clearly came from the front of the warehouse.

Five… Four… Three…

Burnett got into position to kick down the door. We heard another muffled yell.

Two… One… Zero.

I worked the trigger and Burnett kicked the door down. Then all three of us ducked into the warehouse space. It was empty. Without hesitation, we moved quickly across the warehouse floor to the double-doors leading to the second corridor. Burnett got there first, and burst silently through, Mort and I following closely behind. This corridor, too, was empty. And just as the floor-plan had indicated, there were six further doors: one directly opposite us, shut, which led to the first corridor; two on the left-hand side; and three on the right. But two things immediately caught my attention.

Firstly, all these doors, save the partitioning one, had been fitted with heavy-duty locks and peepholes, which seemed to suggest the offices had been converted into cells. Secondly, while the three of these modified doors furthest from us were closed and their bolts engaged, the two nearest us – one on the left, and one on the right – were ajar.

Communicating to Burnett and Mort with my hand, I indicated that I wanted Burnett to cover the partitioning door while Mort and I investigated the open rooms on the left- and right-hand sides respectively. After both men gave me a nod of understanding and Mort darted off towards the left-hand room, I made for the room to the right, and entered with my Glock at the ready. The room was unoccupied, but not empty. There was an army cot in the corner, on which there were handcuffs, leg-shackles, a decrepit suit, and a bomb vest. The window had been covered by a metal sheet.

All this confirmed my suspicions that these offices had been converted into cells.

I returned to the corridor. Mort was already there.

'The room looks like a cell,' I whispered to the men. 'Empty aside from an army cot and a bomb vest. I'm thinking it might've been Francis's cell. '

'The other room also looks like a cell,' said Mort. 'It also has an army cot with a bomb vest on it. But there's also a dead man in there, castrated. I don't recognize him.'

I could tell by the look in Mort's eyes he'd seen something chilling. But there was no time to dwell on it.

I gestured to the locked doors. 'These doors have peepholes. Let's take a look.'

Immediately I made for the second door on the right, while Mort made for the only other door on the left, and Burnett continued to cover the partitioning door. The peephole revealed another room with metal-covered windows and an army cot. But this cot had someone on it – a dazed-looking, middle-aged man in a suit, with his chest in a bomb vest, his hands cuffed, and his leg roughly bandaged.

I recognized him as Ali Haddad, one of the FBI's most senior translators. I'd met him a handful of times during my time at The Office of Intelligence.

I turned round.

'They've got FBI agent Ali Haddad in there,' I whispered. 'He's in a bomb vest; his hands are cuffed; his leg's done in.'

Mort nodded solemnly. 'Francis Bindle's brother, Liam Bindle, is in the other one. He's also a Bureau agent – also in a vest.'

Without another word, I approached the last door on the right-hand side.

The peephole revealed an even more sparsely furnished room, one without even a cot. But what it did have was a chair in its center. And bound to it was Vannevar Yeung.

His face and left hand were caked in blood. His chest was in a bomb vest. But he was alive.

'It's Vannevar,' I whispered to the others. 'Tied to a chair. Also in a vest.'

'What do we do?' asked Burnett.

'We come back for them,' I replied decisively.

With that, the three of us approached the partitioning door. Then Burnett, who was once again leading the way, eased it open.

As far as we could see, the corridor beyond was empty. But we were in no hurry to progress any further, because the scene before us was far from reassuring.

Firstly, the door directly opposite us, leading to the main office, was shut. This seemed to imply that for whatever reason, the agents who entered via the front hadn't gotten this far yet. And if this was the case, it meant that the window of opportunity for catching by surprise anyone who might be in one of the rooms off this corridor had been missed – by this point, they would've realized the warehouse was under attack.

Secondly, the other seven doors in this corridor, of which there were four to the right, and three to the left, were not fitted with bolts and peepholes. In fact, most of them were not even closed. This seemed to imply these room were not holding pens for prisoners but were living spaces for cultists. And if this was the case, it meant that anyone who might be in one was not only aware the warehouse was under attack, but was hostile, too.

It was clear we'd have to progress with caution.

Suddenly, there was movement on the far side: the door to the main office swung open, and a figure holding a semi-automatic stepped through. But a moment later, we realized this wasn't a threat, it was Rodriguez. He looked relieved at the sight of us.

I put my fingers to my lips, indicating the need to communicate without words – if there was anyone in these rooms, we didn't want them hearing what we were planning, nor inferring where we were by the sounds of our voices. Rodriguez nodded his understanding. Then, with his hands, he told us that his team had two cultists subdued in the main office. I signed back that things were all clear behind us. Then we planned our next move. It was quickly established that there would be a countdown from five, after which Rodriguez would investigate the two rooms nearest to him on either side – which the floor-plan had indicated contained the kitchen and bathroom – while Mort and Burnett would investigate the first and second room on the right respectively, and I'd investigate the first room on the left.

With this plan settled, Mort raised his hand, and began dropping his fingers, one by one. When his last finger dropped, we pounced.

I approached my designated room and burst silently in. Given the two camper beds, it appeared to be a bedroom for two and, to my relief, it looked to be unoccupied. But I was determined to be thorough, and quickly set about checking every space within which someone could be concealed, until finally I was satisfied there was *definitely* nobody there.

Only then did I register that I'd heard no commotion. This was a good thing – it implied that none of the other agents had run into trouble. And sure enough, when I returned to the corridor, I found the other agents emerging from their rooms giving the all-clear.

This meant only two rooms remained unchecked: the middle one on the left, and the third on the right.

Without prompting, Mort and Burnett made for the middle room on the left. Then Burnett burst through the door, while Mort lingered outside, ready to provide backup. But he wasn't needed. Five seconds later, Burnett re-emerged, once more giving the all-clear.

Now only one room remained – the one on the right-hand side, with its door a few inches ajar. We all moved towards it with mounting tension.

Surely, behind this door would be trouble. Surely, not every room could be empty.

Mort put himself forward, stepping in front of the door. Then, after a moment's pause, he kicked it aside and trained his Glock into the room.

The concentration on his face turned to puzzlement.

'Dennis Ericson?' he muttered.

Instantly I recognized this name. Dennis Ericson was the son of Richard Ericson, the FBI agent who famously cracked Lockerbie. Parkes, who was a close friend of Richard's, had told me all about Dennis when, two years back, he'd joined the FBI, making him the third generation of the Ericson family to work there.

But whereas all the other FBI agents we'd encountered were locked in cells, Dennis wasn't. And this worried me. Because I reckoned this meant Dennis *wasn't* a prisoner, he was a convert to The Order. And if this was the case – and my gut said it was – then Mort was standing, hesitant, in front a cultist who'd been trained to kill.

Not a moment after I thought this I hurled myself at Mort, barging him out the line of fire. As we hit the floor, I heard a bullet strike the wall behind where Mort had been standing.

My gut had been right.

In the next instant, Mort and I were back on our feet.

'Was Dennis the only person in the room?' I whispered to Mort. He nodded.

I approached the door, remaining just beyond the line of fire.

The difficulty of the situation was obvious. While Dennis had been caught off-guard by our stealth the first time round, he was now completely on guard. And this meant if any one of us wanted to take a shot at him, it would involve putting ourselves in the line of fire of an alert Bureau agent…

'Dennis,' I said, loud and clear. 'It's over, son. The building's under our control. Put down your weapon and come out peacefully.'

The reply was vitriolic.

'False Prophet scum. The Deluge of Euphrates is upon you.'

I took a deep breath. I was talking to a fanatic. But I was also talking to a young man; a wayward son of a FBI agent, just like Samuel. As a result, a part of me wanted to save him.

'Dennis, there is no Euphrates,' I said calmly. 'You've been manipulated by a confidence man. We want to help you.'

'My name's *not* Dennis,' he spat.

'Listen, son. You might think you're about to go down fighting, and that you're going to take one or two of us with you to make it all worthwhile, but that's not gonna happen. While we've been speaking, five men with shot-guns have entered the room next door and they'll shoot you through the walls if need be. What's more, we already have The Zahir, we arrested him shortly after he departed in the sedan. So throw in the towel. It's over, son.'

'*Liar*,' he screamed.

'You'll be safe with us, Dennis. I promise. We can help you.'

I paused, hoping against hope he'd listen to reason. The silence stretched out. But then we heard the snick of a trigger, followed by the sound of a bullet passing through the air. I knew exactly what this meant.

I walked calmly into the room to find Dennis with a bullet in his brain.

WHEN THE FOUR OF US ENTERED THE MAIN OFFICE, WE discovered Sayle and Childs overseeing two cultists – one woman, one man – who were both sitting on the floor, and bound by handcuffs and rope which the agents must've found in the room.

Childs informed Mort, Burnett and myself that these cultists were refusing to speak. In response, I filled Sayle, Childs, and Rodriguez in about the captive agents.

But then, the next thing I knew, my attention was distracted by the equipment in the room. On a desk to one side was a cluster of monitors hooked up to serious computers.

'It looks just like an FBI surveillance suite for a sting operation,' said Mort, his attention having been drawn to the same thing.

I grunted. 'I dare say that's exactly what it is. Think about it – it would explain everything we've just seen. This warehouse was being used for a secret FBI operation. Drexler had a mole inside, Dennis Ericson, and usurped it. Then he kept the agents here as hostages, and used the place as his hideout, because why would the FBI expect their enemy to be based in one of their own classified locations?'

There was a thoughtful silence among the agents. It was a plausible theory.

'So what now?' Mort asked. 'Given that these cultists aren't talking.'

'First,' I said decisively, 'we need to check up on Dotman.'

I withdrew the walkie-talkie from my pocket and held down the button.

'Dotman. You there?'

'I'm here.'

'The warehouse is secure. Update me.'

'Still have them in my sights. We're traveling north up the I-90, passing through Avondale district as we speak.'

'Keep us posted.'

'Will do.'

I put away the walkie-talkie then turned to Mort.

'Now, I suggest we talk to the captive agents.' I picked up the keys on the desk which clearly corresponded to the bolts on the cell doors. 'I suggest you talk to Haddad, while Rodriguez talks to Liam and I talk to Vannevar. Let's see if these agents know anything.'

The three of us headed to the corridor with the cells. Then, once we'd worked out which key opened which lock, Mort and Rodriguez entered their designated cells, and I entered the one containing Vannevar.

As I did so, Vannevar broke into a broad smile. But he didn't ask me how I was, nor how I'd gotten here. Instead, he asked with urgency:

'Has Drexler left yet?'

'Yes. About twenty five minutes ago.'

'He told me his escape plan in brief,' Vann replied.

'But we don't have much time, so come untie me while I fill you in.'

His tone was deadly serious. Quickly, I moved behind him and began unfastening the cables.

'This warehouse was set aside by Muldoon to monitor a group of jihadists in Chicago,' Vann continued, talking fast. 'Drexler took over the joint, then coerced Francis Bindle, the agent in charge of the operation, to convince Muldoon that these jihadists were heading to Yemen to meet with al-Qaeda bigwigs – a couple of their biggest players – and that the Yemenite government would only allow the Bureau to make arrests if Muldoon himself flew out with a $20 million bribe. But this was all a ruse to get Muldoon and a load of cash onto a plane out the country; a plane Drexler intends to be on.

'The flight's due to leave Glenview Naval Air Station about thirty miles north from here, sometime during the early afternoon, today. On this flight, Drex is planning to make a video in which he'll outline his final terrorist attack, which is due to take place tomorrow morning, and execute Muldoon. He plans to release this video after the attack has taken place as a means of proving his responsibility. The timestamp will show it was recorded the day before, and thus that he'd had foreknowledge.'

'Does he plan to outline his final attack before or after killing Muldoon?' I asked.

'He implied after but I can't be sure.'

'Well, on the basis of what the man I have tailing Drexler has just told me, it looks like he's on his way to Glenview now. If he's not planning on any stop-offs, he'll be there within thirty minutes.' I paused in thought. 'We saw him leave here with FBI agent Francis Bindle, who was cooperating without Drexler drawing a gun on him, so I'm guessing his compliance has something to do with the bomb vests the other captives, including his brother, are wearing. I'm guessing Drexler has a remote detonator, and is threatening to activate the vests if Francis fails to play ball.'

Vann nodded, then stretched his arms which had just become free. 'That makes sense: Drexler told me he was planning to detonate my vest remotely.'

'So Muldoon's probably also on his way to Glenview right now,' I said. 'But given that Drexler will need time to stow himself on the plane, I reckon it's safe to say he's organized it so that Muldoon will turn up after him, and thus that Muldoon is still *at least* thirty minutes from Glenview. So there should still be time to contact Muldoon and warn him.' Again, I paused in thought. 'If I can convince Muldoon to knowingly enter the trap *and* smuggle myself on board the flight, then suddenly I'm in a position to derail Drexler's plot.'

'Sounds like a plan,' said Vannevar.

At that, I finished unfastening Vannevar's restraints and walked back in front of him. He stretched his limbs, but remained sitting – he was too sore to stand right away.

I bent down and looked at his vest. On the front, there was a panel with a keypad. Clearly, a digit was required to unlock the straps and deactivate the explosive – a digit that was, no doubt, known only by Drexler.

'However, we're going to need to get you all out these bombs before I confront Drexler, otherwise he'll use your lives as leverage,' I said. 'You'd be able to disable one of these with the right tools, right?'

'I reckon so.'

I looked the embattled Vannevar over. His left hand was in a particularly horrific state: two fingers were grotesquely swollen, and their nails badly mangled.

'I spotted some equipment that'd probably do the trick

in the main office – equipment the agents must've brought along for their original operation. But the real question is: in your current state, will you be able to disable three of these bombs within an hour?'

Vann gave me a smile; then, scrunching his face in concentration, he heaved himself to his feet and shook his limbs.

'You can count on me,' he said.

I nodded.

'One more thing,' I said. 'Did Drexler say if Samuel would be on this flight?'

Vann shook his head slowly.

'He didn't say,' he replied. Then he added, with nothing in his voice: 'Drexler told me Samuel was a paid-up member of The Order.'

I nodded solemnly.

'But I still need to recover him, Vann. He's my son. And Drexler's been killing his followers like flies; so I've no doubt he still intends to execute him.'

Vann regarded me thoughtfully. 'Well, it seems to me there are two possibilities, then. Either Samuel will be on the flight. Or, Drexler has organized some way to have him killed remotely. But even if it's the latter, your best bet is still to get on the plane, because the chances are Drexler will be the only one who knows where he is...'

I nodded. Vann was right.

'What you need to worry about, Saul,' Vann added, 'is getting Muldoon's number. Because I sure as hell don't have it and we need it, fast.'

This comment snapped me to action and a second later, I ducked out of the cell, and into Ali Haddad's.

He was a senior agent, and thus as likely as anyone here to have the number.

Haddad was still lying on his cot, with Mort standing

over him. By the looks of it, Haddad was running a fever – no doubt his leg, which was plainly infected, was to blame – but though he was dazed, he was clearly lucid enough to interact.

'Ali,' I said, interrupting the men's conversation. 'I need Director Muldoon's cell number. It's a matter of top-priority. We need it to thwart the last part of Drexler's plan.'

He looked at me, and recognition flashed across his face.

'Muldoon's number,' I pressed him gently.

He nodded. Then, following a moment's thought, he slowly recited a number.

I thanked Ali; then, without explaining myself further, I left the room, and headed back to the main office, with Mort following quickly behind me.

Within the main office, I found all the other agents – including Vannevar, Rodriguez, and Liam Bindle – already assembled. Immediately, I ordered that the two cultists be removed from the room – a command Child and Sayle quickly carried out. Knowing that calling from the warehouse would increase the likelihood of Muldoon taking the call, since he'd probably recognize the number, I approached the landline and lifted the receiver.

Then I dialed and the phone began to ring. As it did so, I found myself hoping not only that he'd answer, but that he'd do so with an innocuous *hello*. Because there was a chance he was already in the company of someone from The Order. And if he was, and he answered with confusion, or by making reference to where I was calling from, it could be fatal.

Chapter Forty-Seven

'Hello?'

'Director Muldoon. This is Saul Marshall. I need you to listen very carefully, because this is a matter of life and death. The excursion to Yemen you're about to make is a trap. The warehouse you set aside on South Laflin Street to monitor local terrorists was usurped by Ivan Drexler, the leader of The Order of Babylon, and a small band of his accomplices. Drexler coerced Francis Bindle into telling you this lie about Yemen by black-mailing him with the lives of his colleagues, including his brother. In actual fact, this flight is how Drexler is intending to escape the country. His plan is to be hidden away inside the cabin by the time you board the plane and then, once you've taken off, to hijack the aircraft. After this, he intends to make a video in which he will, first, outline his final terrorist attack, due to take place tomorrow morning, and, second, have you executed. He's plotting to release this video the next day, after the attack has taken place, as a means of claiming responsibility.

'Now, what I suggest is that you knowingly enter this

trap, but at the same time, I smuggle myself onto this flight. That way, Drexler, thinking everything's going to plan, will start recording his video, and tell us the details we need to thwart his final attack. Then, once he's done so, and before he can do you harm, I can intervene. But for this plan to work, I need at least an hour to get there from Englewood, so if it's looking like the take-off will take place within the next sixty minutes, you need to stall. And whatever you do, be cautious – treat everyone you encounter over the next hour as a potential Order member.

'Also, bear in mind that Liam Bindle and Ali Haddad are both in bomb vests, and Drexler has the detonator, so Francis is going to be dancing to Drexler's tune. However, I've got Vannevar Yeung disabling these bombs as I speak, so hopefully, by the time I confront Drexler, his detonator will be useless.' I paused a beat. 'I'm aware my name's been dragged through the mud these past few days… but you simply have to trust me.'

There was a short pause.

'Sorry about that. Unfortunate, regrettable news.'

The line went dead.

———

MULDOON RETURNED HIS PHONE TO HIS POCKET. HE was sitting in the back of a Ford Crown Victoria, which was cruising along the northbound lane of the I-294, *en route* to Glenview. Behind the wheel was the young, professional-seeming man he'd met not ten minutes ago at O'Hare Airport, who he'd understood to be FBI agent Dom McElroy.

But now, he wasn't so sure.

Because now, after the message he'd just received from

a man he trusted completely, Muldoon knew that something was terribly wrong; that he couldn't trust anyone.

He also now knew that he needed to find some way to add half an hour to the journey, since he was only twenty minutes from Glenview.

Muldoon looked out of the window and saw that the next exit was in five minutes. All at once, a plan jumped into his head.

Three minutes later, Muldoon started breathing heavily. Then, after forty seconds, he started coughing, too, with steadily increasing intensity. Before long, this had escalated to an all-out, barking, wheezing, teary-eyed paroxysm.

'Asthma attack,' he garbled to the driver while fumbling for his inhaler. He took two ineffectual drags. 'Take this exit.'

The driver – who'd been watching Muldoon carefully for the past sixty seconds in the rear-view mirror – veered to the right and exited the Interstate.

'Pull over,' wheezed Muldoon between coughs. 'Somewhere out of sight.'

The driver hustled the car around a corner and pulled up in a deserted car-park. Muldoon slipped out of the car and continued his coughing from a nearby bench.

The driver also got out of the car. He leaned up against the bonnet and regarded Muldoon with concern.

The final job The Zahir had given Lamed had been a simple one: collect Muldoon from O'Hare and drive him to Glenview. But all of a sudden, it'd gone pear-shaped: Muldoon had been seized by an asthma attack. And Lamed knew that if the attack proved bad enough, and Muldoon required medical assistance, it could derail The Zahir's carefully laid plans.

But while he desperately wanted to avoid bringing in medical assistance, Lamed knew that he had no choice but to offer to fetch some. Because that's what an FBI agent would do.

'Sir, do you require medical assistance?' said Lamed.

Muldoon, who was still coughing hard, shook his head.

'Just give me a few minutes… it'll blow over.'

Though relieved by this answer, Lamed remained tense as he watched the shuddering Director. His coughing fit appeared to come in waves: every now and again, it would subside a little, only to return a minute or so later as bad as ever. Each time this happened, Lamed's nerves took a jolt – he was terrified of letting The Zahir down; of this unforeseen event undermining Euphrates. But then, a long ten minutes later, Lamed was finally given a reprieve – Muldoon's fit began to wind down properly, and, at last, he seemed to stabilize.

'Give me fifteen minutes,' said Muldoon, still short of breath. 'Just so I can compose myself. Then we can hit the road.'

'Yes, sir.'

Lamed breathed a sigh of a relief. Muldoon was going to be alright. And that's all that mattered. Because really, it didn't matter if they turned up thirty minutes later than expected. After all, The Zahir had complete control over the runway for the foreseeable future, so half an hour here or there was nothing to worry about.

And so, back in high spirits, Lamed watched on as the Director paced slowly back and forth, regaining his composure.

Chapter Forty-Eight

M ort and I were in his rental car, Mort was driving, and we'd just joined the northbound lane of the I-94. We'd departed immediately after my conversation with Muldoon because time was of the essence and now that we were on our way, the first thing I needed to do was issue the orders to the men at the warehouse which I hadn't had time to give before leaving.

I pressed the button on the walkie-talkie.

'Agents at the warehouse – the top priority is disabling the vests. Everyone must be on hand to assist Vannevar in this effort and you must keep me updated with the progress. Is this understood?'

'Understood,' came the voice of Rodriguez. 'Vannevar's already made a start on Liam's. We'll keep you updated.'

I lowered the walkie-talkie. Mort gave me a side-on glance. Since departing the warehouse, he'd been concentrating on nothing but getting us onto the Interstate. But now that we were on it, I could see questions forming behind his eyes.

After hearing what I'd said to Muldoon, he knew as much as I did. But he also knew me well enough to know I'd already started thinking about how I was going to execute my plan and undoubtedly he wanted to hear what I was thinking.

But before he could ask anything, the walkie-talkie crackled to life once more. This time, it was Dotman.

'I've got a situation developing. We're on a residential road, round the corner from Glenview NAS. Francis has pulled over behind a second nondescript sedan.' Dotman paused. 'It's your son. He's just gotten out of this second vehicle... And now he's getting into Drexler's car... They're back on the move again.'

This was a crucial development. It seemed Samuel would be on the flight, after all.

'Right,' I said to Dotman. 'As it so happens, we have information that Glenview is precisely where Drexler's heading. We need you to tell us by which gate he enters. Then we need you to keep that gate under observation. We've reason to believe Director Muldoon is being chauffeured there now and we need to know when he arrives.'

'Got it,' said Dotman.

As I lowered the walkie-talkie, Mort shot me a second side-glance. Then he said:

'So we're heading to Glenview NAS, where you intend to smuggle yourself onto Drexler's flight out of the country?'

'Right.'

'And I'm guessing you've thought about the security situation there?'

'Well, I think the overwhelming chances are that Drexler has organized it so that he has autonomy over a runway. But obviously he won't have been able to put his own men on the security gate, so he would've had to settle with giving the Glenview boys instructions. So I just have to hope he's told them to admit anyone with appropriate governmental identification, in which case I'll be fine. But if not, I'll just have to force my way in.'

Mort gave an unconvinced nod. I went on:

'But I'm fairly confident my Bureau ID *will* be enough, because Drexler has also put in place a code word and I imagine Drexler would have thought a standard ID check plus a code word would be plenty secure enough—'

'Wait, how do you know this?' Mort broke in.

'Before Muldoon hung-up, he said to me: "Sorry about that. Unfortunate, regrettable news." At first, I thought this was an odd thing to say. But then I realized it was an acrostic: the first letter of each word spells *Saturn*.

'I reckon that after hearing my plan, Muldoon knew he needed to tell me this word to get me through security. However, he was with someone he didn't know if he could trust; so to communicate this information without it being noticed, he put it in an acrostic.'

Mort gave a low whistle. He was impressed by Muldoon's quick-thinking.

'Okay,' he said. 'So let's say you get through security. But then you have to approach the aircraft without being seen…'

'Right,' I said. 'But I can't imagine that'll be *too* difficult. Not only is it unlikely Drexler will have the place swarming with men, but by the time I get there, Drexler and Samuel will both be hidden on the aircraft so probably won't be in a position to see what's going on outside. And while I concede that the pilots are more likely to spot me, in all likelihood, they'll have no reason to think I shouldn't be there. In all likelihood, they've been told nothing about this mission beyond where they're flying to.

'Who I'm most worried about is the person driving

Muldoon. Seeing that Muldoon felt it necessary to use an acrostic, there's got to be a possibility this person is an Order member. And it seems plausible that after dropping Muldoon off, this driver will hang around. But even if he does, I still have to fancy my chances of pulling it off… it's only one person…'

Mort narrowed his eyes and gave a slow nod. I knew precisely what he was going to ask next. But before he could, he was interrupted by Dotman on the walkie-talkie.

'The black sedan has just entered Glenview via the East Gate on Lehigh Avenue. I'm going to park up on Tanglewood Drive – it's a road parallel to the gate, a half-mile off, from where I should be able to watch the gate through binoculars without arousing suspicions.'

'Keep us updated,' I replied.

As soon as I lowered the walkie-talkie, Mort recommenced his interrogation.

'And how do you plan to get on the plane?' he asked.

'Well, the distance between Chicago and Sana'a is about 6,500 nautical miles so, regardless of where Drexler actually intends to go, he'd have had to organize an aircraft capable of covering the distance for the sake of the ruse. This means he's almost certainly organized a Gulfstream C-37b, the only model of small aircraft the US military has, aside from the two presidential Boeing VC-25s, capable of covering that distance. Obviously, entering via the ordinary passenger entrance is out of the question. But to the rear of the C-37b is a baggage hold, about eight cubic yards in size, which is accessible from the exterior of the plane *and* the cabin. If I can get myself in there, it should do the trick – provided that Drexler hasn't put the cash in there.'

Again, Mort narrowed his eyes and nodded. He could

see that what I was planning was possible but also that there was plenty that could go wrong.

'And then once the plane's in the air, Drexler and Samuel will coerce the pilots at gunpoint... Is that what you're thinking?'

'Something like that,' I replied.

Again, Dotman's voice came through the walkie-talkie:

'I have the East Gate under observation. Will keep you updated.'

'Thanks, Dotman,' I replied.

Mort turned and looked at me hard.

'So, working on the assumption that Muldoon can't yet be there because Drexler would've organized to get there first, we have to hope that Muldoon doesn't turn up until we're extremely close.'

'That's right,' I said. I glanced at the dashboard clock. 'The time now is 11:43, and we've covered about five miles. Twenty-five to go.'

After five minutes, and only another three or four miles, we got a scare as the walkie-talkie crackled to life. But it wasn't Dotman – it was Rodriguez with good news: Liam's vest had been disabled. However, this didn't change our mood as we knew it'd mean nothing if Muldoon arrived too soon. Yet with each mile that crawled by, there was an increase in optimism. And though the increase that came with each mile was small, very gradually it began to mount and by the time Rodriguez contacted us again – twenty minutes after his previous message – to say that Haddad's vest had also been disabled, we'd covered almost twenty-five miles, and were starting to believe that maybe we might actually make it...

Then, before we knew it, we were approaching our exit, still without word from Dotman. And it wasn't until 12:15, by which point we were on a residential road just round the corner from Glenview, that Dotman finally delivered the news:

'A blue Crown Victoria has just entered via the East Gate. I couldn't make-out who they were, but there were definitely two men inside… I reckon it was probably the Director.' 'We're heading over to you now,' I replied. 'I'm going to drop Mort off, then proceed to the East Gate alone.'

Barely had I said this than I ripped the sling, bandages, and splint off my left arm. I knew that approaching a gate at a Naval Air Force Base looking completely wrecked wasn't a possibility. I had to look calm, normal, professional. And by the time I'd coaxed my arm into the jacket sleeve, and made sure I was looking as presentable as I possibly could under the circumstances, Mort had pulled up behind Dotman's car.

Mort got out of the car and I shifted into the driver's seat. Then, after double checking that my Glock, Ka-bar, and ID were all on me, I set off once more, using my right hand to both steer and work the gears.

Soon enough, I was on Lehigh Avenue. And as I closed in on my destination, Vannevar's voice came through the walkie-talkie.

'The final vest has been disabled.'

With that, I pocketed the walkie-talkie. Then, taking a sharp left, I arrived at the East Gate of Glenview NAS.

Chapter Forty-Nine

There were two guards at the gate, both carrying Heckler & Koch MP5s. Beyond the gate was a line of trees, concealing the runway from view.

One of the guards came to my window. Then, before he said anything, he looked at me interrogatively. I'd expected as much – despite my attempt to fix myself up, I was still looking battered, bruised, far from professional – but a moment later, his face relaxed, and it was clear he wasn't going to push the issue.

'Identification,' he demanded brusquely.

I handed him my ID. He looked it over, then swiftly handed it back with a nod.

'Code-word?' he probed.

'Saturn,' I replied with nothing in my voice.

He gave me another nod. Then he nodded at the other guard, who promptly opened the gate.

I drove through, doing my best to make the one-handed driving look like nonchalance, after which, I followed the road as it weaved its way through the trees. To my relief, when I came out the other side there was nobody

360

there to spot me entering the runway's vicinity. And the reason for this was simple: although the runway was directly at the end of the stretch of road I was on – running at right angles to it – the start of the runway, which was to the right, was hidden behind a huge hangar, three times the size of Drexler's warehouse. I had no doubt the aircraft was on the other side of this hangar.

But aside from concealing me as I entered the vicinity, it was clear this hangar was also going to provide me with a place to abandon my car. Because while the hangar faced onto the runway, its rear-wall doubled-up as a large car-park, and was filled with many hundreds of vehicles, both civilian and military, meaning if I left my car there, nobody was going to notice it as not having been there before.

With these thoughts running through my mind, I rolled the car the 350 yards between the trees and the car-park – coasting in order to make as silent an approach as possible – then pulled into a bay, and got out. Then I hurried along the remainder of the rear-wall, and along the right-hand side of the hangar, until finally I reached the front right corner. There I paused, and poked my head round the corner.

Sure enough, at the start of the runway sat a Gulf-stream C-37b. It was a beautiful and diminutive machine – it was 96'5" long, had a wingspan of just 93'6", and on either side of its aerodynamic, sleek white body, was a Rolls Royce BR710 C4-11 turbofan engine – and it was facing down the runway, with its engine idling. Its tail end, where the baggage hold was located, was about 150 yards from where I stood. And as I took in the surrounding scene, two things caught my attention.

Firstly, there was the profile of Francis Bindle's head in the second of the seven small windows lining the aircraft's body, which told me both he and the Director were on board, since I couldn't imagine Bindle would've boarded without Muldoon. Secondly, there was the Crown Victoria parked alongside the aircraft, also facing down the runway, with the guy who'd driven Muldoon sitting behind the wheel. This told me, just as I'd expected, that the main obstacle in entering the aircraft would be this individual. And now the exact nature of the situation was clear: the final 150 yards between myself and the plane, plus the tail-end of the plane itself, were both within his field of vision which meant I had to both cover this distance *and* haul myself into the baggage hold without him once looking in his rear-mirror.

It'd take me fifteen seconds to cover the distance, and maybe fifteen more to get myself inside the baggage hold and attempting it was a big risk. But I had no choice.

Breathing deeply, I fixed my eye on the back of the driver's head, waiting for my chance. Then, fifteen seconds later, I got it – he looked down at something in his lap – and no sooner had he done so than I started bolting across the runway at full-pelt, my eyes glued on my destination, my heart thumping painfully in my chest. The next thing I knew, I was underneath the opening to the baggage hold. Without losing a second, I reached up with my good hand and slid open the portal. Then, clutching the edge of the opening with the same hand, I hoisted myself into the thankfully empty baggage hold at which point, I hastily pulled the portal shut once more.

As my heart continued to hammer, and I gulped in breath, I waited tensely, knowing that if I'd been seen, it was within these next few minutes that I'd be confronted. But the minutes passed, and there was no confrontation. And then the plane started to taxi, and it was clear – I'd made it onboard unseen.

Then, as the plane continued taxiing, I quickly

regained my composure, and, thinking back to a C-37b I'd been on years ago with Parkes, coolly recreated the floor-plan in my head. The cabin space as a whole was just under 44 feet long, just over 6 feet high, and 7 feet wide. Behind the cockpit and the bathroom at the front of the plane, there was the main cabin, furnished with a handful of seats, and a sofa or two. Beyond this, there was a second, smaller cabin. Then, finally, there was a galley, which led to a second, larger bathroom, at the back of which was a hatch by which you could access the baggage hold.

This hatch was just above my head.

Having seen where Francis was sitting, I knew he and Muldoon were in the main cabin. And my guess was that the money was in the second cabin, and that Samuel and Drexler were either also in this second cabin, or in the galley.

However, it was also possible that they were in the bathroom, immediately on the other side of the hatch. But I simply had to hope they weren't. Because as soon as we took off, I had no choice but to get out of the hold and enter the bathroom, since from where I was, it was impossible to get a visual on Samuel and Drexler... And it was crucial that I *did* get a visual, because I needed to know when they set about hijacking the plane, and when Drexler started making his video.

But Drexler and Samuel not being inside the bathroom wasn't the only thing I had to hope for. I also had to hope that in hijacking the plane, Samuel and Drexler didn't kill the pilots... The last thing that was needed was further loss of innocent life.

I was abruptly distracted from these thoughts as the plane started accelerating down the runway. Then, all at once, it lifted off the ground. And as it did so, I suddenly felt emotions rising in my chest – a mix of feelings that came from being just yards away from the man I'd been so desperately hunting and the son I'd been so desperately trying to save. But immediately I squashed them. If I was going to succeed, I had to think of both men in cold, calculated terms.

Drexler was the one I was going to kill.

Samuel was the one I was going to take alive.

I repeated this to myself a couple of times. Then, after taking a long minute to clear my head, I withdrew the Ka-Bar, took a deep breath, and burst silently through the hatch.

Chapter Fifty

To my relief, the bathroom was empty.

I quietly closed the hatch behind me. Then immediately I spotted what I was after: just above the door leading to the galley, which was closed, there was a small air vent in the wall. I crept over and put my eye to it. And though, because of the shape of the vent, I couldn't see through it straight away, after patiently adjusting my angle of observation I eventually found one which allowed me to see the left-hand side of the galley.

Crouching there, not five feet from me, was Drexler. In one of his hands was a Beretta, and in the other was a small electrical device which was undoubtedly the detonator. Propped up next to him was a tripod with a small camera on top.

I adjusted my angle of observation again. Soon I found one which allowed me to see the right-hand side of the galley. Crouching there, opposite Drexler, was my son. In one of his hands was, likewise, a Beretta. In the other was a sap.

His face looked stern, unfamiliar.

I had the two men under observation. Now all I had to do was wait for them to make their move. And that's exactly what I proceeded to do, changing which of the men I had in my sights every few minutes, and holding myself at the ready to make a move of my own.

I was aware it could be hours before they took action. But I was unfazed. I felt patient, calm, focused.

In the end, I didn't have to wait long. Twenty-five minutes later, Drexler gave Samuel a nod. In response, Samuel stood, and moved towards the front of the aircraft, out of my line of sight. Then Drexler followed suit.

It was go-time.

I eased open the bathroom door. Then, without pause, I darted through the galley and poked my head round the door at the end.

The room beyond, which was the secondary cabin, was devoid of life – the two men had already passed through. But it wasn't empty: secured with cables against the far-side wall were neat, shrink-wrapped piles of cash, just where I'd predicted they'd be.

I entered this room and started moving quickly and quietly through it. When I got half way, I could hear – through the door to the main cabin which had been left inches ajar – Drexler address Muldoon and Francis. His voice was icy and mellifluous.

'Gentlemen, how wonderful to see you. Before we get started, let me turn on my camera, I'd hate for something exciting to happen and for us not to have a record of it.'

By the time Drexler finished saying this, I'd reached the door. Because it was ajar, through the gap I could see the left-hand side of the main cabin plus some of the central reservation. And this was where the action was taking place. Francis was sitting nearest to me, maybe six feet away, in a seat facing towards the front of the plane. Opposite him sat Muldoon. And Drexler was standing with his back to the door, behind the camera, keeping his distance. I could see only one leg of the tripod, and his left hand holding the Beretta, but this was enough to gauge where he was.

The Beretta was aimed at Muldoon's head.

'Right, we're rolling,' said Drexler. 'Francis, would you do the honors?'

At that, Francis stood and fastened Muldoon's left hand to his armrest with handcuffs. He then frisked Muldoon. Muldoon played his part well – his surprise looked genuine.

'I'm so sorry, Robin,' said Francis as he sat back down, his voice trembling. 'He has Liam in a bomb vest… Ali, too. But he says he'll let us all live if we comply.'

Drexler laughed a liquid laugh.

'This is wonderful stuff for our home video. But it's true: I plan to let you both live – plus Ali and Liam – provided Francis continues to do everything I ask of him. But Robin, you're very quiet. I trust you know who I am?'

'Ivan Drexler,' said Muldoon tonelessly. 'The architect of The Order of Babylon.'

'Bravo,' said Drexler. 'So now you know for sure it wasn't poor old Saul Marshall, though that *was* Saul Marshall's son you saw pass through just a moment ago, if you're wondering. He's one of my disciples. And if you haven't guessed already, I've had the Englewood warehouse under my control for a week now, all thanks to another of my disciples, the young Dennis Ericson.'

My thoughts turned to Samuel. The sap he'd been holding had been encouraging. It told me he'd probably been intending to knock the pilots out as opposed to kill them. But at any rate, I had no doubt the plane was now under his – and Drexler's – control. Even had Muldoon shouted a warning, the pilots wouldn't have gotten beyond a puzzled exchange of glances before Samuel was upon them.

'Now, while it's true that I'm planning on letting you both live,' continued Drexler, 'that's no reason why we shouldn't have a little fun. So, Francis, I've a request for you – could you please break Robin's nose?'

Francis looked at him pleadingly. Drexler laughed cruelly.

'Come now, Francis, it's not like I'm asking you to *kill* the guy. It's just a little fun for the camera… It's either that, or Liam and Ali get it and I put a bullet through your head for good measure. Your call.'

'It's okay,' said Muldoon calmly. 'Do as he says.'

Francis sighed hard. Then he got up once more, and quickly connected his fist with Muldoon's nose. It burst all over his face. Muldoon released an involuntary groan.

'I'm sorry, Robin,' said Francis as he sat back down. His apology was barely audible over Drexler's laughter.

'That was *too much fun*,' said Drexler. 'I have to see more. How about a couple of black eyes?'

Again, Francis looked at Drexler imploringly.

'Just get it over with,' said Muldoon.

Muldoon's face was calm and stoic, and I was struck by his bravery. Yet what was even more remarkable was his faith. He'd had no confirmation I was on board, but he didn't once glance around trying to seek me out. He simply seemed to take it on faith I was there.

'Just get it over with,' Muldoon repeated with a hardness in his voice.

For the third time, Francis stood. Then, swinging his fists with brutal efficiency, he struck Muldoon twice, once in each eye. Both swelled up to the size of golf-balls.

Again, as Francis sat down, Drexler chuckled.

'Okay, enough of that,' said Drexler. 'I'm satisfied. Now it's time to get down to business. Just give me a moment while I adjust the camera…'

There was a pause, punctuated by the sound of Drexler fiddling with the camera. Clearly, he was rotating it to face him. Then Drexler addressed the camera:

'Hello, America, my name is Ivan Drexler. By now, I'm sure you've heard plenty about the fine work of The Order of Babylon. But, cruelly, you've been left in the dark about who's behind it all. So I'm making this video to put you out of your misery and to tell you that I, Ivan Drexler, am the mastermind behind The Order of Babylon.

'Now, by the time you watch this, it'll be Tuesday afternoon. But as you can see from the timestamp on this video, I'm recording this the day before, on my flight out of the country with my hostage, FBI Director Robin Muldoon, in a plane that belongs to the US Military. And the reason I'm recording this video *now* is because I want to disclose the details of my final attack – due to take place tomorrow morning – in order to prove that I had prior knowledge of it, and therefore that I'm responsible.'

Drexler paused.

I knew what was coming next. Drexler was about the announce the all-important details of his final attack. And I knew that as soon as he'd disclosed what we needed, I had to pounce because his Beretta was still aimed at Muldoon and though his finger wasn't on the trigger, it'd only take a second for it to get there and squeeze. Drexler continued:

'Tomorrow morning, twenty high schools across the eastern seaboard will each be visited by two of my angels of death at precisely 8 a.m. EST. These angels – who'll all be under twenty, and will be carrying Beretta pistols – will kill everyone they encounter. Then, at precisely 8:30 a.m., they'll all take their own lives. A simple yet beautiful finale.'

That was it. That was what we needed.

Time to kill this worm.

With all my might, I slammed my shoulder into the door. It swung inwards and struck Drexler hard in the back, causing him to stumble into the tripod. In the next instant, I was inside the room and before Drexler could react, I slammed my right fist into his left wrist, breaking it one brutal blow, and sending the Beretta skidding under a seat. Then I went in for the kill – I went to grab his throat. But he saw it coming, and jerked his head to the right and as a result, I grabbed his ear instead, ripping it clean off his head.

Suddenly, there was a lot of noise.

Drexler was screaming. Francis was shouting about the detonator in Drexler's right hand. Muldoon was shouting at Francis that the vests were disabled…

But none of this disrupted my focus. I *was* going to kill Ivan Drexler. And with this thought, I went for his throat again, and this time I got it, slamming him hard against the right-hand wall. Then, after allowing our eyes to meet for a fraction of a second, after allowing him to see his executioner, I tightened my grip and ripped out his windpipe.

When I turned around, I found my son sprinting towards me from the direction of the cockpit, his Beretta in hand. He stopped about level with Muldoon, glanced at Drexler lying dead and mutilated at my feet, then, with his eyes manic, with a look like his whole world had collapsed, he trained his gun at my head.

I had no doubt he was about to shoot…

But then, suddenly, Muldoon – who Francis must've released from the cuffs while I was killing Drexler – raised himself from his seat, and struck Samuel hard across the back of his neck just as he squeezed the trigger. Samuel's aim was thrown, and the bullet fizzed past me, through the partitioning wall, and into the next room, where it was thankfully absorbed by the cash on the other side.

I snapped my gaze away from where the bullet had pierced the wall, and back to Samuel, expecting a second assault. But there was none. Muldoon's blow had knocked him cold. He was strewn unconscious at my feet.

And just like that, it was over. The job was done. And though all around me was activity, as Muldoon ran towards the front of the plane and announced the pilots were alive but unconscious, and Francis seized on Samuel's body, and used the cuffs to secure his hands, I knew that for me, there was nothing left to do.

And so I sunk to the floor, and rested a hand on Samuel's cheek.

It felt cold and unfamiliar.

Epilogue

It's been forty-one days since that flight. Forty-one days on the run.

We landed at Andrews AFB that afternoon, and before anyone there had even begun to grasp what had happened, I'd slipped away. I'd had no choice: after the things I'd done, I knew that sticking around would mean facing the firing squad. But while Muldoon had been willing to feign disorientation and hold off ordering my arrest for an hour or so to give me a head start, he'd not let me take Samuel...

From the moment I left Andrews, I listened out obsessively for news on Samuel. But though the botched hijacking was reported, there was no mention of him – clearly a decision had been made to cover-up his involvement altogether. And this worried me deeply. Because when a terrorist is arrested without public knowledge, then anything goes. Beatings, waterboardings, unimaginable horrors.

But on the plus side, there was also no mention of any terrorist events in the days that followed – the information

I'd got from Drexler had been enough. And there was no mention of me, either. National security had clearly made the decision to cover up my activities, too.

But just because they weren't announcing it publicly, this didn't mean they weren't hunting me – they were – and I knew, without a shadow of a doubt, there were certain high-rankers who'd stop at nothing to suppress me. So in those first few days I covered my tracks with manic care. And yet, after a couple of weeks I had no choice but to take risks: my lacerated liver had gotten to a point where either I did something about it, or risked fatal consequences. And so I raised funds by recklessly hot-wiring cars, enlisted a backstreet surgeon in Baltimore to do the deed, and spent the next two weeks with inadequate painkillers, in enormous pain, recovering in a squalid rental property nearby.

But then, once I'd recuperated a bit, it became clear to me I needed to take a bigger risk still. I needed to get in contact with someone in the know in DC because the lack of information about Vann, Mort, Olivia, and most of all Samuel, was killing me. And I decided – since Vann and Mort were both probably being watched, and Parkes was too heavily guarded – that Alex Schneider should be my target, Chief of the Radical Fundamentalist Unit.

So one evening, before she'd gotten back from work, I broke into her apartment, and surprised her with a gun to her head. She was unapologetic about her part in falsely identifying me as mastermind behind The Order, but she talked alright. Mort, she told me, had been suspended, but had avoided anything worse for now, since there was no proof he'd had prior knowledge of the attacks. Vann was under house arrest because he'd clearly had at least some prior knowledge, though just how much remained unclear. And Samuel, thanks entirely to the efforts of Muldoon, had been spared the clutches of the CIA, and had been sent instead to the Kirby Forensic Psychiatric Center – New York's equivalent to Broadmoor.

All she knew about Olivia was what she'd heard through the grapevine – that she loathed herself for ever having trusted me again.

Of course, it was impossible to know if she was telling the truth; but I was aware this was the best information I was going to get.

I left Schneider locked in a cupboard, unable to raise the alarm, and got out the city easy enough. And it was then that I carefully made my way to a motel in rural New York – a run-down, innocuous shack in the middle of goddamn nowhere.

And here I am still, two weeks on, in the same squalid motel, holed up like an animal.

I know it's only a matter of days before I have to move on, before it's no longer safe for me here, but I'm using this time as best I can to recuperate: my liver's still damaged from the shoddy surgery, and I'm exhausted.

And yet, perversely, I'm looking forward to when they come for me. Because at least then I won't have time to sit and think. Won't have time to dwell – as I've been doing compulsively, painfully, agonizingly – on the devastating fallout of that fateful week.

On the fact that my son is brainwashed and broken and languishing in an asylum. On the fact that I've lost everything I'd worked so hard to regain with Olivia.

On the fact that, because of decisions *I* made, dozens of innocent people had lost their lives under the most horrific circumstances – innocent people, whose faces have now infiltrated my nightmares, whose absence have become a part of my DNA.

Afterword

Readers, and the decisions they make, are what determine whether a novel succeeds or perishes. First and foremost, I would like to thank you for giving me a chance. And if you enjoyed what you read, please consider leaving a review online. Word of mouth has a huge impact on any book – to put it bluntly, reviews directly impact on sales – so, in a way, Saul Marshall's life is in your hands!

If I've managed to win you over, you can find links that will speed up the review process at the following URL:

http://tiny.cc/reviewsaul

Thank you so much.

Richard Davis

Get Your Free Book

To sign up to the no-spam Saul Marshall newsletter, and get a copy of NEVER FORGET – the second Saul Marshall thriller – completely free, head over to the following link:

http://tiny.cc/marsh

 facebook.com/richarddavisauthor

twitter.com/dickdavisdavis

Also by Richard Davis

Never Forget - A Saul Marshall Thriller: Book Two

What if terrorists knew your darkest online secrets?

California is witnessing a wave of strange murders: pairs of bodies are turning up under small town landmarks, killed by a single sniper bullet. But ask Saul Marshall – an ex-FBI agent on the run – and he'll tell you it ain't his problem.

But when Saul rescues a young academic from a kidnapping in Los Angeles, and realizes she was in fact next on this mysterious hit-list, he is thrown into the deep-end. And when Saul learns this woman is an anti-China dissident with a secret online presence, it becomes clear they're not just facing some workaday serial-killer.

As Saul finds himself in the sights of a rogue team of Chinese nationalists ruthlessly targeting enemies abroad, he is forced to respond. But his enemy have a powerful weapon. They've found a vulnerability in the Dark Net – the deeply disturbing corner of the internet, where people hide their most explosive secrets – and they're using it to their advantage.

Also by Richard Davis

Riot - A Saul Marshall Thriller: Book Three

**Could a video game convince you to take someone's
life?**

Saul Marshall arrives in Atlanta in the wake of a shocking
incident: a cop with a pristine record has inexplicably massacred
peaceful protesters occupying the iconic CNN Center. But Saul,
exhausted from months on the run from the law, fails to put up
his guard.

But when he is visited in the dead of night by a street gang,
deploying extreme and seemingly unprovoked violence, Saul is
forced to either get his guard up, or perish. And when he
discovers that this same gang has already targeted two of his
team-mates from his days serving in the FBI's elite Hostage
Rescue Team, striking back against the gang becomes not just a
matter of survival, but revenge.

But once Saul realizes that someone else is calling the shots – a
deeply unhinged video-game addict, known only as Red,
obsessed with inciting mass civil unrest – he quickly learns there's
a whole lot more at stake.

To buy a copy, visit http://tiny.cc/riotsm

Printed in Great Britain
by Amazon